I0831227

BLACK SCALES

JAME AGRIPPA AGAPOFF

Black Scales
Book I: The Dragons of Apenninus

v2.0

Dragon Publications

ISBN: 978-0-578-26023-5

PRINTED IN THE UNITED STATES OF AMERICA

Always. Ever. Dragon.

1. Citadel of the Old Kingdom
2. Aggersel
3. Icabus's House
4. Dragon Keep
5. Arkax's Lair
6. Cana's House
7. Gate of the Old Kingdom
8. Northern Wheat Fields
9. Forest Lake
10. Tulia's House
11. Meeting Hall
12. Lake Road
13. Marshes
14. Fig Tree
3 km
E
N
S
W

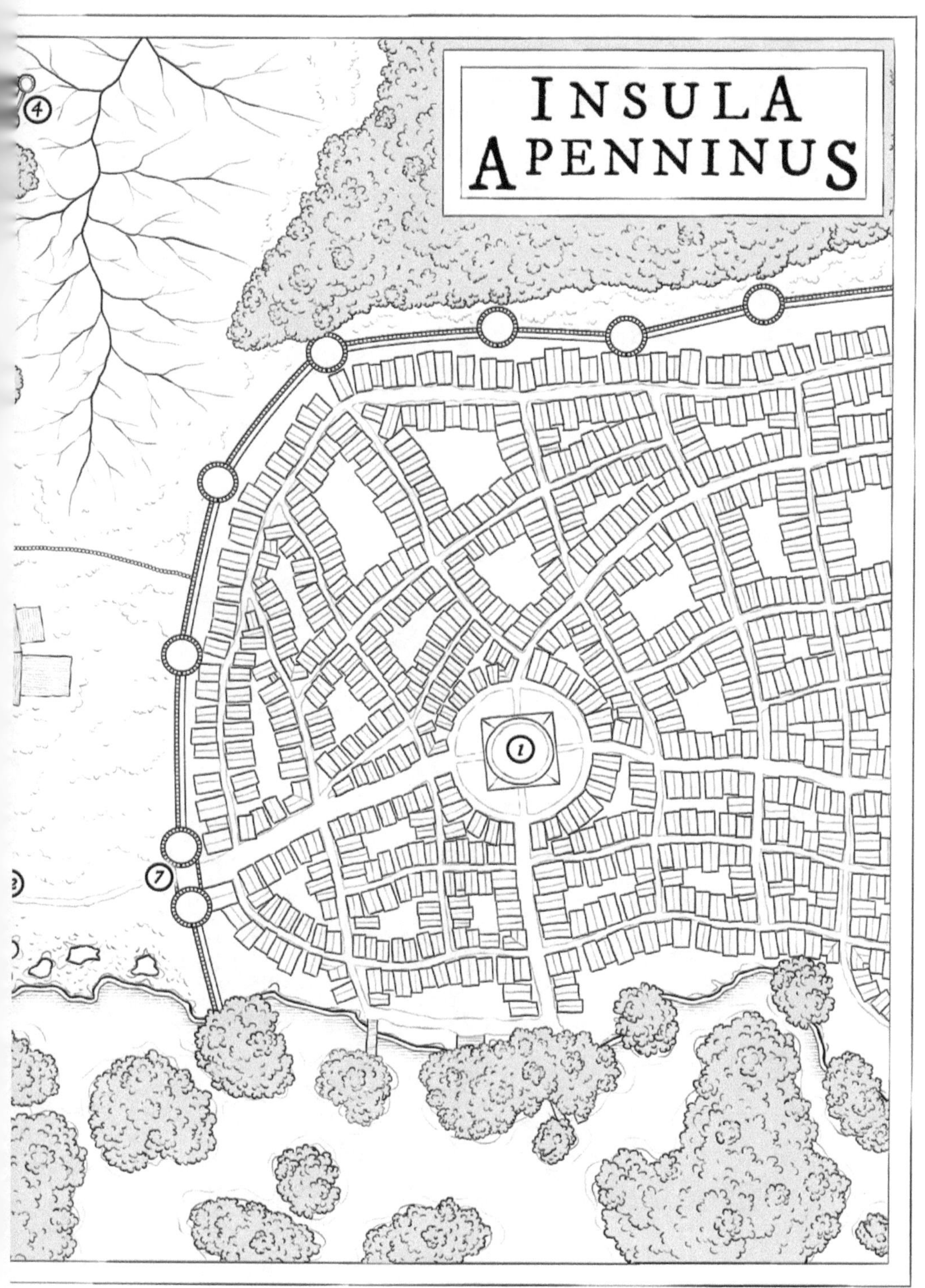
INSULA
APENNINUS
4
1
7

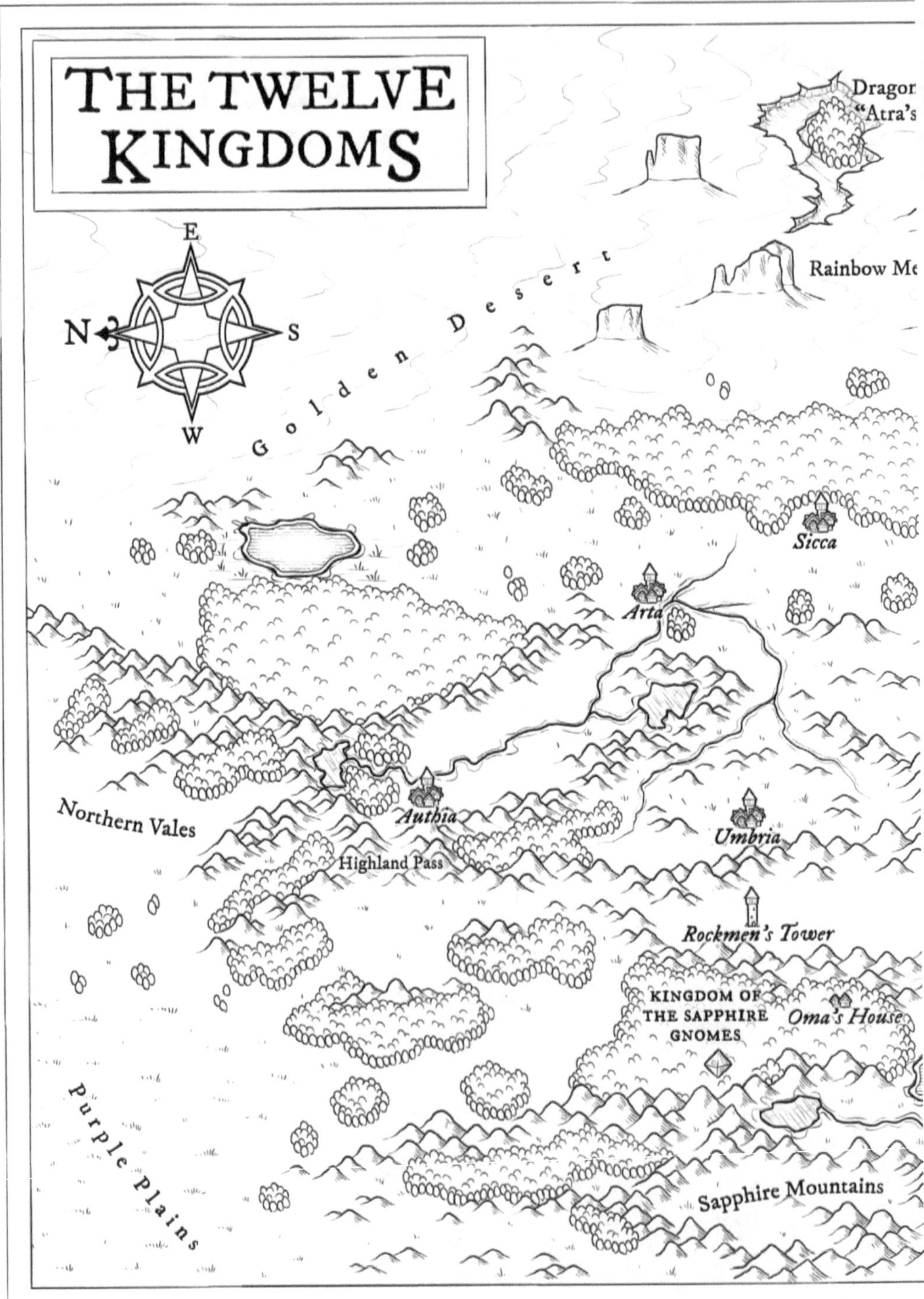
THE TWELVE KINGDOMS
E
N
S
W
Golden Desert
Dragor
"Atra's
Rainbow Mε
Sicca
Arta
Authia
Northern Vales
Highland Pass
Umbria
Rockmen's Tower
KINGDOM OF THE SAPPHIRE GNOMES
Oma's House
Purple Plains
Sapphire Mountains

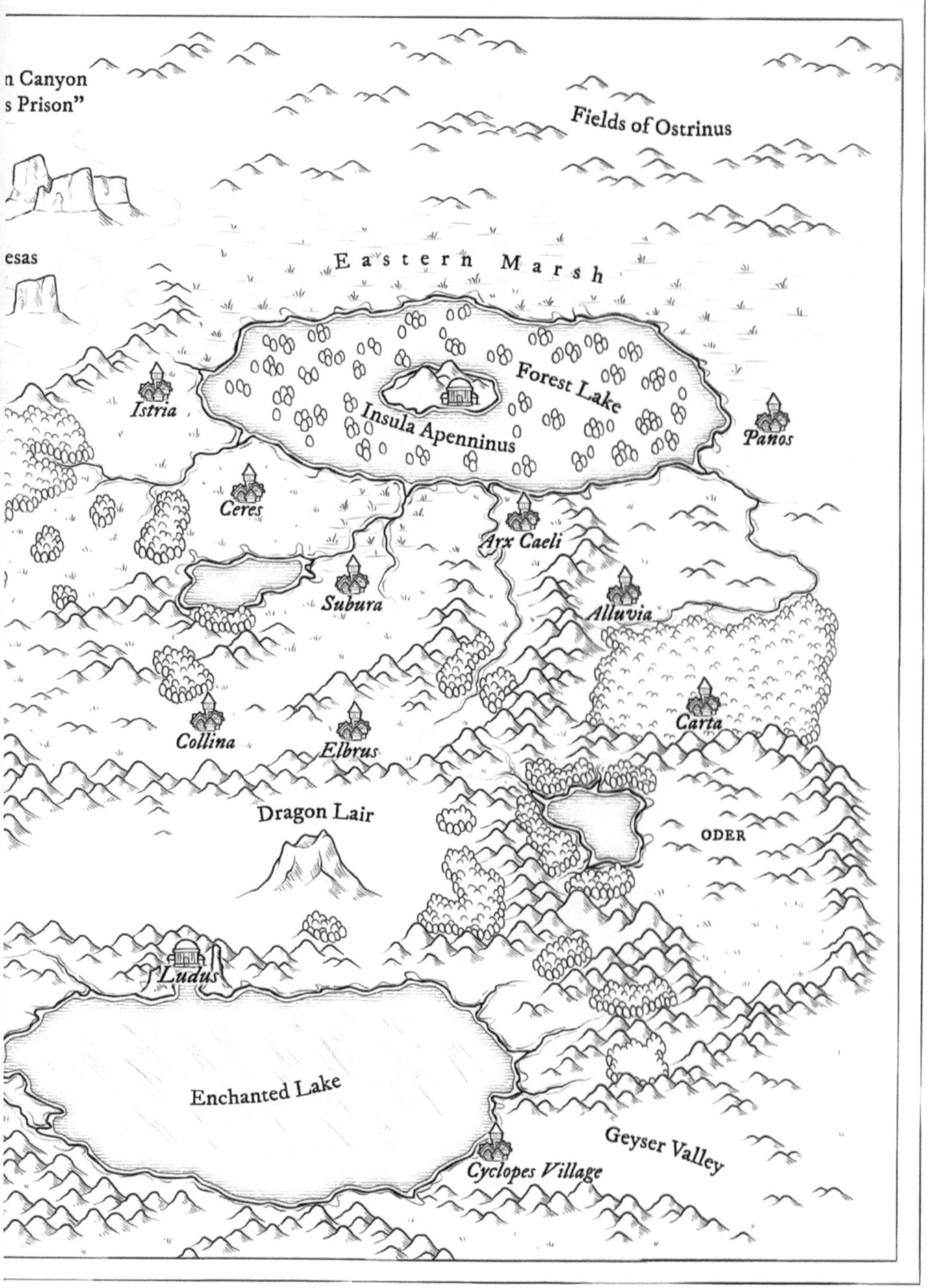
n Canyon
s Prison"
Fields of Ostrinus
esas
Eastern Marsh
Forest Lake
Insula Apenninus
Istria
Panos
Ceres
Arx Caeli
Subura
Alluvia
Carta
Collina
Elbrus
Dragon Lair
ODER
Ludus
Enchanted Lake
Geyser Valley
Cyclopes Village

URMS

Urms closed his gills and raised his face out of the water. Behind him, other Gilian began to surface silently in the shadows of the floating trees. Illuminated by the soft glow of their lanterns, their pale, mostly naked bodies appeared elf-like amid the hard roots of the forest lake.

Across the channel, the three ships were moored together fore and aft, forming a makeshift triangle. The humans of Arx Caeli had sent oared warships into the forest lake before, but never sailed merchant ships. Urms was surprised that, with the support of only two oars, they had made it as far as they did.

Two days had passed since the last human cry sounded over deck. What need or desire drove these men into the forest lake, Urms neither wondered nor cared. For those vessels that sought the island at the center of the lake, the path always ended the same way—in silence and fire.

The Gilian spread out, and Urms clenched his fist, drawing the air through his mouth and expanding his lungs. The pain passed as quickly as it had come, and he forced his breath out through his nostrils, severing the membranes there. Blood trickled onto his upper lip, and he washed it away in the lake.

One by one, the other Gilian opened their lungs, and Urms waded silently across the channel, resting his ear against the hull of the nearest ship. The whir of carrion flies sent a tremor through the wood; Urms drew his face away and frowned. "Bring fire and oil," he said.

The floating trees drifted toward the ships, and Urms took the anchor chain in his hands and climbed up over the deck rail. Above Urms, the furled mainsail creaked on its rigging, while the tattered foresail fretted lifelessly in the wind. Blood stains streaked the wooden deck from the aft cabin over the fore hatch railing, where the flies churned the darkness; their chorus told Urms everything he needed to know.

"Check for signs of life and burn the ships," Urms ordered the Gilian gathering on the adjacent ships.

The planks creaked behind Urms, and two Gilian approached bearing torches. Like others of his Order, these Gilian wore only shark leather shorts.

"Here, Master Urms," said one of the Gilian, handing him a trident and a torch. Already, Urms could feel the moisture leaving his skin. If he stayed out of the water long enough, he would appear almost human.

"Cover the deck with oil," said Urms, pushing open the door to the aft cabin with his trident. Soiled papers littered the table and floor. Urms studied a map drawn in coal dust on the wall.

"This isn't a map... It's a battle plan. Get out now!"

A cloaked man appeared in the doorway. Behind him, the torchbearers lay dead, their throats slit gill to gill. Standing over them was a tall man holding a bloody sword.

"Don't move," said the cloaked man, raising his weapon. Dirt and oil covered his bearded face, but his brown eyes blazed bright with starvation or madness, Urms couldn't tell which.

"Who are you?" Urms managed to say.

"I am Atellus. He's Gurges." Atellus glanced askance to the tall man. "Our master, Furius, has been expecting you."

"You will die for this, Atellus." Urms brought his trident to bear.

"You may want to reconsider that," Atellus said.

Urms heard a creak behind him, and the cold touch of a sword point against his back.

"Time to drop that skewer of yours," said Atellus. "I won't ask you again."

Urms dropped his trident and stepped over his fallen comrades. "You're monsters."

Gurges pushed Urms to the edge of the deck, where the three

interlocked ships formed a triangular pool at their center. He raised the lake boy's chin with his sword point. "Furius's dreams were true after all. You have gills and everything."

Urms regarded the captured Gilian on the other ships and lowered his eyes in shame. This was his first command and likely his last.

"I expected you to be older. You are from the Order of Arms, correct?" came a raspy voice from behind. Urms tried to turn to the speaker, but Gurges backhanded him.

"Look ahead! Speak," Gurges growled.

"Who are you?" asked Urms.

Gurges moved to hit Urms again, but the unseen man placed his hand between them. "I am Furius. I recommend not struggling."

"What do you want?"

"You'll see. Atellus."

"Toss them over," said Atellus, pointing to his men. The soldiers raised the dead Gilian overboard into the pool formed by the interlocked ships. The bodies floated and were dragged under.

"Good." Furius cleared his throat and crossed the deck to face the forest. "I would treat with Arwa, Queen of the Gilian, for the lives of these prisoners. I will begin executions in ten minutes."

"How do you know of our queen?" asked Urms, quickly casting an eye on Furius.

Furius's face appeared younger than his voice, with the gauntness of a man who might have been tortured or plagued with visions. Unlike his men, who wore leather cloaks and armor over red tunics, Furius wore silver-segmented plate and a red cape held fast across his chest by clasps cast in the shape of wolves' heads.

"I dreamed of her." Furius wiped his brow and steadied himself on the ship's railing.

Near the bow of the ship, the floating trees drifted apart, forming a long channel. A small ship, illuminated by a golden lantern, drifted forward. Standing aft were two figures Urms recognized, Queen Arwa and the shaman, Herms.

"Drop a ladder and get me a chair." Furius gestured to the nearest soldiers. "We have guests."

The men did as commanded, and Furius sat motionlessly as Herms helped Arwa over the railing. Intricate scar-like tattoos covered the shaman's body. Unlike Urms, Herms wore a loincloth and an assortment of beads and semiprecious stone jewelry. The queen was less adorned than the shaman, wearing a long, fitted tunic of green sea silk with a braided shark-leather belt and a band of gold crowning her short red hair. Urms saw sadness in the queen's eyes but not fear.

"Welcome, Arwa," said Furius, drawing her attention to him. "I am Furius of Authia. These men are what remain of that brave country. Forgive our scent, savage as we are now."

"You are savage." She glared at the men around her.

"Come, come. Is that any way to treat your host?" Furius regarded her harshly and turned to Herms. "Your scars tell me you are the queen's counselor and head of the Order of Rites. I would recommend you tell Her Majesty to be nice, or I will add more blood to the water."

Herms appeared surprised and whispered in Arwa's ear.

"What do you want?" she asked Furius.

"I think you know the answer to that. Why does any man enter this Gods forsaken place? We seek the island, Apenninus, and the Citadel."

"Passage there is forbidden."

"Yes, I was told you would say that." Furius nodded to Atellus, who stood at his side.

"Minius." Atellus pointed his blade at a short, black-haired soldier on an adjacent ship. Minius stepped forward and slit open his captive's neck. A torrent of blood spilled down the lake man's chest into the water below.

"No!" Urms struggled.

"Shut up!" Gurges silenced him with the hilt of his sword.

"Please." Arwa started forward, and Gurges touched his

blade to Urms's neck, staying her. "The Gods will not forgive you," she said to Furius.

"The Gods." The words sounded sour in Furius's mouth. "The Gods forsook me the day I watched soldiers of Arx Caeli burn the castle where my son slept. Shall I execute more of your people?"

Arwa lowered her face. "I will lead you to the island if you release the prisoners."

"That's better, but this is not a negotiation. Seize them."

Arwa took Herms's hands. "Save Urms, find Nubis, trust your vision."

"No, My Queen!"

"I command you." Arwa drew away and ran to the bow of the ship.

Furius's men collided in confusion.

"Get her, you fools." Atellus raised his sword.

Arwa twisted out of the grasp of one soldier and put her foot over the railing before Atellus seized her by the collar. She cried out, and Atellus threw her down onto the deck.

Furius clapped his hands mockingly. "Pathetic, Atellus, truly pathetic. Bring her here," he said.

"No!" Urms shot up, striking Gurges with the back of his head. The soldier stumbled sideways, but before he could right his sword, Herms wrapped Urms in his arms and carried him overboard into the black waters.

ICABUS

Wind and rain beat against the window in invisible waves. The house groaned, and Amara clutched Icabus's side.

"Do you want me to take you to Mother?" Icabus asked.

"No, I'm not scared," Amara said, peeking out the parlor window at the forest lake.

"Well, little sister, if you're not scared, then release your death-grip. Here, sit here next to me."

Amara slowly edged around Icabus and plopped down beside him, allowing her legs to dangle over the edge of the cushion. She scooted close until their hips touched.

"Icabus, what do the lake people do when it rains?"

"They go under the water I guess. What do you think?"

"I think they turn into frog fishes." She grinned.

"Really? Like this?" Icabus made his best impression of a fish face.

Amara laughed, and a clap of thunder drove her face into his side.

"You know, if you keep doing that I'm going to bruise. You have a lot of muscle for a four-year-old."

"I'm not fat."

"I didn't say that. Never mind. Look, the trees are dancing on the lake."

Icabus could feel the tension leaving Amara's body.

The hypnotic dance of the trees was the only thing Icabus liked about the rain. Otherwise, it simply meant he was trapped inside. The apple orchards sloping downward from his home to the village of Aggersel were muddy and unfit for play; the northern wheat fields, whose tall stalks normally concealed all manner of mischievous play, were wet and droopy; and in the village square, where young and old came together for gossip and an occasional game of chance, there were only mist and the memory of sunnier days.

Icabus shifted in his seat. There was another reason he disliked the rain that had nothing to do with play. The rain was a warning.

"You know why you must never go out in the rain, Amara?" Icabus asked.

Amara tightened her grip on him. "The Taker Monster."

"And where does the Taker live?"

"In the forest."

"And who lives closest to the forest?"

She gulped. "We do."

"And what does the Taker like to eat?"

"Kids," Amara said. Another clap of thunder shook the house, and Amara clutched Icabus's torso.

Icabus smiled, suppressing his own fear. "Don't worry. No one has seen it since Mother was a little girl. The Taker stays in the forest behind the wall, and we stay out here by the lake. It can't get you even if it wanted to."

"Why don't dragons eat the Taker?"

"There are no more left," said Icabus with a touch of dismay.

Amara looked at him with her large grey eyes. "Mama says there was lots of dragons."

"Were, munchkin." Icabus tickled her.

"Stop it." She wriggled away.

Amara's laugh reminded him of his mother, Lucia's. His friend Cana often joked that his sister got the best features of both his parents, Icabus having inherited his mother's pointy nose and his father's freckles. Icabus was just happy he didn't have his mother's rose-colored hair.

"Mama should get a dragon."

"What does Mother need with a dragon?" Icabus laughed.

"So, so, it can eat the Taker Monster and play castle house with me." Amara grinned.

"I don't think dragons play castle house," he said with a smirk.

Amara frowned. "Yes, they do."

"I think you need more friends."

"I have friends." She jumped down from the couch and ran to the corner of the parlor, where three hand-stuffed dolls sat at a miniature tea table. "This is Ara, this is Rada, and this is Stuffy Face. She is sick today."

"I rest my case." Icabus put his feet up and brushed his brown bangs away from his face. Amara sat close with Stuffy Face in her arms.

"Why do the trees float, Icabus?"

"They're hollow, and their roots weave together like little islands."

"Does our island move, Icabus?"

Icabus smiled. "No, we live on a real island at the center of all the other islands. Our island is called Apenninus."

"A-poo-ninus," Amara laughed.

"You're silly. I didn't say poo."

"Poo Island." Amara threw back her head in laughter.

Icabus shook his head. "You're ridiculous. Why don't you go bug Mother?"

"No. I want to wait for the red ships."

Icabus touched her nose. "The ships I told you about were just in a dream I had."

Amara shook her head and pointed to the window. "Uh-uh. The red ships are here."

Icabus looked out the window and his words left him. Emerging from the mist and rain were three ships mounted with red standards.

Icabus got up and pressed his face close to the window. "Mother! Father! You're going to want to see this!"

ATIUS

"Come on, Father, I want to go with you." Icabus handed Atius a lantern from the dock and shielded his eyes from the sun. "These ships look abandoned."

"No, Icabus." Atius climbed out of the rowboat. "Stay onshore with your mother and sister."

"Why can Vescus go and not me?"

"Vescus is not my son. Besides, he's sixteen."

"Wow, two years older. That's nothing. What about my dream?"

"The one where the men on the red ships kill us all? That's not a very good argument to let you come."

Icabus turned to his mother, Lucia, who shook her head. "Ugh! This is ridiculous." He threw up his arms and stomped off.

Lucia lifted Atius's cloak onto his shoulders and helped him fasten it across his neck. She touched the short sword attached to his belt. "Is this necessary?"

Atius eyed the growing crowd and lowered his voice. "It's been a hundred years since the Gilian let any ship cross the forest lake. The last time the Elders even spoke with them was a decade ago. I'm taking every precaution."

"Does that include us?" Mattia called up from the boat.

"You keep my husband safe with that bow of yours, Mattia." Lucia smiled.

"Don't worry." Mattia tipped his archer's hat in her direction. "Vescus and I will keep him safe."

"My fearless and only volunteers." Atius raised his eyebrows at Lucia.

“That’s right,” Vescus spoke confidently. Mattia messed up the boy’s black hair, and Vescus pushed him playfully. The boat rocked.

“Stop!” Piscius steadied himself. He had the rosy complexion of a man taken by cider. “I think we should be off. I’m not partial to the sun.”

Atius leaned forward and kissed Lucia’s cheek. “I don’t think he’s partial to anything,” he whispered.

Lucia bit her lip, and Atius climbed down into the rowboat. He pushed off the dock pole, and Vescus rowed.

“Pull up alongside the nearest of the three ships.” Atius pointed.

“They look like merchant vessels.” Piscius shaded his eyes. Arrows and other signs of battle scored the wooden hulls.

“What’s that smell?” Vescus pinched his nose shut.

Mattia and Atius shared an ominous glance, and Piscius gagged over the edge of the boat. Vescus paddled up alongside the lead ship, where Mattia tied Piscius’s anchor to his rope and tossed it on deck; he pulled it back, fixing it firmly against the railing.

“If that’s not recovered, I will add it to my share,” Piscius noted.

Mattia stood up and tugged on the rope. “If there’s nothing to salvage, will you take it from our hides, Piscius?”

“Can’t a man do a good thing and expect fair reimbursement?” Piscius spoke with offense.

“We appreciate your help.” Atius patted Piscius’s shoulder. “Let’s work together. Aye?”

“Aye.” Mattia turned away.

Piscius hesitated. “Aye. I suppose someone must keep us all together. And if I have to do it, I will.”

“Hush,” said Vescus, placing his ear to the hull.

“What is it?” Atius leaned near.

“Scratching... I’m not sure.”

“It’s probably just an animal.” Piscius waved his hand dismissively.

"Let's find out." Mattia shimmied up the side of the ship. "Watch out," he said, releasing a rope ladder over the railing.

"Thanks." Atius tested the ladder. "Are you coming, Piscius?"

"I will stay here with the boy and protect the boat. We'll be ready for a quick departure should anything happen."

Vescus stood. "Can I come onboard, Atius?"

"No, stay here with Piscius till we have a look around."

Vescus sat down with a disappointed look, and Atius climbed aboard. Streaks of dried blood covered the deck, and Atius stumbled back against the railing.

Vescus shaded his eyes. "You alright, Atius? What do you see?"

"Nothing. Keep watch." Atius covered his mouth and crossed the deck to the fore hatch, where Mattia stared into the darkness.

"Do you think anyone could be alive down there, Atius?" asked Mattia.

Atius didn't answer.

"I wouldn't go down there. You might wake the dead," came a voice from behind.

Atius drew his sword and stepped in front of Mattia. Three men stood in the doorway of the aft cabin.

"Please, we are not armed," said the center man, who was supported by the others. "I am Furius of Authia. These men are Atellus and Gurges. Who are you?"

Atius slowly lowered his sword. "I am Atius. This is Mattia. How did you get here?"

"By chance or fate, I cannot decide. My men and I set out from Arx Caeli and became lost on the forest lake. We had all but lost hope."

Furius's knees buckled, and Gurges and Atellus supported him. "He needs water," said Atellus.

"Aye," said Atius, sheathing his sword.

Mattia touched Atius's shoulder. "I will check the other ships for survivors."

"No." Furius coughed. "These ships are tombs. To disturb the dead is a great dishonor to my people. The ships and all within must burn."

"Burn the ships... Piscius will love to hear that." Mattia smirked.

"Are you alright?" Vescus peeked through the railing. "Gods! Who are they?"

"What, there are survivors?" Piscius shouted.

"Piscius, you're rocking the boat." Vescus slipped back.

Mattia scratched his head and laughed. "Sorry, we don't get many visitors here."

"By that, he means never," said Atius. "Hold the ladder, Vescus. We're coming aboard."

Vescus helped the men into the boat, and Gurges pushed off the hull. He rowed the small vessel to the dock. Gurges stared at him, unblinking.

"Slow it," said Piscius.

Vescus held the oars in the water, and the boat slowed. The villagers moved closer, and Piscius threw a rope over a piling, securing the vessel in place.

Atius climbed out of the boat. "Come on, let's make some room."

The crowd shifted but did not disperse. Atius helped Furius up onto the dock, while Gurges and Atellus supported him from behind.

"Move it, make a path," hollered Vetus, leading the other Elders: Ralla, Silana, Maro, and Cilo through the crowd.

"Thanks, Vetus." Atius wiped his brow. "We need to get these men out of the sun."

"My house, come." Vetus waved them in his direction. "My wife Tulia is toasting apple biscuits as we speak."

"How far is it?" asked Atellus, placing Furius's arm over his shoulder.

Mattia pointed. "It's that tall house at the end of the square."

Gurges supported Furius's free arm and allowed Atius and Vetus to guide them through the crowd. "Is that a cider mill?" Gurges licked his lips and veered left.

"Gurges!" Atellus cursed, steering them back on course.

"It is," chuckled Atius. "Produce, baked goods, meats, cider, we have it all here in the square for trade."

"A remarkable community," said Furius.

"What's that big structure there, past those oaks?" Atellus pointed to a rock building set back from the square to his left.

"Town hall," said Atius. "It used to be a barn long ago."

"I imagine everyone in town could fit in there." Atellus smiled.

"I suppose." Atius followed Vetus past a row of produce carts and up a short stair.

A thin, white-haired woman stood up from her porch chair and blocked Vetus's path. "These men didn't come from those ships, did they?" she asked.

"Where do you think they came from, Tulia, the sky?"

Tulia frowned and opened the door. "What do they want?"

"Food, drink, and less tongue flapping." Vetus made an ushering motion behind her.

"Don't worry, they're always like this," Mattia laughed, holding the door open.

Furius stopped at the top of the steps and glanced back to the square, where most of villagers still lingered. "Atius, who is that boy, there?"

Atius shielded his eyes. "That's my son, Icabus. Why do you ask?"

"It's nothing." Furius smiled weakly. "Your son just has a familiar face... like someone from a dream. Shall we?"

"Aye," said Atius, taking Mattia's place at the door. Lucia raised her hand, and Atius forced a smile before shutting the door.

FURIUS

"That's quite a story." Maro pushed the strands of his white hair behind his ear and sipped his tea. "I am sorry for your loss."

"It's not a reality I have yet accepted." Furius stared at his lap. "Authia was the last of the Twelve Kingdoms to resist Arx Caeli. I would have gladly traded my kingdom for the life of my son, but Praetor Marius took both."

Silana shivered and tossed another log onto the fire. "This new Praetor is a madman to kill the first-born son of each house because of some prophecy. I'm glad the forest lake stands between him and us."

"As long as Praetor Marius rules Arx Caeli, none are safe," Furius spoke flatly.

"Excuse me." Atellus got up and stepped out onto the porch where fireflies twinkled.

"Is he alright?" asked Atius.

"I'll see to him," said Gurges, grabbing a few apple biscuits.

Furius glanced at Atellus's silhouette through the window. "Atellus watched his wife and daughter murdered by soldiers. He has not yet forgiven himself for living."

"You are lucky men, damn lucky if you ask me." Cilo took a bite of biscuit and spoke as he chewed. "You say you never encountered the Gilian during your crossing?"

"No." Furius coughed. "I've heard stories of the lake men my whole life. All we saw were trees and the maze of waterways between them."

"Strange that they should allow you to cross but not aid you." Atius shook his head.

"Not really." Cilo leaned back in his chair and rested his hands over his slightly rotund belly. "Worst neighbors we ever had. Imagine you stop by every twelve years just to say you have nothing to say. That's the Gilian!"

Silana tended the fire and sat on a foot stool facing Furius. Firelight illuminated the length of her waist-long red hair. She glanced at the others and then to her feet.

"Speak your mind, child," said Tulia, who continued to stare into the fire.

Silana eyed the old woman and cleared her throat. "Well, excuse me for asking, Furius, but why attempt a crossing at all? The forest lake is vast. There are other paths you could have taken after losing your pursuers?"

The fire popped, and Furius raised his face to the amber light. "You may think me mad, but I was called here in a dream."

"A dream?" Ralla's expression flattened.

"Yes." Furius cleared his throat. "In the dungeons of Arx Caeli, I became ill and suffered visions of my father. At first, I thought it was madness; but, then he showed me how to free my men and escape. After we lost our captors on the forest lake, I began to dream about Apenninus. In them, my father led me through an abandoned city to a sanctuary holding a fountain of exceptional beauty. He told me that if I rescued the one trapped there, I would find the power to save Authia."

Furius adjusted his position and grimaced. "Later, I began to dream of a dark place beneath the city. There, a voice told me a time of reckoning was near... In Authia, we believe the Gods allow our elders to guide us from the afterlife through dream. I had to come."

Atius stood and rested his arm on the mantle of the fireplace. Years of manual work had given him a stocky, healthy appearance. "My son and wife have also had dreams like you describe. They speak of something dark awakening beneath the Old Kingdom."

"You look pale, Ralla. What is it?" asked Cilo.

Ralla crossed her pudgy arms and shifted in her chair,

making the wood groan. "As you know, I make remedies. Lately, many villagers have been asking for sleeping potions. At first, I thought nothing of it, owing to the change in season and all. The thing is they kept coming back. They described horrible nightmares."

"What about?" asked Vetus.

"About that thing beneath the Old Kingdom. I brushed it off until I had the same dream myself. Scared me half to death." Ralla fiddled with her brown curls.

Furius shook his head. "You speak of darkness and danger, but what I saw beneath the city was someone trapped and needing help. I know what it is like to be cast into a dungeon and forgotten."

Tulia turned away from the fire, and the light appeared trapped in the cataracts of her blue eyes. "Did this prisoner tell you his name, Furius of Authia?"

"He did. He said his name was Galen."

Vetus choked on his tea and spat it back into his cup. "What?"

"I thought so." Tulia held Furius's gaze. "I too have had this dream. In it, I asked the prisoner his name, and he would not answer."

Ralla shook her head. "This is mad. It can't be that Galen."

"There has been no child given that name since," said Tulia.

"Who is Galen?" Furius asked.

Maro straightened his thin frame. "Galen was an alchemist and a sorcerer. He is the reason the Old Kingdom lies abandoned and we live in its shadow."

Furius's hand shook, and he steadied it on his knee. "The sanctuary I described in my dream, does such a place exist in this Old Kingdom?"

Atius and the Elders regarded Tulia, who watched Furius austerely. "You describe the Citadel where Galen once guarded the healing waters of the Golden Land. But that place is no more. Its waters are dried up."

"No. In my dream, the waters ran again. I must go to this place."

“The city is cursed. It can bring only death,” Vetus objected, accentuating his already deep frown lines.

Furius forced himself to his feet. Even in his weakened state, his posture and bearing were kingly. “Death is already taking me. The dungeon illness I contracted in Arx Caeli is progressing. Without a miracle, I soon won’t have the strength to stand.”

Furius regarded Atellus and Gurges through the window overlooking the porch. “I don’t believe it was mere fortune my men and I survived the crossing. Something is awakening here. I only ask permission to follow my visions to their end.”

The Elders regarded each other, and Atius cleared his throat. “I have a map of the city passed down from my grandfather.”

Furius’s eyes brightened. “Your collective visions are a warning. If you ignore them, it is at your peril.”

“And what peril is that?” asked Cilo. “Our ancestors sealed the Old Kingdom for a reason. Why should we do anything different now? Silana, what are your thoughts?”

“It is easy to do nothing and hope for the best. I think we have to do more.” She nodded at Furius.

Cilo frowned. “What about you, Maro? You’re supposed to be the brains around here.”

Maro put his hands together and leaned forward, placing his elbows on his knees and touching his chin to his fingertips. With his long, delicate features, he looked like a brooding wood elf. “As Elders, we are charged with the safety of the community. We are also their servants. Not to include them in such an important decision I think is a mistake.”

“A vote?” Vetus raised a bushy eyebrow.

Maro nodded. “Tomorrow we can introduce our guests to the village and discuss the matter further. Those in favor, say aye.”

“Aye,” said the Elders in broken unison.

VESCUS

From his hiding place outside the window, Vescus could see Tulia leading Furius, Gurges, and Atellus into the kitchen. He turned away briefly as they disrobed and took the steaming pots of water into the bathhouse. Vescus left his hiding place and settled under one of the open windows.

"Your clothes won't be ready till tomorrow," said Tulia. "I may have to boil them with spice bark to get rid of the smell. There are some old tunics and drawstring pants over there in the cabinet. Help yourselves. They're going to be small for some of you, but they'll suffice for now."

"Thank you," said Furius. "We are in your debt."

Vescus heard the patter of Tulia's slippers as she left the room. Lights throughout the house extinguished, and for a while, there were only the sounds of washing and the occasional crude exchange between Gurges and Atellus.

"One of you must go to the ships," said Furius.

"I will do it," said Atellus.

Gurges yawned. "Good. I'm tired."

Atellus cleared his nose. "If Galen is the source of your visions, can you trust him?"

"There is nothing to fear," said Furius. "If not for Galen, all of us would be hung by the neck in Arx Caeli or drowned in the forest lake."

Atellus paused. "And what of these people, My Liege? Do we do to them what Arx Caeli did to us?"

"We will only do what we must. What I need now are loyalty and trust."

"You have it," Atellus said without hesitation. "What would

you have me do?"

"Go to the ships and tell our men to make ready to secure the town tomorrow as soon as the townspeople enter the meeting hall. Gurges will lead a company to bar the door and address any resistance."

"Yes, My King," Gurges yawned.

Vescus crawled around the edge of the house and ran headlong across the square into the cider mill, causing the door to fly back and slam against the inner wall.

"Vescus! Why aren't you at home?" Cilo rose up from his table, surrounded by a throng of drinkers. They looked at Vescus with ire and confusion.

"Father, I need to talk to you. It's important."

Cilo sat back down. "I don't have time for this, Vescus. Can't you see I'm busy?"

"Wait a second, Cilo," said Iulius, smiling. "Maybe Vescus saw the Taker again. Wasn't that what it was the last time he barged in here?"

Vescus felt flushed. "I did see the monster beyond the wall. I swear it. It had yellow eyes that glowed in the dark."

"And hair like needles, I suppose," added Rufus, jokingly.

Cilo smirked and raised his drink. "Whatever it is, Vescus, it can wait till tomorrow."

"There might not be a tomorrow! Furius and the others are plotting to take over the town."

The mill became silent and then roared with laughter. "With what army?" someone called out. Cilo got up and pointed to the door. Vescus stomped out with Cilo at his heels.

"Why are you embarrassing me?" Cilo grabbed Vescus's shoulder, turning him around.

Vescus shook with anger. He looked away, holding back his tears. "I'm not lying, Father. Soldiers are hiding in the ships. They will make their move tomorrow during the town hall meeting. If you don't believe me, then come to the ships. Atellus is going there now."

Cilo rubbed his temples. "No, Vescus, we've been down this

road before. I'm not going to embarrass our guests and us. Go home and stay away from Furius and his men. They've been through enough, don't you think?"

"I think you're a fool!" Vescus pulled away and ran through town into the darkness of the apple grove. He leaned against a tree and wiped away his tears.

"Hey, kid."

"Atellus?" Vescus glanced up. Something hard struck Vescus in the gut, and he hit the ground, breathless and dazed.

Atellus smiled crookedly and lifted Vescus by the collar. "Snoop." He punched the boy in the face, knocking him unconscious.

ATIUS

Atius lifted the soup bowl to his lips and gulped the remaining contents. Amara mimicked him, and stew poured down both sides of her cheeks. Atius chuckled, and Lucia cleaned Amara's face. Icabus and Cana stared at Atius intently.

"Fine, then," said Atius, appearing stern. "Their names are Furius, Gurges, and Atellus. The rest of their crew died during the crossing."

"Yes, I know," said Icabus. "What about Furius's dreams?"

"Dreams? Where did you hear that?" Atius scrutinized Icabus and Cana in turn. "Cana, were you eavesdropping?"

Cana looked at her lap. "Yeah, I'm sorry. I was outside. Furius's dreams about Galen sound a lot like Icabus's nightmares."

"Galen?" Lucia's smile vanished.

Atius raised his hand. "Cana, I think you should go home. I will have to tell Corvus about this."

"Yes, sir." Cana stood up. "Thank you for dinner." She walked around the table and hugged Lucia and gave Atius a remorseful look. Atius looked after her until the house door closed.

Atius rubbed his eyes. "Icabus. I know this may not sound fair, but I want you to stay away from these men until we find out a little more about them."

"That doesn't mean I can't go to the town meeting tomorrow, does it?"

Atius remained silent, and Icabus threw his arms up. "Gods! This is so unfair."

Icabus pushed back his chair and left the room. Amara turned to Atius and threw up her arms and laughed.

"Go upstairs and get ready for bed, and I'll tuck you in."

Lucia patted Amara on the head.

Atius lifted Amara and kissed her on the cheek. She ran out of the room, and Atius sighed. "This Furius character claims to have dreams like yours and Icabus's. Ralla confirmed other villagers are having them too. Furius says the thing in his dream said its name was Galen."

Lucia held his hand. "You don't think it's that Galen, do you?"

"I think a lot of foolish things. What matters is that Furius wants to visit the Citadel and drink from the spring."

"What? It will likely kill him."

"The man is sick. He's going to die either way. The Elders wish to put the matter to a vote. My gut tells me they will not allow Furius to enter the Old Kingdom."

Lucia searched his expression. "You disagree?"

"If there's even a fool's chance that Galen is alive, we need to know. There are no dragons to protect us anymore, and the Gilian want nothing to do with us."

Lucia squeezed his fingers. "Perhaps the Gods will give you a sign."

A knock sounded upon the door, and Atius gave Lucia a long look. "It's in your hands now, my love." She kissed him on the cheek.

Atius got up, and Lucia followed him to the door. Furius, Gurges, and Mattia stood on the porch. Mattia scratched his neck and smiled.

"Pardon the intrusion, my lady." Furius bowed to Lucia. "I am Furius of Authia, this is Gurges, and I think you know this young man."

Atius frowned. "Who is at the watchtower, Mattia?"

"Caelius came a little early. I was heading back home when I came across these two in the apple orchard. I thought they were wild pigs come up from the wheat fields and almost put an arrow in them."

"I'm glad you didn't and happy you came along when you did, as neither of us were quite sure how to get here," said Furius.

"You truly have come far to be here." Lucia smiled. "Atius,

won't you invite them in?"

Furius raised his hand. "No thank you, my lady. My strength comes and goes. Atius, when the Elders said they would put my request to a vote, I sensed your doubt. I request the map and any help you can give?"

Atius rubbed his chin. "You ask me to betray the Elders' decision?"

"You can't betray a decision that has not been made," said Gurges.

Atius eyed Lucia, who rubbed his shoulder. "Do what you think is right," she said.

Atius glanced over his shoulder to the stairs leading to Icabus and Amara's rooms. "I can take you to the Citadel, but if the spring does run, then you must promise to let my wife examine the water before you drink it. Also, if we find anyone or anything alive there, we don't engage it and come back."

Furius bowed his head. "As you wish."

"Wow, this is exciting," said Mattia.

"You're not coming, Mattia." Atius shook his head. "The Elders would not approve."

Mattia laughed. "Don't worry about me, Atius; I've always wanted to see what's in the Old Kingdom. Anyway, it wouldn't be the first time I did something that made the Elders mad. Plus, you may need my bow."

"Let's hope not," said Atius.

ATIUS

Fifteen feet high, the guarding wall ran perpendicular from the shores of the forest lake to the palisades of Apenninus. Midway between the marshes and the cliffs, a single barbican gate offered the only path into the city.

"Spooky." Gurges reached up and grasped the portcullis. "What do you suppose bent this?"

Mattia pulled on the grating. "A dragon, if you believe the story."

Gurges released his hand and frowned. "Dragon? When's the last time one of those was around?"

"Not in my lifetime." Mattia passed under the portcullis and pushed on the barbican doors.

"Good luck breaking through those." Gurges turned away and surveyed the walls.

"No need," said Atius, twirling a grappling hook and rope and releasing it over the parapet.

"Mattia, there should be an old ladder up there on the wall walk. I've seen it from the fig tree above the mill."

Mattia tugged on the rope and smiled. "Now I understand why you brought me along, Atius."

Atius stood below Mattia as he scaled the wall. Minutes passed, and Atius crossed his arms. "Hey Mattia, everything alright?"

"I'm fine," said Mattia, poking his head over the parapet about twenty paces mountainside. "It's pretty dark up here." He lowered the ladder slowly over the edge, where Atius received it.

Gurges shook his head. "That thing looks like it could barely handle the weight of a child."

"I will go first," said Furius.

Gurges held the ladder, and Furius ascended it without difficulty. Mattia reached down and helped Furius over the edge.

"Good," Furius called down to the others.

"You want to go first?" Atius asked Gurges.

"Not really." Gurges grabbed the first wrung, which snapped in two. He gave Atius a fatalistic look and slowly climbed the ladder, cursing each creak. Atius followed after him.

"There is a stair right over there." Mattia lit his lamp. The yellow flame cast long shadows upon everything around them. Furius looked as white as a ghost.

"Are you alright?" Atius asked him.

"Yes," Furius wheezed. "How far is it?"

Atius examined his map. "A league, maybe two, if we don't get lost."

Furius smiled weakly. "Let us not delay then."

Atius took the lantern and turned down the first avenue into the city. Those buildings not ravaged by fire appeared ready to collapse. Black film covered their stucco surfaces and blotted out their windows in moldy cataracts. Atius thought the air smelled like rotting books.

"Stop." Atius froze.

The twisted remains of a building blocked the road. Halfway emerging from the rubble was a skeleton covered in a furry hide.

Gurges squinted. "Is it a wolf, Atius?"

"Not unless where you come from wolves have hands."

"Gods. That thing must have been huge," said Mattia. "It's a Taker, isn't it?"

Mattia reached down to touch it, and Atius grabbed his hand. "Be careful; it may be diseased."

"So, you think this was once a man?" asked Gurges, pulling a tarnished sword away from the monster's hand.

"A servant of Galen." Atius eyed Furius, who was staring beyond the wreckage toward the shadow of the Citadel.

"So, this is what I've been keeping watch for." Mattia shivered.

"Aye, and I hope you never see a living one." He pulled out his map. "Furius, I think we will move faster if we take the side streets."

Furius blinked like a man awoken from a trance. "Very well, Atius. You have led us this far."

Gurges tapped the skull with his boot, and its jaws snapped shut. "Gods!" He jumped.

Mattia laughed. "Careful, friend. Even the dead bite here."

The alleyway opened into a small cobblestone courtyard. Black water filled the fountain at its center.

"It's nice you found someplace creepier than before," remarked Gurges, staring into a broken window. A family of human skeletons sat at a table with their skulls in their laps.

Atius raised his light to the map.

Gurges paced. "Are we lost?"

"No, I'm just deciding which way to go," said Atius.

"How about the fastest way," Gurges pressed.

"Follow me." Atius crossed the courtyard and entered an alleyway. On either side of the road, furniture and rubbish rose in mounds so large they nearly eclipsed the street.

"The air stinks of urine," said Mattia.

"Be quiet, stay close, and don't touch anything," whispered Atius.

They moved through the piles and came to another courtyard filled with junk. A few alleyways were completely impassable, while others appeared barely negotiable.

Atius studied the map.

"I don't mean to be a pest," said Gurges, "but I'd like to be moving."

"The path is blocked." Atius pointed to the debris. "We need to find another route."

Gurges groaned and suddenly stopped. He snapped his fingers, bringing the others to attention. "What is that?"

The thing rose no more than four feet tall but would have been taller except for a twisted spine. It stood like a man with hands and feet fixed with curved, dirty claws. With its narrow snout and black eyes, it had the likeness of a rat. Trailing behind the rat-thing was a long tail, broken and improperly healed at one joint. A few gangly whiskers protruded from its otherwise hairless body covered in folds of pale, droopy skin.

"Alright, everybody," Atius whispered. "Slowly move with me."

"Where are we going?" Gurges spoke through his teeth.

"Out of here," said Atius.

Other rat-things began to appear from the rubbish piles. They hissed at the lamplight and pulled stray pieces of garbage inside their mounds. A few started to follow behind them.

"We have some trouble back here," Gurges said, shaking his sword. One of the rat-things reached for his boot, and he stamped his foot, causing the creature to screech and retreat.

"I think they're attracted to the metal. Let me dim the light," said Atius.

"Don't you dare," Gurges growled. "Keep moving. Be ready with your arrows, lad."

"Aye," said Mattia, reaching over his shoulder.

They came to a fork in the road, and Atius stopped.

"No, keep going, left," Gurges insisted.

Atius hesitated for a moment and took the path. More of the rat-things were gathering close behind, and Atius could hear them moving through the buildings.

"Gurges!" Furius cried.

A rat-thing held Furius by his sigil ring, and Gurges lopped off the creature's hand with his sword. The rat-thing rolled away, shrieking, and all the other beasts screamed in a maddening chorus.

"Run, you fools," Gurges shouted.

"I see it. The dome to the Citadel!" Atius panted.

A rat-thing jumped in front of Atius, and Mattia released a bolt into the monster's eye.

Gurges grabbed Atius by the arm. "Give me the lantern."

Atius did, and Gurges threw it into the nearest nest. The paper within ignited, causing the rat-things to fall over themselves and shriek louder.

"Hurry." Atius ran forward.

The alleyway opened into a wide, circular park. Furius fell onto the dead grass, and Gurges lifted him. "Master Furius, we can't stop."

"Look." Mattia pointed. "They're not following."

Twenty or so of the rat-things had escaped the blaze and were lined up at the edge of the alleyway. The fire was steadily growing behind them, but they would not enter the park.

"What do you think has them spooked more than that fire?" asked Mattia.

"What do you think?" Atius looked to the Citadel.

"What are those creatures?" Furius struggled to find his breath.

Atius watched as the rat-things moved along the edge of the park. "There's a story about the men who chose to loot the city during the fall. It is said they were cursed and transformed into monsters to match their greed. I always thought it was just a story to keep kids from wandering in here."

"I'm glad I never wandered in here," said Mattia.

Atius chuckled. "Too late."

"Are there any other stories you wish to share before we go any farther?" Gurges frowned.

"There's the one about Galen's body being cast into the well of the spring," said Atius.

Gurges's eyes widened. "This spring?"

"Aye," said Atius, leading them across the park and up the stairs to the Citadel's colonnaded portico. Two bronze doors, each four meters tall and half as wide, stood ajar at the entrance. Atius could hear the gurgle of water from within. "I can't believe it... the spring flows. Stay close." He unsheathed his short sword.

Behind the doors, a short hall opened into a circular rotunda supporting a coffered dome. Moonlight fell from the dome's oculus onto a round recessed pool, where water flowed from the mouths of four dragon-faced fountainheads. A dark well drained the excess water at the center of the pool.

"I wonder what it took to build this place?" Mattia smiled at Atius.

"I wouldn't even know where to start." Atius ran his hand over one of the porphyry pillars.

Mattia tugged on Atius's shirt and drew his attention to the fountain, where Furius was kneeling before the water. Gurges guarded him, sword in hand.

"Furius, wait! Don't drink the water," Atius's voice echoed.

Gurges extended his sword.

Atius stopped shy of the point. "Are you mad, Gurges?"

"No madder than you." Gurges smirked.

Furius cupped the water in his hands and stared at it. "Look at this water, Atius. It sparkles even in the dark. It is mana, it must be."

"Gurges, you can't let him do it. It's not safe." Atius held out his hands.

Gurges dropped the tip of his sword and glanced over his shoulder.

Furius let the water fall through his fingers. "Do you hear it, Gurges?"

"What? The water?"

"No, the voice from the well. It sounds like my father."

"Furius, if there is one thing I know, it's that your father is not in that well," Gurges spoke flatly.

"In my visions, Gurges, I saw my father here. He told me Authia was lost, but I could still avenge him and my son. Now, he's telling me to free the one in the well. We need the rope."

Mattia shook his head and backed away. Gurges grabbed Atius by the collar; he put the sword to Atius's neck. Mattia drew an arrow and aimed it at Gurges's face.

"I guarantee I'm as fast as your arrow, kid. Put down your bow and give me that rope."

"This is crazy," said Atius. "Haven't you heard anything we've said?"

"Hush." Gurges pressed the blade to Atius's skin. Mattia

lowered his bow and kicked it over to Gurges, who booted it into the fountain. "Now the rope, boy."

Mattia lifted the length of rope from over his shoulder and walked it over to Gurges.

Gurges took the rope and pushed Atius away. "Thanks." He fastened one end of the rope to a dragon fountainhead and tossed the remaining length into the well.

"I'm here to free you as I promised," Furius's voice echoed. "Help me avenge Authia."

Nothing happened, and Atius sighed in relief. Even Gurges appeared relieved.

"Why don't we return to Aggersel?" offered Atius. "I know you men are under terrible stress. No one has to know of our journey here. Our ways may be simple, but I think you can find peace with us."

Furius fell to his knees and shook the rope in his hands. "I have done all you've asked. Why do you forsake me now!"

Gurges looked back over his shoulder. "Furius, I don't think there's anyone in that well."

"You're wrong! Don't you hear him, Gurges? He calls me to join him."

Furius staggered into the pool, and Gurges reached for him, falling face down in the water. There was a moment of silence, and Atius turned away as Furius tossed himself headlong into the well.

"No!" Gurges scrambled to the edge of the hole. He lifted the rope and shook it in his hand. "Furius! Grab the rope! Furius!"

"I can't believe he threw himself in," whispered Mattia. "Was he mad?"

"I think he was feverish," Atius answered.

Gurges looked back at them with rage. "Why are you both standing there? Do something?"

"There is nothing to be done," said Atius.

The rope in Gurges's hand began to straighten and became taut. He looked into the well and shouted, "Hold on tight, Furius. We'll pull you up."

Atius and Mattia joined him in the water and began to pull on the rope. Mattia used the dragon fountainhead to brace himself.

"Gods, how deep is this well!" Mattia cursed.

"Pull!" shouted Gurges.

Over the lip of the well, a slimy purple robe appeared. Emerging from the shroud, a pale arm held Furius's unconscious body.

Atius let go of the rope and stumbled backward out of the fountain. "No..."

Gurges gave one final pull and dragged the two men into the fountain basin. He grabbed his sword and extended his free hand. "Give Furius to me."

Furius stirred. He smiled and sat up, looking at the man's face beneath the slimy hood. The man cupped the waters in his hands and lifted them to Furius's mouth. Furius drank and laughed. "Put away your sword and get on your knees, Gurges."

Gurges hesitated and slowly knelt. As he did, the man lifted his hands to him. Gurges looked to Furius for encouragement and took a sip. His eyes widened with surprise, and he drank the rest. "Gods! What is in that water?"

"It's mana," Furius laughed.

"Long life," said the man, lifting his cupped hands in Mattia's direction. Mattia took a step to the fountain, and Atius stopped him.

"Who are you?" Atius asked.

The man let the water run between his fingers and lifted the hood from his head. He had sharp, porcelain features with straight, white hair and pale blue eyes that shone yellow in the moonlight.

"I am Galen," he said softly. "Will you not let me give you a blessing for rescuing me?"

Atius stepped back and almost tripped over his own feet. He grabbed Mattia's shoulder and stared at him wild-eyed. "We must go."

They ran down the steps and across the dead park. There was no sign of the rat-things, and Atius was happy to find that the fire had cleared away some of the wreckage blocking the main avenue. They didn't stop running till they reached the gate.

Mattia rested his hand against the wall. "Atius, what are we to tell the Elders?"

Atellus stepped out from the shadows. He gestured up to the wall walk, where six men brandishing bows leaned over the parapet facing the city. "I'm only going to ask this once. Where are Furius and Gurges?"

ICABUS AND CANA

"Where's Father? I haven't seen him this morning." Icabus sat down at the kitchen table beside Cana.

Lucia lifted the lid of her stew pot and tossed in some potatoes. "I don't know, Icabus."

"Icabus and Cana are going to marry!" Amara pressed her dolls together, making a smooching sound.

Cana laughed, and Icabus poked Amara under the arm. "Buzz off, or I'll boil one of your dolls in Mother's stew."

"No," Amara cried, running to Lucia's side.

Lucia patted Amara on the head and handed Icabus a washcloth. "Honey, I think some of the steam hit your face. You're all red."

Cana put her face in her hands and laughed. Icabus blushed again.

"Cana dear, have you seen Mattia or the men who came on the ships today?"

"On the way up, I saw Furius having breakfast with Lady Tulia and Vetus on their porch. He looks healthier. I haven't seen Mattia."

"What about Atius?"

Cana shook her head. Lucia dried her hands and gazed out the window.

"Is there something wrong?" Icabus asked.

"No, dear." She picked up her knife and began chopping vegetables again.

Icabus looked at Cana, who shrugged. "Like I was telling you, Icabus, I heard this screeching sound. Celsus heard it, too, and we ran outside, and that is when I saw the explosion. There was this big flash of light, and then the whole Old Kingdom glowed red. It lasted about an hour."

"Ow," Lucia squeaked, pulling back her hand. A streak of blood coursed down her index finger.

"You cut yourself." Icabus stood up.

Amara began to cry, and Icabus handed his mother a washcloth. She poured water over the wound and covered it. "Don't worry, Amara; it's not that deep. Do you want to see Mama bandage it upstairs?"

Amara nodded and clung to her mother's skirt.

"Thanks for breakfast, Lucia," said Cana.

"Anytime, dear."

"I'm going to walk Cana home, alright?" Icabus asked.

"Icabus, you heard what your father said. He doesn't want you anywhere near the town hall meeting."

"Oh, come on. Cana's house is in the opposite direction of the village. If things are so dangerous, should she be walking home alone?"

Lucia used her forearm to rub the sweat away from her brow. "Very well. Take her home but come right back. If you see Mattia or your father, tell them to come see me."

"Fine, fine."

Lucia began to ascend the stairs and stopped. "If I find out you went to that meeting, you're going to spend the rest of the summer scrubbing floors."

"Yeah, I know," Icabus called back.

"Yes. Now you do," said Lucia.

Amara repeated her mother's words and laughed.

Cana followed Icabus around the front of the house into the apple grove above the grist mill. "You know, Icabus, someday this sneaking around is going to catch up with you. What do you suppose we do when we get to the meeting hall, just walk in?"

"Leave that to me. I have an idea."

"Alright, but we had better not get caught. Atius still hasn't told my father about me spying on Furius."

"Knowing Corvus, he'll probably just laugh. Don't worry. We

can cross over to the other side of town behind Vetus's house. If we can make it to the wheat fields, it should be easy to stay out of sight till we get to the meeting hall."

Cana stopped. "So, your plan is to go in the back door?"

Icabus smiled. "Do you have a better idea?"

Cana rolled her eyes and followed him. The air was warm and smelled like decaying apples. "Oh my Gods, Icabus. I almost forgot to tell you. Last night I saw a lake boy."

"A Gilian? Where?" Icabus asked with an air of skepticism.

"Down by the ships."

"What did he look like?"

"Well, he was fair-skinned, sort of tall, with silver shorts, long blond hair, and a spear thing with three points," Cana replied.

"Sounds like a trident." Icabus looked back. "What was he doing?"

"Just staring at the ships."

"He was standing there, that's all?"

"No, Icabus, I'm serious." She struck his shoulder with her fist. "He looked really sad."

"Well, where'd he go?"

"After a while, he looked in my direction and disappeared. I think he saw me."

Icabus stopped in his tracks. Cana collided with him.

"Ouch. Why did you...?" Cana held her mouth agape. Not ten feet ahead, gagged and tied to an apple tree, was Vescus. He had a black eye and bruises on his face.

Icabus ran over and released the gag.

"Icabus! Cana! Hurry up and let me free. Furius means to sack the town."

Icabus hurriedly loosened Vescus's wrist bonds. "How can they sack the town, Vescus? There're only three of them."

"You're wrong, Icabus. There are a lot more of them on those ships."

"What should we do?" Cana freed the rope around Vescus's ankles.

Vescus shook off the binds and jumped to his feet. "I need to warn the Elders now! You both stay out of sight."

Icabus began to speak, but Vescus was already running down the hill toward town. Cana stared at Icabus wide-eyed.

"I think we should still see what's going on," said Icabus. "If we find my father or one of your brothers, maybe they can help?"

"Don't you think we should go warn your mother, Icabus?"

Icabus looked up the hill and kicked a clump of dirt. "We can warn her after we find someone who can help us. Come on."

Cana didn't object and ran with Icabus through the orchard above the village. "What do you think Vescus is going to do?" she panted.

"Probably make an uproar."

"Wait a second." Cana jumped up and grabbed an apple branch. "Give me a boost."

Icabus locked his hands together and lifted her foot. Cana pulled herself up into the branches.

"What do you see?" he asked.

"Everybody is in the meeting hall already. Gods, Icabus, Vescus is right. There are strange men in red tunics everywhere."

"How many are there?"

"I don't know, lots. Icabus, they're kicking in doors!"

"Do you see Vescus?" Icabus paced.

Cana looked around silently. "Yeah, he's at the meeting hall doors. Gurges won't let him in."

Icabus heard Vescus's voice rise in the air and fall silent. "What happened?"

Cana scrambled down from the tree. "Gurges hit him in the face. What should we do?"

Icabus raised his index finger to his mouth and pointed through the trees to where Atellus and another soldier moved up the hill. The other man was fat and out of shape and made all sorts of disagreeable sounds.

"Come on, Bassus, you pig," Atellus ordered.

"Of all the houses he could have in town, why does Furius want this house?" Bassus moaned.

"It's farthest from the lake and easy to defend: a good place to secure our special Gilian prisoner."

Bassus wiped his forehead with his dirty red tunic. He sighed and continued his ascent.

Cana pulled on Icabus's shirt and spoke into his ear. "They're talking about your house, Icabus. We have to do something."

"We have to find my father."

"I've got an idea..." Cana ran into the avenue and held her arms above her head. "Hey, fatso, I'm going to get my brother, and he's going to put an arrow in your butt."

Atellus pushed Bassus. "Get that little brat!"

"Hurry, Icabus, we can hide in the wheat fields."

Bassus lumbered into the avenue like a runaway dung cart, and Icabus took off behind Cana. He heard Bassus's curses in the distance as the fat man struggled to keep up and quickly fell behind. They zigzagged through the trees and sprinted down the northern slope into the wheat.

Icabus and Cana knelt and peered through the grass. Bassus was nowhere in sight. Icabus fell onto his back and breathed deeply. He turned his head to Cana. "What kind of plan was that?"

Cana panted. "It seemed like a good idea at the time."

Icabus rolled over and crawled to the edge of the field. Soldiers wandered between the houses. Some carried jewelry boxes and other trinkets, but most held food, which they forced into their mouths until their cheeks bulged.

"These guys are starving," said Cana, peering over his shoulder. "We could probably walk right through town, and they would pay us no mind."

"I'd rather not." Icabus crept out of the grass, leading Cana between the houses to a hedge behind the meeting hall.

Five soldiers huddled near the back door. They rested on their haunches, swords drawn.

Bassus entered the clearing and nearly collapsed. He rested one hand on an oak tree and leaned forward, trying to catch his breath. "Have any of you seen two kids? A girl and a boy?"

"No, what did they do?" asked one of the soldiers.

"They taunted Atellus. If I get my hands on them, Minius, I'll—"

"What, pass out on them?" Minius laughed.

The other Authians jeered, and Bassus waved his hand and stumbled off. Looking back up the hill, he groaned. "Gods save me."

"The Gods will never forgive us for this," said a thin soldier resting his chin on the hilt of his sword. "What a cruel hand fate has given us."

"The Gods already curse us, Seius," said Minius. "How many of us prayed at the temples of Authia even as our villages burned? Some good that did us, *Priest of the Gods*."

Seius brushed the long strands of his gray hair away from his face. "To commit the same sin against others as has been inflicted upon us is not a path to salvation, it is a road to damnation."

"I think the Gods delivered us here so that we might have our revenge," said another soldier, stroking his peppered beard. "Furius's visions, the Gilian, Galen, none of it is by chance. The Gods favor us, I'm sure of it."

"Thank you, Salvius," said Minius, smiling. He was shorter than the other soldiers, with olive skin and black, fierce eyes. "How about you, Licinius, what do you think of our newfound fortune?"

Licinius shifted uncomfortably and looked up. He was an older man beset with deep wrinkles. "I overheard Atellus say that Furius believes that if we cross into the Golden Land, we will grow young and live forever. A new start... I want that."

Minius winked at Seius. "You can't damn what lives forever."

"Damnation is forever," Seius answered flatly.

"You know what I think, priest? I think you're jealous. You have lost Furius's ear and most of us as well. Now you're just a soldier like the rest of us."

Seius lowered his head and said nothing.

Minius made a satisfied grunt and addressed the others. "So, have any of you seen this Galen chap?"

"I have," said Gurges, appearing around the edge of the

building. He knelt between Salvius and Seius and squeezed Seius's shoulder.

"I hear he is as fair as a woman." Minius winked.

"With skin as soft and white as snow." Gurges grinned, revealing a missing cuspid.

Salvius crossed his arms and chuckled nervously. "What's he doing on the weapons ship?"

"Making weapons." Gurges smirked and rose to his feet. "Are you men ready to work?"

The soldiers grumbled in assent; Gurges led them into the back of the hall and closed the door behind him.

"Let's go," said Icabus, leaving the shadows.

Murmurs reverberated through the stone walls, and Icabus parted the door and peeked inside. Two short opposing staircases led backstage, where stacks of crates and other supplies used for town festivals rose nearly to the rafters. Gurges and the other soldiers were nowhere in sight.

Icabus tapped Cana on the shoulder and pointed stage left to a seam of light in the curtains. Cana nodded, and they crept toward the opening.

ICABUS

The town hall was more crowded than Icabus had ever seen. Villagers stood along the walls and sat shoulder-to-shoulder on benches running from the hall doors to the stage, where the Elders took their seats behind a wide oak table facing the townspeople. At the center of the table, seated in a high-backed chair, was Maro, flanked by Silana and Vetus to his right, and Cilo and Ralla to his left. Standing beside Vetus was Furius, who appeared healthier to Icabus.

Maro struck his gavel against a wooden block. "Quiet down, everybody. Quiet down."

"You heard the man," added Vetus, striking his hand against the table.

Maro waited for the chatter to dissipate. "Thank you, Vetus. As all of you know, a thing happened yesterday that hasn't occurred in a century—we have visitors."

"Is it true they came from Arx Caeli?" called a voice from the crowd.

"Did they see the Gilian? Is the path across the lake now open?" shouted another.

"Please." Maro raised his hands. "The man before you is Furius of Authia. Please give him the courtesy to speak without interruption."

The villagers whispered and shifted nervously in their seats. All eyes, including Icabus's, fell on Furius.

Furius bowed slightly to Maro; holding his hands behind his crimson cape, he crossed in front of the table. The dull click of his boots rapped ominously on the wood as he covered the distance of the stage.

"Thank you, Elders," Furius spoke evenly. "A hundred years ago, when darkness fell upon these lands, its shadow also reached the Twelve Kingdoms. Faith in the Gods diminished, and in every village, the stench of alchemy could be found."

Furius lowered his gaze. "Fanaticism spread through the nobility like a plague. Blinded by desire and fear, the rulers of the Twelve Kingdoms installed the alchemist, Marius, as Praetor of Arx Caeli, who promised to extend their lives in exchange for their servitude and the sacrifice of their firstborn sons. A few kingdoms, including Authia, resisted, and it cost us everything..."

Furius rested his hand on the edge of the table and scanned the assembly. His expression was stoic, but his eyes blazed with anger. "My own bannermen betrayed me. Those and I loyal to Authia were marched to the capital for execution. All appeared lost. Illness and grief stole my strength, and I began to suffer a dying man's visions. In my fever, I saw the spirit of my father, who told that to avenge Authia, I must cross the forest lake and find the one trapped in darkness."

Icabus shivered, recalling the dark presence in his nightmares.

Furius smirked. "My men thought me mad until my visions helped us escape Marius's dungeons; we boarded the ships you saw and set our sails to Apenninus. By the time the harbor soldiers fired their arrows at us, we were beyond capture. Eighty-six of us set out from Arx Caeli—the last free men of Authia."

The room erupted into chatter, and Maro struck his gavel. Icabus saw Furius look toward the curtains, where Gurges and his men hid near the center of the stage.

"What's happening?" Cana whispered.

"Nothing good," Icabus said in reply.

"Do you see Atius out there?"

"No, I don't see Father." Icabus sighed.

Maro raised his hands and the hall again wound down into murmurs. "My friends, I know you have a lot of questions. I do too. It is no secret that many of us have experienced nightmares of late. Furius believes there is a link between our dreams and his visions."

"What link?" shouted a villager.

The Elders regarded one another and Maro slowly let out his breath. "Galen."

The villagers gasped and the hall grew so loud Icabus could feel their voices reverberate through the floorboards beneath him. Maro struck his gavel.

"My friends... My friends!" Maro pushed back his chair and stood up, drawing attention to him. "Ever since the fall of the Old Kingdom, we have made decisions together. Last night, Furius made a request that we believe can only be decided as a community. Please let him speak and we can debate the merits of his appeal."

Furius bowed his head and scrutinized the villagers. "You are the descendants of the most powerful kingdom to exist since fabled Ludus. Swear fealty to me, and we can rebuild the Apennine Kingdom to its former glory and restore balance to the Twelve Kingdoms."

The Elders shared exasperated expressions and Cilo stood up. "This is not what we discussed."

"What say you?" Furius asked the Elders.

"This is mad," said Silana.

Furius shook his head. "Gurges."

From behind the curtains, Gurges led Licinius, Seius, Salvius, and Minius onto the stage. In front of the hall, soldiers entered through the main doors, brandishing swords and spears.

"What is the meaning of this?" Cilo raised his voice.

Gurges pointed his sword to Cilo's chest. Cilo sat back in his chair, mouth agape.

Ralla eyed the men sourly. "Who are these soldiers?"

"They are a small part of the eighty-six Authians who are now protecting your village," said Furius.

"Eighty-six? You lied to us," said Ralla.

"I am sorry." Furius addressed the villagers. "My friends, thanks to one of your own, Atius, I have already confirmed my visions. Galen lives and he has granted me the authority to return this island and its inhabitants to greatness. I do not want bloodshed." Furius extended his sigil ring to the Elders. "Kneel and swear allegiance to me and together we can destroy Praetor Marius and bring peace to the Twelve Kingdoms."

"You're insane!" Vetus pushed back his chair and pressed his hands against the table. "We will not be ordered around by thugs like you."

Furius slowly lowered his hand. His demeaner was calm but Icabus saw fury in his eyes. "I did not wish for this to happen, but it is what Galen said would come to pass... Minius."

Minius forced Vetus into his seat. Furius made a slicing motion across his neck, and Minius cut Vetus's throat.

Icabus started but could not look away. Vetus gasped for breath as blood poured down his tunic. Throughout the hall, townspeople shrieked and held one another as the Elders pressed their backs to their seats.

Cana reached out and embraced Icabus. Icabus felt her touch him, but he could not bring himself to comfort her. The sight of such violence left him numb.

"We have to go." Cana tugged on Icabus's shirt. His mind told him to run, but he felt frozen in place.

Furius rested his hands on the Elders' table. "Swear allegiance. Save your people." He spoke forcefully.

Silana rose from her chair with balled fists. Icabus could see her brother, Cyprian, shake his head at her from the crowd, pleading with her not to speak. "Aggersel has no king." She spit in Furius's direction.

Furius touched the spittle on his face and shook his head. "Licinius."

Licinius seized Silana by the hair and drove his blade through her back. She raised her hand to Cyprian and fell limply to the ground.

"No!" Cyprian rushed the stage. He tripped on the steps, and two of Furius's soldiers threw him to the ground and began to kick him.

Ralla positioned herself behind her chair.

"Get behind me, Ralla." Cilo placed himself between her and the soldiers.

Salvius took him by the collar and threw him to the ground.

"No. Stop!" Cilo covered his face.

Salvius turned to Furius, who nodded, and stabbed Cilo in the gut. Cilo doubled over and Salvius took him by the hair and slit his throat.

"Such a shame. Seius." Furius pointed to Ralla.

Seius raised his blade and stepped forward.

"Please. You don't have to do this." Ralla began to cry. "You don't."

Seius stopped and looked to Furius, who nodded. He tossed the chair aside; and, again, he hesitated.

"Come on," Gurges spat. "The locals are getting restless. Finish her."

"Get away from her!" Maro knocked his chair against Gurges and threw himself at Seius. Maro struck him, and together they fell to the floor. Blood filled Maro's mouth, and he moved his tongue as if to speak; he seized Seius's hand holding the hilt protruding from his gut. "Curse you. Curse you all..." He fell limp.

Ralla tripped over her own feet and ran for the curtain. Icabus's eyes met hers, and she stopped suddenly. With her lips, she mouthed, "Run."

Time seemed to fracture before Icabus's vision. He saw Gurges behind Ralla, and then the soldier's sword point protruding from her chest. Ralla grimaced, and Icabus caught his terrified reflection in her eyes. She fell to the floor, and Gurges freed his sword from her back. He wiped the blade on her dress and sheathed it.

"Hey, kid," said Gurges, smiling at Icabus. "Come here."

Icabus stumbled back into Cana. "Run," he said, allowing her to take the lead.

Behind him, Icabus could hear Gurges toss around the boxes behind the stage. They emerged from the hall and ran to the cover of the orchards.

"I gotta go home, Cana," said Icabus.

"Me too." She trembled. "When am I going to see you next?"

Icabus shook his head. "I don't know."

Cana leaned over and kissed him on the cheek. "For luck," she said, sprinting off.

Icabus watched her disappear into the shadows of the apple grove. Somehow, he knew from this moment on, neither of them would ever be the same.

ICABUS

Icabus knelt below the portico window. There were no signs of Atellus, Bassus, or any of the other soldiers.

A limp body hung lifelessly over the railing of the watchtower. Icabus took a deep breath and tiptoed around the edge of the house.

"Got you," Gurges growled.

Icabus spun around, but Gurges had him by the tunic.

"Don't struggle, or I'll break your face, you hear?"

"Where's my father?"

"Atius? Tied up somewhere. Very useful your father."

Icabus allowed Gurges to pull him toward the porch. His father was alive. That's all that mattered to him.

Gurges kicked open the door and pushed Icabus inside. "Mother, Amara!" Icabus shouted.

"Icabus?" Lucia choked.

Gurges guided him toward the kitchen. Atellus and Bassus sat at the table with bowls of soup and bread before them. Lucia stood near Atellus with a decanter of hard cider in her hands, while Amara sat in the corner playing with her dolls.

"Icabus." Amara raised her teacup. "The knights have come for lunch. They are here to save us from the evil Takers."

"Uh-huh." Icabus didn't move.

"Aye," said Bassus, slurping a cabbage leaf out of his bowl. "Wait. You're that brat I chased down the hill. You got something coming to you."

Icabus opened his mouth, but Lucia shook her head ever so slightly, and Icabus held his tongue.

"You need the exercise, Bassus." Atellus smiled, lifting his glass. Lucia did not notice, and Atellus grabbed her arm and pulled her forward. "Cider!"

"Don't touch my mother," said Icabus.

Lucia's eyes grew wide. Atellus raised his napkin and cleaned the corner of his mouth. Amara began to cry.

"I expect an honorable boy to defend his mother. That is why I haven't broken your jaw. Speak again without my lead, and I will."

Atellus pushed Lucia backward. "More cider and shut up that child," he said, not taking his eyes off Icabus. "And where have you been tonight, Icabus?"

"With a friend."

"A friend. That would not happen to be in town, would it?" Atellus asked.

"No," Icabus muttered. He didn't sound convincing even to himself. "Down the ridge to the south."

"The south. Are you sure? There was a report of two children spotted near the town hall: a boy and a girl. Sound familiar?"

Icabus shook his head.

"No?"

"No," said Icabus.

"You weren't the boy hiding behind the curtain?" asked Gurges skeptically.

"No, that was another boy."

Gurges gave Atellus a doubtful look and took his seat. Lucia gave him soup, bread, and cider. Bassus pinched Lucia's thigh as she passed. She flinched, and Icabus suppressed his anger. Lucia went to the corner and picked up Amara. The little girl was flush with tears but was quickly comforted in her mother's embrace.

Gurges smiled at Amara. "What a lovely little girl. Gurges likes him a pretty girl. Want to come and sit on my lap, darling?"

Amara hid her face, and Bassus snickered. Icabus felt his stomach turn.

Gurges looked at Icabus and then to Atellus. "This boy appears like a kettle ready to boil over, Atellus."

Atellus nodded. "Aye. What do you think, Bassus?

"I think he needs to loosen up a bit." Bassus raised his bowl to his lips and burped. Broth, cider, and bits of meat clung to his beard and dripped onto his already stained tunic. "There are more than a few ways to break a young buck like this."

Lucia picked up Amara and placed her hand on Icabus's shoulder. "May we leave this house as ordered and go into town?"

Icabus regarded Lucia with disbelief. "They're forcing us to leave?"

Lucia did not reply, and Atellus leaned back in his chair. "Good food, good drink, but I think your boy needs a lesson. I am sure he's the one Bassus was chasing through town and also the one Gurges saw in the village hall. Am I right, boy?"

The soldiers pushed back their chairs and eyed Icabus like hungry dogs cornering a fox.

Lucia shielded him and led him from the house. "Please, we've done as you asked. Let us leave in peace," she pleaded.

Atellus removed his belt and wrapped the buckled end around his hand. "You and the child may leave, but the boy stays. I don't know why, but our new friend Galen wants to meet young Icabus, here."

Lucia shook her head and turned to her son. "Run, Icabus."

"No," Icabus protested.

"You must," she said, placing her hand on his cheek. "Do you remember your dream about the black dragon?"

"Yes... But what does that have to do with anything?"

"Icabus, I never told you, but I think it was a vision. Trust me. You have to run. Now."

She kissed his head, and his eyes began to water. "I can't leave you with them."

"Yes, you can. Go!"

Gurges pushed Lucia to the ground and reached for Icabus. Amara screamed, and Icabus jumped forward, kicking Gurges between the legs. The soldier dropped to his knees.

"That's for your sick thoughts," Icabus shouted.

"Kill him," Gurges groaned.

"Come here." Atellus seized Icabus's shoulder and back-handed him. Icabus fell onto his side, dazed.

"Icabus..." Lucia reached out her hand to him.

Icabus staggered to his feet, but before he could regain his balance, Atellus hit him again. Everything seemed to be moving too fast, and he lost all sense of direction as he hit the ground. Atellus kicked him in the stomach.

"That's just the start." Atellus took off his gloves and helped Gurges up.

Gurges placed his hands on his knees and leaned over. "Argh! Give me a second." He grimaced.

Icabus's head felt heavy, and his muscles burned down to the bone. Down the pathway, the voices of men could be heard ascending the ridge, whilst a few others could be heard searching the orchards below. There was nowhere to run.

"Looks like Furius is coming to check on us." Atellus followed Icabus's gaze. "Compared to me, boy, that man's the fire of Hell itself."

"Let me get a few licks in before he gets here," Gurges huffed.

"Icabus." Lucia embraced Amara and lowered her voice. "Go." She pointed to the guarding wall.

Icabus could feel his heart in his throat. The one thing he was taught never to do, the one thing no one in Aggersel dared to do, was cross the guarding wall into the woods.

Icabus scanned the horizon, seeking somewhere, anywhere he could run that wasn't the woods. The men were very close now, and he could make out Furius's crimson cape over the rise. Beside him was a man in a purple robe—the same man who haunted his nightmares.

"Galen..." Icabus whispered.

Gurges reached down, and Icabus spun toward him, punching him square in the groin. The soldier doubled over for a second time; Icabus leaped over Gurges and made for the watchtower ladder.

Shouts rose up behind Icabus as the arriving soldiers broke

into a sprint. Atellus maneuvered in front of Icabus, extending his reach with his sword.

"Yield and keep your foot. Otherwise, I promise you it will be the least of your handicaps," Atellus threatened.

Icabus pivoted right but immediately shifted his weight and ran in the opposite direction. A shout and a thud sounded behind him, and Icabus turned long enough to see Atellus lying flat on his stomach with Lucia's hands around his boot.

"Run!" cried his mother.

"Grab the brat!" Atellus cursed, pushing himself to his knees.

Icabus heard Bassus swearing behind him, but it only motivated him to move faster. He reached the ladder and climbed hurriedly to the platform above. A waist-high railing surrounded the square lookout, and Icabus pulled himself over it facing the forest.

He looked up at the dark forest rising ominously before him. Behind him, the ladder creaked below the trapdoor. Icabus took a deep breath, gave Aggersel a final look, and leaped toward the nearest tree branch. His distance was good, but the strength of his grip was not, and the limb slid through Icabus's fingers like a wet fish. He hit the forest floor and found himself partially buried in a pile of leaves.

Above him, the soldiers leaned over the platform and pointed at him. Icabus rolled out of the leaves and stumbled away. The thick loam of the forest floor deafened his footfalls, and he zigzagged through the labyrinth of trees until all sight and sound of the soldiers were far behind him.

Bands of sunlight penetrated the forest canopy, and Icabus followed them to a wide chasm bridged by a fallen oak. Claw marks scored the bark and reminded Icabus of where he was at.

"I can't stay here," he whispered.

Something moved in the underbrush behind him, and Icabus scurried over the chasm. He hid in the shadow of the fallen tree and pulled his knees to his chest. Nothing stirred in the forest, and for a long time, he watched and waited until exhaustion took him and he slept, dreamless and afraid.

ICABUS

The wood was dark and cold when Icabus awoke. Across the reach, a low mist covered the ground and spilled over the chasm in a spectral stream. If anyone had followed him, they had turned back or gone another way.

"What is that?" Icabus muttered.

Not far from his resting place, a pile of tattered cloth lay strewn against the side of a tree. Icabus lifted a soiled bonnet with a stick. He touched the fabric and fell to his knees.

Icabus blinked, and the world brightened. Bees hummed and apple blossoms fell into a creek before him. The image reflected in the water was not his own but that of a young girl with red hair and freckles. Another girl, who looked very much like a younger version of his mother, Lucia, ran ahead laughing.

Young Lucia spun around in a circle with her arms outstretched. Her yellow and white dress fluttered around her like sunflower petals caught in a breeze. Icabus ran up behind her and seized the bonnet from her head.

"Lepida, give that back," Lucia laughed.

"Now you see me, now you don't," said Lepida. She pulled the bonnet over her head and ran around the apple trees, giggling, zigzagging any which way to avoid Lucia's grasp.

"I'll get you, you'll see," panted Lucia.

"No, you won't," said Lepida. She reached the top of the ridge and entered an old grove littered with stone ruins.

"Ha, you're trapped," giggled Lucia.

"No, I'm not." Lepida dashed to the edge of the forest. "Will you follow me in there?" She pointed to the wood.

Lucia's smile vanished "Lepida, don't. Mama says there's a

monster in the woods."

"I don't see one, do you?" Lepida stepped into the shadows and hid behind a tree. "Boo! Now I'm the monster."

Lucia froze. "Lepida, come back."

"Fine, scaredy, I'm com— Wait, do you hear that? I think I hear somebody crying."

"Lepida, no..."

"But somebody's crying." Lepida parted the thicket and came to a ring of boulders. "Hello, who's there? Do you need help?"

Silence settled over everything, and Lepida stepped away from the boulders. A terrible cackle broke the silence.

"And where are you going, you brave little thing?"

Lepida gasped as a clawed hand slipped around the edge of a boulder followed by a snout overflowing with sharp teeth.

"If the dragons don't watch and the Gilian are far away, we eat," laughed the monster. His eyes were yellow like a bad liver.

"Leave me alone!" Lepida ran, ignoring the branches that battered her face and arms.

Through Lepida's eyes, Icabus could see Lucia's sunflower dress beyond the trees; he could smell the apple blossoms and feel the warmth of the sun's rays passing through the forest foliage.

Lucia ran forward.

"No, Lucia. Run! Get away!" Lepida leaped over a branch, but her toe caught its bark, and she fell to the forest floor.

"Lepida, give me your hand. Lepida!"

Icabus could feel the monster's grip on Lepida's ankle. There was a sense of weightlessness, and the world spun upside down. Lucia's horrified face told him everything: the monster had them.

Icabus dropped the bonnet, and the dark wood came back into focus. "Mother... You knew it was out here. It took your friend. How could you send me here?"

Across the chasm, a stick broke, and a monstrous form shifted in the darkness. Whatever it was, it now stood between Icabus and the path back down the mountain.

"Bassus, is that you?"

Icabus's heart pounded in his ears as he shifted his gaze over the twisting forest shadows. Somewhere out there, something began to cry.

Icabus backed away, almost tripping over the pile of rotting garments.

The cry morphed into a tittering laugh. "It's been a long time since one so young has wandered into my wood."

"Stay back!" Icabus shouted. "I have a sword."

"It doesn't have a sword." The monster clawed his way atop the fallen tree.

"Gods, you... you're a Taker."

"A Taker... yes, but you may call me Arkax if you wish." The Taker licked his nose and sniffed the air in Icabus's direction.

Icabus continued to back away. He looked for a weapon—something, anything. Even the rocks seemed to have abandoned him.

"No sword, no stone, only skins and bones," laughed the monster. His eyes glowed in the dark like yellow flames.

"Go away!" Icabus dug his fingers into the earth and scrambled up the hill. The forest was very dark, and everything in it looked the same. He spun around in disarray and froze.

There amid trees was Lepida, the girl from his vision. Her pale dress hung limply over her thin body, which appeared translucent. A look of sadness covered her face. She waved him in her direction.

"Come here!" The Taker leapt and knocked Icabus to the ground.

Icabus struck his back and kicked the monster in the muzzle. The beast tumbled backward down the hill and hit a clump of jagged roots; he yowled in pain, and Icabus pulled himself up and ran in Lepida's direction.

Out of the corner of his eye, Icabus could see Arkax angling toward him in an attempt to cut him off. Bristly fur like a porcupine's needles covered the monster's body. He ran partly on all fours and partly like a man, with grotesque paw-like hands and feet bearing curved claws that reflected the starlight like obsidian.

Lepida continued up the hill, disappearing behind one tree and reappearing around another. As fast as Icabus ran, he never seemed to get any closer to her. Then suddenly, she was gone.

Icabus heard the flopping of the monster's enormous feet as he closed in on him. "No! Not this way. Come back!" Arkax snarled.

Ahead of Icabus, a low wall of white stone girded a field filled with moon flowers. He fell over the wall, cutting his back and shredding his shirt. The Taker clawed at him from over the wall; he wailed as if mortally injured.

"Come back!" Arkax snatched up a piece of Icabus's shredded tunic and held it to his nose. He shifted his gaze between Icabus and the ruins beyond.

"Go away!" Icabus scrambled backward on all fours; he looked behind him but couldn't see what gave the monster pause.

The Taker began to crawl over the wall but then retreated. "You fool. Can't you smell him? He will tear you limb from limb, and you will pray for death."

Icabus got to his feet and moved farther away from the wall.

"Come back to us," the Taker whimpered, resting his jaw against the stone and extending his clawed hands like a child begging for his favorite toy.

"No." Icabus shook his head.

Arkax took a deep breath and disappeared behind the wall. Icabus could sense the beast's presence lurking behind the stone, wishing and wanting.

A cold breeze blew down from the cliffs, and Icabus held himself and stumbled across the field. Where the granite cliffs narrowed, an emerald vein of pine and fern continued up into the mountain.

Icabus pushed aside the veil of branches and entered the grove. He felt listless and sore all over. Roofless stone ruins filled the wood. He tried not to think about being alone, but every broken door and empty window reminded him of home, and when the first tear escaped, it was as if a dam of emotion had broken, and he wept there against the ancient walls until exhaustion took him and he slept.

ATIUS

"The boy's father." Atellus shoved Atius to his knees.

"Unbind him." Galen spoke softly, sifting through the bottles on the table. Beside him, Furius leaned against the inner hull of the ship and rubbed his eyes. To Atius, he appeared like a man under a spell.

"Give me your hands," said Atellus, cutting Atius's bonds.

Atius massaged his wrists and looked around. The table, like the rest of the room's furnishings, reminded him of the decaying relics of the Old Kingdom. "Why am I here?"

"To choose," said Galen, drawing back his sleeve. He took a shallow breath and cut into his right wrist with a paring knife. Blood trickled from the wound, which he added to a small cauldron elevated over a tabletop flame.

"A hundred years ago, my followers and I found the source of the sacred spring in the dragons' caves. The dragons called this place the Golden Land. There was an invisible power there—a mana, unlike anything that now exists in this world. It infused our bodies, granting us long life and other abilities. We became transformed by our thoughts, and in our anger, we assumed terrible forms."

Galen stirred the mixture. "The creature in the woods that your people fear is, in fact, a disciple of mine named Arkax. When the dragons drove us from the Golden Land, he left me for dead. He is a coward and a beast, and his form reflects it. Even now that mana returns, I doubt he will ever assume a human form again."

"Why are you telling me this?" Atius asked. The floor creaked and Atius looked over his shoulder where two guards wearing butcher's smocks blocked the door. One had a gangly black beard, whilst the other was hairless save for two patches of curly red hair behind his ears. Their hungry smiles made Atius uneasy.

"Because it gave me an idea." Galen glanced up. "Anger, hunger, lust, envy. These are the emotions that turn men into Takers. Using these herbs, I can invoke any emotion I wish. Adding a small amount of my blood will induce the potential for a single, irreversible change."

"You're making monsters."

Galen rested his pale hands on the table and smiled delicately. "You are fortunate, Atius. What happens next is your choice. I'm ready, Furius."

Furius addressed the guards behind Atius. "Villus. Ulpius. Bring the prisoner."

"My lord," said Villus, moving his beard up-and-down. Iron bars separated Galen's lab from a narrow hallway running fore to aft down the center of the ship's hold to a locked door.

Villus took the lead and unlatched the door. Ulpius followed behind him, holding a lantern and a small hand ax. The door creaked open, and a foul smell, like animal excrement, struck Atius's nostrils. The soldiers disappeared inside, and Atius felt a shiver go up his spine as chains rattled and something within growled.

There was a protest and a human cry followed by silence. Villus emerged with a boy slumped over his shoulder."

"Is that Icabus?" Atius gasped.

"No." Atellus placed his hand on Atius's shoulder, staying him. "That's not your son."

"Leave him there, Villus." Furius pointed to the floor beside Atius where a collection of parchments soaked up a puddle of drying blood.

Villus dropped the boy, whom Atius recognized as Pelagus, son of Piscius, the boatman. "You are a lucky man." Villus stared down at Atius like a heretic. "Galen's creations are beautiful."

"How are the other... creations?" Furius asked Villus.

"Well enough for traitors and would-be deserters, my lord. They follow commands with a little persuasion." He patted the club at his side.

Furius crossed his arms. "These monsters are uncontrollable, Galen. They would just as soon bite off your hand as speak."

"Any art, including this kind, requires practice to perfect." Galen dipped a flask into the cauldron, filling it with a brown, putrid liquid. He placed it on the table in front of Atius. "Your son has injured one of Furius's guards and is in hiding. The guard will recover, but his pride is wounded. The penalty for attacking a soldier is death... or worse." Galen touched the top of the flask.

"I won't let you hurt my son," said Atius.

"Nor do I want that," Galen replied. "Your son's dreaming awakened me. I would like to meet him. Furius has agreed to pardon his crime in exchange for your allegiance and assistance in maintaining order."

Atius looked at Furius. "The Elders are the leaders of the village. Nobody will follow me over them."

"Your Elders are dead," answered Furius. "You can lead in their absence."

"Dead... How?" Atius tried to say more, but the words escaped him.

"This potion is for you or the boy." Galen regarded Pelagus, who began to stir. "He killed a soldier trying to search his house. He was brave, but all actions have consequences. Accept Furius's offer, and your son will be pardoned. This boy will receive the potion for your son's crime and his own. Refuse, and Villus will give you the potion. The boy will be your first meal."

"He's just a boy. Furius, please."

Furius frowned and regarded Atius with a sullen gaze. "It is also my will. Choose."

Atius eyed Pelagus. The boy was not much older than Icabus. "And what of the rest of my family?"

"They will all be under my protection," said Furius, extending his sigil ring.

Atius hesitated and shook his head.

"Time has run out for you, Atius. I will not offer this again," Furius spoke flatly.

Atius glanced from the ring to Pelagus. He took a deep breath and shut his eyes. "Gods forgive me," he prayed, kissing the ring.

"Rouse the boy, Villus." Furius waved his hand.

Villus kicked Pelagus in the gut. The boy started and coughed; he stared frightfully at the men in the room and fixed his gaze on Atius.

"Atius?" Pelagus began to cry. "There are monsters down here. Help me. I want to go home."

"Give it to him, Atius," said Galen, gesturing to the potion.

Atius's eyes widened. "No. Why must I do this?"

Pelagus reached for Atius's trousers. "Atius, what are they talking about?"

"Villus, Ulpius, help Atius with the boy," instructed Galen.

"Like the last one?" Ulpius asked Villus.

Villus nodded and grabbed a funnel and some rope hanging from a hook on the doorpost. Ulpius put the lantern on the table and took Pelagus by the collar.

Pelagus cried out, and Ulpius pressed his face to the planks. Villus handed Ulpius the rope, and the bald man bound Pelagus's arms behind his back. He sat Pelagus up and stood behind him, placing one hand under the boy's chin and the other across his forehead.

"Atius, help me. Atius!" Pelagus sobbed.

Villus tried to place the tube in Pelagus's mouth, but the boy resisted, so Ulpius smothered the boy's face with his hand. Pelagus became red and began to thrash. Villus placed the funnel near his lips and Ulpius relaxed his grip. The boy gasped for breath, and Villus forced the end of the funnel into Pelagus's mouth.

Galen offered the potion again, and Atius fell to his knees, touching Furius's feet. "Please, Furius. Do not make me do this."

Furius stepped aside and regarded Atius abjectly. "You have your order."

Atius trembled and took the flask. Pelagus struggled and made a series of garbled groans, pleading to Atius with his watery eyes.

"I'm sorry," said Atius, turning away and pouring the potion into the funnel.

Villus released the tube and Ulpius held Pelagus's mouth shut. "Swallow, and you get to breathe," said Ulpius.

Pelagus did, and Ulpius released him. The boy gagged and gasped for breath.

"Place him in shackles and a neck collar like the others. He will begin to change very soon," said Galen.

Ulpius lifted Pelagus by the collar, and Villus patted the boy on the face. "I envy you," said Villus.

Ulpius drug Pelagus out of the room, and Villus followed. Atius covered his face and wept.

"You made the right choice," said Galen.

"Atellus, take Atius back to his family." Furius waved his hand. "Inform Gurges that when we find Atius's son, he is not to be harmed and should be returned to Atius immediately. Am I clear?"

"Aye. Come on, Atius." Atellus appeared unsettled. "Let's get out of this place."

"Atius!" Pelagus cried with a voice not his own. "Atius!"

ICABUS

Caw!

"No!" Icabus lurched forward.

A shiny crow, the largest Icabus had ever seen, regarded Icabus from the windowsill.

"Seriously?" Icabus fell back and covered his eyes with his arm.

Caw!

"Be quiet."

Icabus waited for the bird to make another sound, but it was silent. He lifted his arm, and the crow cocked its head and blinked.

"Is this your house or something?" he said, noticing the array of small animal bones strewn about the room.

The crow ambled back and forth along the sill. It lifted one leg into its plumage and closed its eyes.

"I think that's a yes." Icabus sat up and stretched. A dull ache permeated his muscles, and he felt lightheaded. "Gods I'm hungry. Crow, where can I find some food?"

The crow blinked thoughtfully and waddled to the edge of the sill, where it lifted a dead mouse with its beak and tossed it onto Icabus's lap.

"Gross..." Icabus raised the mouse by the tail and placed it back on the sill. "I can't eat that. Do you know where any fruit is? Gods, of course you don't."

Caw! The crow flew to a nearby branch and repeated its call.

Icabus staggered out of the ruin onto an overgrown avenue leading deeper into the canyon. Ahead of him, the crow glided from branch to branch, occasionally looking back in his direction. In the morning light, Icabus thought the forest ruins looked more lonely than scary.

"Well, isn't that something," Icabus whispered, looking up.

Built against the canyon wall and sharing the sky with the treetops was a turret covered in vines. Its wooden top had long rotted away, but the tower rose mostly intact.

"Is that a castle back there, Mr. Crow?" Icabus passed under the crow's branch and looked up. "Aren't you coming?"

The crow gazed down at Icabus and then at the castle and ruffled its feathers.

"I guess not." Icabus crossed his arms and shivered. The valley shadows were cold, but he felt like someone, or something, was watching him. "I hope you're sending me where I can find food and not where I can be food, Mr. Crow."

The trees thinned, and Icabus saw that the tower was not part of a castle but of a guarding wall closing the canyon's end. At the center of the wall was an arched gate large enough for a dragon to pass through; the wooden doors were rotted away to the hinges, but the iron portcullis remained shut.

Icabus tore a hole in the vine-covered grating. A single avenue lined with apple trees led to a meadow at the canyon's end surrounded by natural caves. The trees there were older than any Icabus had seen in Aggersel, but to his surprise, they appeared to have been pruned in the last season.

"Well, I suppose I could climb it." He glanced up. "On the other hand, do I have a choice?"

The vines provided numerous handholds, and Icabus scaled the wall with a mind not to look down. He hoped he might see Aggersel, but all he saw were the treetops and the distant waters of the forest lake.

Icabus faced the canyon. "Hello!"

"Hello… Hello," the canyon echoed.

"That was stupid," Icabus whispered to himself. "I should have just said, 'Here I am, come and eat me.'"

Icabus crossed the wall walk and entered the turret. A stone stair led to the avenue below, and Icabus tiptoed down the steps to the shade of the apple trees.

Past the trees, the canyon walls joined and rose in a stepwise fashion like a giant's stair. At each level, caves and other stone ruins dotted the cliffside. There was no stair up or down. If you wished to reach the caves, you had to fly.

Icabus walked along the trees and entered the meadow. At the center of the park, surrounded by broken columns, was a round stone altar covered with fresh apples, berries, and root vegetables.

"Hello, is anyone here?" Icabus turned around.

A soft wind whistled down the granite, stirring a collection of chimes hanging from one of the apple branches. Again, Icabus felt eyes upon him and saw the fat crow perched atop one of the broken columns.

"Thanks for leading me to this food, Mr. Crow. It looks like an offering. I'm not sure I should eat it."

Caw. The crow landed on the table and began pecking at a red apple.

Icabus entered the circle and looked at the fruit. The apples still had green leaves on their stems, which surprised him because apple season wasn't for another two months. In fact, none of the fruit on the table was in season.

"Today is Ostara, isn't it, Mr. Crow? The spring festivals would have begun today if Furius hadn't..." Icabus rested his hands on the edge of the altar table and allowed the wave of emotion to pass.

"You wouldn't happen to know any great warriors or dragons that can help rescue my village, would you?"

The crow stopped pecking and cocked its head.

"I didn't think so." Icabus walked away from the altar.

A flattened trail of grass led to a crop of boulders along the cliffside. The crow left his perch to sharpen his beak on the tallest stone. Icabus followed the trail around the rocks to an earthen stair descending into the mountain.

"Hi, I'm Icabus. I'm from the village down the hill. Is anyone in there?"

Icabus hated caves. Ordinary people didn't live in caves. Monsters lived in caves.

The ground inside the cave was moist and fell away steeply like a muddy slide. Icabus held on to a root and leaned forward. Along the wall, a sloping stair twisted downward in an uneven, narrow spiral.

"I'm going to eat one of the apples on the table. Alright?"

Icabus shifted his weight, and the root broke. He flailed his arms and fell backward, letting out a feeble cry. The ground beneath him rushed away, and there were no handholds or roots to slow him. If he was afraid, he was too scared to know it, and he greeted oblivion as most men do—thoughtlessly.

ATIUS

"Not that way," growled Atellus.

Atius looked at Atellus quizzically. "That is the road to my home."

"It's Furius's house now."

"Where's my family?"

"The Lady Tulia's." Atellus took the lead.

"Why are you doing this? What does Furius want?"

"Those are two different questions," said Atellus. "I'm doing this because nothing matters. Furius wants vengeance. Pray that you keep your family, Atius. The world is a dark place without them."

"Atellus, I don't think you are an evil man. You could help us."

Atellus pushed Atius under the shade of a storefront. "If you know what's best for you and yours, Atius, you will never test my loyalty again."

Atius parted his lips but held his tongue.

"Good, I like it when you don't talk. I'm going to fetch Gurges and put together our guard. Say hello to your pretty wife for me. I'll come by in an hour. I want all of Aggersel to see you stand with us."

Atellus left him, and Atius ambled through the empty square to Tulia's porch. Feeling ashamed and mostly numb, he knocked.

"Who is it?" Tulia answered through the door.

"Atius, my lady."

Lady Tulia parted the door and quickly scanned Atius and the porch. Her face was red from tears.

"Lady Tulia." He bowed. "My condolences for your loss. Are

my wife and daughter here?"

"Papa!" Amara shouted.

"Amara, wait," came Lucia's voice from the distance.

The child slipped through the crack in the door and into her father's arms. "My baby girl." Atius smiled, kissing her on the forehead.

"Papa, where is Icabus?"

Atius held back his anger. "Icabus will be coming home soon. I promise."

"Come inside," said Tulia. Her hand trembled against the door latch. Atius touched her shoulder and went inside.

The anteroom was warm and smelled like butter and nutmeg. Lucia stood before him, her face flushed from old tears. She covered him in her arms and held him tightly.

"Atius, when you didn't come home, I was so afraid something had happened to you."

"I heard Icabus ran away. Atellus tells me a soldier named Bassus has also disappeared. What happened?"

Lucia squeezed Atius's fingers. "They wanted the house. Icabus came home from Cana's, and things escalated. He fled into the woods."

"The forest! Was he mad? How could you let him go in there?"

"There were soldiers everywhere. He didn't have a choice."

Atius rubbed his chin. "Icabus is smart. He's likely crossed back over the wall and is hiding somewhere in the village. Have you seen Cana?"

Lucia shook her head.

"Papa, Papa." Amara tugged on her father's trousers.

Atius patted her on the head, and Tulia took her hand. "Come, little love. Help Tulia make some cookies. Your mama and papa need to talk."

"Does Papa want cookies?" asked Amara.

"Yes, Amara, Papa would love some cookies."

"I help makes." Amara smiled, scampering into the kitchen.

Lucia looked into Atius's eyes. "Atius, what happened to you?

Atius led her to the fire and sat down beside her. He recounted how they came to the Citadel and how Furius and Gurges betrayed them and freed Galen.

Lucia covered her mouth. "So Icabus's dreams were true. Galen lives."

"Aye." Atius squeezed her fingers. "Mattia and I escaped, but Atellus ambushed us.

"Lucia, they threatened to kill Icabus for what happened last night. I agreed to help Furius in exchange for our protection."

Lucia pulled away. "You're helping them?"

"What would you have me do? I would do anything to protect this family."

Lucia shed a tear. "I should never have encouraged you to help Furius find the Citadel. I thought in some way it might help stop Icabus's nightmares, but it has only made them a reality."

Atius rubbed away her tear with his thumb. "Even you can't see the future." He forced a smile. "We need to find Icabus before Furius and Galen."

Whack! Whack! Whack!

"Atius! Are you in there?" Gurges shouted.

Lady Tulia appeared in the kitchen doorway, holding Amara by the hand. Atius and Tulia's eyes met, and he shook his head.

"I'll be out in a minute!" Atius shouted.

"Will they not even let you eat?" Lucia frowned.

"I suppose not. I don't have an appetite anyway." He kissed her on the forehead and sighed. "Don't let anyone in here."

Whack! Whack! Whack!

"I won't," she said.

"I'm coming!" Atius got up and swung open the door.

"About time," Gurges spat. "It's hot out here."

"Where's Atellus?"

"At the lookout." The soldier waved his long arm in the direction of Atius's house. "He sent me to fetch you. Let's go." He stomped across the porch.

"Your mood has worsened since we met, and your gait. Did you trip?"

Gurges swung around with his sword drawn. "You'd better pray I don't find your son before you. I'll make sure he never feels anything down there ever again."

Atius pushed the blade away with his finger and leaned forward. "Harm my son or family and Galen will make you as hideous on the outside as you are on the inside."

Gurges sheathed his sword and grunted. "I was hoping you wouldn't come back from that ship. Pity me." He cleared his nose on the porch stair. "Come on."

Atius trailed behind, keeping his eyes on the northern fields as they went. They crested the ridge, and Gurges laughed. "Now, aren't you glad you aren't doing that?"

Over fifty villagers, brandishing axes, saws, and ropes, were spread in a long line before what remained of the guarding wall. Behind them, an equal number of soldiers forced them forward into the forest where they cleared the trees and underbrush. "No. What are you doing? Are you mad?" Atius gasped.

"Do you really think there are monsters in the woods, superstitious fool?"

"What do you think happened to my son?"

"Your brat son is probably hiding somewhere around here, which I'm sure you already know."

"No. You don't understand. This is wrong. Listen to me." Atius reached for his arm.

Gurges spun around and seized Atius's collar. "No. You listen. No one wants to hear your ghost stories. So, shut up, do what we say, and you might not get worked to death. Understand?"

"Why are they taking down the wall?"

"Go ask Licinius." Gurges pointed up the hill with his sword. "His company is a bunch of gullible halfwits, but boy do they like to talk. He seems to think Galen is trying to capture something?"

"Capture what?"

"Maybe a monster... Boo! Ha-ha! It could be more of those rat-things for all I know. I guess we'll find out soon enough now, won't we?"

Atius held to Gurges's shadow and averted his gaze as they

passed the villagers. He felt ashamed among them.

"Atius? What in the Gods...?"

The voice was that of Cana's father, Corvus. He looked haggard and worn in the midday sun. Beside him were his three sons: Celsus, Caius, and Caelius.

Atius shook his head at Corvus discouragingly.

"Shut up!" Gurges stared down the villagers. "Did we permit you to talk? Come here." He pointed to Corvus.

"Father?"

"No, Celsus. I'm fine. Don't any of you say or do anything." Corvus eyed his sons sternly.

Gurges grabbed Corvus by the back of the tunic and pushed him past the line of soldiers.

"Atius, what's going on?" Corvus asked.

"Shut up! Get against that tree." Gurges shoved him.

Atius took Gurges by the shoulder. "Gurges, please. I know this man."

Gurges smiled. "As you said, Atius, I can't hurt you or your son, but your friends—I can hurt them." He signaled to the closest soldier. "Tie him to the tree and cut his shirt up the back."

Corvus eyed Atius with disbelief. "Atius, have you betrayed us?"

"Shut up!" Gurges raised his voice for all to hear. "Atius has chosen to serve King Furius. That's why he's standing here nice and happy, and you're over there getting worked like animals."

Gurges patted Atius on the back and laughed. "Do you know how to use a whip?"

"No."

"Well, I'm going to show you, and then you get to try. I want three good lashes from you." Gurges leaned over and whispered in Atius's ear. "And, if you don't put some muscle in them, I'll make you do them over and over."

"No."

Atellus walked down the line from Atius's house. "What's going on?"

"Just a little motivational punishment. I want Atius here to give this fellow three lashes, and he's having second thoughts."

Atius pointed to Corvus. "Atellus, this man—"

"I don't want to hear it. Give the lashes and come to the house. That's an order."

"That's an order," repeated Gurges, squeezing Atius's shoulder.

Atius could barely swallow. All the men of Aggersel had stopped and turned their eyes on him.

"Watch me," said Gurges. "Now hold the whip loose like this. It's all in the wrist. You shouldn't feel any strain whatsoever. Like so."

Crack!

"Ah Gods!" Corvus fell to knees. The weal on his back stretched from buttocks to shoulder. Blood quickly streaked his back.

Caelius, Corvus's eldest son, started forward and found the tip of a soldier's blade at his neck. Celsus and Caius found the same.

"Shall I demonstrate again, Atius?"

"No," said Atius, taking the whip from Gurges's hand.

Gurges leaned close. "Now remember what I said. Make it count, or I'll make you do it again."

Atius let the loose end of the whip hit the earth. He shook his wrist, loosening it, and took a deep breath. "I'm sorry," he said, cracking the whip.

Corvus cried out, and a fresh gash crossed the one Gurges made.

"Harder," Gurges snarled.

Atius cracked the whip again, tearing into Corvus's back. Corvus cried out and Atius struck him again without pause.

"Good." Gurges pointed to the soldiers. "Cut him down and string up the youngest boy."

Atius scoffed. "The boy? No! I won't. You can't make me do it!"

"I guess your son doesn't mean that much to you." Gurges winked. "Bring the boy. Get the father out of my sight!"

Corvus struggled as he was dragged back to the line. "Atius, you can't! Atius! No!"

Atius's hand shook. They tied Celsus to the tree, and he sobbed. Gurges used his knife to cut the shirt from Celsus's back and slapped the skin, leaving a red mark.

Celsus flinched and whimpered.

"Like father like son, eh, Atius?"

Atius ignored him and walked over to Celsus. "Don't tense up, Celsus. It will only make it worse." Atius couldn't even recognize his own voice. It sounded distant, empty.

Gurges yawned. "Three lashes and hurry it up. I'm hot."

Atius walked back to position and relaxed his shoulders. He stared into the sun, allowing it to bleach his vision, and struck the boy three times. Celsus's screams passed over him like wind over cold stone.

"Back to work, everyone!" Gurges shouted.

"Here's your whip," Atius said.

"I think I'll let you keep that. Just in case one of these peasants slows down again. Now come on."

Atellus and Furius rested in the shade of what was once Atius's porch. Gurges bowed slightly, and Atius reluctantly followed his lead.

"You're a natural, Atius," Furius said distantly.

Atellus regarded Gurges sourly. "Was whipping the boy necessary?"

"Just trying to maintain order," said Gurges.

Furius fanned himself with a piece of old parchment. "Don't be so harsh, Atellus. Wasn't I just saying I couldn't decide who would be bait for Galen's trap? The smell of blood and exhaustion is already on the boy."

"That is his youngest son," noted Atius.

"I'd gladly replace father for son, but Galen says this creature prefers younger meat. One of the villagers even referred to it as the Taker of Children. Enlighten me if I am incorrect."

Atius looked away into the hot noonday heat. "The boy is just a decoy, right? If the monster comes, you're going to kill it, aren't you?"

"What else would we do with a monster?" Furius regarded him apathetically.

Father its children, thought Atius.

"Atius, go fetch us some cold water," Gurges ordered. He took a seat beside Atellus and wiped his brow. "You know your way around inside, don't you?"

"Stay away from upper level," Furius warned. "The guards are not the typical sort."

Atius stopped at the door. "What's upstairs?"

"You mean, who?" Furius stared ahead.

"Arwa, Queen of the Gilian," said Gurges. "Furius's visions helped us capture her. Once that was done, it wasn't so hard getting here."

Gurges made a shooing motion with his hand, and Atius entered the house, shutting the door behind him. The stairway to the upper level was dark, but Atius could make out the shadowy outline of two sentries at the top of the run. They stood unmoving, their heads downcast and their hands loosely gripping bronze spears. They stunk of old death.

"Who are you?" Atius whispered.

The soldiers did not answer nor move, and Atius did not tarry. He went into the kitchen, where dirty dishes filled the washing basin and covered the table. The scent of Lucia's spices still hung in the air—cinnamon and sweet maple bark—but overlying those fragrances were the more obtrusive odors of rotting vegetables and meat. The tea set Lucia had made for Amara was crushed and kicked into a corner. A handmade doll lay soiled and turned over in the waste.

"Gods save us," he mumbled under his breath and exited the back door. Behind the house, the guarding wall was torn away, revealing an overgrown glen that Atius hadn't seen since his youth. At the center of the meadow was an old well covered with vines and surrounded by forest. Atius started around the side of the house when a splash sounded in the well.

"Hello? Gurges, if that's you, I'll push you down that well."

Atius unfurled the whip and left the path. The wooden crank

that lifted the bucket was rotted and broken, but the waxed rope itself was intact. A mark in the dirt on the rim of the well showed where a bucket and length of rope once rested.

Keeping his eyes on the woods, Atius grabbed the rope and lifted the bucket out of the well. He pulled it over the edge and immediately fell back, throwing the contents aside; a man's head rolled lifelessly into the tall grass.

"A present," came a voice from the wood.

Atius scuttled backward. Two yellow eyes stared at him from the darkness of the forest.

"It brings me food, and I give it presents," said the Taker, pointing to the onyx ring in Bassus's mouth.

"I don't want your gold. I want Icabus. Did you kill him?"

"What's an Icabus?" The monster shifted in the underbrush. It was huge.

Atius grabbed the edge of the well and lifted himself to his feet. "My son. He ran into the woods."

"Icabus... Icabus is bad!"

"Where is he?"

"Dead."

"You're lying." Atius trod into the grass. "I can hear it in your voice."

The Taker snickered. "The boy is hiding, but not for long."

Atius placed his hands together and got on his knees. "Please, I beg you, don't kill him. I'll do anything."

The monster growled low. "You want this boy?"

"Yes."

"You will die for this boy?"

"Yes."

"You will kill for this boy?"

"...Yes."

"Good... Bring me young ones, and I will not eat the Icabus."

"No, I will not bring you children, but I will bring you as many soldiers as you like, younger than the fat one." Atius pointed to Bassus's head.

The monster fell silent, and Atius was afraid it would refuse, but after a moment the beast grunted. “Bring me the red shirts here at night, and I will make them disappear. In exchange, I will not eat the Icabus.”

“I will feed you until every last soldier has left these shores. Now, where is my son?”

“In the mountain. I cannot go there, but when the Icabus comes out, I will bring him to you.”

“Why can’t you go there?”

“Shut up! If the boy comes out, I will bring him, not limp, not chewed.”

“Why ‘if’?”

The Taker extended his snout, showing off his collection of teeth. “I do not enter the caves. Do not ask me again!”

Atius felt his legs wobble beneath him. He didn’t trust the Taker. In fact, he expected it to lie. Icabus could be hiding in the village. He could also be dead, but it wasn’t Icabus’s head that had rolled out of the bucket. After what he did to Pelagus, feeding this creature Furius’s men seemed like a small inconvenience. He might even enjoy it.

“I’ll do it, and you will bring me Icabus unharmed. Agreed?”

“Not chewed,” said the Taker. From the distance came the sound of a falling tree. “Why do the red shirts cut the wood?”

Atius thought about his answer. “It’s a trap for you.”

“I know.”

“Then why did you ask?”

“To see if you lie and I should eat you.” The Taker gnashed his teeth.

“I need to return.” Atius kicked the head back into the woods. “Don’t leave scraps around.”

“Worse for you than me, I think,” said the monster.

“That depends on how much you like eating.”

The Taker closed his eyes and receded into the shadows. “Bring me a red shirt now.”

Atius brushed off his clothes and started back to the house. “Be patient.”

ATIUS

"Where have you been?" Gurges picked his ear and flicked the wax in Atius's direction.

Atius struck a carafe on the table with an assortment of mugs. "The cups were dirty; I had to wash them."

Gurges filled his glass, emptied it, and wiped his bristly face with his sleeve. "I hope you cleaned your hands before you fetched this. You peasants are unclean."

"To new friends." Atellus raised his mug in Atius's direction and smirked.

Furius ignored the toast and raised his hand. "Licinius!"

"Master Furius." Licinius came forward and bowed. To Atius, the man appeared exhausted and a little out of his element.

"Leave that large oak and clear the underbrush four meters around it. Have the men dig a pit trap facing the forest and tie the boy to the tree facing it. I want snare traps set along the back and rear of the tree and a net set high that can be released if those should fail. Smoke the area when you're done to hide our scent. Be quick about it; nightfall is nearly upon us, and Galen will not tolerate failure."

"Master Furius." Licinius bowed, quickly striding back to the line. A flurry of activity ensued, and Atius felt a moment of guilty relief that he was not caught up in that labor.

"The pit trap won't work," said Atius after a while. "You have a chance with the snares, but you'll be lucky to catch anything, having altered the environment so drastically."

"We're not trying to capture an ordinary animal," said Furius, still watching the men work.

"And what are you trying to catch, Master Furius?" Atius asked.

Furius turned to Atius, and Atius regretted being the focus of his attention. "I think you know. Enlighten us."

"All I know is that it's big, mean, and eats people." Atius crossed his arms. "There's nothing much else to say."

Furius grinned smugly. "This pit is a diversion. The snares are my idea, but Galen doesn't think this animal will come anywhere near this trap."

"Then why set it?" asked Atius.

"To get its attention. It's probably watching us right now. I set the real traps hours ago, there and there." Furius motioned to the forest with his chin. "The snares are rope braided with metal thread. They're strong enough to hold a bear hog."

Atius made a mental note of the location of the traps. "Hold but not kill. Why?"

Furius gave Atius a weary look. "Galen's request. He wants to torture it, I think."

"Sadistic." Atius shook his head.

"Perhaps. You've seen the power of Galen's blood. If this creature's blood has half the potential, it would be very valuable. Atellus, gather the villagers. I have an announcement."

It took only a few minutes for Atellus and Gurges to break the lines and bring the villagers in front of Furius. Atius thought they looked like a herd of unkempt sheep. They stared at him, some with anger, others with confusion. His shame made it hard to look them in the eyes.

Furius clapped his hands drawing the attention of the assembled.

"People of Aggersel. Long have you lived in the shadow of your forebears. Your great kingdom lies abandoned and filled with vermin; in your forest, a monster holds dominion and steals your children; even this great lake, which your ancestors traversed freely, is restricted to you by water-breathing zealots.

"Today, I again offer you a choice. Swear fealty to me, and these things that were once yours shall be again. Already one of you has joined us. Atius stands beside me as a friend and ally. He has glimpsed the greatness of my vision and now enjoys the rewards of service."

Furius beckoned Atius forward with his fingers and addressed the crowd.

"Join me, and your families will be under my protection. Join me, and you and your children will be masters of a new kingdom where death is an illusion. Join me, and let us reshape the world in our image." Furius extended his sigil ring in Atius's direction.

Atius glanced at the townspeople, knelt down on one knee, and kissed the sigil. Furius touched him on the head, and Atius rose and stood beside him.

Whispers trickled through the crowd. Atius saw anger and desire in the townspeople's eyes. He guessed they hated him more than they hated Furius.

"What say you, people of Aggersel?" Atellus shouted.

"I will join you," came a voice from deep within the crowd.

"Us too," said another voice.

Atius's heart skipped a beat as Corvus, Caius, Caelius, and Celsus stepped forward. The two boys supported their younger brother between them, and Corvus held on to Caelius's shoulder. Celsus looked pale; neither he nor Corvus would look Atius in the eyes.

Corvus cleared his throat. "My sons and I are willing to swear oaths to you in exchange for the protection of our family."

Furius nodded with measured pleasure. "I can accept your vows, except for your youngest. He is too sickly to serve.

"Minius. Salvius. Take the boy to the forest."

Minius and Salvius stepped away from the line, and Caelius shook his head at Corvus. "No, Father," Caelius protested.

Corvus fell to his knees and edged forward to Furius. "Please, spare my youngest son. I beg you."

Furius leaned close. "I am helping you save two," he whispered. "Show them the right course. If the trap works, no harm will come to your youngest."

Furius lifted his sigil ring. Corvus looked at the ring and back at his sons. He hesitated and kissed the sigil.

Celsus began to cry. "Father?"

Caius shook his head and stood in front of Celsus. "Father, we can't."

"As your elder, I command you." Corvus wiped a tear from his eye.

"This is wrong," cried Caelius.

"Do as I say!" Corvus demanded.

Minius and Salvius took Celsus's arms and began to drag him to the forest edge. His voice cracked as he wailed.

Caius and Caelius stared dumbstruck at their father. Anger, sadness, and disbelief were a few of the emotions Atius recognized in them. He felt them, too.

"Take your oaths!" said Corvus.

Caius and Caelius stepped forward. Many of villagers shook their heads in disbelief. Caelius got down on one knee and gave his father one long, lasting look. Corvus nodded, and Caelius kissed Furius's sigil. Caius did the same, and they stood beside Atius.

Gurges leaned over and whispered in Atius's ear. "I guess you're going to have to find someone else to whip."

Atius imagined Gurges getting torn apart by the Taker and smiled.

"My son is missing. I will join you if you help me find him," said Piscius.

Furius nodded and extended his ring. Atius leaned over to speak in Atellus's ear. "That is Pelagus's father."

"Who?" Atellus asked.

"The boy on the boat."

Atellus snickered. "Well, at least we know where to find his son."

Piscius kissed the sigil ring and took his place beside Corvus. To Atius, he looked quite pleased.

The men in the crowd began to stir and whisper among themselves. Atius could sense their resolve crumbling.

"What say you?" Furius spoke over them.

Atius could see the mood in the crowd shift. Men began to move forward and push past one another to kiss Furius's ring. Atellus separated and embedded them in various companies serving under Furius's guard.

A majority of the townspeople refused to acknowledge Atius. Those who did regarded him with contempt.

"Well, I think half is a good start," Furius said to Atellus. For those who have sworn oaths, have them paint their houses with red X's. Our men may evict any other whom they wish. I want our new soldiers to be responsible for administering punishments. If anyone refuses an order, kill him in front of the others. Understood?"

"Aye," said Atellus. "I will tell the other captains."

Furius regarded the remaining villagers who had not taken oaths. Some were relatives of the slain Elders. There was Livius the butcher, husband of Ralla, and Cyprian, who was Silana's brother. Mattia stood with them, too. He was married to Julia, Maro's second born.

"Who is that boy there?" Furius asked Atius.

"That's Vescus. He's Cilo's son—the Elder."

"Well, at least he has a reason for that awful look he's giving us. Vescus, come here!" Furius commanded.

Vescus looked at the men at his side and stepped forward. "I won't join you. I'd rather die."

"Alright," Furius said without conviction. "Gurges."

"Wait," said Atius. "Let me handle this."

"By all means." Furius motioned to Vescus with an open hand.

Atius stepped forward and struck Vescus in the face with his fist. The boy stumbled backward, and Atius struck him again, first in the stomach, then in the temple, driving him to the ground.

Vescus gasped, breathless.

Atius could taste the tension rising in the air. The villagers around him were restless. To resist now meant certain death. He couldn't let that happen. Without them, there was no hope.

He pushed Vescus's face into the ground and leaned close. "Listen to me," he whispered. "Apologize now. You don't honor your father in death."

"You're a traitor," Vescus wept. "My father loved you, all the Elders did, and you betrayed them."

Atius wished he could fill his ears with cloth. The boy was older than Icabus by only two years, but Atius thought them so much alike.

"You can't hate me as much as I hate myself. If you want to do something good, help Celsus. Now apologize."

Atius lifted Vescus to his feet. Vescus was bleeding from one nostril and covered in dirt but otherwise uninjured.

The boy looked to Atius and then to the ground. "I'm sorry."

Furius leaned forward. "What did you say? Look me in the eyes."

Vescus lifted his head. "I apologize."

Furius turned to Atellus who nodded agreeably. Furius leaned back. "Very well. Consider this a warning to you all. To attack or defame a soldier or person under my protection brings with it a punishment worse than death."

"Master Furius. Shall we place him in the trap with Celsus? Two are better than one," Atius said.

Furius lifted the corner of his mouth in a crooked smile. "You surprise me, Atius. Make it so."

Atius handed Vescus over to the nearest soldiers and rejoined Furius.

"Minius. Salvius. Take these men who have sworn oaths back to town and brand their hands to identify them among the others. The rest of the men can sleep together in the town square under guard. Have them erect a corral for themselves and post a watch."

"Yes, sir," said Minius, bowing slightly.

Furius addressed Atellus. "Have your men set a watch tonight on the trap. This thing Galen wishes to capture can be harmed but not killed. Am I clear?"

"Aye, perfectly, sir." Atellus nodded.

"Raise the alarm if anything happens. I will be upstairs with Galen and the prisoner. Do not disturb us."

ATIUS

"No. I shall not eat. I have not the will for it." Seius stared into the fire.

Atellus tore a piece of goat from Licinius's stick and tossed it before Seius's feet. He regarded Seius sourly. "Eat it. It's an order. You may have been a priest once, Seius, but none of us are quite what we used to be. Accept it."

Seius picked up the meat, brushed it off, and nibbled on it.

Licinius took another bite and regarded Atius. "So, why do your people live here when you have an abandoned city right beside you?"

Gurges chuckled. "You wouldn't ask that if you saw what's living inside it."

"We don't live in the Old Kingdom for the same reason we don't live in the woods. Anyone who enters these places disappears," Atius replied.

Atellus leaned back against a tree and scratched his chin. "Have you ever seen this monster, Atius?"

Atius looked into the woods. "Aye. When I was eighteen, I manned the watch. I didn't take the position very seriously and often fell asleep. The Gods must have favored me because, one night, I awoke to a twig breaking. I didn't see all of the beast, but I saw enough. Its head was like a wolf's, with yellow eyes that glowed in the dark. By the time I put arrow to bow, it was gone."

Seius shook his head gravely. "Cursed are these lands where demons still walk."

Licinius regarded the woods apprehensively. Atius said nothing, and the group fell into their thoughts. It was Gurges who broke the silence.

"Yesterday, when I was chasing your snot-faced son into the woods, I thought I saw something. Bassus had been running beside me. I thought the fat loaf had fallen or was just fatigued, but when I turned around, he was just gone. No Bassus. No nothing."

Gurges paused and tossed a small log onto the fire. "I will say this, though. There was something out there with us besides your boy. I could hear it in the underbrush. Whatever it was, it was big, bigger than a man, even bigger than Bassus. I was going to call out, but my instincts told me otherwise. For a moment, I thought I saw yellow eye shine in the distance."

"You didn't tell me this," said Atellus.

"Would you have believed it?"

Atellus grunted and shook his head.

Thwap!

"What was that?" Licinius jumped up.

"The traps!" Atellus scrambled to his feet. "Gurges, you're with me."

Gurges drew his sword and cursed.

"Pair up and stay within earshot," Atellus ordered. "Seius, check the house and be ready to sound the alarm on my signal."

"I will." Seius moved off.

Atius threw his whip to the ground. "I need a better weapon."

Licinius drew a curved blade with a white coral handle from his belt. Atius had never seen anything like it. "This is special. I took it from a dead lake man. I want it back."

"Very well," said Atius, taking the blade. It was as light as a feather.

Thwap!

"Gods, another snare!" Licinius peered into the wood.

"Minius, Salvius, go left." Atellus pointed. "Gurges and I will go right. Check the traps and circle back here."

Atius watched as the men moved in opposite directions and entered the wood. The light of their torches only seemed to accentuate the forest darkness rather than diminish it.

Vescus pulled at his bonds. "What's out there?"

"Shut your trap!" shouted Licinius, entering the shadow of

the forest. "Atius, do you hear that? It's like a child's cry. Do you think one of the men got hurt?"

"Yes, you!" Atius drove the dagger into Licinius's flank.

Licinius arched his back and shrieked. "Gods... you... stabbed me," Licinius stammered; he reached for the knife and stumbled back.

Atius shoved him toward the forest.

Licinius fumbled with his sword and dropped it. He fell to his knees and began to crawl toward the tree line. "Help me! Help me!"

"There's one thing you should know about the Taker, Licinius... It's always hungry." Atius reached down and pulled the blade from Licinius's side.

"Ah!" Licinius cried, holding the bloody wound. "I hear them. They're coming back. You're done, Atius!"

"That's not who you think it is." Atius stepped back.

Licinius looked up and whimpered. The Taker's shadow fell over him, and Licinius rolled over, holding out his hand to Atius. Atius blinked, and Licinius disappeared feet first into the underbrush.

"Atius, what happened?" Seius stood at the edge of the forest, staring at the dagger in Atius's hand.

Atius sheathed the blade. "Sound the alarm. The creature took Licinius."

Seius gave Atius a long look and ran back toward the house. Atius could see the torches of the other men in the distance.

Vescus struggled against his bonds. "Gods, what was that, Atius?"

Atius cut the ropes binding Vescus and Celsus. Vescus yelped as his arms dropped after being suspended for so long.

"Why are you helping me?" Vescus asked.

"I..." The words seemed to evaporate in Atius's mouth. He wanted to tell Vescus that he wasn't a monster, that somehow his actions would redeem themselves in the end, but Atius didn't believe that anymore. Even if Icabus returned, things would never be the same. He would never be the same, and there was nothing to say about any of it.

"The men are returning." Vescus gestured to the forest.

"Vescus, take this dagger. Help Celsus. You must go to the Lady Tulia's. My wife is there, and she will hide you. You must do as I say."

Vescus nodded slowly and accepted the blade. He supported Celsus by the shoulder, and together they crossed the clearing into the apple orchard.

Near the house, Seius rang the bell, which was answered by a horn. Torches ignited throughout Aggersel and coalesced into a river of fire as Furius's soldiers made their way up the hill.

Atellus and Gurges burst from the underbrush. "What happened?" Atellus panted.

"Look, Atellus." Gurges pointed to the trap.

Atellus grabbed Atius's shoulder. "Where are the boys?"

"I don't know. Whatever it is, it got Licinius, too. We heard Vescus scream, and then something struck me in the head. When I came to, Licinius and the boys were gone. Seius came, and I told him to ring the bell."

"Gone?" Atellus said under his breath.

Minius, Seius, and Salvius entered the torchlight.

"Seius, did you see what happened?" asked Atellus.

Seius regarded the empty trap and Atius in turn. "I heard a scream and came. Atius told me to sound the alarm, and I did."

"Gods, curse me." Atellus kicked the dirt. "Minius, did you and Salvius find anything in the snare?

Minius nodded. "Bassus was in the trap, but not all of him. We found a leg in one trap and part of a torso in another."

Salvius turned to Atius. His salt and pepper beard trembled as he spoke. "What did you see, Atius?"

"Nothing. I was struck in the head."

"Furius is not going to like this," Atellus grumbled.

The first group of soldiers crested the ridge, and Atellus set off to meet them. Gurges followed close behind.

"The Gods curse us." Minius kicked the dirt.

Seius shook his head. "We curse ourselves."

Somewhere in the darkness, the Taker laughed.

CANA AND VESCUS

"Vescus." Cana stepped out from behind an apple tree.

"Cana?" He lowered his knife and sighed. "What are you doing here? Furius's men are coming."

"I was going to help you. Was that a Taker?"

Vescus glanced back over his shoulder and shivered. "Yes, I think so."

"So, the stories are true. The Takers are real!"

"We gotta run," said Vescus, turning toward the road.

Cana grabbed Vescus's arm. "Wait! Where are you going?"

"Atius told me to hide at Lady Tulia's."

"That's in town. You'll never make it past the soldiers. You can stay in Father's barn. There are lots of places to hide inside, and nobody ever goes in there."

Vescus regarded the line of torches cresting the hillside. "Alright. Let's go."

Cana smiled and helped support Celsus between them. Her brother was sweaty and moaned as they moved.

"He needs medicine," said Cana, leading them farther into the orchard. The earth crunched beneath their feet in rhythmic discordance.

"Do you know where you're going?" asked Vescus.

"Yeah. Icabus and I made a path in the canyon. By the way, have you seen him?"

Vescus slowed. "You haven't heard?"

Her face glowed like old porcelain in the moonlight. "What?"

"Icabus is gone."

"What do you mean, gone?"

"Icabus attacked several soldiers and ran into the woods. He and a soldier, Bassus, never came out."

Cana shook her head. "Icabus would never go in there."

"I don't think he had a choice. Maybe the Taker has Icabus, and Atius knows it. Why else would Atius feed it soldiers?"

Cana stared ahead blankly. "I shouldn't have left him last night."

Vescus stopped. "Cana, you can't blame yourself. If anyone can get out of there, it's Icabus."

"You sound like him, only older." She offered him a meek smile.

Vescus reciprocated. "I'm only two years older. He's a brave kid."

"Yeah, he's stupid, too."

Vescus's gaze made her feel self-conscious and she looked away to the stream. "Let's go. We can cross right over there." She pointed.

Together, they helped Celsus across the creek. The path led them up a shallow rise, giving them a bird's-eye view of the forest lake.

"Wow, that's spooky," said Vescus. "You and Icabus really go tromping around here at night?"

"It's not so bad. Do you wanna see something special?"

"Is it far?"

"No, but we should put Celsus down."

"Alright." Vescus slowly lowered Celsus onto a bed of leaves. "My arms are tired anyway."

"Follow me." Cana led Vescus up the hill to a lookout surrounded by a tangled growth of fig trees. "We gotta climb," said Cana, lifting herself up into the nearest tree.

Vescus scratched the back of his neck. "You know, I'm kind of afraid of heights."

"Come on. Don't be scared. Look how easy it is."

Cana purposefully ascended into the canopy, and Vescus followed behind. He checked and rechecked each branch for sturdiness, careful not to look down or even up if he could help it.

"See? That wasn't so bad."

"Speak for yourself." Vescus's hands shook as he held the branches. "What did you want to show me?"

"Icabus and I always liked looking at the Old Kingdom from here. One day, he noticed you can see something from this spot you can't see from anywhere else. Take a look."

Vescus followed Cana's finger to a point far above the city, where the mountains became steep and the rocky slopes rose in perilous palisades. There among the trees and rocks was a collection of caves.

"Wow, are those dragon caves?"

"Dragon caves. That's what Icabus thought, too." She smiled. "You can only see them from this spot. Icabus used to dream a lot about dragons..."

Vescus nudged Cana gently with his shoulder. "It sounds like you care a lot about him. He's lucky to have you as a friend."

"I'm sorry about Cilo." Cana wiped her eye and regarded him warmly. "I liked him. He could always make me laugh."

Vescus looked down. "Sometimes, I wish I could have been his friend and not his son. The last time we talked, we fought."

"Families fight. At least, that's what Father always says."

"I guess so." Vescus exhaled. "Now how do we get down without falling?"

Cana giggled. "Follow me."

Celsus was still asleep where they'd left him. He stirred as they lifted him off the ground. "What's happening?" He blinked dazedly.

"We rescued you," Cana whispered. "Just try to move your legs a bit more. You're heavy." Celsus complied, and they followed the stream past the gristmill to the lake road.

The moon was high, and no soldiers were on the road. They turned away from town and headed in the direction of the Old Kingdom.

Cana breathed a sigh of relief at the sight of the barn. "Almost home, Celsus. Father is going to be so happy to see you."

ICABUS

The light of the cavern entrance fell away, and Icabus slid so fast he couldn't find the breath to scream. Coldness such as he had never known enveloped him, and he thrashed, realizing that it was neither earth nor ice that he struck but water.

The water stung his skin like needles, and he kicked, drawing himself to the lake's surface. A column of light shown in the distance, and he swam in that direction.

"Next time, I'll take the stairs," he muttered, clawing his way up the moist bank. White stalactites hung from the ceiling like dragon's teeth, and along the floor, stalagmites rose around a collection of springs feeding the underground lake.

Icabus pulled off his wet shirt and wrung it out. His entire body shivered, and he found it hard to focus. "I need the sun." His teeth chattered.

Beyond the stalagmites was a natural rotunda honeycombed with caves. Icabus stumbled into the sunlight and raised his face. The light was dim but warm, and he fell to his knees savoring it.

"What are these?" Icabus traced the parallel lines etched into the floor. "Claw marks," he whispered, taking a fresh inventory of his surroundings. Stalagmites did not surround the cavern—bones did: giant, bleached bones rising above him.

Something shifted in the darkness, and Icabus slipped between two dragon ribs. He couldn't see anything in the light; however, he could make out the faint scratching of claw on bone. He moved away from the sound to a wide arched passage. The cave was blacker than obsidian, and Icabus placed his hand into it and quickly pulled it away. He rubbed his fingers and slowly extended them again into the void. To his amazement, they disappeared.

"What kind of darkness makes your hand disappear?"

Caw!

Icabus spun around and tripped over his own feet. He fell backward, and for a brief second, he saw the fat crow perched atop a giant rib. Then there was only blackness.

Icabus screamed, but no sound reached his ears. He moved, but there was nowhere to go. Memories washed over his mind like waves breaking on a fast-moving ship. His life had never felt so short or insignificant before.

A point of light appeared in the darkness, and he was drawn to it like a ghost to the afterlife. What he saw was not a memory but rather an image that appeared conjured from a story. The scene was that of a man in black leather armor facing a waterfall. He sat cross-legged with his back to Icabus. His reflection was hazy and indistinct in the fall, but his eyes shone brightly, glowing inhumanly with a wash of green and gold like a dragon's.

Icabus tried to turn away, but he could not stop himself from being drawn forward. Out of the liquid silence, birdsong and the roar of the falls deafened him, and he fell forward on hands and knees, crying out like someone being born, dying, or both.

Blinding, hot sunshine stung Icabus's skin, and he blinked, casting the sunspots from his vision. The world came into focus, and the man in the black armor approached, sword extended.

"Don't... hurt me," Icabus choked. It hurt to speak.

"Look at me," said the man.

"I can't." Icabus's whole body felt like a sack of wet potatoes.

Using the tip of his blade, the man lifted Icabus's chin. "You are not Arkax. Did he send you ahead as a diversion?"

"No." Icabus shook his head.

"Don't lie to me!" He kicked Icabus onto his back.

"I'm not lying. I got lost in the woods. Arkax chased me, but he wouldn't cross the rock wall."

"And how did you come to be here? Speak!"

"There was a fat crow... It led me to the Ostara offering. I slipped and fell into the cave. I was trying to find my way out when the crow spooked me, and I got sucked into that." Icabus shifted his attention to the gate.

The man searched Icabus's expression and sheathed his sword. "The crow's name is Cales."

"Cales?" Icabus's voice quaked. "Who are you?"

"Nubis," he said, facing the gate. "Senile bird. He should not have led you here."

Icabus struggled to sit up. "Why? Where is here?"

"Why? Because the last humans who passed through the gate became monsters like Arkax. This place has many names, but the dragons called it the Golden Land."

Icabus tried to stand but fell to one knee. His left arm tingled, and the rest of his body felt as heavy as lead. "I don't want to be a monster. Let me go back. I will never return."

"It's too late for that. The weakness you are experiencing is part of the change. You are now as much part of this place as you are a boy. Soon you will become a reflection of your heart. If you are a Taker, as most men are, then you will not leave this valley, but you will not suffer either. I promise that."

Icabus tried to get up again and fell onto his side. He forced himself into a sitting position. "Are you a dragon knight?"

Nubis regarded him austerely. "I have been called that."

"Then you must know where to find the dragons."

"They are all dead or gone far from this place. I am all who remains."

Icabus shook his head despondently. "My village is overrun by Authians who crossed the forest lake. They killed our Elders. Everyone is in danger."

"What you say is not possible." Nubis turned to the falls. "The forest lake is protected. None may cross."

"You're wrong! Aggersel is overrun, and Galen is alive!"

Nubis spun around and seized Icabus by the neck. "I'm tired of these lies. I did not think Arkax was so cunning."

"It's not a lie. I swear it on my life."

"Enough!" Nubis released him and drew his sword again.

Icabus fell to his knees and raised his hands to his face. "I don't want to die. Please."

"You would beg while those you love suffer?"

"How can I find someone to help them if I'm dead?"

Nubis tossed Icabus's shirt aside with his sword. "Take off your shoes. The feet and hands usually change first. Sometimes there is a tail. The face is last."

Icabus did as instructed and sat in the grass facing Nubis. "What now?" He wiped his eyes and sniffled.

Nubis sheathed his sword and returned to the flat stone at the edge of the reflecting pool. "We wait."

ATIUS

Furius stalked the edge of the wood like an angry wolf. Atius thought that if the man had a tail, he'd be flicking it.

"You say you saw nothing, not a thing?" Furius asked.

"No." Atius shrugged.

Atellus cleared his throat. "Master Furius, you saw Bassus's body. If this creature had more hands, I don't think any of us would be left to talk about it."

"Talk? About what? That you saw nothing! That you heard nothing! It may as well have eaten all of you!" Furius stomped away.

"May the Gods have mercy." Seius rubbed the stubble on his face.

Atellus frowned. "Come on. Let's not let him get too far ahead, or he'll tie one of us to that tree."

Furius stood over Bassus's collected remains and looked around. "Where's his head?"

"Not found," noted Atellus. "The tattoo on his shoulder is his family crest."

"Build a fire and burn the body," Furius ordered. "We don't need any other vermin coming around here. What's this?"

Furius picked up Vescus's discarded bonds and examined them. Atius could feel the hairs on his neck stand on end.

"These bonds look cut by a blade. You said the monster took the boy, didn't you, Atius?"

Atius shifted nervously. "I didn't see the boy taken, but that's what happened. This monster may have used a blade to lessen its work."

"None of that was done with a blade." Furius pointed to

Bassus's corpse. "Why use a blade when your teeth and claws cut flesh like razors?"

"Then perhaps this is the work of its claws or teeth." Atellus examined the rope.

"Pray that Galen agrees with you." Furius moved off in the direction of Atius's house.

Atellus wiped his brow. "Gods, what a mess."

"I need a sword," said Atius.

Atellus looked at the ground and laughed, shaking his head. "Those bonds looked cut, and if I remember correctly, Licinius let you borrow a nice dagger he took from one of those fish heads. Where did it go?"

Atius shook his head. "I don't know. Remember, I got hit in the head."

"Very convenient. Gurges!"

"Yes, Atellus." Gurges sauntered over.

"Give Atius one of your blades."

"Alright," Gurges said with noticeable displeasure. He chose a medium length sword from the four he had secured to his belt. "If you live long enough to kill someone with a blade, I want this one back; otherwise, I'll take it back when you're dead."

Atius accepted the short-sword and threaded its sheath through his belt. Gurges tossed a torch on Bassus's remains and set off down the hill. Atius thought he could hear Gurges cursing under his breath.

"Thank you, Atellus," said Atius.

"Don't thank me. Our heads look no different to Furius as they roll off the chopping block. Remember that."

ARKAX

The skinny man was funny.

Even with his throat crushed and his arms dislocated, he continued to struggle like an albino carp pulled from the lake bottom. He flopped, he writhed, but mostly he gasped wide-mouthed for each ounce of air that trickled through his pencil-sized throat.

"You're going to die," Arkax chuckled.

The resilience of humans intrigued the Taker. Even in the face of death, they fought against their inevitable fate. Some took longer to break than others. Once they gave up, there was no reason to keep them alive. The game was over, and Arkax was always hungry.

Settling onto his haunches, Arkax inhaled deeply. He could no longer smell the lake men. Their fishy stench usually covered everything, but since the ships arrived, the Gilian no longer protected the town. The stupid villagers didn't seem to notice. Didn't they have noses?

Even the Nubis's scent was absent. The stupid villagers probably didn't know he was here either. That foul boy knew, the Icabus. He didn't care what bargain he had made with the Atius; if Arkax ever saw the Icabus again, he would tear his face off and let him run around the woods without eyes. The Atius could have him that way.

The Nubis would probably kill the Icabus; he would kill him and let the flesh go to waste. The Nubis was cautious and fearful. He would decapitate the Icabus in his sleep before the boy became a Taker. The Nubis and the lake men had killed all the others like him. Arkax was the last because he was patient.

The Nubis never forgave him for killing Kail. Arkax thought the Nubis would eventually pass on like the rest of his kind. But the Nubis didn't leave; he just changed. He was weaker and slower than he once had been, but Arkax would not take that for granted. He was still the Nubis, the slayer of Galen.

Their hunt had been a long, mostly silent battle of attrition. There were pursuits and close encounters, but Arkax knew this forest like the length of his claws, and there were always places he could go where the Nubis could not follow.

In his isolation, the Nubis was going mad like him. Arkax could smell it—the chronic stress, the yearning, the hating. It was devouring Nubis from within. Arkax's plan was simple: he would wait for the Nubis to lose his mind and then kill him. He only had to wait. Fear tasted good, but madness and hatred tasted even better.

Arkax licked his teeth and sighed longingly. The skinny man had wandered off again. He could hear him shuffling in the leaves over the rise. All this thought of the Nubis and the Icabus made him ravenous.

"Where are you going? The village is the other way, stupid."

He could hear the man wheezing. The sound had begun to annoy him.

"Come here and let me fix you."

Arkax sauntered over the rise, and Licinius shook his head. Exertion and lack of oxygen distorted Licinius's movements, and he stumbled away like a drunkard.

"Come here, now!"

He grabbed Licinius's ankle and flipped him onto his back. Licinius yelped and waved his arms incoherently.

"Stop it. You act like a man who's never had his shoulders dislocated before." The Taker took Licinius's hands in his own and leaned close. "If you thought that hurt, I can't wait till you feel this."

With a swift upward pull, Arkax abducted Licinius's arms and set his dislocated shoulders with a pop. Licinius gasped and lost consciousness.

"Wake up." Arkax patted Licinius's cheeks. "Almost done. I want to fix your throat. "Try not to look so scared," he laughed. "If I miss, you bleed out, and your inconsequential life will be over."

Using his thumb claw like a hook, Arkax cut into Licinius's neck. There was a rush of blood and then a whoosh as air rushed into Licinius's lungs.

Arkax licked up the blood pooling around the breathing hole and smiled. "Nice and clean. Do you feel better? Your heart was getting so quiet I thought you were going to die. Now listen to it." The Taker put his pointy ear to Licinius's chest. "It's like a caged bird that wants to be free."

Licinius coughed, releasing fresh blood and mucus from his wound. The Taker licked it up hastily.

"The village is that way." Arkax motioned with his snout. "A boy could run the distance in ten minutes, and that's how long I'm going to give you before I come after you. If you can escape, then the little bird stays in your chest, tweet, tweet. If you don't—I eat the bird. Got it?"

Licinius coughed again, and the Taker laughed. He hadn't had this much fun in years.

"Fly, fly, little bird. Fly, fly." He reclined against a rock. "Your time starts now."

The skinny man disappeared over the hillside for the second time, and the Taker licked his thumb claw. When he tasted the man's blood, he fantasized that he was tasting the Icabus. Just thinking about the Icabus made him excited and angry. He'd never lost his prey before, and if it weren't for that foul little ghost, the Icabus would not have escaped.

The ghost. Arkax hated her almost as much as he hated the Nubis.

She tormented him like a bone splinter stuck in his gums. Most things just died; not this spirit. It kept coming back.

Sometimes he would wake and find her staring at him. Other times she stalked his peripheral vision, disappearing only long enough for him to divert his attention before returning again and again.

Such a significant haunting would have bothered most creatures, but not Arkax. Once he concluded she wasn't a hallucination, a part of him was flattered. She was his audience and at other times his unwilling accomplice. He wanted to punish her for helping the Icabus. The skinny man would help.

The Taker flared his nostrils and took the forest air into his nose. He curled his toes in delight as a rush of images flashed before his mind. The secret to smelling was not the 'what' but the 'where' and the 'when' of a scent. The 'what' was easy: even the stupid humans could detect 'what' if they got their noses close enough; however, the 'when' and the 'where' of a scent were much more challenging.

The Taker's nose told him the skinny man was now stopped less than a quarter mile away. The anxious hope he smelled from the man a moment before had now been replaced by foreboding and dread. The Taker laughed and licked his teeth.

He did not lie to the skinny man. The village was close, very close, but lying between the man and his goal was a gorge five meters wide and many times as deep. It had been dug long ago by the engineers of the Old Kingdom as a way of bringing fresh water to the city and diverting water away during periods of flood. He should know since he designed it, but Arkax no longer remembered that. He had long ago forgotten his human life. This was part of his madness.

In the corner of his eye, the ghost appeared, and the Taker knew it was time to go. "Go and try to help him, you little sprite. Unless you can fly him over the gorge, he's dead."

Lepida disappeared, and the Taker shot off in pursuit. Ahead of him, Arkax heard Licinius scream. Lepida had come to the rescue.

The ghost appeared again in the corner of his eye. She was trying to distract him and give the skinny man more time to get away. He wasn't going to play.

Licinius coughed a word that might have been, "No," and scrambled to the cliff's edge. Arkax waved his finger in warning and slowed to a stop.

Lepida appeared on the opposite ledge of the cliff. The Taker's audience had arrived.

Licinius shook his head and peered over the edge of the ravine. He scrambled left then right in desperation. There were no handholds or footholds.

Arkax watched with a twisted smile. From across the ravine, Lepida held out her hands.

"I think she wants you to jump. I'm not sure you want to do that. It's a long fall but not one sure to kill you. If you make me go down there and peel you off the rocks, I promise a very unpleasant end."

Licinius covered his face and sobbed.

"Let's make a deal. Given the unique circumstances, I promise not to tear your still-beating-heart from your chest if you come here and offer your neck to my teeth."

Licinius edged closer to the cliff edge. He looked from Lepida to the dark chasm below and back again.

Lepida nodded, but Licinius shook his head.

"Good. Come here." Arkax extended his arms. His breath quickened with expectation. "Let me see that sweet neck. Just one little bite and no more pain, just sleep."

Licinius shuffled forward, partly upright, partially using his hand to guide him over the sharp slag that separated him from the Taker.

Lepida lowered her arms, and the Taker threw back his head in a victorious cackle. His immoral victory over her was nearly complete. It would be too easy just to kill the skinny man now. The meddlesome ghost needed a lesson. Licinius would suffer for her intervention.

"Come here, you wretch." Arkax pointed to his hairy feet.

Licinius stumbled forward, and Arkax watched Lepida with malign satisfaction.

"Now, watch as I tear him apart, you sprite."

Licinius jumped forward, revealing a shard of black granite, and stabbed the monster's collar. Arkax wailed in pain and anger; he lashed out blindly, knocking Licinius backward. The skinny man hit the ground with a soundless thud.

"You stabbed me?" Arkax gasped, pulling the spike from his hide and holding his hand over the wound. Warm blood coursed through his fingers like a handful of wet ribbons. Lepida's frown became a smile.

"You knew it, you vile little ghost. You led him to that shard!"

Licinius edged away, and Lepida held out her hands again.

"Hairless swine, you stabbed me! I'm going to break every piece of you for doing this to me."

Licinius pulled himself upright and stumbled to the edge of the ravine. Lepida nodded.

"No! I forbid you to jump. I forbid it. I'll tear you open and eat your insides. I'll—"

Licinius, son of Junius of Authia, jumped to his death.

"You," the Taker growled, leaping across the ravine. He held his jaws wide, hoping to capture Lepida's spectral head in his grasp. The little ghost lowered her arms and disappeared.

Arkax hated that ghost.

ICABUS AND NUBIS

"No!" Icabus lurched forward. Nubis stood over him, and Icabus looked down at his hands and feet. He took a deep breath and fell back upon the grass. Cold sweat drenched his body, but nothing had changed.

"I made a fire." Nubis pointed to a small pit beneath a shelf of stone.

Icabus wobbled to his feet, and Nubis guided him to the fire. The heaviness he experienced when he crossed the gate had passed. Now, he simply felt sore and a little woozy.

Nubis sat across from him. "You were dreaming."

Icabus warmed his hands over the flames and shivered. "It's a nightmare that won't go away."

Nubis watched him silently, and Icabus scratched the back of his neck.

"It's always the same. I'm in a dark place like a cave filled with cold water. There's someone else there with me, but I can't see him. Then he grabs me, and I wake up."

"How do you know it's a he?" Nubis's voice was calm, but the firelight reflection in his eyes made him look inhuman.

Icabus regarded him timidly. "Sometimes, instead of grabbing me, he talks. He says I woke him up and he's trapped and needs my help."

"Did he say his name?"

The hair on Icabus's arms rose and he mustered the strength to meet Nubis's penetrating emerald gaze. "He said his name was Galen."

The fire popped, and Nubis was unblinking. Beneath his stoic stare, Icabus wondered if it was sadness and not anger that he saw in the dragon knight's eyes. "What else do you dream about?" Nubis asked, after a while.

Icabus considered the question. "I used to dream a lot about dragons."

"Many boys dream about dragons."

Icabus thought to agree but something about Nubis's bearing made him believe he would know if he was lying. "In my dreams, I only dream about one dragon."

"Only one?"

Icabus nodded slowly. "He's black, like onyz. We fly together and go on adventures. They used to scare me, but not anymore."

"Why?" Nubis blinked.

"Because dragons are protectors."

Nubis got up and walked back to his sitting stone facing the falls. Icabus watched him for a time and then curled up next to the fire and slept. In his dreams, a black dragon circled overhead.

CANA AND VESCUS

"Hey there, sleepy face." Cana peeked at Vescus from the loft ladder.

Vescus rolled over and grimaced. "Gods, I'm sore."

"How'd you sleep? I thought you would never wake up."

"Alright, I guess. Is it midday?

Cana laughed. "It's afternoon."

"Afternoon." Vescus lay back and groaned. "At least that explains why I've got to pee so badly. Have any soldiers come by?"

"Not here, but there's been a lot of them going toward the Old Kingdom. Father says Atius is building a trap there for the Taker. He just left again with Caius and Caelius. Are you hungry? I brought some food."

"Starving." Vescus climbed down the ladder behind Cana.

"Here." She offered Vescus a handful of bread and a glass of goat's milk.

"First things first." Vescus poked his head out of the barn door, then scuttled around the corner of the building. He came back and sighed.

"Better?"

"A thousand times better." He smiled. "Wow, this bread's still warm."

"Yeah, I made it myself. I milked Missy, too. She's so fussy. I practically had to chase her around the yard just to get that."

Vescus giggled and immediately choked.

"Hurry, drink the milk."

Vescus gulped the goat's milk.

"You're like Icabus. There's always something going wrong with him, too. It's patho..."

"Pathological?"

"Yeah, he's mental."

Vescus put down the milk cup. "We're going to find him, Cana. I promise."

Cana nodded. She kicked a clump of hay and put her hands in her back pockets. "I know I said it already, but I'm sorry about Cilo. He was the one Elder who always made me laugh."

"Father was good at that." Vescus's smile lessened but did not fade. "Are you meaning to tell me that Ralla never put you in one of her bear hugs? That was pretty funny."

"No, but I saw her do it to Icabus. I thought his eyes were going to pop out of his head."

"They were, I promise." Vescus stuffed the last chunk of bread into his mouth and washed it down with a gulp of milk. "Thanks," he said, clearing his throat. "How's Celsus doing?"

"Not great. His back is all swollen and red, and he has a fever."

Cana bit her lip, and Vescus touched her shoulder. "I'm sorry, Cana. I'm sure he'll be fine."

"I hope so." Cana reached for the metal cup but not before their fingers touched. "Ouch, you shocked me."

"What makes you think it was me?" Vescus laughed.

"If you don't stop it, I'll never bring you milk again."

"I'm sure Missy won't complain about that."

Cana blushed and avoided Vescus's eyes. She felt silly whenever he looked at her. It made her want to reach out and get shocked by him over and over again.

"So, has Corvus told you why they're trying to trap the Taker?"

Cana shrugged. "I overheard Father say that Galen and Furius have been spending a lot of time on one of the ships. Should we look while everyone's away?"

"That sounds dangerous."

"Do you wanna just hide in here forever?" Cana crossed her arms.

"No. I just don't want you to get hurt."

Cana relaxed her arms and giggled. She liked him again.

"If we're going to do this, there's something I want you to have... for protection."

Vescus pulled out the ornate dagger Atius had given him and handed it to Cana. It seemed bright even in the darkness of the barn.

"Licinius was carrying it. I think it's special."

"Whoa. It's pretty, Vescus. Where do you think it's from?"

"I don't know."

"I think Father has a sheath that will fit it. Let me get it, and we can go."

"Better check on Celsus, too."

"Of course." She smiled, and Vescus reciprocated. She thought she might be in love.

CANA AND VESCUS

Cana parted the reeds. Vescus knelt beside her and heaved a sigh.

"Are you alright, Vescus? You look pale."

"I've just got this weird feeling, that's all. Don't worry; I'm fine."

Cana gave Vescus a fretful look then turned her attention to the harbor. "Father told Caelius that Furius anchored his weapons ship to the floating trees. If we can get onto one of the islands, we can walk right up to it."

"Get down, Cana." Vescus pulled on her tunic.

A convoy of men stopped on the bridge below the mill. A man in a purple robe placed his hands on the railing and stood there in silence. Furius whispered something in the man's ear, and the convoy began to move again.

"Phew. That was close," said Vescus. "Who was that creepy guy in the robe?"

"Galen," said a voice from behind.

Vescus shielded Cana. "Mattia?"

Mattia stood up from his hiding place, and Vescus embraced him.

"You escaped?" Vescus asked.

"Aye, myself along with Livius, Cyprian, Iulius, and Rufus to name a few. Furius has sent patrols to the northern fields to look for us, but we are held up in the marsh."

"Where do you plan to go?" Vescus whispered.

"We haven't decided, but we can't stay here much longer."

"You could go to my father's barn," offered Cana.

Mattia raised an eyebrow. "But your father has sworn an

oath to Furius."

"He only did that to protect us."

"What about your older brothers?"

"Same," said Cana.

Mattia rubbed the stubble on his chin. "I will tell the others. I know your father has secret storage areas in his barn. Where are you two going?"

"To check out that ship." Vescus pointed.

"You should reconsider it," Mattia spoke gravely. "You would not believe the sounds I've heard coming from that ship."

"We'll be careful," said Cana.

"Very well. Just don't get too close." Mattia patted Vescus on the shoulder and crept through the reeds.

Cana and Vescus waited till Mattia was out of view and made their way to the lake. To their right, the mast of Furius's lead ship rose above the reeds, and ahead of them, the wall of floating trees covered them in afternoon shadow.

"Let's do some island hopping," said Cana, wading out into the water. Where the reeds thinned, a floating clump of trees drifted near, and Cana grabbed it and hauled herself aboard.

"I can't believe we're going into the forest lake. People disappear here." Vescus took Cana's hand and joined her.

Cana cracked one of the hollow saplings and sounded the lake bottom. She pressed firmly down, propelling the floating island out into the lake. "Don't worry. Icabus and I have been over here before. As far as I know, there are no furry monsters."

"No, but maybe some other kind." Vescus peered into the dark waters. "My father used to say the lake people have claws like fishhooks."

"Do you promise not to laugh at me if I tell you something?"

"Sure, what?"

"The night the ships arrived, I saw a lake boy out here."

"Really?" Vescus asked, skeptically. "What did he look like?"

"Fair-skinned, sort of tall, with long, blond hair, and a spear thing with three points. He was wearing these funny silver shorts. I barely blinked, and he was gone."

"Your eyes could have been playing tricks on you. The lake is like that."

"No, Vescus, that wasn't it."

"So, he might have been a frog prince." Vescus winked.

Cana hit him in the chest. "You promised not to laugh. I'm never telling you anything ever again."

"Sorry, I couldn't help myself. Two days ago, I would've thought you were crazy, but now I'm not so sure."

"Do you believe me?"

"I'm sort of afraid if I don't." Vescus grinned. "Hold on."

The floating island struck the greater collection of trees, causing the smaller ones to shake. Vescus jumped onto the floating island and helped Cana over the roots.

"Do you hear that?" Cana whispered.

"What, the trees creaking?"

"No. Listen."

Vescus listened, and his eyes widened. "My Gods. What is that? It sounds like moaning and... growling."

"It's coming from that ship, Vescus. I changed my mind. I don't think we should go over there."

Vescus bit his lip and shifted his attention from the shore to the ship. "No. Somebody might need our help. Why don't you wait here and keep watch for me?"

Cana fidgeted anxiously. "I'm coming, but I won't look."

"Alright, stay close." Vescus tiptoed through the trees.

The weapons ship was wider than Furius's other two ships, with a prominent deckhouse and a square mainsail set high on a central mast. A small headsail extended beyond the prow to maintain the ship's heading in good winds.

"Vescus, what's that smell? It's making my eyes water."

"I know. Gods, Cana, don't look."

Hanging over the edge of the ship was a line of corpses. Not all the bodies were human—counted among them were Gilian.

"Like the one you saw?" Vescus pointed.

Cana nodded and covered her nose. "Gods, Vescus, they look butchered."

"Get down, Cana. There's someone on deck."

Two men in bloody smocks came into view. Between them was another man Cana recognized: Piscius, father of Pelagus. Piscius's face was as white as a ghost.

"Give him the blade, Villus." The bald soldier nudged Piscius forward with the butt of his ax. "Piscius, your boy is hungry. Cut him some meat."

"Aye, Ulpius." Villus pulled a bloodstained cleaver from the deck rail and handed it to Piscius.

Piscius's hand shook and he began to weep.

"Stop fussing, Piscius. Cut your boy some fish man meat," said Ulpius. "It's good and hearty. Makes 'em strong for the change."

Piscius grabbed the rope suspending one of the Gilian and pulled the corpse up over the railing. The smell must have been terrible because he wretched overboard and nearly dropped the cleaver into the water.

"Be careful!" Villus sneered. "Lose that blade, and I'll have you hanging over the edge with the rest of these unfortunates."

Piscius covered his mouth and cut into the flesh. Cana could hear him sobbing.

Ulpius pulled a dirty rag from his belt and blotted the sweat from his head. "Are you going to cry every time you feed him?"

"But what's he becoming? It's horrible," Piscius wept.

"Master Galen says all men are monsters." Villus leaned against the railing.

Piscius wiped away his tears with his sleeve. "Galen doesn't look like a monster. Will my son ever look like himself again?"

Ulpius sighed. "Galen says in the Golden Land all things are possible."

The snarls from below deck had diminished to a painful whimpering. Piscius cut away the biceps, triceps, and part of the Gilian's right deltoid.

"I'm coming, Pelagus!"

Piscius and the two soldiers disappeared from view. Vescus took a step toward the ship, and Cana grabbed his tunic.

"Seriously, are you crazy?"

"I've got to see what they're doing in there, Cana."

"Why? If even half of that craziness we just heard is true, then Galen is a lot more dangerous than anyone thought. We need to tell Atius."

"Atius? Atius is a traitor. Look what he did to your brother. He whipped him like an animal. You shouldn't trust him."

"He saved your life, Vescus. I know it doesn't make sense, but I know he's on our side," she whispered.

Vescus clenched his fists at his sides. "Cana..."

"What, Vescus? Say it."

"The only thing Atius cares about is Icabus. Sometimes, I think that's all you care about, too."

"That's not true, Vescus. Take it back, or I'm leaving."

Vescus turned toward the ship and said nothing.

"You're mental, Vescus." Cana stole into the floating forest.

ICABUS

"Wake up."

Icabus opened his eyes and saw Nubis's silhouette in the morning light. He sat up and quickly examined his hands. "I didn't change. What does that mean?"

"It means you're a boy and nothing else. We must go."

"Where?"

"To the ocean. If what you say is true, the Gilian will come to warn me."

"There are Gilian, here?" Icabus asked.

"There is a path to this land in the deep of the forest lake. It connects to the sea beyond this valley."

Icabus looked to the gate. "I can't come with you. I need to go back to Aggersel."

"I can't let you do that. You could still change. You're coming with me."

"And if I refuse?"

Nubis rested his hand on the hilt of his sword.

"Didn't you hear anything I said? Galen is alive."

"I doubt that."

"Why?

Nubis came close. "Because I killed him and threw his body down the well of the Citadel."

"But what about my dreams? What about Furius and the other Authians? Every minute I'm here is a minute lost."

Nubis exhaled slowly and regarded the morning sky. "If only that were true. Days here are only hours across the gate. Besides, there is no honor in throwing your life away. You told me you dreamed of dragons. They once roamed these lands. Perhaps you will find one to aid you."

"Why would they do that?"

"Because dragons are protectors." Nubis offered his hand.

Icabus took it reluctantly, and the dragon knight lifted him to his feet.

"Come." Nubis headed upstream.

Icabus scratched his head. "Wait. If you're trying to reach the ocean, shouldn't we go downstream?"

"The stream leads to the sea, but the coastline there is perilous. To reach the shores we seek, we must leave this valley. I hope you're not afraid of heights."

"No, just falling to my death." Icabus eyed the cliffs above the fall with apprehension.

A spiderweb of exposed tree roots made an imperfect ladder up the rockface. Icabus tried his best not to look down, but where the trees thinned, Icabus's curiosity overcame his fear, and he marveled at the greater canyon and sea behind him, which appeared golden under the fading daylight.

Above the canyon, a flat highland marsh formed the headwaters of the stream. The hills ringing the marsh were arid and grassy.

Nubis dropped his pack near a flower bed of crystals and sat cross-legged. "Tonight, we rest here."

"Can I start a fire?"

"If you like. Do not wander far. This land does not favor your kind."

"Don't you mean our kind?"

Nubis nodded, and Icabus left him.

Past the arid rim of the marsh, the land sloped downward into a vast wooded valley. Kindling was abundant, and Icabus quickly collected what he needed and made a fire.

"Ugh, I'm starving." Icabus poked the fire with a stick.

"I brought some cooked roots." Nubis reached into his pack and pulled out four purple potatoes.

"Do you have any dried meat in there to go with them?"

"I rarely eat meat," said Nubis, tossing the spuds into the embers.

Icabus raised an eyebrow. “Why? Are you allergic?”

“No. Humans don’t need to eat animals, so I don’t.”

“But they’re so delicious.”

“What if a dragon said that to you? Is deliciousness worth your life?”

Icabus laughed nervously. “That’s silly. I’m not an animal.”

“Aren’t you? Some must kill to live; most humans kill out of desire. I think life is worth more than that.”

Icabus turned his potato noting its sweet, honey-like aroma. “Do dragons eat people?”

“No,” said Nubis, unfurling a wool sleeping mat. “What do you know of Galen?”

Icabus thought about it. “Not much. I know he’s the reason the Old Kingdom fell, but the villagers don’t talk about it. Even after a hundred years, I think most of them are still afraid.”

“As they should be.”

“What did Galen do?”

The dragon knight’s expression remained stoic, but Icabus saw sadness and anger in his eyes. “He poisoned the dragons and set ruin to this land; he was a heretic and a murderer and deserved a far worse death than he received,” he spoke firmly.

Icabus pretended to find interest in the ground between his legs and cleared his throat. “My mother says Galen was the Steward of the Citadel. She told me the spring there could make people live longer.”

“She speaks true.” Nubis’s tone softened. “Sickness and death were not common things in the Apennine Kingdom. The waters there flowed from the Golden Land. In small amounts, it brings long life and wellness, and in larger quantities, greater change.”

“Like turning you into a monster?”

“Yes. In this land, there is no difference between who you are and what you are, Icabus.”

Icabus tried to put this idea out of his mind. He never felt so concerned about his own thoughts. “Did you know Galen?” Icabus shifted nervously.

"Not personally," Nubis replied indifferently. "He was a charismatic and popular steward. There was an allure about him that caused many people to follow him blindly."

"Why did he hurt the dragons?"

Nubis watched the flames with detachment. "Galen wanted to live forever. He used his position as steward to petition the dragons to be a gate guardian like the dragon knights. It was an unconventional request, but one that the dragons could not ignore. Galen was granted a test to see whether he would serve himself or others. He failed that test and retaliated."

"How did the Old Kingdom fall?" Icabus warmed his hands over the fire.

Nubis exhaled slowly and scrutinized him. Icabus couldn't tell whether he was angry, annoyed, or both. "Sometimes the past is better left where it is, Icabus. We have a long journey tomorrow. We should eat and rest."

"My father always said that history repeats itself if people don't learn from it." Icabus poked one of the potatoes with a stick and rolled it in Nubis's direction.

Nubis broke the spud in two, releasing a puff of fragrant steam. "If I speak of this, you will not ask me about it again?"

Icabus nodded.

"Very well. After Galen returned from the mountain, a sickness fell upon the Apennine Kingdom. First, the old succumbed, then the young, until young and old were piled equally in the streets. Galen's followers claimed the sickness was a sign of the Gods' anger. They convinced the people that Galen could make a cure in the Golden Land."

Nubis regarded the fire emotionlessly. "Words and reason became meaningless at that point. The dragons refused to allow Galen to enter the Golden Land, and rioting broke out in the streets. In the confusion that followed, Galen poisoned the dragons and passed through the gate with his disciples. He used fire powder to seal the entrance behind him."

Nubis paused and looked up. "After we buried our dead, the dragon knights broke into Galen's workshop and found it filled with poisonous herbs. We discovered the same plants in the well of the Citadel."

Icabus shook his head. "Galen was poisoning everybody?"

"Yes, but that was not the end of it. After decimating the ancient races here, Galen and his followers returned to the Apennine Kingdom, but they were no longer men but beasts. They ravaged the city, killing and setting fires. Your ancestors were among the few who escaped.

"Most of Galen's followers were hunted down and killed. Galen and Arkax were presumed dead in the fires, but I was wrong." Nubis tossed his spud to Icabus and lay on his back. "I think I lost my appetite."

Icabus watched him patiently, and the dragon knight hummed a tune.

"Wait. You're not done telling the story, are you?"

Nubis glanced toward Icabus and then back to the stars. "I said I would tell you how the Apennine Kingdom fell, nothing more."

"But I want to hear the rest. What happened to Galen and Arkax? How did you end up here alone? I want to know."

"Perhaps another time." Nubis closed his eyes and began to hum again.

Icabus flopped down on his back. "There's no way I'm going to sleep tonight," he groused.

The dragon knight continued to hum, and Icabus listened. The melody carried him somewhere between dream and memory, and when Nubis fell silent, Icabus began to hum in turn, completing the dragon verse only a knight should know.

VESCUS

A fat crow plucked maggots from the eyes of one of the dead Gilian. He cawed loudly at Vescus as if speaking.

Vescus put his finger to his lips. To his surprise, the crow did not caw again.

"Was that a friend of yours?"

The crow chortled mournfully and swallowed a few more maggots.

"Gross." Vescus wrinkled his nose.

The guttural cries from below deck had ceased. Vescus could hear several muffled voices he recognized, including Piscius and the bald butcher, Ulpius, and a few he did not. These latter voices gave Vescus pause. They sounded guttural and inarticulate. Vescus didn't know what afflicted them, but he was certain that whatever had been growling moments before now seemed to be striking up a conversation.

The crow cocked its head toward the ship and ruffled its feathers.

"Yeah, I don't like the sound of that either," said Vescus. "I wonder if you have a name?"

"Cales," said the bird.

Vescus's eyes widened. "Cales."

Cales lowered his head and lifted his feet one after the other.

"Well, Cales. Let's see how smart you are. Can you jump up onto that railing and tell me if it's all clear."

The bird made a mocking chirp and hopped onto the deck railing. He scanned the deck, turned his head 180 degrees, and nodded.

"Alright, I'm trusting you. If I get caught, it's on you."

Cales squinted his eyes and ruffled his feathers.

"Don't get offended. We just met, and you're a bird. Where I'm from, this sort of thing gets people talking. By the way, has anyone ever told you that you might be the biggest crow ever?"

Cales cocked his beak, and Vescus scaled the side of the boat. Vescus pulled the cleaver from the railing and sliced the air in front of him. The blade was as long as his forearm and curved along the cutting edge to a point.

Cales cawed nervously and flew over his head. He landed on one of two lantern posts on either side of the deckhouse entrance. The bird pecked purposefully at the hook suspending one of the lamps.

"What? You want me to torch the place and run?"

Cales bobbed his head up and down.

Vescus unhooked a lantern and peered into the deckhouse. Shelves lined with jars rose to the ceiling. Between them, a trail of dried blood led to a descending stairwell. A dim light flickered from the space below. Vescus's heart quickened.

"I gotta see if there's anyone down there who needs help before I burn the ship."

Cales squinted at him incredulously and pecked at his shoulder. Vescus pulled away.

"Ouch. No cracker for you, angry bird. Keep quiet and get out of sight."

Cales retook flight and landed on a branch overhanging the ship. The limb dipped under his weight.

"Keep eating maggots, and the next time it will break, fatso."

The bird picked through his plumage, and Vescus stepped into the deckhouse. The sound of footfalls halted Vescus in his tracks, and he quickly returned the lamp to its hook and hid behind a row of jars.

"You see, Piscius, your boy grows stronger by the day," Ulpius said, following Piscius up the blood-soaked steps.

"What happened to his eyes?" Piscius wept. "They've turned yellow."

"'Tis the human meat," said Villus. "It changes the mind and is reflected in his eyes. It makes him stronger, hungrier."

"His appetite is insatiable. He said he wanted to eat me."

"Feed him then, Piscius." Ulpius patted the man's back. "He's still your son."

Vescus held his breath as the three men stepped passed him to the deck. A chill went down Vescus's spine. Someone below deck was crying, and it sounded like a child.

Vescus tiptoed out of his hiding place and descended the stair trying not to step in the blood. The scent of urine stung his eyes and threatened to extinguish the small lantern hanging from the rafters.

The bloody path continued down the center of the ship to a fore door with a small barred window at eye level. Two storage holds, walled above waist level with iron bars, lined the hall between the stair and the forward hold. Potions and parchments filled the starboard room, while the port hold resembled a butcher's shop. The floorboards beneath Vescus's feet creaked, and the crying stopped.

"Hello? You don't have to be afraid. I'm here to help you," Vescus spoke softly.

Vescus unhooked the lantern and extended the wick. He raised it to the bow door window. Light illuminated the center of the hold where something hairy drew itself back into the shadows. Whatever it was, it was bigger than a child.

"Help us," said a voice.

"Release us, before they return," said another.

Chains rattled behind the door, and someone began to weep. "The keys. Please. Open the door and gives us the keys so we can be free."

A key ring hung from a hook beside the door. Vescus exchanged the keys for his lantern; he released the bolt lock and tried several of the keys before finding the one that fit the lock and pushed open the door. The trail of blood continued into the hold where flies and maggots feasted on the larger pieces of gore and bone. Vescus covered his mouth and nose with his arm and reached for the lantern.

"No, please, the light hurts our eyes. The keys. The keys."

A terrible foreboding held Vescus. "What has Galen done to you? Tell me."

"He's hurt us. That's all you have to know. Give us the keys!"

Vescus glanced at the keys and then at the darkness. He lifted the lantern from the hook. "No, I must see."

The crying stopped and whoever had been weeping now began to giggle. "He wants to see."

"Pelagus are you in here?" Vescus lifted his lantern and caught the flash of yellow eyeshine ahead. He stopped, and to his right something rushed forward from the darkness.

"Give me the keys!" The Taker snapped his jaws shut at the edge of the light.

Vescus stumbled back. Behind him, chains rattled and Vescus jerked forward, feeling the swift raking of claws brush his tunic. He recovered and retreated to the door.

"You fool!" growled the Taker to Vescus's left. "You didn't scare him enough, and now he's still alive!"

"Shut up! Now look what you've done. He's leaving! Are you happy?"

"Not until your limp throat is in my jaws!"

Vescus had seen enough. He turned to Galen's laboratory and lifted the lantern above his head. The ship and everything else with it would burn.

"Vescus? Vescus, is that you?"

The growling turned to silence as quickly as it had begun. The voice was familiar to Vescus but distorted, like that of someone who was sick.

"Pelagus?"

"Yes, it's me! I need your help, please! Give me the keys."

"What has Galen done to you?"

A giggle arose in the darkness followed by a collection of whispers. Pelagus growled, silencing the chatter. "You said you want to see, Vescus. Follow the trail of blood."

"No, come over here," said the beast to Vescus's left.

Vescus extended his lantern's wick and pretended not to see

the hairy monsters shift in his peripheral vision. Their eyes were twice the size of an average man's and glowed a sickly yellow against the firelight.

"Pelagus, where are you?"

"Here."

Near the bow of the ship two yellow eyes opened. Vescus stopped.

"Can you see me?" Pelagus's eyes became slivers.

Vescus nodded. "What have Furius and Galen done to you, Pelagus?"

"This." Pelagus's chains rattled and he moved into the edge of the light.

Vescus could not find the breath to speak. Pelagus was a Taker, but it was not that image that took Vescus's breath away, it was the blood—blood that covered Pelagus from snout to toe.

"Yes, we are monsters. Help us," pleaded one of the Takers.

"Please, free us before they return," added another.

"Please, please, please," said a third.

"Shut up!" Pelagus growled.

Manacles, held fast by chains, bound Pelagus's neck, wrists, and ankles to the hull. Bits of gore that didn't reach his mouth dangled from his hairy chest.

"Galen's potion did this to me, Vescus." He rested on his haunches and showed Vescus his clawed hands. "At first, I refused to eat. Gods forgive me Vescus, the pain and hunger were too much, so I ate, and the more I ate, the more I changed."

Pelagus reached into his mouth and pulled out a human tooth and tossed it aside. The tooth rolled into the corner where Vescus saw a severed hand. "Release me, Vescus, so I may have my revenge."

"No." Vescus shook his head. "I can't release you."

"Vescus! Give me the keys now!" Pelagus pulled against his chains.

Vescus slowly backed away. "I'm sorry."

Pelagus panted and sat back on his haunches. "No, brother, it's you who will be sorry. I wanted to spare you my fate, but I can't let you kill me."

The floor groaned behind Vescus, and before he could turn, a fist pummeled him in the face. He fell onto his hands and knees, losing his lantern and cleaver. All around him chains rattled, and a contemptuous laughter filled the hold.

"And who might you be, young'un?" came a booming voice, which Vescus recognized as belonging to the bearded butcher, Villus.

"It's a Vescus," said one of the Takers.

"A bad boy," growled another.

"Yes, give him to us fresh. He was going to burn the ship!"

Ulpius kicked Vescus's cleaver aside. With one hand, he grabbed Vescus's fallen lantern, and with the other, he took Vescus by the hair and lifted him to his feet. "Going to burn the ship, eh? I want a better look at you. What should we do with this boy, Villus?"

Villus stroked his beard and smiled. "I can think of a few things, Ulpius."

"Piscius, help me?" Vescus cried.

Piscius did nothing.

"He won't be doing you any favors," laughed Villus. Using a match, he transferred the fire from Vescus's lantern to a large lamp hanging at the center of the hold. The wick sputtered then blazed to life.

The monsters shrieked.

Gore and dried blood covered every visible surface. Pelagus and the other Takers cowered, hiding their faces from the light. A few reacted hysterically, shrieking, lashing out, and clawing at the hull.

"Yes, a fine specimen," said Ulpius, running his hands up and down Vescus's body like a horse trader.

"No! He's defective," cried one of the monsters.

"Yes, not worth saving," shouted another.

"Please, let us have him," whimpered a third.

"No." Ulpius smiled. "This one is brave. He will make a powerful Taker."

"Feed them, Piscius!" Villus stepped aside, allowing Piscius to enter the room.

"Piscius, help me," said Vescus.

Piscius kept his eyes to the ground, ignoring Vescus's plea. Scraps of decaying meat dangled from Piscius's trembling hands, and he threw some to each of the monsters. Pelagus reacted with disdain to his father's presence. He growled and spat a mouthful of frothy yellow sputum onto Piscius's foot as the man offered him a handful of meat.

"I'll get the potion ready," said Villus.

"Should we wait for Furius and Galen?" Ulpius raised a brow.

Villus shook his head. "Master Galen intends to bless all the children of Aggersel with his potion. This one's just a little early."

Vescus struggled as Ulpius lifted him higher off the ground by his hair. Ulpius squeezed Vescus's cheeks. "Now listen here. You can be a good lad and drink the potion, or I can ram the metal tube down your throat, and you still drink the potion. No difference to me, but soon you'll be real hungry, and Gods help you if you can't eat because your throat is cut up and swollen."

Ulpius grinned, and Vescus could see the brown stumps of his decaying teeth. "Ask Pelagus if you don't believe me. I didn't let Daddy feed him for a whole day because I feared he might choke. He's still grumpy about it."

"No, I'll never do it!" Vescus protested. He dug his nails into the bald butcher's forearm, and the man barely flinched. Around them, the creatures sniffed the air and stirred restlessly.

Ulpius frowned. "The table and the tube then."

"Vescus, give me the keys now!" Pelagus held out his hand.

Vescus tossed the keys underhand. Ulpius batted Vescus's arm, but he was too late. The keys flew through the air and slid to a stop a claw length from Pelagus's grasp.

"Piscius, you fool, get those keys!" Villus cursed.

Piscius's face slackened, and he looked as white as a ghost. "No, my son, no!"

Pelagus fought against his bonds with a ferocity that made

the hull groan. The steel manacles tore into his flesh, and he snarled in agony as he fought for each millimeter of reach.

Piscius fell to his knees and grabbed the keys. He pulled them away from Pelagus but Piscius's momentum drew him forward. Pelagus raked his father's face with his ebony claws.

"Pelagus?" Piscius gasped. He touched his face and dropped the keys. Strips of flesh dangled from his cheeks. Vescus could see Piscius's teeth through the holes.

Pelagus grabbed the keys and cackled wildly.

"Stop him, Villus!" Ulpius gasped.

The bearded man drew his sword and pushed past them. Pelagus had already removed the manacle from his right wrist and was unlocking the one around his neck when Villus shouted, "The keys, or else."

"Or else what?" snarled Pelagus.

Villus made to stab Pelagus in the leg, but the beast drew back and laughed.

The manacle around Pelagus's neck hit the floor with a thud, and he immediately went to work freeing his other wrist. Villus cursed intelligibly and stabbed at Pelagus's chest.

Pelagus shifted left, and the blade stuck squarely in the hull. Villus gasped, but before he could react, Pelagus was upon him. His jaws closed around the man's neck, and suddenly Villus had no throat, only a void with a spine and blood enough to paint the ship twice over.

Villus stumbled sideways, and Pelagus pushed him toward one of the Takers, who cackled gleefully.

"Gods, no, no!" cried Ulpius. He dropped Vescus and the boy drove his heel into Ulpius's foot. The bald butcher snarled in pain and punched Vescus in the face.

Vescus fell to his knees and lost all sense of orientation. Blackness stole his vision, and the horrible sounds around him became muffled. Vescus's consciousness was slipping away, and he grasped onto the memory of Cana's face to stay present. He felt Ulpius brush against him and he struck out, punching the man squarely in the groin. The butcher doubled over.

"Free us!" called one of the Takers.

"Give us the bald man and let us eat him," screamed another.

Vescus ignored them and unhooked the large lantern hanging at the center of the hold.

"Oh, no you don't," said Ulpius, grabbing Vescus by the ankle.

"Oh, no you don't," said Pelagus, grabbing the butcher by both legs and yanking him away from Vescus.

"No! No! No!" Ulpius begged.

Pelagus chuckled through serrated teeth. "Now, now, don't fuss. You always wanted to become a monster, didn't you? Now you'll become four after we eat you."

Ulpius shrieked, and as much as Vescus had wished him harm, he didn't wish this fate on anyone. Around him, the Takers rattled their chains and howled in a hungry frenzy. Hands, feet, and chunks of muscle sailed through the air and entered the monsters' jaws. There was so much blood, and still the butcher shrieked, arching his body and flapping what remained of his arms and legs like bloody flippers.

Pelagus didn't seem to notice. He buried his snout in Ulpius's belly, and the more the butcher fought him, the more ferocious Pelagus feasted on his bowels.

Vescus seized the lantern and ran. He slammed the door behind him and fastened the bolt lock in place. Above deck, there came a hollering. Vescus could discern three, maybe four, sets of boots on the planks above him.

"Curse the Gods," he muttered under his breath. He looked back through the small barred window where the Takers still chomped contentedly on the bald butcher's flesh. The meat cleaver was lost somewhere under the gore.

Vescus unfastened the door and swung it wide. "Pelagus, we have company."

Pelagus lifted his snout. Fresh blood painted his face and hands, and where humanness once resided in his eyes, a hungry madness now reigned. He licked the flesh from his lips and laughed. "Tell me, Vescus, did you open the door only so I could save you? You should know by now that no door can hold me."

"I'm going to burn the ship. Be ready."

"I am. Here, I know you want this." Pelagus pulled the meat cleaver from below a blossom of intestine and slid it toward Vescus.

Vescus picked up the blade and wiped its bloody handle on his trousers. He turned away, and before he could move, a huge hairy hand held his arm to his side.

"Be seeing you, Vescus," said Pelagus, licking his face.

Vescus stumbled away, partly in shock at Pelagus's speed, but mostly because the monster had tongued him like a salt lick. Lights appeared on the stairwell and Vescus put down the lantern and ducked beneath the table in Galen's lab.

"Ulpius, Villus! It's Pio. Are you down here? Why aren't you on deck? Give us report so we can get off your accursed vessel."

Pio stopped at the door to the lab. "Gods, what's that smell? I think I'm going to be sick."

Vescus held his breath as two other soldiers joined the group. Beyond the monsters' door something giggled.

"Ulpius, is that you, bald brute?" Pio began to draw his sword but dropped it back into its ring. "Do you hear that? It sounds like a child is crying"

Vescus slowly exhaled as the soldiers approached the bow of the ship.

Pio placed his hand on the Takers' door and Vescus stepped into the light. "Hey!"

The soldiers spun around and drew their swords. Vescus recognized one of the men as Germanus, a villager who had raised sheep before swearing allegiance to Furius. Just seeing him in one of Furius's red tunics made Vescus angry.

Germanus's jaw slackened in disbelief. "Vescus?"

Vescus nodded and picked up the lantern. "Your friends are dead. I killed them."

"Impossible," said Pio.

"You're right. He's lying. I ate them!" Pelagus threw back the door and raked the flesh from Pio's face.

The man dropped his sword and spun around screaming. "My eyes! My eyes!"

They were gone.

"This way," chuckled Pelagus. He seized the faceless Pio and threw him into the Takers' hold.

Vescus could barely hear him scream before the Takers devoured him in the dark.

"Now you," Pelagus said to the second Authian. The man turned to run, but Pelagus leaped onto his back and drove him into the floor. Vescus thought he heard the man's neck snap before Pelagus began to eat him. He could see the soldier's eyes staring up at him, fully aware, pleading for help.

Germanus stood plastered against the bars, between Vescus and Pelagus. He was white as a ghost, and his trousers were wet down one leg. He looked to Vescus and then at the stair.

Vescus shook his head. "No, I can't let you go."

"Get out of my way, Vescus!" Germanus moved like a man without a hope. A part of Vescus wanted to step aside and let him pass. He'd known Germanus his whole life, but Germanus had made a choice, just as Vescus had; Germanus chose Furius, and now he had to pay.

"Germanus, stop or I'll..." Vescus held his ground.

Germanus struck him and Vescus reacted in defense. Warm blood poured down Vescus's hand where the cleaver had entered Germanus's neck. "Curse you, Vescus." His lip quivered. "You're a monster."

Germanus collapsed and Vescus pushed him away. In the background, the monsters reinstated their howls for freedom.

Pelagus regurgitated a chunk of thigh, chewed it, and swallowed it again. He gave Vescus a toothy grin and entered the lab, where he sifted through the bottles on the table, sniffing their contents.

"Takers," said Pelagus. "That is what Galen says the dragons called us before they killed us all. Part man, part beast—smarter and stronger than both.

"Galen was the first Taker. He became that way after he

entered the Golden Land. From his blood, Galen created the first potion that causes the change. He wanted to transform the Old Kingdom in his image, but the dragons stopped him. Now he's here to finish his work."

Vescus got up and raised the lantern above his head. Pelagus's yellow eyes widened. "No, you fool, don't!"

Vescus threw the lantern and Pelagus jumped. The Taker moved so fast, Vescus feared he would pluck the lamp out of the air, but his claws caught only air, and the lamp shattered, pouring oil and flame across Galen's table. The heat came so fast Vescus could smell his eyebrows burn. Blue, green, and orange light flashed in blinding bursts as vials filled with combustible powders and liquids exploded in a hellish rain.

Pelagus covered his face, and Vescus shoved him toward the fire. The wall of parchments ignited, knocking Vescus to the ground and engulfing Pelagus in flames. Pelagus screamed: a horrible, painful howl that was more animal than human. The other Takers answered in turn, recognizing, at last, the painful death that would soon consume them, too.

Vescus rolled over and scrambled up the stairs and out of the aft hold. The touch of the sunlight never felt so welcoming, but when it surrounded him, the humidity and stench of the rotting dead triggered a wave of nausea, and he dry heaved over the starboard railing, unable to expel the chemical smoke still burning his lungs.

Below him, the ship juddered, tilting the deck more port side and pushing the starboard side higher into the air. The ropes securing the hanging dead dangled within Vescus's reach, and he used them to climb up onto the starboard railing.

The railing beneath him cracked, and he fell headlong off the ship. One of the ropes caught his ankle, and he dangled there, upside down, coming mouth to mouth with the hanging dead.

"Vescus! Gods, you're alright."

Vescus opened his eyes. The 'alright' part was debatable, but he wasn't about to argue. "Hi Cana," he answered. His throat felt coarse like sandpaper. "Mind cutting me down?"

The tilt of the ship made it possible for Cana to jump onto the starboard hull. She handed him a rope, which he wrapped around his wrist, and cut free the rope binding his ankle. Vescus spun around; his feet grazed the water, but he didn't fall in.

"Why did you come back?" he asked.

"I decided you didn't know what you were talking about." Cana helped him to his feet. Beneath them, something clawed at the inside of the hull and yowled. Cana's eyes widened.

"We should get off this ship," said Vescus.

"Yeah, I think you're right. You first."

Vescus didn't protest. Even though the distance was less than three feet, he almost didn't make it to the floating trees. Cana sheathed her blade and jumped across.

"What was that sound?" she asked.

Vescus coughed. "Worse than you can imagine. I'll tell you after we get out of here."

Cana led Vescus through the thicket of floating trees. Around Aggersel, horns sounded and men hollered. Furius's forces moved about the docks in utter disarray. Some boarded rowboats, while others simply gawked with their swords in hand.

The weapons ship's hull was disappearing below the waterline, and Vescus only wished it would sink faster. Cana stopped, and Vescus nearly knocked her over.

"Vescus, look."

In the shadow of the wood stood a Gilian boy. He regarded them silently and pointed to the coral hilted dagger on Cana's hip.

"I think he wants this knife," said Cana.

"I don't think that's a good idea," Vescus whispered.

"I'm pretty sure he could have hurt us already if he wanted to, Vescus. I think this blade means something to him. I'm giving it back."

"No." Vescus grabbed her arm.

Cana shrugged him off and walked forward. She presented the dagger with both hands. "Here," she said, searching lake boy's pale features.

He took it and examined the sharp edge. "The blade will never dull, so long as you don't try to sharpen it. May it bring you more protection than its former bearer." He handed it back to Cana and looked at Vescus. "Thank you for burning the ship."

Vescus nodded and the Gilian boy turned away.

"Wait." Cana took a step toward him. "What's your name?"

"Urms," he said, without facing her.

"I saw you the night the ships came. I'm Cana. That's Vescus. Have you come to help us?"

Urms regarded them over his shoulder. "I was supposed to stop you."

Cana drew back. "Why?"

"So Furius would not think we acted against him. He holds our queen, Arwa, prisoner."

Vescus frowned. "That's how Furius got here, isn't it? You led him here. He would never have made it this far if you hadn't shown him the way."

"We didn't have a choice."

"There's always a choice." Vescus touched Cana's shoulder. "We need to go. Galen and Furius's goons will search these islands for sure."

"Galen?" Urms's expression became grim.

"Come on, Cana." Vescus took her hand.

Cana hesitated. "If you won't help us, Urms, then who can?"

Urms looked away. "There is one who lives in the mountain, but he is no longer himself."

"Cana... Furius's men are coming. We have to go," Vescus urged.

Cana wavered and then half-heartedly allowed herself to be led away. When Vescus turned back, Urms was gone.

ICABUS

"Hellos."

"Ah! Nubis, wake up! It's a monster," Icabus screamed.

"Rhah! Nubis wake! It is bads."

Icabus shoved the creature back, and it made a squeaking sound. Firelight reflected in its black eyes, but Icabus fixated on its curved fangs.

"You won't suck my blood." Icabus pulled a burning stick from the fire pit. The thing gasped and hid its nose behind a leathery wing.

"Stop!" Nubis plucked the firebrand from Icabus's hand.

The creature peeked over its wing and squinted disagreeably at Icabus. Slung across its shoulder was a leather strap attached to a wicker basket brimming with fish. "Rhah! No fish for yous."

"I'm sorry, Shrail. Icabus has never seen your kind before," Nubis explained.

Icabus could still hear his heartbeat in his ears. "You're a giant..."

"A bat, stupids," Shrail screeched.

Nubis sat cross-legged and stirred the coals in the fire pit. "Shrail is still frightened by you, Icabus."

"He's afraid?" Icabus gawked.

Nubis glared at Icabus and tossed the firebrand onto the glowing embers.

Icabus rolled his eyes. "I'm sorry, Shrail. You scared me, too."

The bat blinked curiously at Icabus and slowly unwrapped himself from the cloak of his wing. "Sorry, too, for the pees," said Shrail, wiggling his nose and allowing the hair on his back and neck to fall.

"Gross." Icabus shook the beads of urine off his pants.

"When Shrail is scared, Shrail pees."

"Shrail does." Nubis smirked.

Shrail squatted and gutted two fish using his thumb talon. Icabus relished the thought of a fish meal after eating Nubis's tasteless potatoes.

"Want the sweets?" Shrail offered Icabus the guts.

"No, throw them out."

"Throw? The sweets are bests?" The bat scooped the organs into his mouth and handed the rest of the fish to Icabus.

Icabus skewered the fish with a stick and set it over the fire. Shrail handed Nubis a cleaned fish, which the dragon knight placed scales-down on the coals.

"You're going to eat that?" Icabus asked Nubis.

"It would be rude to refuse." Nubis bowed his head to Shrail.

"Would you like me to cook one for you?" Icabus offered Shrail.

Shrail pursed his lips, revealing the tips of his fangs. "Fire fish stinks like Flkrulk."

Icabus turned to Nubis, who shook his head. "Ask me when you're older."

Shrail cackled and cleaned another fish. "Bats tell Shrail Black Scales leave valley but is not alones. And then Shrail sees this stupids with Black Scales, and we think, can it be Kails, but Kails is dead, and we are afraids." The wet tip of Shrail's nose wriggled as he sniffed the air in Icabus's direction.

"Who's Kail?" Icabus asked.

Nubis ignored the question. "Tell me Shrail, have the Gilian come out from the ocean?"

"Not."

"Icabus and I are going to the Giants City. Can your people set a watch on the valley to ensure Arkax does not cross the gate?"

"Shrail cans."

"Do any Giants still live in this city?" Icabus asked Nubis.

"Birds and bugs and snakes," answered Shrail.

"Any dragons?"

The hair above Shrail's forehead rose, and he looked to Nubis.

Nubis shook his head without looking up. "The city is abandoned. The bats prefer the comforts of the mountains, as do I. For training, the solitude of the city will suit our needs while we wait for the Gilian."

"What training?"

"You must learn to meditate to protect yourself from change. And if we have time, I can teach you how to use a sword. Unless you wish to go with Shrail and learn to fish." Nubis glanced up at Icabus.

"No. I mean, yes. I would like to learn how to fight." Icabus suppressed his smile.

Shrail fidgeted. "Bats need Black Scales help, too. Taker hunts bats."

"That's impossible," Nubis replied. "Arkax still hides on Apenninus. Icabus himself has seen him."

Nubis's words were calm, but Icabus noticed a frightening change in his eyes, which blazed like a green flame. It reminded Icabus of the first time he saw the dragon knight's reflection in the falls.

"Nots Arkax," said Shrail, avoiding Nubis's gaze. "Another..."

Nubis raised his hand, and the bat chirped and fell silent. "How do you know it is another?" he asked.

"Dragons scars on its backs." Shrail made a slashing motion with his claws. "Many bats die protecting babies, but Taker too strongs... takes babies and eats."

"It is true then..." Nubis stared off into the darkness. "Mana returns. Things are waking up again."

Icabus turned his fish. "What's mana, Nubis?"

"A building block of life. It's what causes the change. It is also why the spring in the Apennine Kingdom brought long life. Excuse me." Nubis stood up and walked to the edge of the ridge. He looked out over the forest and the sea in silence.

The bat watched Nubis and whimpered. “Shrail needs dragons, but Kails is dead, and Black Scales is sads. Icabus fix?” Shrail blinked.

“I need a dragon, too, Shrail.”

ATIUS

"Where's the fire?" Atius panted, bounding up the wall walk stairs. A column of smoke and ash rose up from the harbor. He sighed with relief, seeing the fire was not in the village.

Atellus shielded his eyes. "It's from one of the ships."

"Which one?"

"Which one do you think?" Atellus cursed under his breath. "Wait here. I'll inform Furius."

"I can go."

Atellus raised a brow. "Very well, Atius. He's in that villa down the road with Galen. Look for Valens and Tatius."

"Aye." Atius bowed slightly.

"Wait." Atellus blocked Atius's path with his sword. "How goes your trap?"

"Everything is on schedule."

"Sounds dangerous. We'll be crushed or burned to death if the buildings don't fall as you say."

Atius held the man's stare. Atellus had been watching him closely since Celsus and Vescus disappeared. "That won't happen."

"That won't happen..." Atellus repeated slowly, allowing the silence between them to become uncomfortable.

"May I go?"

Atellus lowered his sword and offered Atius a desultory smile. "Give Galen a kiss for me."

Atius left him, taking the stairs two at a time. Beyond the gate, villagers dug trenches in the shadow of the ancient buildings. They cursed Atius under their breath. Atius pretended not to hear them and moved up the avenue to where

Tatius and Valens stood on the stoop of one of the stately houses. Atius thought they shared enough of a resemblance to be brothers.

"State your business," said Tatius, extending his spear. Unlike the other soldiers, his uniform was clean and smelled of honey and orange.

"There's a fire on one of the ships."

"What?" said Valens.

Tatius glanced over his shoulder and frowned. Atius thought he looked afraid. "Furius is upstairs," he said, withdrawing his spear.

Inside the villa, a dried corpse sat against a stair. Atius tipped his hat to it and climbed to the second floor, where Furius stood on a terrace facing Aggersel.

"Yes, Atius." His voice was deeper and stronger than Atius remembered.

"I came to report on the trap and a fire."

"I've seen it." Furius entered the room.

A hairy hand seized Atius's neck and held him from behind. He winced, feeling claws cut into his skin.

"Tell me, Atius, where might I find Vescus, son of Cilo."

"Galen?" The claws dug deeper. "Gods! I don't know."

"Really?" Galen growled.

"I swear it." Atius tried not to move. He could feel the sorcerer's hot breath against his cheek.

"Who is this girl who slinks about the shadows with your son? Her scent is everywhere in your house."

"Who? Cana?"

Furius stood before Atius. "Cana, who?"

"Her father is... Corvus."

"The man you whipped?"

"Aye." Atius felt faint.

Galen shoved Atius onto his knees. Atius touched his neck and examined the blood on his fingers.

"You will find the boy and the girl together." Galen stepped past Furius and faced the terrace. Beneath his purple robes, the sorcerer's form was hidden, save for his feet, which resembled a demon's paws.

"I will find her," said Furius. "I grow tired of failure. She will burn in Atius's new trap."

"No Furius, please." Atius placed his hands together. "This girl is like family to me."

"But she is not family, is she? I surely hope none of them are involved in this."

Atius felt as if his breath was stolen away. "No..."

"No." Furius regarded him fiercely. "When I get back, this trap had better be ready."

Atius nodded.

"Good." Furius stomped down the stair.

Atius got up and moved dazedly to the landing.

"Where are you going, Atius?" asked Galen.

Atius rested his shaking hand on the banister. Galen's voice barely sounded human to him. "To tend to the trap."

Galen laughed. "Don't take me for a fool. You came here with a purpose. Ask your question."

Atius considered his words. He wished he'd never come. "Why are you doing this?"

"This is why, Atius." Galen lifted his hood and faced him.

Atius expected Galen to be hideous, but what he saw could not match his wildest fear. Teeth, too many to count, filled the sorcerer's wolf-like snout, which was deformed and partially collapsed on one side, where scars and open bone marked his ancient wounds. The violence of the injuries made Atius believe that whoever and whatever inflicted them had wished upon the sorcerer a fate worse than death.

Atius looked askance, trying to shirk the hungry madness in Galen's yellow eyes. "Why go back? Why not leave this island? You have no one to stop you now."

Galen came so close that Atius could taste the metallic stench of his breath. "Because the dragons deceived me, Atius. They tricked me into believing the Golden Land would reveal my true form, but instead it turned me into a monster! I will not leave Apenninus until I am restored." Galen stroked Atius's cheek with the back of his claws. "Go, and make sure your trap doesn't fail. Your son may be in hiding, but your family is in plain view."

ICABUS

"Nubis? Shrail?" Icabus stretched. Morning dew clung to his clothes, making him feel sticky.

Nubis's bedroll and pack were gone. Two potatoes sat on a rock beside Icabus.

"Did they leave me?" Icabus sat up and looked around uneasily. As much as the dragon knight frightened him, Nubis's presence made Icabus feel safe in this strange place.

Icabus suppressed his angst and ate one of the potatoes as the sun climbed over the sea and cast its early light over the misty forest. "Well, I'm not going to wait here. Nubis was going to the sea, so that's where I'll go, too."

After packing his things, Icabus set off down the ridgeline. His body was still sore, but there was new strength in him that put a spring in his step; and, for a while, he forgot his troubles and walked in tranquil silence, noting the woodsy fragrance of the mist and sapphire brilliance of the sea. He'd traveled less than an hour when a shadow covered him from above.

"Where does it goes?" screeched the bat. "Shrail went back, and it was gones? Go with Shrail, not go alone, Black Scales says!"

Icabus placed his hands at his sides. "How can I go with you if you aren't there when I wake up? Where were you, anyway?"

"Fishing." Shrail landed in the needle grass and showed Icabus his catch.

"Why didn't you fly up the ridgeline like last night?"

"Shrail was scared and went a different way."

"Why does that not surprise me?" Icabus shook his head. "What else do you like to do besides fishing?"

"Vorluck," Shrail said with a fanged smile.

"Vorluck? What is that?"

"It is what you do when another smells very goods. Fish?"

"I'm not sure what you're getting at Shrail, but I think I just lost my appetite. Where is the Giants City?"

The bat made an incoherent gesture with his wing toward the forest then the sea. "Very far for yous."

"Why 'very far' for me?"

"No wings." The bat cackled.

"Great. Do you have any water?"

"Not. Water is theres." Shrail pointed with his chin down the ridge where the stream entered the sea.

"Gods, that is far. Can we go down into the woods and find some?"

Shrail eyed the forest and began to shake.

Icabus waved his hand. "Gods, you're no help. Stay here if you like, but I'm going down there."

Shrail followed Icabus on foot and wing, hissing incoherent curses or prayers, Icabus could not tell which. Underneath the cool canopy, Icabus could taste the salty moisture in the air.

"Hear that?"

Shrail moved his ears. "Whats?"

"Running water."

Icabus trudged through a thornless patch of thimbleberry to an open glen surrounded by a ring of redwoods. At its center was a clear pool fed by a trickling spring.

"Thank the Gods." Icabus dropped his things and knelt before the pool. The water was like glass and reflected his image. He looked older and more insipid than he remembered.

"Do not drink!" Shrail huddled in the bushes.

"Why? Is the spring poisoned?"

"Water Spirits."

"Water Spirits! You've got to be kidding me! You know, I'm surprised you're not afraid of flying." Shrail seemed to consider this for a moment, and Icabus groaned. He placed his hands in the face of his reflection and drank it. "See, nothing to be afraid of."

Shrail slowly edged away, and Icabus shook his head dismissively. He turned back to the water, and to his surprise, the trees and sky were reflected there, but not him. He waved his hand over the water. Nothing. Slowly, he reached out a finger to the mirror-like surface, and to his shock, the water evaded him.

"The water must be poisoned, Shrail. I'm hallucinating."

Icabus reached out to the surface, and the water recoiled like an animal; it shot out, hitting his chest. He fell back, and the water rose from the pool in a terrifying column.

"Gods!" he cried, slipping on the muddy bank. Two streams of water erupted from the column and pinned his hands to the ground. The pillar of water leaned over him, assuming the shape of a dragon.

"Taker..." spoke the water dragon. Its voice came not from its mouth but reverberations over its entire surface.

"I'm not a Taker. I'm a boy... Icabus!"

"You drank of me. My waters course through your veins. Do not lie."

"I'm not a monster!"

"Liar!"

Icabus felt a searing pain in his stomach as if the water he drank was now boiling. He screamed and struggled, but the Water Spirit's grip tightened the more he resisted.

"What are you?" Icabus moaned.

A ripple spread over the water dragon's body, and it released its watery arms. Icabus rolled over and vomited into the mud. The expelled water slithered away like two serpents and joined the Spirit's body.

The water dragon raised its long neck heavenward and growled.

High above the pond, Shrail hovered. With astounding precision, the bat pelted the Water Spirit with fish. The Spirit dissolved its dragon form and stretched its wispy arms hopelessly into the sky.

"Run, stupids!" screeched the bat.

Icabus scrambled to his feet and sprinted from the clearing.

There was a splash and a moan, and Icabus didn't dare look back. He kept running until he reached the edge of the forest where he met Shrail perched on a low hanging branch.

"Wow, that was a Water Spirit! I think I'm in shock."

From his branch, the bat glowered. "Not talking."

Icabus touched his tunic and looked over his body. "This is amazing, Shrail. I'm as dry as apple skin. When the Water Spirit had me pinned, I was soaked. It's like every drop of water was part of its body. Crazy."

"Not talking." The bat turned his back on him.

Icabus smiled and came close. For being a scaredy bat, Shrail was brave. "You know, you saved my life. I will never forget that."

The bat shrugged as if disinterested.

"And I promise I will never doubt your word again."

Shrail turned his head to Icabus without moving his body. "You are stupids. Shrail does not know why Black Scales likes."

"That's not the first time you called Nubis, Black Scales. It's those weird tattoos on his shoulders, isn't it?"

Shrail squinted disapprovingly. "Shrail almost dies and now Shrail has no more fish and stupids talks scales!"

"Sorry. We're fine now, aren't we?"

"Not! Shrail is still scared! Shrail almost dies! Shrail has no fishes!"

"Alright, alright. Don't talk then and stay scared. Thanks for helping me. Are there more of those things?"

"Not. Spirits need manas. Takers trick Spirits and stop manas. Most Spirits dies. Some sleeps."

"If they're waking up, then mana must be returning. Maybe that's why Galen woke up, too. Do you know Galen, Shrail?"

"Not. Is he bads?"

"Yeah, he's bad. He's the reason I'm here. He's some kind of monster."

"Taker?"

Icabus nodded. "I thought Nubis was going to come out of his skin the first time I mentioned his name. I think he hurt somebody close to Nubis."

Shrail shifted nervously and eyed Icabus. "Nubis tells Shrail to keep secrets. Shrail keeps. But Nubis not say this. Nubis stays because Takers kill Kail and Black Scales sads. Others go, but Black Scales stays."

Shrail looked at Icabus with sorrowful eyes. "Kails was Black Scale's friend, but Takers kill Kails, and Black Scales never fly again."

"Was Kail Nubis's dragon?"

Shrail did not answer and looked toward the sea. "Too much talks. Drinks." Shrail handed Icabus his fish basket.

Icabus peered inside and saw a few liters of water at the bottom. A small fish swam inside.

"Water fresh. Fish lives," said Shrail.

"Fish lives," Icabus sighed, taking a gulp. "A little fishy but not bad. What happens if I drink the fish?"

"Then stupids must catch Shrail a new fish."

Icabus took a few more gulps and handed the basket back. Shrail looked inside and fastened the lid in place.

"Hurries," Shrail said, taking flight.

CANA AND VESCUS

Furius used the tip of his sword to raise Celsus's chin. "Where is your sister? Where is Vescus, son of Cilo?"

"I don't know where they are. And if I did, I wouldn't tell you," said Celsus. Sweat beaded on his forehead, and he shivered despite the evening heat.

Furius lowered his sword and looked around. Soldiers scoured the barn and house, overturning furniture and creating havoc as they went. "Any signs of the rest of the family?"

"No, sir," Gurges called from the house.

"Nothing, Master Furius," Seius called from the barn.

"Your family are traitors. Do you know what the punishment for that is?"

"Death?" Celsus coughed and leaned forward.

"Worse. Bring him, Gurges."

Gurges took Celsus by the collar and dragged him away. The boy struggled, and Gurges struck him across the temple with his sword hilt. Celsus fell limp.

"Let's go," said Furius.

Vescus rose up above the gooseberry bushes, and Cana pulled him down. "No, Vescus," she whispered.

"Cana, if I give up, Celsus might be spared."

"No, I need your help. Remember what Urms said: there's someone in the mountain who can help."

"There's no time for that. I have to do this."

"No, you don't," said a voice from behind.

"Atius." Cana started and then wrapped her arms around him.

"What is this business with the ship? Did you burn it?" Atius asked.

"Yes." Vescus nodded. "Galen was making Takers there."

"Did any escape?"

Vescus shook his head.

"That was a dangerous business. You are both lucky to be in one piece." Atius examined them. "Lady Tulia and Lucia will hide you. I will find Corvus and your brothers, Cana.

"No, Vescus and I are going to the mountain. There's someone there who can help us."

"Who told you such a thing?"

Vescus and Cana looked at each other. "We aren't supposed to say, but the source is good," said Vescus.

Atius rubbed the stubble on his chin. "Vescus, you've seen what lives in the forest. It's fast and cunning and will kill you without hesitation. I can't let you two do this."

"You can't stop us," said Cana. "Let us help."

"You're not helping by throwing your lives away. Vescus, I know you have more sense than this."

Vescus eyed Cana. "I think Cana has more sense than both of us. I'm sorry, Atius, but I'm with her."

"Damn kids... At least give me till morning to see if I can draw this creature away from the woods to the Old Kingdom. I believe it might be holding Icabus prisoner somewhere in the forest. I need you both to find him. Can you do that for me?"

Cana smiled broadly at Vescus, who nodded. "We can do that," she said.

ICABUS

The Giants City gave Icabus the creeps. Vines dangled from the forest cliffs, strangling the balconies and carved facades. Lichen clung to every surface, glowing dimly green in the fading evening light.

"Shrail! Look at this."

The bat stopped. "Yes, moon mosses. Do not eat. Taste bads!"

"I wasn't going to eat them." Icabus rubbed the lichen, which increased in fluorescence under his touch. "Wow! Look! My fingers are glowing."

The bat squinted incredulously. "Comes." He led Icabus across an expansive courtyard to a tower facing the sea. "Towers smell like dragons, and Takers afraid."

"You don't mean that vanilla scent, do you? I've smelled it before."

"Shrail does not know vanillas only dragons. Are dragons vanillas?"

"No, dragons are not vanilla. Hey, Shrail, hasn't it been a long time since the dragons left? Why would the towers still smell like them?"

"Mosses take safe smells and make more. If mosses hurt, old ones tell new ones not to make smells."

"Weird." Icabus followed the bat up a spiral stair. Each step was a meter high and likewise deep. As much as he tried, Icabus could not establish any rhythm to his ascent. Shrail didn't seem to mind and crawled up each rise with casual ease.

After what felt like endless climbing, the stair terminated in a domed chamber with a colonnaded wall open to the sea. Icabus wiped the sweat of his brow and scanned the beach. Small flicks of yellow light appeared and disappeared among the sands and the trunks of the trees. "Those aren't more spirits, are they?"

The bat squeaked in what Icabus thought was laughter. "No stupids, fire butts."

"Fire butts? What are they? Some sort of animal?"

"Bugs... with fire in butts."

"I suppose those aren't good for eating either," Icabus joked.

The bat gawked. "Crunchy and delicious. Shrail gets."

Shrail poised himself to take flight, but Icabus held out his hand to him. "No. I think I'll take your word for it. Say, what is that strange blue glow moving in with the tide?"

The bat spat. "Soft heads. Very bads. No faces—only hair that stings and kills."

"It looks like there are hundreds of them."

"Thousands." The hair on the bat's neck rose.

"They are beautiful though, aren't they, like stars in the sea."

Shrail considered this and eyed the heavens warily. "Shrail is scareds."

"What are you afraid of now?"

"Sometimes, star falls."

"Really? Is that even possible?" Icabus gazed at the heavens.

Starlight entered through an oculus in the ceiling onto a blackened fire pit recessed into the floor. A heap of armor, similar to Nubis's, was piled against the back wall. Swords and shields stuck out of the mess like pins in an oversized pincushion.

Icabus plucked a sword from the pile. "This armor belonged to the dragon knights, didn't it?"

The bat quietly surveyed the woods below. "Yes, knights leave. Armor too small."

"Well, that doesn't make any sense." Icabus combed through the pile with the end of his sword. "How fat could a knight get? Shrail?"

The bat was gone.

"Shrail! Where are you?"

Above him, bark and other detritus fell through the oculus. "Ah! Bads!" The bat screeched.

Icabus tightened the grip on his sword. “What’s happening, Shrail?”

“Rhah!” The shadow of the bat appeared and disappeared from the oculus’s opening. From what Icabus could see, Shrail struggled desperately against some unseen menace.

Icabus braced himself and jumped backward as Shrail curled his toes around the edge of the oculus and hurled his mysterious adversary toward the fire pit. “Take that!” Icabus swung his blade overhead in a deadly arc.

Shrail poked his head through the oculus. “What’s you doing?”

Icabus blushed. “Nothing.”

The bat’s head disappeared, and Icabus tried desperately to free his sword before the bat returned; it would not budge. It was stuck in the firewood.

FIREWOOD PRINCESS

Shrail wrapped himself in his wings and nestled by the fire. His eyelids drooped with weariness. "Try agains."

Icabus stood up and pulled on the sword. "Still stuck."

The bat chortled with amusement. "Wood is very deads."

"I thought someone was attacking you."

"Yes, wood monsters."

"Be that way, fur face. At least I'm not afraid of the sky falling on me." Icabus put the sole of his boot on the free end of the burning log and pulled on the sword. "There." He raised it.

"Dragon sword strongs. Metal never hots, always sharps."

Icabus examined the edge of the blade and touched the metal. "You're right. It isn't even warm." He twirled the blade in his hands. "So, how long do you think Nubis will be, Shrail?"

Silence.

"You're not asleep, are you?"

The bat stirred. "Not. Shrail was thinkings. Black Scales says he looks for Taker who kills bats. Takers only found when Takers want to be founds. Hard to tracks."

"So, what are you saying, hours... days?"

The bat shrugged, and Icabus's jaw dropped.

"You can't be serious. Days! What are we supposed to do here while we wait?"

"Practice swords. Shrail can bring fishes and woods in the nights."

"So, you're going to abandon me, too. I'm beginning to feel like a damsel in distress."

"Firewood Princess," Shrail squeaked.

Icabus stared out over the shore where moonlight reflected

upon the white sands. It might have been the most beautiful sight he'd ever seen except for the uncertainty in his heart.

"Shrail... something's coming."

The bat opened his eyes, and Icabus stepped back. The thing was flying unsteadily toward them. Icabus picked up his sword.

"Waits!" cried the bat.

"What is it, Shrail?"

"Bats."

Shrail screeched, and the approaching bat answered in turn. It landed on the edge of the opening feet first, allowing its wings to touch the ground in support. Cuts crisscrossed its face and chest, and Icabus noticed a tear in the membrane of its right wing.

The injured bat squinted disagreeably at Icabus and said something to Shrail that Icabus couldn't understand. Shrail looked to Icabus and shook.

"What is it Shrail?"

"The Taker has Black Scales."

The injured bat hissed at Icabus and took flight over the trees.

"No. Wait!" Icabus shouted. "Where's he going, Shrail?"

"To tell other bats."

Icabus paced. "What are we going to do?"

Shrail whimpered.

"Come on, Shrail, think. We have to do something."

Shrail buried face under his wing. "Stupids needs army not swords."

Icabus placed his hand against one of the columns and scanned the forest. "What are those blue lights in the treetops?"

The bat waddled over and spat. "Vlorkas."

"What are Vlorkas?"

The bat wiggled his nose. "Lizard mens. Lives in treetops. Bats no like."

"Are they trackers, warriors?"

The bat nodded slowly, and Icabus smiled. "I have an idea."

"This is very bads."

CANA AND VESCUS

"Do you think our path will be clear?" Vescus gazed into the forest.

"Yeah, why wouldn't it be?" Cana yawned.

Vescus frowned.

"Are you afraid?"

"Sort of. Aren't you?"

Cana yawned again. "I'm too tired to be scared yet."

Vescus sighed and turned his attention back to the forest. "I can't see five feet ahead."

Cana looked past him. "I can see the trees."

"And not much else."

"Gee, Vescus. You're such a weirdo." She nudged him toward the forest edge. "You went on board that crazy ship, but you won't go in there."

"It's because I went on that crazy ship that I'm afraid to go in there."

Cana stepped past him into the forest. "If we find a dragon, it's mine."

"What if we find a monster?"

"It's yours." She smiled.

"Ha-ha, keep moving." Vescus ushered her forward.

Brambles, boulders, and fallen trees prevented any straight path to the mountain. Cana kept her eyes to the canopy, looking for any break in the foliage to see the mountain.

Vescus tugged on her shirt. "What?" she asked.

"Look," he said, pointing toward her feet.

Not two steps ahead was a chasm. Long, lush branches overhung the reach, hiding it in shadows.

"Yikes. I'm glad you were paying attention. How are we going to cross?"

"How about that?" He pointed to a fallen oak.

"Creepy." Cana rubbed the goosebumps on her forearm.

The oak tree was old and dead. Rain, wind, and the summer heat had stripped away its rippling bark, leaving behind only the smooth, white wood beneath. The few branches it had reached hideously upward and back toward itself like a dead spider's legs.

"I'll go first this time," said Vescus.

Cana didn't object, and Vescus led the way. Claw marks etched the wood, giving their steps traction. Muddy paw prints, the size of Cana's hand, joined some of the fresher markings. The sight of them made Cana's heart race. "Look, Vescus. Don't those look like boot-prints?"

"Could be." He paused. "Do you realize we haven't heard a bird or anything since we came in here?"

Cana's eyes widened. "You'd better not be just trying to scare me, Vescus."

"I wish I were." He leaned close. "I feel like someone is watching us."

"We should go back," Cana whispered.

"Go back where?" came a voice from behind. "Good to see you again, Vescus. You look... intact."

"Pelagus?" Vescus gasped.

"In the flesh, or what's left of it." Pelagus tore a piece of eschar from his muzzle and placed it in his mouth.

"Cana, get behind me," said Vescus.

"Not so fast." Pelagus bounded onto the tree and yanked Cana out of Vescus's grasp.

"Vescus, help me!" The roasted musk scent of Pelagus's body made her want to throw up.

"Let her go!"

"Oh, you want me to let her go?" Pelagus held her over the chasm. "I sort of like her the way she is. Don't you?"

"Vescus!" Cana shut her eyes.

"Stop it, Pelagus! What do you want with us?"

"Us? I want you, Vescus." Pelagus revealed a bottle covered in burned leather. He uncorked it with his teeth and smiled. "The last of Galen's potion, perfected with his blood. Your little fire took my eye. Now I want something from you."

"You can't have Cana."

"I don't want Cana." He held out the potion. "Don't look so conflicted, Vescus. The choice is quite simple: either you drink the potion, or I force her to drink it and push you to your death."

"Why are you doing this?"

"You betrayed me, Vescus. Now you will help fix what you did to me. Galen's powers come from the Golden Land. He thinks someone still protects the gate. I need your help, and you're no use to me in your present form. Drink!"

Vescus looked around for something, anything that could help him. There was nothing.

Pelagus sighed and took Cana by the neck. "Now hold still, darling. It burns a lot going down and does a nasty bit on the head. But take it from me—in a few days, you'll feel great."

"No, Pelagus! Stop! I'll do it! I'll drink the potion."

Cana shook her head. "Vescus, don't—"

"Shut up!" Pelagus barked. "Come closer, Vescus. A little closer. Just a bit more now. Good, come here!"

Pelagus threw Cana behind him and hammered Vescus's left shoulder with his fist. There was a "pop" that brought Vescus to his knees. He cried out feebly and Cana saw agony on his face.

"Oh, don't be such a baby, Vescus." Pelagus choked him. "It's just your clavicle. I'll make sure you're good as new in no time. Now open wide!"

Vescus gasped, and Pelagus pushed the neck of the bottle into his throat. He gagged, but Pelagus held him. A single tear rolled down his cheek and evaporated before it reached his chin.

"Vescus, no!" Cana cried.

"Good. All done, Vescus. I wish I could tell you the worst is over, but it's not."

Cana pointed the Gilian dagger at Pelagus. "Let him go."

"Run Cana. Ah!" Vescus doubled over and held his stomach.

Pelagus turned his yellow eye to her and licked his teeth. "No, Cana. Don't go. Stay for dinner."

She backed away. The blade trembled in her grasp.

"No, Pelagus!" Vescus grimaced. "You touch her, and I'll throw myself over. I swear I'll do it."

Pelagus swung his head around and lowered the pointy ear not melted to his head. He settled onto his haunches and did not take his eye off Cana. "You say that now, Vescus. Let's see what you think about little Cana's flesh when you look like me. Either way, it's a race against time. Tick tock, tick tock, Cana. You best run before it's too late."

Cana shook her head, and Pelagus cackled madly.

"Run!" Vescus screamed. He pulled off his poncho and threw it into the chasm. The clothes beneath were splitting at the seams. Tufts of fine hair grew from his shoulders and extended down his arms and chest where muscles swelled and contracted asynchronously. He howled, and in a single snap, his sternum separated, bringing his ribs forward.

"Don't scream, Vescus. Bones must break to grow. And don't you dare fall into the chasm, or I'll eat your little friend whole."

Cana covered her ears to deafen Vescus's screams and stepped backward toward the forest.

"Tick tock, Cana."

"I'm sorry, Vescus! I'm sorry," she sobbed.

Cana began to run and didn't look back. Twigs and thorns battered her face, but she felt none of it. Nothing in life had prepared her for what she had seen. Had she a thought to think, she might have chosen a different course, but fear and instinct drove her forward, and she ran headlong out from the forest into the apple grove.

A fat crow flew in front of her, and she tripped, falling into the dirt. Several meters away, a soldier entered the grove.

"Did you hear that, Atellus?"

"It was that crow. Come on, Gurges."

Cana watched Gurges's feet. The soldier stood still, and Cana held her breath.

"Gurges!"

"I'm coming." Gurges cursed under his breath.

Cana waited until they were out of sight and pulled herself up. She looked around and headed down the hill toward the lake road. Morning fog covered much of the town, but still, Cana moved with stealth and purpose, careful to avoid open spaces.

The house she sought stood alone like a looming giant in the mist. She had always been afraid of this house for no apparent reason. It was large and old, that was all. Now it just felt like a house.

Cana crossed the street and ran up onto the porch. She stopped and listened. Nothing. Not a stir, not a whisper. She rapped on the door, and the sound seemed to echo everywhere and nowhere.

The door cracked open, and Lucia covered her mouth. "Cana!"

"May I come in?" Cana asked, choking on her emotions. The tears, which before seemed lost, now streaked her face.

"Yes, of course." said Lucia, embracing her.

ICABUS

"I can't believe I thought this might be a good path." Icabus forced his way through the underbrush. "You know, if you would stop eating all the fire bugs, then I might be able to see."

The bat grinned, and the inside of his mouth glowed like a jack-o-lantern.

"You know, Shrail, there isn't a word to describe just how gross that is."

The bat chirped and gestured ahead with the end of his wing. "Vlorka stink like birds. Go that way."

Icabus ducked under a fern frond and skirted the edge of a wide redwood. "So, the Vlorka live in the redwoods?"

"Very old trees have houses. Vlorka lives on tops and insides."

"Do the bats also live in trees?"

"Not! Branches could falls and crush."

"Has that ever happened?"

"Not! Because bats live in caves. Very high, very strongs."

"But if the bats never lived in the trees, how do they know the limbs will fall on them?"

Shrail's eyes widened, and his jaw hung open loosely.

"Hey, don't look at me like I'm crazy. Think about it."

"Everything you says is crazies. Shrail almost dies today, and now Shrail maybe dies again. Only stupids walks into woods at night and looks for Vlorkas."

"Never mind. We can talk about this some other time. And I said I was sorry about—"

"Downs," hissed the bat, grabbing Icabus's shirt with one of his talons.

"What is it? I don't see anything," Icabus whispered.

The bat peered through the ferns and Icabus saw the faint flicker of blue firelight in the distance.

"How do they make the flames glow blue?"

"Dry soft heads," said the bat. "Good for keeping chalklas aways."

"What is that, some kind of animal?"

"Not animals, chalklas are bugs that bites. Remembers, Vlorkas challenge with eyes. Don't looks unless you wants to fight." Shrail filled his lungs with air and pressed his chest against Icabus's.

"What are you doing?" Icabus laughed.

"Vlorkas moves close, always looks down for challenges."

"So, I shouldn't look up? But how will I know the leader if I'm always looking down?"

"Shrail will helps. Leader is very strongs, very means, and lives in biggest tree."

"That makes me feel a whole lot better." Icabus parted the ferns to get a better view.

Under the blue torchlight, the redwoods glowed purple. Spiral staircases climbed the largest trees to the canopies above.

Shrail nestled beside Icabus. "Vlorkas."

Near to the base of the closest stair, a yellow light shone between the roots where a piece of rawhide covered a subterranean dwelling. Voices and shadows stirred within.

"Are they the ones I have to challenge?"

The bat shook his head. "Only Vlorkas losing challenges lives in tree bottoms. Very bads. Monsters walks the woods at nights."

"Like us?" Icabus winked.

"Not." the bat wiggled his nose. "Thizzles and Glitkhas."

The door-flap opened, and Icabus could feel the hair on his forearms rise. "Oh Gods, that's a Vlorka?" Icabus murmured. "I'm going to die."

Standing on his toes, the lizard man was nearly seven feet tall. He sneezed, causing the other Vlorka inside the tree to cackle. With a few growls of rebuke, the lizard man scanned the forest and focused on the bushes where Icabus and Shrail hid. His fleshy nostrils undulated as he investigated the forest breeze, and he approached, spear in hand.

Icabus tensed and reached for his sword, and Shrail silently shook his head. The lizard man stopped at the edge of the undergrowth and lifted the edge of his loincloth, releasing a warm spray over the fern. Most of it slid down the arms of the fronds, but some of it fell on Icabus's neck and tunic. The Vlorka hissed in apparent relief and bounded back into the dwelling.

"Oh my Gods, did that just happen?" Icabus covered his mouth and gagged.

"You luckies. Vlorka is sicks, nose is bads."

Icabus carefully tried to shake the beads of Vlorka pee off him.

"Don't," urged the bat. "Vlorka pee hides smells."

"Shrail, only you would think getting urinated on is a good thing. Believe me, if I don't get some of this off, it will be worse for both of us."

"Comes," said Shrail.

Icabus followed Shrail past the dwelling and up the nearest spiraling stair to a platform overlooking the sea. Cool breezes wandered through the canopy and whispered through hundreds of hidden chimes. The entire city seemed asleep.

"Remembers, if you see Vlorkas, no look in eyes unless you want to fights. Shrail knows leader, so Shrail tells to look. If stupids picks wrong Vlorka, then stupids fights for nothing. Shrail finds leader. You stays in the shadows."

Icabus nodded, and the bat disappeared above him like a wraith. He walked to the edge of the platform and tried to lose himself in the scenery. The cold touch of steel against his neck shattered the spell.

"Nubis?" said an unfamiliar voice.

Icabus pivoted around the point of the spear, all the while looking down. The shiny green scales and sharp toe claws of the Vlorka were all he needed to see. "No. Do you know Nubis?"

"Stop moving! I'll ask the questions. Are you a Taker?"

"Why does everyone keep asking me that? Have you seen

one of those things? They're hideous."

"Answer, or I'll kill you. To trespass here carries the penalty of death."

The point of the Vlorkan spear pressed firmer against Icabus's skin. "Whoa! I'm not a Taker."

"I don't believe you."

"I promise. I'm Nubis's... friend."

Icabus could see the Vlorka's leg muscles relax and feel the spear point pull away from his neck.

"If that is true, who are you and where do you come from?"

"My name is Icabus. I come from Aggersel beyond the gate."

"Then you are a Taker!" She brought the spear back to his neck.

"No, I'm a human, like Nubis and the dragon knights. Soldiers from Authia attacked my village. I escaped and found Nubis guarding the gateway."

"Lies! I don't believe any of it. Nubis would not allow another of your kind to pass the gate, not after..."

"Kail."

"How dare you say his name. What do you know of him?" She pressed the cold point of the spear to his neck, drawing blood.

Icabus gritted his teeth. "Only that Nubis still mourns him."

"Stops!" The bat swooped down from the shadows.

Icabus sighed. He never thought he would be so happy to hear the bat's voice.

"Shrail," said the Vlorka. "What are you doing here?"

"Shrail comes to rescue this stupids who Shrail tells not to moves."

"You know this Taker?"

"Yes, Shrail knows," he answered with disdain.

"Do you both know each other?" Icabus asked.

"Shut up," they both exclaimed.

"Yes, Black Scales likes, but Shrail does not know whys. This one always making troubles for Shrail. Very stupids. Shrail almost dies." Shrail began counting his claws.

Icabus shook his head, and the Vlorka grunted.

"Look at me," said the Vlorka to Icabus.

"I don't want to challenge you."

"Don't be foolish. I'm a female."

"Oh, does that matter?"

Shrail chirped with amusement, and the Vlorka pulled her spear away. "Of course, it matters," she said.

Icabus raised his face and met her diamond-shaped pupils. Against the pattern of her green scales, she wore an assortment of silver jewelry studded with shells, animal teeth, and semi-precious stones. "What is your name?" he asked.

"I am Zrilla."

"Where did you learn my language?"

"Nubis taught me, but that is irrelevant."

"Alright," Icabus shifted anxiously. "How do you know Nubis?"

"Our relationship is personal. Why are you here?"

"I need your people's help to rescue Nubis. The bats say a Taker has captured him."

Zrilla pointed her spear to Shrail. "Is it true?"

"Bats say and Shrail thinks," he whimpered.

"You will have a hard time convincing the king to rescue Nubis. My people fear him almost as much as the Taker."

"Why?" asked Icabus.

"Because he is powerful in their eyes. But you know that Shrail..."

Zrilla focused on Shrail, who began to tremble.

"You aren't here to ask for our help, are you?" She curled back her lips. "You're here to challenge the king?"

"Wait Zrilla, let us explain." Icabus raised his hands.

Zrilla let out a guttural bark, and a cacophony of calls answered in return. Torches lit up the canopy, and a line of colorfully decorated sentries jumped onto the deck. They hissed and bared their pointy teeth as they circled Icabus and Shrail.

Zrilla raised her spear to Icabus's chest. "Now would be a good time to lower your head. Do not speak my name, or I'll run you through."

"But..." Icabus began, but Zrilla was already backing away. "Shrail, who is she?"

The bat shook under his wings. "Zrilla is Azfrell's daughter. Azfrell is king."

"Great. That could have gone better."

Spears poked Icabus's back and chest, and he fought to stay still and not look up.

"Azfrell comes," said the bat. He spoke something in Vlorkish that Icabus could not understand but which led the surrounding Vlorka to hiss and poke him more violently.

"Ouch. What did you say, Shrail?"

"I told the Vlorkas you think theys are very weaks, and that's why you don't looks."

"Why would you say that?"

The bat grumbled but did not respond. Icabus saw a pair of scaly feet enter the circle and approach him. The sickle-shaped toe claws flexed expectantly.

"Now looks," said the bat.

Icabus raised his head and met Azfrell's angry grin. The Vlorkan king towered over him, and Icabus felt his heart sink as Azfrell closed the distance between them and struck his chest against Icabus's, knocking him back.

"Get ups!" shouted the bat.

The circling Vlorka cackled in amusement. Icabus pulled himself to his feet and wiped away the blood from his lip.

"Now do sames to Azfrell," Shrail directed.

Icabus groaned and thrust his body against the Vlorka's. His chest barely reached the top of Azfrell's abdomen, but the lizard king's glare let him know he had made his point.

"I accept your challenge," Shrail translated for Azfrell. "At first light, we fight. First blood to rule, death to rule, whatever comes first."

ATIUS

"The trap is set, Atius," Minius reported. His olive complexion appeared darker in the shadow of the firelight.

Seius brushed his hair away from his eyes. "Aye, it is set, but this fog is a bad omen. I fear the worst."

Atius dropped a fresh bushel of myrrh branches by the gate. "Add these to the torches to mask our scent. Are the timbers soaked and brushed as I instructed?"

"Yes," said Salvius. "We used all the oil we could find. Once the wood burns, the foundations will collapse, and the buildings will trap the monster between the guarding wall and the standing structures."

Minius scratched his head. "Atius, I know you're a carpenter, but I'm not sure the buildings will fall as you expect. It seems to me—"

Atius waved his hand. "I don't have time for this."

"For what?" Atellus approached. Gurges lingered close behind looking bored and annoyed.

Minius regarded Salvius and Seius, who both looked away. "It's nothing, sir."

Atellus placed his arms at his sides and stepped close to Atius. "I've had the villagers bring all the nets from the docks as requested. They're in a pile in front of the gate. Do you need any more supplies?"

Atius shook his head.

"Alright." Atellus studied Minius and waved to Gurges. "Let's go."

The two soldiers entered the shadow of gate and Atius visualized himself stabbing both men in the back.

Atellus tapped his temple with his finger. “Oh, I almost forgot to tell you, Atius.” He paused to face him.” That boy, Celsus, the one who mysteriously vanished, has been captured. Furius wants him to be the bait for this new trap of yours. Just thought you should know.”

“Aye,” said Atius.

Atellus winked and led Gurges out through the gate. Atius scratched his chin and stared at the ground.

“You alright, Atius?” Salvius asked.

“Fine. Bring the nets to the rooftops. I will be along soon.”

A cloaked person passed Atius, and he followed the man into the nearest alley. “What do you plan to do with that sword, Corvus?”

Corvus raised his face just enough to show Atius his bloodshot eyes. “I will run it through Furius and Galen’s hides and then through yours if I live to see the day. You are the worst of traitors, Atius. I curse you.” He spat on Atius’s boot.

Atius glanced behind him. “If you try this madness, all that blade stands for will be lost.”

“If I do nothing, my son will die. I cannot let that happen.”

“Celsus will not die, and I swear to you that, if by morning I am still breathing, then Galen and Furius shall be dead. Do not do this thing. I beg you.”

Corvus’s lip trembled, and he raised the point of his sword to Atius’s gut. “I hold you to this. If my boy dies, you will not live to love yours again.”

Atius nodded slowly. “The Gods be our witness.”

GALEN AND FURIUS

Furius climbed the stairwell and sneezed. "You need a housekeeper, Galen."

"Hello, Furius." Galen stood on the balcony with his hands resting on the railing. Fog and torchlight surrounded him in a blanket of eerie brilliance.

"You've changed again?" Furius noted the sorcerer's clawless hands.

Galen offered him a gentle smile. Beneath his hood, Galen's face appeared human, save for his eyes, which still shone yellow in the torchlight.

"I ate," said the sorcerer, gesturing to the corner of the room where a bloody skull and other human remains lay. "I think I now understand why Arkax eats the young. Their flesh is full of potential."

"So, are you a man...?" Furius carefully considered his words. "Or something else?"

"Are you asking me if I'm a beast, Furius?" He chuckled, exposing his straight, white teeth.

To Furius, it felt like a challenge.

"The truth is ugly, Furius. This city was once the jewel of the Twelve Kingdoms. Now, like me, it is only a shadow of its former self: cursed, broken, and betrayed. Are we any different?"

Furius crossed his arms and frowned. "I am not a beast."

"Of course not," said Galen. "Is the trap ready?"

"Atius says it is." Furius leaned on the railing and watched the men toil in the alleys below. A boy in a red tunic crossed the road; the way he dithered, Furius thought he appeared lost. "Tell me again why we must capture this monster?"

"The villagers say the dragons have left, but I am not convinced. I believe Arkax haunts these shores because the gate is still protected. Once I extricate the information we seek, we can use what's remains of him as bait."

"Enius!" Furius hollered down to the boy. "Come up here."

Enius stared up in surprise. "Yes, Master Furius." Several moments passed and the fair-skinned boy appeared at the top of the stair.

"Make me a fire. Use some of this broken furniture," Furius ordered.

"Yes, sir." Enius went to work, not taking his eyes off Galen or the pile of human remains in the corner of the room.

Furius crushed walnuts in his hand and watched Enius toil. The boy reminded him of his son, Dagan, who died by Marius's hand. Even the good memories of his son could no longer be recalled without sorrow and anger. Only his fantasies of revenge seemed devoid of grief.

"Anything else, Master Furius?" Enius asked.

Furius looked up from the fire and smiled without showing his teeth. "Yes. Galen wants a back rub."

The boy's jaw slackened, and he grew a lighter shade of pale. Furius laughed and tossed Enius a walnut. "I'm joking. Find Atius and bring him here."

"Yes, sir." Enius bowed and disappeared below.

Furius quietly picked through the shells and chewed on the nuts. "My father used to give me walnuts as a boy. Enius lost his father to war, as I did. He is the youngest firstborn son of Authian decent still alive. Loyalty runs in his blood. I would trust him with my life."

"The boy would serve you better if you gave him my potion."

Furius glared at the sorcerer. "You have an odd sense of humor, Galen. Those things you made on that ship were as mindless as they were hideous, like this monster in the woods."

"Arkax is not mindless."

"Then why not reason with the beast? He could be an ally."

"If Arkax knew I was alive, he would flee or try to kill me. He knows I could never forgive him for betraying me."

"You never told me the tale?"

Galen's smile that was not a smile flattened. "There is little to say. After we lost the Golden Land, Arkax abandoned me to save himself. I fled to the Citadel, but I could not escape. The rest in insignificant."

Furius suppressed his laughter. "Is how you ended up at the bottom of that well, Galen?"

"My enemy thought it a fitting grave, but I took more from him—much more." Galen's smile returned; this time, Furius thought it was genuine.

"So, you plan to torture this beast for information and then use him as a lure."

"Yes, but first I need Arkax to make more potion. I grow weak from bleeding myself. Until your men cross the gate, we need a mana source to make more Takers."

"Why would I lead my men into this Golden Land if it will turn them into monsters?"

"The Golden Land only reveals what is already inside a person. Men have become many things or nothing at all. Whatever your men become, they will be far stronger than they are now."

Furius took the last walnut from his pocket and turned it in his hand. "Let's say you get what you want, and we take this Golden Land. What then? How are we going to return to Arx Caeli and kill Marius as you promised?"

"You're short-sighted, Furius. The Golden Land is everything. What man would not pledge his life to the one who controls the gate to immortality? If the path across the lake opens again, this Praetor of men you despise will bow before us like a servant. The Twelve Kingdoms will be ours. You will have everything."

"So, what are we waiting for? This foreplay and idleness are not to my taste. Do we or do we not have the strength to take this gate?"

"Only Arkax and the Gilian queen know for certain."

"Shall we try new ways to motivate her majesty?"

"No. Arwa shares a mind connection with the other Gilian, just as the dragon knights once did with their dragons. If she is harmed, they may act, and your forces as they are now would fall. Arkax is the key."

"Then why are we trusting Atius to deliver? A knife, not claws, cut those ropes. Celsus proves it."

"If Atius tries to trick us, it only supports my choice to make him a Taker."

"I've seen how your potion works. That would only make Atius more dangerous."

"Perhaps. Beast or man, if Atius's son becomes my pupil, Atius will obey me."

"Why the obsession with this boy? You haven't even met him."

"We have met. The same way you and I met, in dreams. That is why I know we must find him at any cost."

"Including my men?" Furius crushed the nut in his hand and clenched his fist, drawing blood.

Galen lowered his head. "You would have all hung before the crowds of Arx Caeli if not for me. Your lives are already mine. Don't forget it."

"I did not free you to be enamored with some boy, son of a traitorous peasant."

Galen waved his hand dismissively. "I don't expect you to understand."

"I think I do. You would rule with this boy. Powerful, is he? Maybe he should be my pupil." Furius threw the bloody walnut shells into the fire and tossed the kernel into his mouth.

"I think you're choking," Galen said.

Furius felt the walnut shift in his throat and enter his windpipe. He spun away, pounding his chest and gasping for breath. He crashed against the ancient dining table, knocking Galen's experiments onto the floor. His head swam, and he fell headlong onto the edge of the triclinium, striking his stomach. With a pop, the nut ejected from his mouth and rolled onto the floor.

Furius jumped up, panting for breath, and reached for his

sword, but before his toes could steady him, Galen threw the triclinium aside and drove him against the hearth. Furius gasped, and Galen lifted him, one-handed, by the neck.

"You freed me from my prison, and for this, I have ignored your arrogance." Galen tightened his grip. "You think you're special, but you're just a beast like the rest of your men. Let me show you."

Galen bit down on his own wrist and offered the oozing wound to Furius. "Open your mouth."

Furius shook his head. "No... I won't become one of those things."

"You may hide behind a handsome face, Furius, but I'm no fool. I see the monster inside you. Don't you feel him? He wants to be free."

"Liar!" Furius seized the dagger from his belt and drove it through Galen's forearm.

The sorcerer barely flinched, but out from his hood, a rudimentary muzzle extended, brimming with teeth. "Stop resisting me, Furius," he sneered, tightening his grip.

Furius's vision began to dim, and he grabbed at Galen's purple robes, feeling the velvet slip through his grasp. He could no longer perceive the sting of Galen's claws, nor the foulness of the monster's breath. Oblivion called to him, and in the yellow reflection of Galen's eyes, he saw the hell awaiting him.

"Let go, Furius!"

"No!" He kicked the sorcerer in the chest, driving him back.

Furius dropped to his knees and nearly fell over. The fate he saw in Galen's eyes was undeniable. He left Authia a martyr, but Galen had used his grief and anger to make him a murderer. In life and in death, he was damned.

"Now you see, don't you Furius," Galen cackled.

"This ends now!" Furius staggered to his feet and unsheathed his sword; it felt clumsy and unbalanced in his weary grasp. Cold sweat and blood stung his eyes, and he rubbed it away with his arm, summoning all his hatred and directing it to the sorcerer.

Galen's palms grew dark and calloused, and he grabbed the

cutting edge of the blade with his hand. "When I finish with you, Furius, you'll be so hideous that not even the Golden Land will be able to mask your disfigurement." He bared his growing canines.

Furius pulled him forward, crushing the monster's toes under his boot. The sorcerer yowled like a wounded animal, and Furius freed his sword and brought it down, severing Galen's hand.

"Ah!" Galen clutched his vacant forearm.

The severed hand grabbed Furius's ankle, and he kicked it into the fire where it contracted violently before succumbing to the flames.

No!" Galen lunged with open jaws.

Furius clobbered him in the nose, and the sorcerer stumbled back. Blood painted Galen's face and chest, and Furius attacked again, driving his blade through Galen's side and bisecting the sorcerer's lungs and heart.

Galen threw up his arms, knocking Furius against the hearth stone. He spun away wildly, twisting, flailing, and reaching hopelessly for the blade bisecting his body. Even as he spun, his flesh continued to morph, changing into what first resembled a Taker and then shifting into something less—a living malignancy given form.

Furius scrambled back as chunks of flesh fell from Galen like a tree losing leaves in the autumn. The globs twitched angrily on the floor and came to rest in bloody, gelatinous heaps.

Galen stopped and focused on Furius with a single, yellow eye.

Furius tried to get up, but the monster pinned him to the floor. Mouthfuls of clotted blood fell onto Furius's puckered lips.

"You can't escape me Furius. We are one."

Furius turned away and gasped for breath. A drop of gore reached his tongue, and he laughed, having gotten everything he ever wanted without ever realizing he wanted it. "This blood!"

ICABUS

Icabus flipped over the feather pillow and beat it with his fist. "Gods, I've barely slept a wink."

"Tries mores," said Shrail, who hung upside down from the rafters.

"What am I doing, Shrail? I've never fought anyone in my entire life, and now I'm about to duel with a king born with claws. Have I lost my mind? What should I do?"

"Not dies," said the bat, without opening his eyes.

"Thanks. That is very helpful. I feel better already."

The bat purred quietly in his wing cocoon. "Good. Shrail likes to helps."

Icabus stared at the ceiling. Everything felt out of his control. It now seemed almost sure that he would never see his family again.

"Icabus."

"Is it time already?" Icabus sat up facing Zrilla's silhouette in the doorway.

"Soon." She paced before him. "My father injured his right foot on a recent hunt. He has tended the injury in secret. It is healing, but it prevents him from pivoting quickly to the right."

"Why are you telling me this?"

"I told my father about Nubis. If you lose the battle, he will not try to rescue him."

"Are you doing this just for Nubis?"

"For Nubis and the Vlorka. The longer we wait to face the Taker, the stronger it will become. My people are afraid. We can't continue to hide in these trees and pretend what we fear does not exist."

"What if I lose?"

"Don't." She stepped aside for the sentries. "These Vlorka will lead you. Come."

Vlorka lined the rope bridges connecting the canopies. Some hooted and bared their teeth at Icabus, while others looked on thoughtfully. A few Vlorkan children sat on their fathers' shoulders. They hid their snouts when Icabus passed.

"Cute huh, Shrail?"

Shrail sucked his lip. "Nots. Vlorkan babies bads."

"How can you say that?"

"Once Shrail leaves fish basket next to seas. Shrail comes back and basket very heavies and making bad sounds. Inside is Vlorkan babies eating Shrail's fishes."

"Ha! I hope you didn't threaten to eat them."

"Not. But Shrail screams, and babies very scared."

"You're terrible."

"Not terribles, hungries."

The sentries stood aside, and Icabus stepped past them into a wide painted circle lined by Vlorka. As he crossed the threshold, the Vlorka began to hoot and rap their spears against the deck.

Across from him, a path opened, and Azfrell stepped into the ring. The Vlorkan king wore a leather battle-skirt and studded arm and ankle bracers. Red, gash-like markings crossed his back, flank-to-flank, and continued down his tail. Icabus had never seen a more fearsome scale pattern.

Azfrell's appearance energized the crowd. He raised his spear, and their calls rose in a dizzying crescendo before collapsing into the steady thump of scaly toes.

Icabus felt a tug on his tunic. "Give Shrail swords. King chooses weapons."

Icabus unclasped his sword belt and gave it to Shrail. Behind Azfrell, Zrilla appeared holding a carved redwood box. She knelt before the king and opened the box. Azfrell pulled out a short scimitar and held it at his side. He bared his perfect set of serrated teeth at Icabus.

"Great. A weapon that favors his reach," Icabus mumbled.

Zrilla knelt before Icabus and opened the box. Under her breath, she muttered, "The weapons are designed for flesh wounds. If you kill my father, I will put a spear in your back." Turning to Shrail, she said, "You too."

The bat squawked, and Icabus lifted a scimitar from the box. Zrilla slapped the lid shut and disappeared behind Azfrell. The crowd grew silent.

Azfrell bent forward and stalked into the ring. His tail twitched as he circled the edge of the arena in sync with the steady rap of the Vlorkas' feet. Icabus mimicked his movements, maintaining the distance between them.

The king hissed something to the crowd, leading them to hoot and shake their spears. Shrail and Zrilla looked on in silence, and Azfrell tossed his scimitar to the ground and raised his clawed hands, drawing a chorus of reptilian applause.

Icabus held the scimitar in front of him, and the Lizard King crouched down and pounced, reaching with claws and open jaws for Icabus's face. Icabus fell against the wall of Vlorka, who pushed him back into the ring. Azfrell's claws cut the air in front of Icabus, and he ducked under the strike, forcing Azfrell to pivot on his injured foot. The Lizard King snarled in pain and took a knee, causing the Vlorka around them to fall silent.

The mood in the arena had shifted, but Azfrell didn't seem to notice. The Lizard King's pain only seemed to intensify his ferocity, and he struck out angrily, driving Icabus back against the crowd and batting the scimitar from Icabus's hand.

Icabus wanted to dive for the blade, but instinct warned him otherwise, and he twisted away, using Azfrell's own momentum to evade the strike and force the king onto his injured foot. Azfrell's claws scored the deck, and he stumbled, drawing hisses and boos of disappointment from the crowd.

Icabus circled the king, keeping his head low and his hands outstretched. Below his scales, Azfrell's leg muscles tensed and twitched. The Lizard King could no longer place his full weight on his right foot and held it slightly off the ground.

Icabus knew this was his chance.

Azfrell lunged again, and Icabus ducked into the attack. Surprise filled the Lizard King's eyes, and Icabus grabbed Azfrell's forearm and crushed the king's injured toe beneath his boot heel. Azfrell collapsed with a gut-wrenching cry, and Icabus picked up his scimitar and put it to the king's neck.

The Lizard King panted between outstretched hands. Icabus looked up at the crowd and saw Zrilla staring back. She shook her head, and Icabus pulled back the blade.

Azfrell reached up and grabbed Icabus's wrist. It happened so fast Icabus didn't even recognize the sky as his feet left the deck and he fell like a flour sack onto his back. Hot breath and a slimy row of serrated teeth hovered above him.

The scimitar was still in Icabus's hand, and he struck out blindly, feeling the Lizard King's claws close upon his neck. The king howled and snapped his jaws shut.

The crown of redwood twigs upon the king's head fractured and fell upon Icabus's chest. Surprise filled Azfrell's eyes, and Icabus pushed him back, causing the king to fall off to the side. The scimitar in Icabus's hand was bloodless, but lying beside it in a puddle of blood was a small vestigial toe, still twitching.

Zrilla rushed to her father's side. Two Vlorka joined her and helped lift the defeated king.

Icabus's back ached from the throw, but he managed to straighten himself and face Azfrell. Shrail crept to Icabus's side to translate.

"The right to rule is yours. May your reign be longer than the length of your claws," said Azfrell. He lifted his head and exposed the white scales of his neck. The assembled Vlorka followed suit.

"What are they doing, Shrail?" asked Icabus.

"This is signs of respects. Neck is soft. Vlorka always guards necks against attacks."

"What happens next?"

"Party, stupids."

CANA

"Gods, where on earth have you been?" Lucia wrapped her arm around Cana and led her into the kitchen.

"Is anyone else up?" Cana inquired, seeing two cups on the table.

Lucia sat Cana down and pulled their chairs close. "No, dear. They're asleep. I just had one of my feelings that someone would be coming and that they'd need tea. Have you seen Icabus?"

"No." Cana shook her head and began to sob.

"There, there, dear." Lucia pattered her hand. "Tell me what happened?"

"You won't believe me. It sounds crazy."

"You forget I live with Atius, dear. Half the things he says are crazy." Lucia smiled.

Cana cupped her teacup in both hands, savoring its warmth. "It started the night after Icabus went missing..."

She told Lucia of how Furius had made the men of Aggersel swear oaths to Furius in exchange for the protection of their land and families. Lucia shed a tear when she heard how Atius was made to whip Corvus and Celsus and place Celsus in the trap.

"Father swore oaths to Furius to protect my brothers and me, but we didn't want him to. I thought Atius had turned against us, but then he freed Vescus and Celsus from the trap and told them to come here. I made Vescus bring Celsus home because of all the soldiers."

"You saw all of this?"

Cana nodded. "And Atius gave Vescus this dagger, which he gave to me." She pulled out the Gilian blade and put it on the table.

Lucia looked at the knife in disbelief. "Where on earth did this come from? It's unlike anything I've ever seen."

"It's Gilian."

"How do you know that?" asked Lucia, touching the coral handle.

Cana explained how she hid Vescus in her barn and how she rescued him after he set fire to the weapons ship.

"Gods, that was you two? Why did Vescus burn the ship?"

"There were monsters inside, like the one in the woods. Vescus and I were running away when I saw a Gilian boy.

"He said his name was Urms and that the dagger's owner had been killed by one of Furius's soldiers during the crossing. He told me I could keep it. Vescus got mad at him for letting Furius's ships cross the forest lake, but Urms said they had no choice because Furius kidnapped their queen. That's why the Gilian haven't helped us. Furius told them if they did anything, he would kill Arwa."

Lucia looked into her teacup like a mystic. "Arwa... Since Furius arrived, I've been having these dreams about this strange woman in my house. She's imprisoned and alone and asking me to help her."

"We need to free her, Lucia."

Lucia took a sip of tea. "That may be difficult."

"Lucia, we have to. She might be able to help Vescus."

"What happened to Vescus?"

Cana tried to speak, but the words would not come. Lucia pushed her chair close and rubbed Cana's back.

"It's alright, dear, what is it?"

"Pelagus... Galen turned him into one of the monsters and he escaped the fire. He found Vescus and me in the woods. He was going to hurt me, but Vescus stopped him. Vescus drank Galen's potion so that Pelagus would let me go."

"Gods, is he...?"

Cana nodded. She wiped the tears from her cheek. "Arwa might be able to help him. I have to try. I have to do something."

Cana made to stand, and Lucia grabbed her forearm. "Cana,

sit down. If you're going to help anybody, you can't go rushing off under the light of day."

Cana looked at the table blankly. "First Icabus and now Vescus. Why is this happening?"

Lucia pulled Cana close. "You don't have to be afraid anymore, dear. You're safe right here."

"Do you think Icabus is alright?"

Lucia thought about the question silently for a moment. "In my heart, yes."

ICABUS

"No, Nubis, stay away! There's something else in that pit!" Icabus lurched forward. Sweat poured from his brow, and he gasped for breath. Above him, Shrail snoozed amid the rafters, tucked tightly in his wings. A shadow rose near the doorway.

"Who's there?"

Zrilla stepped into the firelight. "Did you have a bad dream?"

"Zrilla... Yes. I dreamt Nubis was in a city, but it wasn't like any city I've ever seen. It was covered in yellow smoke. There were skeletons everywhere, and the roads were like rivers of boiling mud. I saw a Taker there and something else like fire." Icabus shook his head in thought. "It's hard to describe."

Zrilla rapped her spear against the floor. She walked behind Icabus and lifted the hides covering the windows. Far in the distance, a plume of smoke rose above the forest canopy.

"What is that?" Icabus asked.

"The ruins of a great city destroyed by the Takers. The Spirits built it. Now it is their tomb."

"Do you think Nubis is there?"

"I've already sent trackers. Nubis's scent is known to my people. Soon we will know."

"We should go there, too. I've wasted too much time here already. Don't you want to find him?"

Zrilla nodded slowly. "We will go, but first you must meet the ones who live in the First Tree. Come."

Zrilla led Icabus down a poorly lit stair to the forest floor. The sweet scent of burning resins surrounded them, and they followed the trails of smoke to an ancient tree at the center of the others. It had no branches, and what remained of its trunk rose into the air like a fairy king's crown. Despite the loss of its main body, the tree showed new signs of life with hundreds of small shoots emerging from its bark.

"The tree is alive?" Icabus touched one of the new shoots.

"Mana returns to the land," said Zrilla.

"And so do our enemies," said an old Vlorkana, supporting herself with a wooden staff. She wore feathers, bones, and semi-precious stone beads, which hung from her neck, waist, and wrists by leather strings. Icabus was surprised she could sneak up on them.

Zrilla bowed and struck Icabus on the back of the calf with her spear. Icabus dipped his head and smiled.

"Giza, shaman, and protector of the Spirits. This is Icabus. He defeated my father in open combat."

"Did he?" Giza grabbed Icabus's left hand and traced the lines on his palm with her index claw.

Icabus giggled with surprise. "Did Nubis teach you to speak my language too?"

"No, I speak many tongues, even the barbaric ones. It is a gift to me from the Spirits." She took Icabus's face in her scaly hand and turned it from side to side. "I hear you took advantage of Azfrell's disability. Strange that an outsider should find our king's injury so easily."

"Icabus is a warrior. His master is Nubis."

"Is he?" Giza sniffed Icabus's ear. "Strange he does not smell like his master."

"I have brought Icabus to the First Tree as is the tradition for our new leaders," said Zrilla.

Giza released Icabus's face and rapped her spear against the ground. "Usually, you come in the light of day and not in the hour before dawn. Did you wish to evade me?"

"No. Of course not." Zrilla exposed her neck. "Icabus had a dream about Nubis. He wishes to meet the Spirits before our trackers return."

Giza flared her nostrils. "Nubis is in the dead city. I have seen it in a vision. You don't need the trackers."

"What else have you seen?" asked Icabus.

"Fire and flesh as one. Would you face this enemy?"

"If that's what it takes to get Nubis back, yes," Icabus said without hesitation.

"Then enter the tree. The Spirits are expecting you." Giza pointed with her spear.

Between the folds of bark, a narrow passage led into the tree. No light entered there, and Icabus could see nothing within but blackness. "Are you coming with me, Zrilla?"

"No, only Giza and the leader of the Vlorka may enter."

"Should I be afraid?" Icabus asked Giza.

"Only if you fear yourself," she replied

Icabus sighed softly and stepped sideways into the narrow passage. The center of the tree was completely hollow and open to the sky. White morning glories covered the floor and the inner wood of the tree. Icabus held his breath as they silently opened their petals for him.

"Hello?"

Silence answered him. He crossed the small meadow and looked at his reflection in a vernal pool. The face he saw appeared sadder than the one he used to know.

"Hello," said a voice.

Icabus turned but saw no one. The wind rustled through the grass and wrapped him in its cool touch. He thought he could hear whispers in the breeze.

"I'm Icabus."

"We know," spoke the wind.

Icabus tensed.

The breeze laughed. "Do not be afraid. Our home is a place of peace and reflection."

"Who are you?"

"Who? What? We just are."

A gentle wind spun around Icabus and tickled the skin beneath his clothes. "You're Air Spirits?"

"Yes," several whispers laughed at once.

"I met a Water Spirit once. It wasn't so nice."

"He was afraid of you," said one Spirit.

"Forgive him," said another.

Icabus watched as the strands of incense smoke pooled before him. Five amorphous apparitions stepped from the haze, and Icabus felt his heart rise in his throat. "Elders?"

The figures looked at each other and nodded with a smile.

"How can this be? I saw... I saw Furius's men murder you."

"We know, Icabus," said Maro. "We are less and more than the men and women you knew."

"Are you ghosts?"

"No," said Ralla.

Icabus fought the urge to step away as Ralla reached for his shoulder. Icabus flinched as her fingertips grazed him. Her skin was warm, and she smelled of lemon oil and crushed flour, just as he remembered her. Ralla hugged Icabus, and he felt weak.

"There, there, Icabus. It's going to be fine."

"I wanted to help you, but I was too afraid."

"There was nothing you could have done," she said.

"I feel so lost. I don't know what to do."

Maro touched Icabus on the shoulder. "When you passed through the tree, we touched your mind. We know of your journey, your struggles."

Icabus released Ralla. "But you are not the Elders. You are... copies."

Silana stepped forward. "Whatever the Elders were to you, we are, but we are also Spirits."

"Do you have the Elder's memories?"

Ralla shook her head. "We are only the reflection of them from your memories."

Icabus looked at his feet, and Vetus cleared his throat. "You blame yourself for our deaths and the fall of Aggersel. This is a terrible burden to carry and one you must let go of if you are to return and defeat Furius and Galen."

Icabus looked up. "How can I do that? There are no dragons left on Apenninus, and I've lost the one person who might have any idea where to look.

"I don't even know why I'm doing this. You saw my memories. Nubis doesn't even want me around."

Ralla rubbed Icabus's back. "He needs you more than you know. You need each other."

"How does Nubis need me?"

Silana took Icabus's hand. "Icabus, we have touched Nubis's mind as we have touched yours. He is noble and courageous, but he has become a reflection of his grief. You can help him, Icabus. In your brief time together, I've seen it working—we all have. Don't give up. We would not send you into danger if we did not believe there was hope."

"What if I'm scared?"

Cilo winked. "Then you have more than rocks in that skull of yours."

Icabus managed a smile. "I'm so sorry, Cilo. I didn't want you to die."

Cilo squeezed Icabus's shoulder. "I know. I forgive you, son. Let this pain go."

Vetus placed his hand on Icabus's other shoulder. "I forgive you."

"I forgive you," said Maro, placing his hand next to Vetus's.

"I forgive you, too," said Silana, squeezing Icabus's hand.

Ralla lifted Icabus's chin. "Are you ready, Icabus?"

"For what?"

"To receive our blessing. The enemy is here, Icabus. The Vlorka need their leader. Kneel."

Icabus knelt, and the Elders gathered around the pool. They placed their hands in the water and together lifted a simple crown of redwood twigs. Maro took the crown in both hands and held it above Icabus's head.

"This crown shall never wither as long as you are fit to lead the Vlorka. Do you vow to rule the Vlorka as you would rule over your own family?"

"I do."

"Then accept this blessing of the Spirits."

Maro lowered the crown onto Icabus's temples. It felt as light as air.

"There is no destiny for you, Icabus, only choices. Choose well. You fight not only for Aggersel but the Golden Land itself. Remember that." Maro took Icabus's hand and lifted him up. "Go now. And do not give in to fear."

VESCUS AND PELAGUS

Constant, endless pain held Vescus like a vice. He cried out a pitiful, reproachful whine that was more animal than human.

Pelagus laughed. "Yes, it's terrible, I know, but it will pass. You'll see."

Formed thoughts were beyond Vescus, but his emotions were clear. Had he the ability, he would have torn Pelagus apart.

"My, my, Vescus, what big feet you have." Pelagus grasped Vescus by a toe claw.

Vescus's jaw twitched. He willed it to tear out Pelagus's neck, but a twitch was all he could muster.

Pelagus tugged on Vescus's toe. "Focus on it, stupid. Try to move it. It will make you feel better."

Vescus focused on the toe. The motion that followed was insignificant, but the relief was a hundred-fold greater.

"Now your finger. Resist me." Pelagus pulled on Vescus's clawed finger.

Vescus did, and a rush of endorphins washed over his body like a warm cloud. The hair that now covered him stood on end.

"I found this trick much later in my transformation than you. I wish someone would have shown me. Now say something, I know you can."

"I... rill... kill... you."

"Ha-ha. Good."

Vescus bared his teeth and made a feeble growl.

"My, my, Vescus, what big teeth you have."

"I... rill to tear y... your f... ace off."

Vescus did not recognize his own voice. His lips were drawn

tight against his gums and retracted only to reveal the jumble of serrated teeth behind them.

A jolt of pain shot from Vescus's snout down to the tips of his toes, making his back arch and his jaws snap shut. The bones in his chest and back were changing again, and the experience was agony.

"Come on now," said Pelagus. "Stop your thinking and keep moving. You're only halfway to perfect."

Vescus focused on his fingers and toes. The muscles there were weak, but millimeter-by-millimeter, his range of motion increased and his strength grew.

"I... ah going... to kill you, l... legus." He struggled with letters, like 'm' and 'p,' that required the use of lips.

"I told my father the same thing, but in the end, I killed him because he was in the way, not because of what he did to me. Once you taste human blood, you'll understand what I mean."

"No!" Vescus cried. Already, he could sense his desires changing. The shift was effortless, and yet the drives of his previous life lingered before him like a hungry specter, no longer alive but unforgotten.

Pelagus rolled his eyes and yawned wide. "When you're done being a such an insufferable wimp, Vescus, I think you'll thank me."

Pelagus sniffed around and grabbed Vescus's traveling sack. He tore open the bag and dumped the contents before his muscular paw-like feet. "Smells like Atius. I hope he packed something edible in here before he sent you to your doom."

Pelagus pulled out a small wrap of dried goat meat and leaned back against a tree. He bit into the jerky and chewed it greedily. "Everything tastes better fresh and bleeding. Trust me."

Strange appetites eclipsed Vescus's attention and filled his mouth with drool. Some of his desires disgusted him, but others he would not deny. "Give..."

Pelagus licked his teeth and threw Vescus a piece. Vescus swallowed it whole. "I want a goat. Now!"

"Well, well. Aren't we feisty? Do we really need to work our way up the food chain? There are so many of Furius's soldiers running about. Why don't we just eat one of them?"

Vescus's stomach growled. "No."

"Your mind says no, but your mouth says, 'Yes, yes, yes.' Are you done moaning and groveling around in the dirt?"

Vescus steadied himself. He tried to stand upright but fell forward again.

Pelagus chuckled. "Easier to walk on all fours now. Come on. We can look for a goat, but if I find a soldier along the way, I'm eating him."

Weakness had replaced the heavy feeling in Vescus's legs. He wobbled forward like a mutant puppy learning to walk, taking in shallow breaths through his nostrils and out his mouth. The rush of sensation almost made him fall over.

"I see you've discovered your new nose. Intriguing, isn't it?"

"Strong." Vescus exhaled.

"Even my senses were overwhelmed entering this forest after being chained up in my own filth. This place is a temple of decay, Vescus. Take it in."

Vescus breathed lightly. Not only had the sensitivity of his olfaction increased but also its range. He could smell the musk of a beetle hiding in the tree leaves above him. He didn't know how he knew it was a beetle—he just did, as if he always had known it, but lacked the nose to remember it. When he focused on the scent, his ears twitched, and he found he could hear the beetle, too. To his satisfaction, he found he could also do this in reverse order.

He turned his senses to Aggersel where the scent of the fires overwhelmed his nose. He exhaled deeply with a puff of steam. "Fire," he spat.

"Yes, foul, isn't it?" Pelagus grunted.

Vescus turned his ears toward the north end of town, where the apple orchards gave way to wheat fields. A particular sound made him extend his neck eagerly.

"What do you hear?"

"Goat... bell." Vescus shook the drool from his mouth. 'B'

was another one of those letters that gave him trouble.

Pelagus turned his head in the direction Vescus's ears were pointing. "Yes. Wait for the wind to blow this way, and we'll be able to smell them, too. Are you ready to hunt?"

Vescus grunted in the affirmative. He wanted to deny Pelagus the pleasure of his carnal excitement, but he suspected that the subtle shift in his own scent already gave away his eagerness.

"Come on." Pelagus picked up his pace.

Vescus ambled forward in a gangly fashion. The weight of his head drew him forward, and he tripped over his forepaws, striking his face. He growled, shaking the dirt from his nose.

"Stop running like you're a hairless, flat-footed weakling. Bound!"

Vescus stopped thinking about moving and let his body do it for him. The shift was almost effortless, and he picked up the pace behind Pelagus.

They came to the edge of the forest and stopped. Wet detritus pushed up between Vescus's toes and cooled his entire body. The torchlight in the distance distorted his night vision and made him squint. Pelagus brushed past him. "Follow me."

Vescus exposed his teeth in momentary disapproval for being touched and took up position behind Pelagus, who danced in and out of the shadows like a wraith, leaving no tracks as he went. Where orchard became wheat, Pelagus slowed and crouched in the grass. Six goats grazed behind a farmhouse at the edge of the field.

One goat had a large bell around its neck that Vescus thought was very annoying. He imagined himself tearing the goat to pieces and eating every bit.

Vescus took the lead and parted the wheat with his snout. The wind was blowing uphill carrying his scent away. Even so, the goats shifted restlessly.

The fear Vescus sensed from them was intoxicating. He could hear the uncertain quickening of their hearts and smell the rush of hormones priming them for flight. Their anticipation mirrored Vescus's own, and he was content to hold them there until fear or lack of fear betrayed one of them to move and become his prey.

"Hey goats, why are you so spooked?"

The voice belonged to a boy, Blandus, son of Laelius. Vescus was so fixated on the goats he had not heard him approach.

Vescus's stomach twisted in a knot. Perched above Blandus was Pelagus. The Taker had climbed one of the old oak trees and now loomed over the boy. Tails of saliva hung from his jaws.

Blandus moved under the branch, and the spit fell onto his forehead. "Yuck. What's that?" He looked up.

"No!" Vescus cried, leaping out of the darkness.

The goats scattered, and Vescus struck Blandus with his forepaws, driving him backward onto his face. "Run, or I'll tear out your throat!"

Blandus stumbled to his feet and began to run. Pelagus pounced from the tree with a blood-curdling howl, but Vescus moved with him and seized him by the ankle, allowing the boy to flee.

"Idiot!" Pelagus cried, reaching back and clawing Vescus in the face.

Vescus released Pelagus's ankle and lunged for the Taker's throat. Pelagus grabbed him by the neck, midair, and drove him against the trunk of the oak tree. Vescus felt a jolt of pain, followed by tingling in all his extremities.

"I should have tied you up and fed you human meat like Galen did to me. One taste and you'll never settle for anything less, you fool."

"No," Vescus snarled.

"We'll see about that," Pelagus growled, releasing him. "Where did those goats go?"

"Here," came a voice from the field. Pelagus and Vescus turned, and two goat carcasses, necks torn out, landed at their feet.

Pelagus bared his teeth at the darkness. "Show yourself!"

Vescus didn't care who was there. He seized a goat and brought his muzzle to its neck. The taste of the blood only intensified his hunger, and he plunged his snout into the goat's belly and feasted on its organs. Nothing had ever tasted so wonderful.

"How is this possible?" said the voice, which had moved. "I did not make you."

Pelagus held up his ear. "We will unmake you if you don't stop moving around."

The voice in the darkness laughed. "You can try, but you will fail. Have some goat. Your friend is enjoying it. How old is he? A day? Less?"

Pelagus regarded Vescus, who appeared completely oblivious to the conversation. The young Taker had moved from eviscerating the goat's belly to fileting its flank.

"You're not much older yourself, are you?" asked the voice, which was closer this time.

Pelagus tensed. "Old enough to rip out your throat."

"Old enough to... no. The way you went after that boy tells me you've tasted one. I should warn you, friend, it's safer to eat the old; the young ones don't always stay dead."

"He's crazy," Pelagus whispered under his breath. He scanned the wheat field and caught a glimpse of yellow eyeshine.

Vescus grabbed Pelagus's goat and began devouring it. Pelagus ignored him and stared ahead.

"Why are you hiding downwind? Are you afraid we will recognize your scent?" Pelagus asked.

"No... I'm deciding."

"What?"

"Whether to kill you," said the voice. "By what path did you enter the Golden Land?"

"I don't know what you're talking about," Pelagus responded.

"Liars! Then how did you come by these forms?"

Pelagus nipped Vescus in the shoulder. "Focus, you fool, or we'll both be dead in a minute."

Vescus lifted his head from the goat carcass. Gore covered his snout, and he licked the bits off. "I'm paying attention. What is it? Dragon?"

"Dragon," scoffed the voice in the shadows. "If I were a dragon, then you'd already be dead."

Vescus sniffed the air and sighed. "We were transformed by Galen's blood. What is it to you?"

The thing in the field fell silent, and Pelagus growled at Vescus.

Vescus picked up the goat carcass again and began cleaning the meat from between the ribs with a row of pointed molars he just discovered in his mouth.

Pelagus sniffed the air. "Is he...?"

"Still here?" Vescus chewed. "Yes."

Several meters into the field, the two yellow eyes appeared again. "Galen is alive?"

"Yes," Pelagus backed away.

"Do you serve him?"

"We serve ourselves. Who are you?"

"I am Arkax, but you may call me Master."

ICABUS

"What happened?" Icabus covered his mouth and coughed. Fire and smoke engulfed the lower tree dwellings of the village, trapping the Vlorka above.

A handful of lizards stood with Zrilla and Shrail, guarding the entrance to the First Tree. They acknowledged Icabus's redwood crown with approving grunts.

"Taker attacks," said Shrail.

"It's worse than that," added Zrilla. "A dozen eggs were taken. One of Giza's apprentices is dead, and another is badly injured. Many others are unaccounted for."

"Is the Taker still here?"

"Not," said Shrail.

"Alright, first things first. Zrilla, tell all the warriors and any lizard on the ground to stop whatever they're doing and focus on putting out these fires. Tell them to focus on the trees whose canopies are isolated.

"Shrail, I need you to fly up there and carry anyone in danger to an adjacent canopy. Can you do that?"

"Shrail cans," said the bat, taking flight.

Zrilla barked a few orders to the surrounding Vlorka, who dispersed. Icabus took up a bucket and joined the line. Many lizards appeared confused or scared, but when they saw Icabus's crown, their fear vanished, and they joined the effort.

Zrilla pulled Icabus aside and knelt over the charred remains of a Vlorkan child. "We should assemble trackers and warriors and go after the Taker now!"

"Yes, it looks like the fires are almost under control."

"First, you need protection." She barked a few calls, and two

Vlorkan warriors stepped forward. Icabus had noticed them close behind him from the moment he exited the First Tree. One bore two orange stripes that ran from head to tail tip, while the other had a series of red, gash-like, markings that bisected his green back at regular intervals. From the shape of their jaws, Icabus though they might be brothers.

"You look familiar to me," said Icabus.

The Vlorka with the red markings exposed his neck. Zrilla translated as he spoke. "I am Sercxal, and this is my younger brother, Hress. Azfrell is our father, and Zrilla our sister."

Icabus cleared his throat. "You don't have a problem serving me?"

Sercxal and Hress looked at each other in surprise. "We serve to protect the king. That is why you chose us, no?"

Zrilla leaned close. "They are the strongest warriors in the village, and as long as they are on your guard, they cannot challenge you. It is a great honor, and since you have no heirs, it places our house in the position to rule again if you die."

"What if I die under their guard?"

"If you die an unnatural death, then the guards are buried alive with you."

"Well, I suppose that's a deterrent. Tell them I am honored to have the strongest Vlorka as my protectors."

Zrilla translated, and her brothers bobbed their heads agreeably. Hress took up position behind Icabus, and Sercxal in front.

"How did one Taker create so much destruction?" Icabus examined the scorched trees.

"I do not know," said Zrilla. "Let us ask Giza. This way."

On the other side of the rookery tree, two Vlorka held down another, while Giza applied a white balm to the lizard's chest and face.

Giza lifted her snout and motioned with her finger to Icabus to come forward. "My apprentice tried to stop the monster and was attacked."

Shrail had told Icabus that a Vlorka's hands and feet

continued to grow through life. Giza's fingers were longer than Icabus's hand.

Icabus stood over the injured Vlorka, who had a burn that cut across the right side of his face, obliterating one eye, and transecting the length of his chest. The wound was deep and, in some places, still smoldering.

"Hold him," Giza said, rinsing her hands in a bowl of milky water. She dipped her claws into a boiling liquid and then began to claw away bits of the apprentice's charred flesh. The apprentice hissed and rose up, but his strength was not enough to fight the other Vlorka holding him. Giza pulled out a still burning ember from his chest and tossed it into the cauldron. To Icabus's surprise, the ember made a popping sound and what Icabus thought was a cry.

"He can't talk if he passes out," Zrilla said.

Giza waved her hand dismissively.

"Giza." Icabus heaved a sigh. "Can you to stop what you're doing and let me ask him a few questions?"

"These wounds still burn, young king. Every moment you waste with your questions, the deeper I must dig into his flesh to rid him of this unnatural flame."

"Respect," hissed Zrilla.

"Respect is earned," countered Giza.

Zrilla growled, and Icabus raised his hands. "Please. I only want to know what happened."

Giza gave Icabus a blank, weathered look. "Then ask your questions and let me return to my work."

Icabus took a knee and leaned close. The stench of burning flesh permeated the air. It made Icabus sick to his stomach. "How did the Taker do this to you?" he asked the apprentice.

"Taker... is... fire," Giza translated.

"How is the Taker fire?"

The apprentice struggled to free his arms, and Icabus motioned to the others to release their grip. Taking Icabus's hand in his own, the injured lizard pulled an ember from his chest, and dropped it on Icabus's palm.

"No," shouted Giza.

Icabus gasped in pain and tried to pull his hand away, but the apprentice held it like a snare. On his palm, Icabus felt a searing pain, unlike any burn he had ever felt before.

"Fire Spirit... is... Taker!" The apprentice spoke in Icabus's tongue.

Icabus pulled away and tried to throw the ember from his hand. It didn't budge and began burying itself deeper into his skin.

"Give me your hand!" shouted Giza.

The old healer grabbed Icabus's forearm and scooped out the ember using her thumb claw. Icabus let out a feeble cry and fell back. Giza dropped the ember into her cauldron and applied some poultice to Icabus's wound, cooling it instantly.

"Do you know enough?" Giza hissed.

Icabus nodded in shock.

"Are you damaged?" asked Zrilla, appearing concerned.

Sercxal and Hress sniffed Icabus's hand.

"Yes, I mean, no, I'm fine. It didn't go very deep. What kind of fire eats flesh?"

"The bad kind." Zrilla flicked her tail.

ATIUS

"I don't like the way your thoughts smell, Atius. Where's my dinner?" Arkax growled from the shadows of the alleyway.

"You'll have plenty to eat once you spring the trap. The buildings will fall away from you and cut Furius's forces in three. They should be easy enough for you to pick off after that."

"Is there anything else you want to tell me?"

"No. What else is there to say?" asked Atius.

"When were you going to tell me that Galen was alive?"

Atius opened his mouth but said nothing.

"You can't play both sides, Atius. Did you think Galen might be able to kill me? Did you believe that we would kill each other, and you would walk over our corpses?"

"I don't know what you're talking about. We have an arrangement."

Arkax lifted his muzzle to the air and emitted a throaty cackle. "Was it part of our agreement to send those children into the woods to look for your son while I was away? I'm surprised, Atius. You would risk their lives for your ends. Maybe I underestimated you. I think we would look very much alike if you entered the Golden Land."

"What have you done with Cana and Vescus?"

"Me? Nothing. The boy is looking a little shaggy. You might find pieces of the girl in his teeth still if you look closely."

"Vescus would never hurt Cana. I don't believe anything you're saying."

"You're out of cards, Atius. Lead Galen and this false king, Furius, here to me. If I suspect you have betrayed me in any way, I will let you watch as I eat your son alive. Understand?"

"...Yes"

"Good. Now get out of here!"

Atius turned a corner and leaned his hands against a stucco wall. He kicked it with such force that the old plaster fell away. "You're a fool, Atius," he whispered, closing his eyes.

"Atius."

Atius spun around. "Enius. Where did you come from?"

Enius stood unmoving. "Master Furius requests your presence."

"Are you alright? You look pale."

"Yes... I'm fine."

Atius followed Enius through the empty streets. The boy stopped at the entrance to Galen's villa and lowered his head. Atius lifted Enius's chin. The boy's eyes were distant and terrified.

"Upstairs," said Enius.

The air in the villa was hot and tasted metallic. Atius picked up an oil lamp and ignited the wick. A bloody slick ran up the stairs. Atius followed the trail to the landing where it spread out in a black pool. Something dripped into the pool from above, and Atius lifted his lamp and extended the wick.

"Gods," he gasped.

Globs of flesh attached to bits of fabric hung from the ceiling and dripped onto the floor below. Bloody streaks crisscrossed the old plaster where someone had painted the walls with blood.

Atius put his hand to his mouth and shuffled back. The marks diverged from a collection of bone and viscera in the corner of the room. In the center of the mess was a human skull with one blue eye gazing back—Galen's eye.

"Gods, did Arkax devour him?"

Atius knelt before the skull and touched the blue eye. He pulled a short dagger from his boot and worked his blade around the socket. An instinct as potent as thirst drove his hand, and he wrapped the eyeball in a piece of Galen's purple robe and forced it into his pocket.

Galen's vacant eye sockets gawked at him silently.

"Atius."

Atius jerked around and lowered his dagger. "Furius?" The man's voice and red cape were unmistakable even in the darkness. "I didn't hear you approach. Are you hurt?"

"No, I'm not injured." Furius moved closer.

Atius looked back at Galen's corpse. "What happened here?"

"An accident."

"How is this... an accident?"

"You're right. There are no accidents. Everything happens for a reason, doesn't it?"

Furius moved into the lamplight, and Atius felt his heart quicken. Furius's face, mouth, and chest were covered in blood. Atius pulled a handcloth from his pocket and offered it to Furius.

"Thank you, Atius." Furius wiped the blood from his mouth and cheeks and handed the cloth back.

"Keep it," Atius insisted.

Furius cleaned his hands, took a deep breath, and dropped the cloth onto the ground. "You know, Atius, I feel much better now that Galen is dead—lighter, really. You can't imagine how much he disappointed me. My men and I sacrificed everything to free him, and for what? I think he would have turned us all into monsters if he had his way. Vile sorcerer." Furius cast an eye on the corpse.

"Did you know that he planned to kill your son, Atius? It's true. I heard it from his very lips. Galen was afraid of him. I can't imagine why. He is just a boy." Furius reached out and squeezed Atius's shoulder. "I promise we will find him."

Atius nodded slowly.

Furius patted him on the cheek. "Good."

There was a shuffling on the stair, and Enius appeared carrying a steaming pail of water and a set of fresh underclothes. He bowed his head slightly at Furius without making eye contact. Atius thought he looked terrified.

"Ah! Enius. Put that down near the hearthstone. Good lad." Furius smiled with an air of madness.

Enius did as instructed and kept his gaze down. "The Taker,

Arkax, has been spotted entering the city," said the boy.

"Thank you, Enius; we don't want to keep him waiting. You know, Atius, I've had a change of heart about this trap of yours. I think we will try to bargain with this creature. He can't be any worse than Galen, can he?" Furius laughed and squeezed Atius's shoulder.

Atius's mouth slackened. "Furius, you can't reason with this monster. It's a beast, a taker of children."

Enius released Furius's cape and began unlacing his armor. "That didn't stop you from bargaining with it," said Furius.

"I don't know what you're talking about."

"Yes, you do. Galen saw you the day the creature crept out of the woods behind your house. He watched you from the upstairs window. Strange that I should know this. Galen never told me."

"Then you must believe me that this thing cannot be trusted. Kill it. The trap will work."

Enius loosened Furius's chest and shoulder plates, which Furius lifted over his head and handed to Atius. He unbuttoned his tunic and threw it to the floor. Enius went to work loosening Furius's bracers.

"'The trap will work.' Yes, Minius has told me how your trap would work. I'm sure you'd like to watch my men crushed under burning rubble. No, I think not.

"Now be of some use and fetch me the rag from that pail. I can't go out in public covered in Galen's blood."

ICABUS

"Yuck. What is that, Shrail? It smells like a big you-know-what."

"Shrail does not know whats is a big-you-knows." The bat sneezed. "Gases."

"Ugh. Gas is right." Icabus pulled his tunic over his mouth and nose.

A yellow haze hung over the valley like a stagnant pond. Those trees that penetrated it were gray and dead.

"Where is it coming from?" Icabus rubbed his eyes.

"The land's belly," answered Zrilla. "Stay to the left. There are cliffs ahead."

"You've explored here?"

"When I was a hatchling, I came here. It was forbidden, but I wanted to see the Spirit City. In my foolishness, I became lost and injured. Nubis found me and returned me to the village."

Icabus kicked a loose stone. "What's your relationship with Nubis? Are you, you know, together?"

Zrilla looked to Shrail, who spoke something in Vlorkish that made her eyes widen.

"No, we never did that. I would visit him at the falls when the duties to my clan allowed it. He taught me about the ways of the dragons. Sometimes, he would speak of the lands beyond the gate. Your Twelve Kingdoms are like the great Vlorkan houses.

"Did he ever talk about the Apennine Kingdom or Galen?"

Zrilla shook her head. "We did not talk about these things. They caused him too much pain.

"You are from this Apennine Kingdom like Nubis?"

"What's left of it. We no longer live there. It's a dead place like the Spirit City.

"I'm glad to hear that Nubis has visitors sometimes. I can't imagine sitting in that valley all alone, waiting for something to come through the gate."

"The Vlorka guard the gate when he is away. You are fortunate he was there when you passed through. We have orders to kill anything that enters the Golden Land."

Icabus stopped in his tracks and pointed to the distance. Protruding from the ground and stretching as far as his eyes could see were hundreds of bones. There were the remains of Giants, Vlorka, Takers, and many other creatures Icabus could not identify.

Zrilla flared her nostrils. "The Rotten Hallows. It's where the final battle took place between the Takers and the dragons. Long ago, a balance existed between the races. But when the Takers came, they corrupted the Fire and Earth Spirits and promised to make them stronger than the other elementals. The war that followed eventually consumed all the races and led to the destruction of the Spirit City."

"How did the Takers promise to increase the Fire and Earth Spirits' strength?"

"To penetrate the source of the mana spring inside the Spirit City and draw directly from it. This land has always been strong with mana, and the Spirit City was once its greatest reservoir." Zrilla gazed into the distance. "Our elders believe it was from these springs that the first groves were born and the cycle of life began. The dead forest before us was the first and oldest. Other mana springs have been found scattered throughout the land. The First Tree is an example."

"And the spring where Shrail saves stupids from the Water Spirits."

Zrilla gasped. "A Water Spirit lives?"

"Yes. It almost drowned me."

"Gods. Giza will be pleased to know a Water Spirit lives. Stop!"

Icabus looked around. "What?"

Zrilla picked up a stone and tossed it into the collection of bones sticking out of the earth. The rock hit the ground and sank.

"Quicksand?"

"Worse. It is a sinking bog. The earth beneath is like fire. Even if you escaped, the injuries would be unspeakable."

"What is that at the center of the moat? It almost looks like a castle."

"Spirit City." Shrail shivered. "Very bads."

"Yes, we must be careful," Zrilla added.

"Looks," said the bat.

Three Vlorka approached at a steady pace through the haze. They slid to a stop and bobbed their heads in greeting. Zrilla translated.

"I am Herh, and this is Freh of House Srehk. This is our sister and tracker, Erilla. We have searched the Hallows and believe the Taker has taken refuge in the ruins of the Spirit City. How should we proceed?"

Icabus walked to the edge of the bog and surveyed the ruins in the distance. There was no bridge over the boiling mud, only the petrified corpses of trees. Given time, Icabus knew the Vlorka could find a path across the reach, but time was against them.

"Shrail, I have an idea, but we are going to need the help of the bats."

FURIUS AND ARKAX

"Furius, you're making a mistake. This creature cannot be trusted," Atius pleaded.

Arkax entered the square and approached them on all fours. Firelight revealed the bulk of his muscular form. He darted his head back and forth, scanning the soldiers. Behind him, two Takers lurked in waiting.

"Hideous," Furius observed.

Drool dangled from Arkax's chin. He licked his lips and sniffed the air. "Yes, I've seen you all—tasty little morsels at the edge of my wood. And now here you are in my kingdom, brandishing swords, the blood of my old enemy on your breath?" He focused on Furius. "Tell me, was Galen still alive when you ate him?"

Furius's men whispered around him. He cleared his throat, bringing them to silence. "Galen suffered well enough if you must know. I am Furius, King of Authia."

Arkax yawned, showing off his many teeth. "Hi, Atius. You've looked better."

Furius glanced at Atius and back to Arkax. "Galen told me you were alone, but I see two others."

"You don't recognize your own trash, red king. Tsk, tsk. I found them wandering the woods, cold and alone. A shame. I almost had to give them blankets because their fur was so short."

"Survivors from the ship?" Furius squinted.

"I must admit, Galen's new potion works well. What did he use as the catalyst? Poison? Physical pain?"

"Both," Furius said, causing his men to shift uncomfortably. "He went too fast with some, and they lost their minds. Do these creatures know their names?"

"The stupid one who looks like he fell into a fire pit calls himself Pelagus. Pelagus calls the other one Vescus. He talks, but I find him a little dull."

"Vescus? The only Vescus I know about is..." Furius turned to Atius, who was staring at the golden eyes in the darkness. Furius laughed. "That little troublemaker got what was coming to him. Was there a young girl with him?"

Arkax regarded Atius with a toothy smile. "Dead. Vescus could not restrain himself. By the time I found them, there was nothing left but hair and bone."

"Monsters!" Atius struggled.

Minius struck Atius in the gut and he doubled over.

Arkax growled. "Your prisoners have rabid tongues, red king. You should cut them out."

"Take Atius and this boy, Celsus, if you wish. I no longer have need for them. All I ask in exchange is safe passage through the gate of the Golden Land."

Arkax approached the fountain where Celsus was bound. The boy moaned but did not look up. Arkax exhaled discontentedly. "This boy is half dead with blood sickness. I have two mouths to feed. They'll need more than a shifty man and a sick little boy to sate their appetites."

Furius crossed his arms. "What arrangement would suit you?"

Firelight shadows danced over Arkax's body like demon apparitions. "You will bring me all the children in the village old enough to hold a sword but too young to use it. Do this, and I will show you the way to the gate."

Furius glanced back to his men, who regarded him with weary reservation. He nodded slowly. "Very well. For this, you will lead us through?"

"For this, I will point the way and not kill you."

"Is there something there to fear... a gatekeeper?"

Arkax growled. "What do I need to fear? If I wanted to, I could paint this city with your corpses."

"Galen spoke of one named Nubis."

"Galen was a fool. Why do you think he ended up where he did? I am the guardian of the gate on this island. Don't forget it."

"And what about on the other side. What will we find there?"

"The Golden Land is filled with disagreeable creatures. Lucky for you, Galen and I killed most of the dangerous ones long ago."

"You can't trust this monster, Furius. It lies," Atius pleaded.

"Yes, unfortunately, Atius is right." Arkax faced him. "I did lie. I told him his son was alive, but I ate him. Did you think anything could escape me, Atius?"

"Liar!" Atius screamed.

"Enough." Gurges struck Atius in the temple with the hilt of his sword.

Atius fell to his hands and knees. He shook his head like a drunk man.

Arkax approached on all fours. The soldiers drew their swords, and Furius raised his hand, halting them. The beast raised his snout to Furius's nose so that they shared the same breath. "You think me foul. You think me inhuman. You think you can avoid this fate—you are rushing to it, red king. Bring me my children, and I will allow the Golden Land to show you what you are."

"We are not alike," Furius spoke impassively.

"Really?" Arkax turned his large head in Atius's direction and grinned. "What did Atius do? Did you find out he was planning to bury you all in fire and rubble? Keep him. I will take the boy."

"No, take me instead." Atius tried to stand and Gurges kicked him in the gut. Atius fell facedown onto the dusty earth.

Arkax ran his claws through Celsus's hair. The boy woke up and shuddered and tried to pull away. "Hush. It's going to be fine," Arkax cooed. He held Celsus by the jaw and rubbed the boy's cheek with the rough pad of his thumb. The boy struggled, but Arkax paid him no mind. The Taker stared into Celsus's eyes and purred. The boy's muscles relaxed, and his lips parted in a smile.

"He hypnotized him," whispered Atellus.

The bite was so quick Celsus barely flinched. He fell limply into Arkax's arms.

Atius began to sob. "Celsus!"

Arkax tore away Celsus's bonds and flung the boy over his shoulder. At the edge of the courtyard, he turned to face Furius. "Bring my children to the forest edge—alive and healthy."

"I will," said Furius.

Arkax raised his ears and snarled.

"What's that sound?" Minius asked.

"The ground is shaking," said Gurges.

"Get down!" Atellus screamed.

Brick and mortar exploded into the square, striking some dead and maiming others where they stood. Arkax retreated as fast as he could.

"No, wait! Lead us out!" Furius cried.

The Taker ignored him and vanished into the shadows. Behind him, one building crumpled and a second fell, blocking the closest alleyway and filling it with burning timber and brick. Another building imploded, spilling its contents into the square and burying the archers stationed on its roof. Screams rose up all around them as the flames and rubble sealed off entire blocks.

"Somebody has sprung Atius's accursed trap! We have to get back to the wall. Now!" shouted Furius.

"No!" cried Minius. "These buildings could fall at any moment. We must go deeper into the city."

Furius clenched his fists. "Lead."

Minius coughed and pointed to the path Arkax had taken a moment before. "This way."

"Go," came a voice from within Furius's head. "If you want to live, let go. I know the way."

"Never!" Furius screamed.

Enius frowned. "Master Furius, are you alright?"

"Yes, move. I will follow. Go!"

One by one, they disappeared into the darkness of the city. Ashes filled the air like hot snow. Furius could hear the voice in his head laughing; it was a voice he knew well—Galen's voice.

ICABUS

"Higher, Shrail!" Icabus tightened his grip on the bat's ankles.

The bat beat his wings and lifted them over the rotten trees. "If stupids keeps squeezing, Shrail will not feel feets and Shrail will drops!"

"Sorry." Icabus relaxed his grip.

"Shrail does not like plans."

"Do you have a better idea?"

"Not, but Shrail still does not likes. Firewood princess will be eatens."

"Let's hope not."

Shrail wiggled his nose. "Or boiled in muds."

"Only if you drop me."

"You are skinnies, like princess. Shrail will not drops."

"You'd think that after me becoming the leader of the Vlorka, you'd call me something different than stupid or firewood princess."

"Lizard brains," the bat chortled, losing altitude.

"Watch out, Shrail!" Icabus lifted his feet. The sharp arm of a dead redwood passed harmlessly beneath.

"Don't makes Shrail laugh. Shrail must use chests for flying not laughing."

"How did you convince the bats to help us? They didn't seem to like the idea of coming here."

"Shrail says stupids has black magics like Spirits and is very bads."

"Seriously?"

"Shrail also says stupids eats bats, and Shrail is very scared."

"You didn't!"

"Shrail does. You are very bads, and Shrail is very scared."

"Great. Thanks for helping me make a good impression. You know, Shrail, you shouldn't lie. It's not good."

"If Shrail is alives after battle, then Shrail not sorrys because Shrail is alives. If Shrail is deads, Shrail does not cares, because Shrail is deads."

"You're hopeless."

"Not."

The bat descended, and Icabus felt a chill pass over him. The city was in a state of slow decay. Rivers of bubbling mud liquefied the organic contents of the buildings. What stone remained was mottled and stained like rotten teeth. Near the center of the city, one of the towers had exploded from within, casting its red and black rubble over several blocks. Icabus looked for any signs of life. Nothing remained there, not even the memory of death.

Icabus focused on the center of the city, where the towers surrounded an amphitheater recessed into the hillside. Within the mist, a single light flickered and vanished.

"Did you see that, Shrail?"

"Whats?"

"I saw a light in that theater."

"This is bads. We should go backs."

"And do what? No, we can't leave now. Put me down somewhere over there, outside the walls."

Icabus savored the last breath of fresh air before they passed into the sulfurous mist. His eyes stung, and his lungs burned, and he wondered how anything could live in the fumes.

"Can I count on your people, Shrail?"

"Bats think plan is dangerous and stupids but will do."

"If your people are careful, they shouldn't be in danger."

"Only you thinks flying into poisonous mists to Taker's house is safes. Bats thinks you crazies, and Shrail thinks so, too."

"Well, at least you're consistent. Honestly, I felt your people were more opposed to working with the Vlorka than flying into danger. Who knows, maybe this will be the start of a new friendship?"

"Not. Bats do for stupids because Black Scales always helps bats. Vlorka only steal fishes and stinks."

"That's funny; the Vlorka said the same thing about the bats. If my mother were here, she would say you both need some quiet time to talk out your differences."

"It will be quiets when Vlorkas stop playing stupid drums in the forest."

Icabus sighed and observed the ground between his feet. Deep fissures surrounded the amphitheater where boiling mud eroded the earth inside the arched entrances.

The bat's toes tightened under Icabus's armpits. "Ground looks bads."

"Hey, how about that archway over there." Icabus gestured with his chin to a shelf of earth extending out from the wall.

Shrail lowered Icabus onto the rock, which immediately crumbled and slid into the moat.

"Bads. Arches too small. Shrail can't fly insides."

"I don't think we have a choice. All the other entrances to this place have been buried or collapsed. Can you toss me inside?"

Shrail hovered in midair and grumbled. "Rights, but if you dies, it's not Shrail's fault."

"If that happens, I don't think I'll have much to say about it."

The bat angled toward the passage. His wings nearly scraped the walls as he lowered Icabus into position. Icabus tried to extend his legs toward the safe earth within, but his toes barely scraped the edge.

Icabus breathed deeply. "Alright. On three. One... two... three!"

With a labored screech, the bat swung his torso and released Icabus over the reach. The stone shelf held Icabus's weight, but its slimy surface assailed him, and he slipped over the edge, grabbing the edge of the stone shelf with his hands."

The bat gasped, and Icabus pulled himself to safety. He turned to Shrail and smiled. "That was close."

The bat frowned and looked down the passage. "Shrail will not knows if something happens if you goes this way. How can Shrail give the signs if Shrail does not knows?"

"Do you still have a dried soft head jellyfish the Vlorka use to tend their torches?"

The bat landed on a broken column and dug in his fish basket. First, he produced a small perch, which he smelled and immediately threw into the moat, followed by a soft head. Tossing the jelly in Icabus's direction, he said, "Not so dry anymores, but smelling nice."

"If you say so," Icabus cringed, placing it in his bag. "I want you to fly up and hide near the top of the theatre. If I find Nubis, I will light the soft head, and you can fly down and get him out of here. If I find the Taker, I'll blow the tracker's horn."

"What happens if Taker gets Icabus and Shrail does not sees or hears?"

"If you don't see or hear from me by nightfall, I don't want anyone coming after me. You and the Vlorka need to protect one another and the gate."

The bat took flight and whimpered. "Find Black Scales and don't dies."

"I'll try." Icabus gave him the best smile he could. He watched Shrail rise into the mist and disappear. The bat was fearful, but he wasn't a coward. Icabus hoped he would see him again.

CORVUS

The Taker killed his son, and Corvus could only watch.

He turned away from the rooftop and bit down on his knuckle until he tasted blood. He wanted to scream, the way he cried the night his wife died of fever. That night, he cursed the Gods. He knew he would pay for his sin someday, but he never imagined it would be with the life of his son.

"Atius, you promised he wouldn't die. Gods are our witness." He staggered down the stair.

Somewhere in the village, his daughter Cana was hiding. It was only a matter of time before Furius found her. Aggersel was small, and to leave the village was too dangerous to consider.

"They all have to die," Corvus whispered, crossing into an alley facing the guarding wall. The torches there were extinguished in anticipation of Atius's trap. Banners rested against the buildings where the men had abandoned their posts to get a glimpse of the Taker. A few voices carried over the wall, where the bonfires burned down to glowing mounds of cinders. Corvus leaned his shoulder against the wall and listened.

"I think Galen is dead. I think Furius killed him," Seius said.

"You have to be careful what you say, Seius. You were once a person of importance in Authia, but now you are just a soldier like us. There are rumors you helped Atius free those brats from the first trap. If you don't mind yourself, you might end up as monster bait."

"Salvius, I saw Atius leave Galen's villa with Furius and Enius. Atius and Enius were as white as bone dust. I went upstairs and..."

"And, what?" Salvius threw up his arms. "You found Galen dead?"

"If you had seen him, Salvius, by the Gods you wouldn't scoff. There was no flesh left on his bones, and the walls... Gods, blood covered everything!"

"It may not have been Galen. The man survived in a well for a century for Gods' sake."

Seius shook his head. "The robes were tattered, but they were Galen's. I'm certain."

Salvius looked down and stroked his beard.

"What are we doing Salvius? Arx Caeli imprisoned us for refusing to participate in human sacrifice. Now we offer up children to monsters. This is madness."

"It's still better than death. I wasn't ready to be hanged, Seius, guilty or not."

"Guilty? If I was once an innocent man, I am no longer. Those Elders were not sorcerers as Galen and Furius claimed. Their blood has stained our hands. Now the blood of children, too. Gods forgive us."

Salvius spit on the fire. "The Gods. You were a priest to the Gods, and how have they rewarded you? Where are your robes, your temples? Furius has done more for us than any God. Perhaps it's a good thing Furius killed Galen. Damn sorcerer."

"And what of this monster Furius treats with, Salvius? Even Galen hated it."

"If it can help us get our revenge against Arx Caeli, I can live with that."

Corvus slid back into the shadows. The city still lay paralyzed in silence, and Corvus skirted the firelight and made his way along the inner guarding wall to where the men had unburied the foundations of the houses surrounding the square. Not a soul was in sight. The darkness seemed to collect everywhere like dirt, and permeating it was the heavy scent of lamp oil.

Corvus knelt beside the foundations and struck his flint. The sparks died in the air almost as quickly as they formed.

"Damn me. Come on!"

He struck the flint again, and a rain of blue sparks ignited the oil.

"Hey, you there, what are you doing?" Salvius shouted, drawing his sword.

"You're too late!" Corvus laughed.

Fire erupted from the pit, driving Salvius backward and setting his beard alight. The fire spread beneath the buildings, igniting the foundation timbers.

Salvius rolled away, extinguishing his beard. "You damn fool. What do you think you're doing?"

"For my son! For Aggersel." Corvus edged back into the shadows.

Already the screams of Furius's men could be heard rising above the fire in a hell's chorus. Two men, an archer and a swordsman, jumped from a nearby roof. Flames covered the archer's back, while the swordsman's hands and face blistered from the heat. Corvus drew his sword and ran toward them.

"Help us," pleaded the archer. He groped Corvus's trousers, and Corvus buried his sword in the archer's neck.

"You, you did this?" the swordsman stammered. He tried to lift himself but fell to the ground with a scream of agony. "Please, my leg is broken, help me. I'll do anything."

"That's the problem," said Corvus, bringing down his sword on the swordsman's shoulder, partially decapitating him—dead.

Along the guarding wall, a villa collapsed, sealing off one avenue and spilling its burning rubble into the alley. Glass panes exploded under the intense heat, sending shards hurtling through the air in every direction.

A cool breeze stung Corvus's cheek, and he ran toward its direction. He stopped, seeing fire ahead and behind him.

"Corvus," came a voice from the darkness.

Corvus started and raised his sword to the voice. It was familiar but altered somehow. "Who goes there?"

Two golden eyes opened in the distance. "Don't be afraid. It's me, Vescus."

ICABUS

Icabus turned around in a circle. "Gods. This is the biggest place I've ever seen."

From the edge of the amphitheater floor, the theater seating fanned out behind him. Parts of the balconies and floor had collapsed into the center of the space, where yellow steam, hot enough to wash skin from bone, billowed from a cavity in the earth.

Icabus slowly traversed the fractured ground to a smoldering fire pit at the edge of the crater. What coals remained still burned defiantly amid a confluence of cracked bones and seared flesh.

To Icabus's surprise, he could see Shrail perched high up on the colonnaded walk above the seating. Icabus waved, and the bat did not move.

"This is bad. This mist must reflect the light from above. You can see out but not in."

Icabus backed away. He took only a few steps when a booming voice rose from the crater.

"Where do you think you're going?"

Icabus drew his sword. "Show yourself!"

Over the lip of the pit, a single yellow eye appeared. "Hello, young one," the Taker wheezed.

Four parallel scars cut across the bridge of the monster's muzzle where only the frayed edges of his lower lip remained. The gums beneath were leathery and receding, exposing the roots of the teeth.

Icabus stepped back. "Where's Nubis?"

"Who?"

Icabus extended his sword. "The dragon knight you captured."

"Dragon knight? Is that what you think he is? I tore off his head and cooked it over the fire."

"I don't believe you." Icabus tried to hide his doubt.

"I don't care what you believe. But now you're here all alone except for your pet bat."

"I'm not alone. Release Nubis, or I'll call my warriors."

The Taker chuckled. "A dragon knight who can't hold a sword. That's something I haven't seen before. The one you came here to find, he could fight. But you... I guess you're his servant. How about you become mine?"

"I would rather die than be your servant."

"That can be arranged. What is your name, boy?"

"...Icabus."

"I was called Prax before your master did this to me."

Icabus took a step back as Prax pulled himself from the pit. Scars and open sores covered the monster's body. Some wounds appeared to give off their own steam, which stunk like seared meat.

"You're skinny," Prax snickered, circling Icabus on all fours and chomping at the air. "Come. I have something to show you."

Icabus hesitantly followed the Taker around the crater. Where the seating came together, a three-tiered stage rose up from the floor. Each level was colonnaded and adorned with pseudo doorways and ornate niches occupied by statues of anthropomorphic creatures. Time and the mist had dissolved their defining features, transforming them into grotesque, deformed things. Amid these nameless figures was Nubis.

The dragon knight's wrists were bound above his head and secured to a hook in the attic of the central niche. His head fell limply between his arms. Claw marks and dried blood covered his chest. A sparkling layer of black scales covered his shoulders and parts of his upper arm.

With an effortless leap, Prax joined Nubis on the second tier. He lifted Nubis's chin with the back of his claw. "Doesn't he look helpless when he sleeps?"

"Get away from him! Nubis, wake up!"

Prax placed a sickle-shaped claw to Nubis's chest and held it there. "Who are you?"

"I told you who I am."

Prax growled and cut into Nubis's chest with his claw. Nubis cried out.

"Stop it!" shouted Icabus.

Prax twisted his claw and pulled it free. He lifted the dragon knight's face in Icabus's direction.

"Icabus, you fool, run. There is a Fir—"

The Taker struck Nubis on the temple, and the dragon knight slackened. "Hush! Don't ruin my surprises."

"Leave him alone!" Icabus gritted his teeth.

Prax placed his claws to Nubis's throat. "I will tear out his neck unless you tell me who you are!"

Icabus edged back and lowered his sword. His whole body trembled. "My village was attacked by soldiers from Authia. They have enslaved my family and killed our Elders."

The Taker chuckled, and Icabus glared back.

"I fled into the forest to save my life and found the gateway to this land. The dragons and the knights are gone. Nubis sent them away. I was trying to convince Nubis to help me when he went off looking for you. The bat flew me here. I am alone."

Prax patted Nubis's cheek and began to laugh. "So, you're all alone after all, Nubis.

"Foolish child, listen now and listen well. Do you think swordplay alone will help you overcome your enemies? How many are there, ten, a hundred? Would you kill them all? I'd like to see that.

"Look at your master. He is a pathetic reflection of all he's lost. He can't even protect himself. Tell me, how will the two of you, a scrawny boy and the rogue shadow of a dead kingdom, overcome such odds?"

Icabus opened his mouth, but Prax growled, silencing him.

"You will fail! Do not deny the fear in your heart. You will fail, your family will die, and everything you know and care for will turn to ash."

"Leave my family out of it!" Icabus snapped.

"Good! Be angry! If you love them, then abandon this charade. This is not a legend, you are not a dragon knight, and your scaly friend here cannot save your village. Everything you hope for is a fantasy. Accept it. You want vengeance. I... am... vengeance!"

Icabus's felt his heart in his throat. "And what would you have me do?"

"Abandon this charade." Prax unhooked Nubis and pushed him off the edge of the stage.

The dragon knight hit the ground hard on his side and rolled to Icabus's feet. Nubis regarded him with recognition and then slipped back into unconsciousness.

"Only I can give you the power to save the ones you love." Prax exposed his twisted, decaying teeth. "Kneel and run that blade through Nubis's heart. Save yourself and become the Taker you were always meant to be."

Icabus looked back in Shrail's direction and lowered his face.

"Choose!"

"You're right, Prax. I only have one choice." Icabus knelt. "I would do anything to save my family. I am a fool to have any even considered otherwise." Icabus raised his eyes. "I kneel before you, Prax because you are my greatest master."

Prax smiled.

"Sometimes our enemies teach us what we must never become." Icabus stood and pointed his sword at the Taker. "I have chosen. I choose Nubis."

ATIUS

Atius rolled over and shielded his face from the heat. He lifted his head, and the world spun around him. He steadied himself, and slowly the scene came into focus.

The entire square was in flames. It was like a scene from a demon's fantasy, and Atius was in the center of it, trapped.

"Atius!"

The voice was familiar, and Atius spied the wolf-like outline of a Taker looming over him. "Arkax, haven't you tortured me enough? Must you murder me before the flames do it for you?"

"I'm not Arkax," said the voice. "We must go. Let me carry you."

Atius did not resist. As he lay cradled against the monster's chest, the hell around him fell away. His consciousness became a series of blurry images shrouded in darkness.

The cold ground brought Atius back to himself. "Where am I?"

The beast's golden eyes focused on him. "Safe, near the water."

Atius shivered and rubbed his shoulders. He looked at the creature, who avoided his gaze. "Your voice... Gods, Vescus, is it you?"

Vescus lowered his head. "Yes."

"And Cana... is she?"

Vescus shook his snout. "Arkax lied to you. Cana is safe."

"Where is she?"

"In Aggersel somewhere. I tracked her scent there."

"Thank the Gods."

Vescus fidgeted uncomfortably. "I need to go."

"No, wait. You haven't told me how this happened to you."

"It was Pelagus. He escaped the ship and trapped Cana and I in the woods. He made me drink one of Galen's potions in exchange for Cana's safety."

"Does it hurt?"

"Not anymore. The hunger is hard to control. That's why I need to leave."

"You will return then?" Atius asked.

"If it's safe." Vescus sniffed the air.

Atius embraced him.

Vescus tensed, then relaxed.

"Thank you, Vescus. Once this is over, I will find a way to restore you."

"What makes you think I want you to?" Vescus pulled away.

"Vescus?" Atius watched him slink off into the shadows. Everything, he felt, was slipping out of his control.

ICABUS

"Fool!" Prax bounded over Icabus's head.

Icabus raised a bone horn to his lips and blew loudly.

"A tracker's horn," Prax growled. "I hope you don't think that makes me believe any of your lies."

"Leave or die. Your choice." Icabus steadied his sword in front of him.

Prax sprang, batting aside Icabus's blade and driving him against the ground. The impact stunned Icabus and sent waves of prickling numbness down his limbs.

"You fool. It would take an army to kill me."

Icabus flinched as Prax held him by the neck and licked the blood dripping from his nose.

"So sweet. This will be a treat. I'm glad you chose to disobey me. I tire of the taste of reptile and bat."

Icabus panted. "You're going to die."

"No. I don't think so. Just so you know, this is going to hurt."

Prax pulled Icabus forward and closed his jaws on his left shoulder. Searing pain stole Icabus's words; each tooth burned into him, and the Taker punished each act of resistance with a deeper, harder bite.

Cold sweat and goosebumps erupted over Icabus's body. Darkness collected in his peripheral vision, and he knew he had to act quickly to survive.

Reaching out blindly, Icabus found the warm leather hilt of his sword and assailed the Taker's head with the pommel. Prax barely flinched and shook his massive head, forcing the blade from Icabus's hand.

Jarred, bleeding, and helpless, Icabus's whole being became

a blur of fading senses; a warm nothingness enveloped him, melting away the harsh contours of the world. He could no longer feel the sting of the Taker's jaws, only the dull scratch of tooth on his bone.

Suddenly, the weight of the Taker left him, and he thought himself dead. Only the return of pain told him otherwise, and he summoned his senses, feeling the world to be too bright and too loud. He blinked, not believing his eyes.

Shrail was attacking the Taker. His shriek shook the mist like a silver trumpet on a cold morning. With his toe claws clasped into the Taker's neck, the bat flapped his wings ferociously, partially lifting the creature from the ground. The Taker growled and flailed but to no avail.

Fighting nausea and dizziness, Icabus regained his sword and forced himself to his feet. Pain was the only thing keeping him conscious. The Taker spun before him like a demon cast suddenly into flames, and Icabus thrust his sword forward. He aimed for the monster's heart, but his reflexes were too slow, and the sword planted itself in Prax's shoulder. The monster wailed and backhanded Icabus, who fell against the dirt, losing his breath but not his sword.

"Nubis, wake up!" Icabus shook him. "We need to leave."

Nubis remained unconscious.

The bat dropped his wing, and Prax seized it, throwing him forward. Shrail fell in a crumpled pile of wings beside Nubis.

Icabus rested a weary hand on the bat's shoulder. "Shrail, are you alright?"

The bat blinked resignedly but did not move. "Sorries. Shrail is not very strong."

"Don't say that. You saved my life, again."

"Yes, Shrail always saves stupid's life."

"I'm sorry for getting you into this."

"Yes, you will be sorry," Prax snarled, shaking the blood from his pelt. "You will be the sorriest fools that ever fell into my grasp. Even the Gods have not invented names for what I will do to you."

Icabus staggered to his feet using his sword as a support. Around him, the ghosts of the amphitheater were silent. The yellow mist swirled through their empty bodies and collected around the living. The Taker tensed and Icabus positioned himself in front of Nubis and Shrail.

The patter of scaly feet broke the silence.

VESCUS

"Stay back, you disgusting monster, or I'll run my blade through your damn hide," Corvus screamed.

Vescus ambled closer. "These buildings are going to fall. Follow me to safety."

"Liar, you would kill me, just as you killed Celsus."

"Arkax killed your son. Nothing could have saved him, anyway. He stunk of blood sickness."

"Bastard! You killed him like an animal! Like an animal!"

The crash of the floors within the buildings surrounding Corvus sent shockwaves through the ground. He fell to his knees.

"You idiot, you're coming with me," Vescus snapped, striking the sword out of Corvus's hand and grabbing him.

Corvus struggled. "Let go of me."

"Shut up." Vescus struck him in the face. He draped Corvus over his shoulder and bounded out of the alley. The buildings behind him bowed then collapsed into several tons of hot rubble.

"Vescus?"

"Yes, Atius, it's me." Vescus dropped Corvus before his clawed feet.

Atius limped forward. "You found Corvus?"

Vescus nodded. "He started the fires. I didn't think he had it in him."

"He's a stubborn old fox."

"The fool tried to fight me as a building was about to collapse on his head."

"Aye, that sounds like him."

Vescus eyed the harbor. "Wake him."

"Should we wait a while?"

"No," said Vescus, raising his pointy ears. "It's not safe to stay here any longer."

Along the waterfront, the floating islands drifted near. Vescus could smell the Gilian approach the shore.

"Corvus! Wake up. It's me, Atius."

Corvus blinked dazedly and opened his eyes wide. He grabbed Atius by the arm. "Atius? You would not imagine what I just saw."

"Who, me?"

Corvus turned his head and gasped. "Gods, Atius, he has us both."

"Saved us is more like it."

"No, Atius! I saw this monster murder my son."

Vescus snorted and looked to the harbor.

"No, it wasn't him. I know this to be true. Vescus is as much a victim as you or I."

"And yet both of you watched my son die."

"Corvus, I'm sorry. I tried..." Atius shook his face.

"Spare me your apologies, Atius." He pushed himself to his feet and faced Vescus. "Where is my daughter? Is she dead?"

"No, she's in the village."

Corvus blocked Vescus's view of the lake. "If she is hurt, I swear by the Gods and my ancestors you will suffer."

Atius touched Corvus's shoulder. "She is probably with my wife. We should go see, aye?"

Corvus held his gaze on Vescus. "You deserve this curse, Vescus, for the harm you have brought to my house. I hope time forgets you and you find yourself eternally alone."

"Thank you," Vescus said. "I'll remember that the next time a burning building is about to collapse on your head. In the meantime, I think we should go."

Corvus stepped aside, and Vescus could see the Gilian among the trees. They were spread evenly in a wide semi-circle with their weapons held at the ready.

"We should keep going toward the lake," offered Atius. "This smoke will suffocate us."

Vescus cleared the smoke from his nostrils. “No. We should go to the wall. The docks are not safe.”

“There’s too much smoke that way.” Corvus coughed.

“Are you sure, Vescus?” Atius rubbed his eyes.

Vescus nodded.

“Come on Corvus. He’s led us this far.”

Corvus cursed under his breath and followed Vescus. The paths between the buildings were lightless, but where the roadways intersected, moonbeams cast eerie shafts of light through the smoke. The guarding wall lay directly ahead.

“And how in the Gods’ names are we going to get over that?” Corvus asked.

Vescus looked up. “I’ll carry you over.”

Corvus stopped. “You most certainly will not.”

“Corvus, don’t be a fool,” Atius spat. “Think of Cana and your sons.”

Corvus looked at the wall, which rose almost four meters. “Don’t pretend you have done me any favors, monster. If time permitted, I would find another way.”

“If time permitted, I would let you,” said Vescus. “Now climb onto my back before I change my mind.” He knelt, and Corvus put his arms around Vescus’s neck.

Vescus stood and knelt again. “You can’t just hang from my neck.” Wrap your legs around my body, so you don’t strangle me.” Corvus did, and Vescus rose on his hind feet. “I will come back for you,” he said to Atius.

ATIUS

Atius watched Vescus scale the wall and disappear. He heard a scream, and a body struck the ground beside him.

"Gods! Corvus?"

The man was not Corvus but one of Furius's guards. In his neck was Corvus's dagger.

Atius knelt down and freed the dagger.

"Are you alright?"

Atius spun around and gasped. "Damn, you startled me, Vescus. Aye, I'm fine. But this one isn't. Not your work, I'm guessing?"

"If it were me, you wouldn't have heard a scream."

"Where's Corvus?"

"At the top of the wall. We must go. This racket will alert others to our presence."

Atius climbed onto Vescus's back. "Is there something out there we need to be worried about, Vescus?"

"No..."

Atius held on tight as Vescus ascended the wall. Near the top of the wall, they passed out of the smoke layer and into the fresh night air. "Well, now that's a sight."

"Yes," said Vescus without much emotion.

A layer of smoke covered the city. It lingered beneath the parapet and balconies, giving the impression of a city floating among the clouds. Beneath the fume, the red glow of the fires throbbed like an ashen heart. The sight was both ethereal and terrifying. The city of the dead was living up to its name.

Vescus climbed over the parapet and crouched, allowing Atius to slide off his back. From where they stood, the wall extended out into the forest lake, separating the marshes of Aggersel from the once-great harbor of the Old Kingdom.

Atius put his hand on Vescus's shoulder and leaned close. "Arkax told me the lake people hunt him. Leave us if you must."

"Thank you for your concern, Atius. I can see why Cana trusts you. I will leave once you are safely over the wall."

Atius patted Vescus on the shoulder. "Alright."

"Can we get on with this?" Corvus growled.

"With pleasure," Vescus said through gritted teeth.

Vescus carried Corvus down the wall and returned. Atius was staring at the forest lake with his jaw slightly hanging down.

"What is it?" asked Vescus.

"We must go, Vescus. The islands just aligned along the banks. Something is coming ashore."

"Your eyes are good," Vescus said, focusing.

"What are they doing?"

"Carrying Furius's dead to the shore to burn. Let's go."

The ground on the other side of the wall was wet and muddy. Between land and water, marsh reeds extended all the way to Aggersel; their tall stalks chattered in the wind like summer-crazed insects.

Vescus sneezed, clearing his moist nose.

"Now what?" said Corvus.

"We go," said Vescus. "These animal paths lead all the way back to the docks. They will hide us from any of Furius's soldiers on the lake road."

Vescus sniffed the air again and looked at Atius. "What's in your pocket?"

Atius removed the cloth holding Galen's eye. Vescus seized it and swallowed the contents.

Atius gasped. "Vescus!"

Corvus frowned. "What was that?"

"Galen's eye." Vescus licked his upper lip. "You were drawn to it, no?"

Atius took the cloth from Vescus and threw it on the ground. "Yes, I couldn't explain it; I just wanted it."

"Galen entered the Golden Land. His body, like the Golden Land itself, holds the potential for transformation. It is a powerful force that draws men to him. It would have harmed you."

"But why eat it?" Atius asked.

"I was transformed by a potion made from Galen's blood. He is already a part of me. The eye might make me stronger."

"Or drive you mad and make you kill us!" said Corvus.

Vescus sighed and sauntered ahead on all fours. "Shall we?"

The path was dark, and soon Atius lost all sense of direction. Ahead of him, Vescus moved as silently as a wraith; his large hind-paws barely left impressions in the soft earth.

In the distance, water lapped against the reedy bank. Atius could see Vescus keep one ear cocked in this direction at all time. When the wind died down, he would stop and listen until the wind returned and the chorus of reeds began a new melody.

"I can see the ships," whispered Atius.

Vescus stopped and sniffed the air.

"Do you sense something?" Atius knelt beside him.

Vescus squinted. "Soldiers with long spears. They don't smell right. Galen must have revived them after death."

"How many are there?" Corvus asked.

"I can't tell," said Vescus. "Their scent is also on land. They went that way." Vescus pointed his snout uphill.

"To guard Arwa, I bet," said Atius.

"Who's Arwa?" asked Corvus.

"The queen of the Gilian," said Vescus. "That's how Furius made the crossing. As long as the Authians hold her prisoner, the Gilian won't attack."

Corvus threw up his hands. "Then we must free her. Let those Gilian frogmen take their vengeance on Furius's rabble."

"At this point, do you trust that the Gilian can separate Furius's men from our own?" Vescus's right ear twitched.

"Vescus is right," said Atius. "We must defeat Furius first and then release the queen. It's the only way to prevent a massacre."

Corvus paced back and forth. "And what if Furius kills us all before then or turns us into monsters like Vescus? What then?"

"It's a risk we have to take," said Atius.

"There is no hope." Corvus put his hands on his hips and shook his head. "We are trapped on this island on all sides."

Vescus licked his nose. "We should go now. Follow me."

They crossed the lake road and made their way along the orchard's edge away from the water. Where the lumpy, tilled earth touched the cold night air, a thin layer of mist rose off the ground to surround their waists like a spectral skirt.

Vescus stopped between two houses and looked back over his shoulder. His eyes glowed a pale gold in the dark. "The Lady Tulia's house is ahead. Go now while it is clear."

Corvus set off between the buildings, and Atius looked at Vescus. "Thank you. Where will you go now?" he asked.

"They will hunt for me if I don't return. I don't want my scent too close to Aggersel."

"I see. Do you want Cana to know I saw you?"

Vescus furrowed his brow and lowered his face. "Tell her I'm alright and it wasn't her fault."

"I will." Atius patted Vescus on the shoulder. He turned to leave, and Vescus grabbed his wrist.

"Atius. Arkax did not kill Icabus."

"What?"

"I found his scent in Arkax's lair and followed it to an abandoned fortress at the edge of Arkax's territory. Arkax did not follow him."

"Gods!" Atius held his hand to his mouth. "Did you find any trace of him?"

Vescus shook his head. "I lost his scent, but there was another scent there I didn't recognize."

"Then he's alive."

"I don't know."

"Vescus, you must take me there, now! What if he's hurt?"

"It's too dangerous, Atius. Arkax will not allow his territory to go unprotected for long. He would find us."

"Then you must find him, Vescus, please. All that I have done has been for him. If he dies while I am idle here, I will never forgive myself."

Vescus looked over his shoulder to the mountain. "I will search for him if you promise to protect Cana. Do not allow her to leave the Lady Tulia's."

"Alright. I promise. How will I find you again?"

"I'll find you." Vescus disappeared into the shadows of the apple trees.

Atius watched him go and then set off between the buildings. He joined Corvus at the edge of the town square.

"What took you so long?" Corvus asked, visibly annoyed. "I was afraid Vescus ate you."

"We should go."

Corvus nodded, and together they skirted the edge of the square. Darkness covered Lady Tulia's house except for faint lamplight flickering between the shutters.

"Someone is awake," Corvus said, pointing at the light.

"Aye," said Atius. He gave the knocker one brief thrust and waited.

The door cracked open, and Lucia's familiar face glimmered in the candlelight. Fright, excitement, and joy crossed her porcelain features in an instant. She blew out the candle and threw open the door, embracing him. "You're safe," she said, kissing him.

"Aye, I'm safe. Is Cana here?"

"Hiding in the pantry."

Corvus bowed slightly and passed by them to the kitchen. Lucia shut the door and fixed the latch.

"Celsus?" Lucia whispered under her breath.

Atius shook his head, and Lucia covered her mouth.

"Father!" Cana stood in the kitchen door.

Corvus knelt on one knee, and Cana ran into his arms. They embraced, and Corvus could not hold back his tears.

ICABUS

"*Kisch*!" Icabus shouted, using the Vlorkan word for attack. Spears erupted from the mist, and the Taker summersaulted sideways. Icabus ducked and covered Nubis as a few spikes whirred past him and splintered against the stage house.

"Don't let the Taker get away!" Zrilla cried.

Sercxal and Hress leaped forward, attacking simultaneously. Prax batted away Sercxal's spear, but Hress's hit its mark and stuck in the monster's shoulder.

Prax yowled and threw the spear aside. Hot blood ran down his chest.

More bats entered the amphitheater carrying in Vlorka with their feet. The joining Vlorka surrounded the monster in a ring of spears.

"I'm glad you brought your spears," spat the Taker. "Now I don't need to find a spit when I roast each of you alive."

Icabus entered the circle and held out his sword. "You're surrounded. Surrender."

"Never!" Prax sprang forward.

"*Kisch*!" Icabus cried.

The Vlorka thrust their spears forward, but Prax was too quick; he struck Icabus in the chest, knocking him onto his back. The Vlorka faltered, and Shrail attacked. The monster backhanded the bat and seized Nubis with one arm, draping the dragon knight over his shoulder like a human shield. "Fools!" he cackled and bounded off into the mist.

"Don't let him get away!" Icabus spit the blood out of his mouth. "He's heading for the pit!"

The Vlorka regrouped, forming a line between Prax and the pit. Blood coursed down the Taker's left leg, where a spear had cut through his thigh. With Nubis pressed against his chest, the monster spun around on three paws, snarling, clawing, and lunging at the growing ranks of hissing Vlorka. At the edge of the fray stood Zrilla, panting.

"You're wounded," she said to Icabus. Her tone was observing more than concerned.

Icabus touched his neck. In the fervency of battle, he'd nearly forgotten his injuries. "Did you wound the Taker's leg?"

"I would have aimed for his heart, but he's using Nubis as a shield."

More armed Vlorka emerged from the mist and surrounded Prax. Above them, the entire retinue of bats responsible for carrying the Vlorka into the Spirit City hovered, screeching. Shrail repeated their call.

"Many bats who lose families find strength," the bat affirmed.

"Release Nubis, and I promise you won't suffer," Icabus said to Prax.

The Taker's fur stood on end, and his chest heaved. He scrutinized the spears, nipping and growling at the points if they moved too close. Bloody punctures dotted his legs and back where lucky Vlorka had pierced the monster's defense.

"Fool. Look at me! My existence is suffering, and it's your master's fault."

"You can't blame Nubis for what you and Galen did here. Hand over Nubis—now!"

"I shall if you grant me a final word."

"You are in no position to bargain."

"Shall you risk his life then? I will twist his neck and dash his body against a spear if it suits me."

Icabus considered this. "Release him and I'll let you speak."

The Taker tossed the dragon knight's body at Icabus's feet. Icabus knelt and put his hand to Nubis's nose. Faint breath touched his fingers.

Icabus stood, and the Vlorka rattled their spears; they

showed off their teeth and hissed expectantly. "*Asach*," he said, using the Vlorkan word for hold.

The Vlorka scratched the earth with their toe claws and focused on Prax. Icabus could see their muscles twitching beneath their scales; they were ready to strike upon Icabus's command.

"Speak," said Icabus.

"You call me Taker, but I am no more a Taker than you are a dragon knight. That part of me died when your wretched master threw me into that pit. What is left is what you see, but what you don't see will be your end."

The Taker backed away toward the pit, and the ground beneath Icabus began to shake. The Vlorka shifted uneasily, and above them, the bats swarmed higher with fearful squawks.

"Bats say something moving in pits!" cried Shrail.

"*Asach*! *Asach*!" Icabus pleaded. The Vlorka held their ground. For the first time since the battle started, they looked afraid.

The bat leaped into the air amid the rumble of earth. Boiling water erupted from the cavity, causing the Vlorka to retreat from their positions. The Taker laughed.

"You see, I wasn't alone in that pit. There was another much older and stronger than I. In our desperation, we joined our dying essences together. Our bond became one of mutual agony. Death forgot us, but so did life. His hot breath sealed my wounds, but they never healed. The stench of my sores attracted to us the lesser forms of life, which I devoured. For centuries, this is how we survived. Only now that mana returns do we have the strength to rise. Your master did this to us, and now we will have our vengeance!"

"*Asach*!" Icabus screamed. Cracks fractured the theater floor, releasing hot steam, which scattered the lines of Vlorka. Above them, the bats retreated higher into the air.

"You must act now," Zrilla shouted.

Pointing to the bats, the Taker cackled. "Look! Your allies flee and with them your only means of escape. No matter... After this feast, I will be strong enough to hunt them down anywhere."

Shrail took flight to join the other bats above the pit. They appeared to argue among themselves. Icabus watched in shock as Shrail led the bats out of the city.

"Where is he going?" cried Zrilla.

"I don't know. Stay together."

Two lines of Vlorka formed their ranks around Icabus. They aimed for Prax's chest, but Icabus focused on the monster's eye.

"*Asach*," Prax growled. The earth stopped shaking, and the Vlorka looked to Icabus expectantly. Prax watched Icabus and winked. "*Kisch*!"

A rush of heat knocked Icabus from his feet as fire, earth, and boiling liquid exploded from the pit. "Get back!" Icabus yelled, not hearing his own words.

Molten rocks rained down, leveling some Vlorka and disarming others. The devastation was surreal, and the world seemed to slow and grow silent amid the ringing in his ears. Uninjured Vlorka rushed passed him away from the pit; some tried to speak to him, while others pulled at his arm to flee, but nothing could summon him to move from what he saw.

Iron boulders supported by tentacles of liquid fire rose from the pit. They crashed upon the earth like great fists, crushing some Vlorka and sweeping others into the boiling cavity. A great molten sphere made up the body of the inferno, which was blue at its core and streaked with yellow and orange flame like a dying sun.

"Fire Spirit!" Zrilla hissed. "Run!" She lifted Nubis, and Icabus placed the dragon knight's arm over his shoulder.

"Zrilla, tell the Vlorka to make for the stage house. There might be an exit there," Icabus ordered.

Zrilla translated Icabus's command, and the Vlorka scurried toward the stage. Around them the mist hovered, blurring their forms. "Where is the Taker?" she asked.

"Right here." Prax drove his hind paws against Zrilla's abdomen, sending her flailing backward. She recovered her footing and lunged at the creature with her claws and teeth. The Taker shielded his face, and Zrilla clawed at Prax's forearm. The monster yowled and backhanded her across the jaw. She fell to her knees, dazed.

"Before the day is over, you'll know what that feels like, little Vlorkana. But for now, I'll take my prize." Prax seized Nubis by the arm and pulled him away from Icabus. "Thank you."

The Taker made for the pit, and the Fire Spirit's iron hands crashed down, blocking Icabus's path. "No! I won't let you have him!"

"Icabus." Zrilla pulled him back. "Come! You are no use to him dead."

Icabus glared after Prax and grudgingly allowed Zrilla to lead him up onto the stage, where the other Vlorka were funneling into a passage. Behind them, the Fire Spirit grated its iron hands against the ground as it drew itself toward them.

"We're too late. Retreat!" Zrilla cried.

The Vlorka scattered, and the Fire Spirit struck the stage house with its iron fists, burying those Vlorka still in the passage and sealing it.

The Vlorka regrouped around Icabus. Waves of heat emanated from the Spirit's body, devouring the mist and revealing the full carnage left upon the amphitheater floor.

From atop one of the Fire Spirit's iron fists, Prax surveyed the destruction with the twisted reverie of an untamed demon. Unconscious, before his hairy feet, Nubis lay.

Icabus grabbed Zrilla's arm. "Zrilla, tell the Vlorka that the Spirit and the Taker are one. If Prax dies, so does the Spirit!"

Zrilla pointed to Prax and translated Icabus's words. The Vlorka shifted nervously and focused on the Taker.

"*Kisch*!" shouted Icabus.

Spears split the air, and Icabus fought back the urge to blink. He held his breath as the volley converged on the creature's chest. Fear, disgust, and a host of other venomous emotions crossed the Taker's already twisted face.

Prax raised his arms, and the Fire Spirit mimicked the movement and brought its burning arm up to shield Prax. Spears ignited like twigs in a hot kiln, destroying some instantly and dashing others to the ground in a burning heap of ash.

Prax cackled. "You should have killed me when you had the chance. Now, I'm invincible. You think you know suffering—you know nothing. After I squish these pathetic reptiles, I'm going to make your wounds feel like scratches." Prax raised his snout to the heavens. "What's that sound?"

VESCUS

Outside, in the cold, Vescus listened to the reunions occurring inside Lady Tulia's house. The warmth of a hearth, the satisfaction of companionship: these were the things he had taken for granted before his old life ended. He hoped becoming a monster would help him forget his loss, but, on the contrary, it magnified his pain.

Instead of no longer having a father, he no longer had a community. All those who might love him were now afraid of him. Even Atius and Cana would never accept him as they once had. How could they? He didn't even trust himself anymore.

Everything in Aggersel was now a reminder of what he would never have again. Even if Furius was defeated and Aggersel freed, there would be no celebration for Vescus, son of Cilo. His reward would be one of ageless hunger and ruminations of what was or what could have been.

Tears rolled off the edge of Vescus's muzzle onto his lips. Their salt reminded him of blood, and already his mind was turning to his next kill. His flesh hurt for it like a thirsty man following the mirage of water in a desert. He wanted to fight the craving, but he feared what might happen if he did. As long as he ate, he could control his thoughts; however, the longer he waited, the more insatiable his desires became.

The scent of swine and smoke reached Vescus's nostrils, and he followed it away from the house to a smoldering fire pit on the edge of the town square. A half pig, burnt to a crisp on one side, and raw on the other from lack of turning, roasted on a spit.

Vescus pulled the flesh off the skewer and held the uncooked side with his teeth. The taste of the fat against his tongue dissolved the tension in his muscles, and he trotted on all fours between the buildings until the darkness of the apple grove surrounded him and he was high above Aggersel with a view of the town below.

He ate voraciously, barely perceiving the view. To his left, a steady stream of torches now returned to Aggersel from the Old Kingdom. Those who didn't die by fire or smoke would live to fight another day, and Vescus would be ready for them.

With one bite, Vescus swallowed a chunk of pig flank. He burped and licked the fat from his claws. Something marine crossed his nose from up the hill.

"Arwa?" Vescus spied Atius's house in the distance.

The house itself was lightless. Four of Furius's guards stood at the corners. Metal masks covered their faces, hiding their real features. They stood silently, their shoulders and heads slumped forward as if they were scarecrows. To Vescus's nose, they smelled dead, but he knew better.

Vescus took a twig in his hand and cracked it in two. The soldier closest to him turned in his direction and remained fixated on his position.

After a few seconds, the guard dropped his chin, and Vescus doubled back, moving along the edge of orchard and into the forest. The glen behind the house was empty and bathed in starlight. Dew covered the grass and fogged the kitchen windows. Vescus focused on the kitchen door, which was ajar and creaked on its hinges; not trying to hide himself, he stepped into the clearing.

A shriek, like a demon siren, stunned Vescus's hearing. Two metal-masked soldiers burst from the kitchen door, and two others converged with them from the sides of the house, swords and spears at the ready. Vescus smiled and bounded back into the woods.

He leaped nimbly between tree and boulder, looking briefly over his shoulder to size up his pursuers. The soldiers did not have Vescus's animal litheness, but what they lacked in form they made up with speed, making Vescus continually increase his own pace to maintain the distance between them.

A flash of steel sparkled in the filtered starlight, and Vescus ducked as a blade swished past his head. The two guards from the front of the house had ambushed him. Vescus struck the attacking soldier in the chest, driving him into the other soldier behind him. He sprang away just as the remaining guards converged on his position.

The soldiers shrieked, and Vescus changed direction and bounded deeper into the woods. He hoped to drive them away from their prize for a closer look, but he was the only thing driven away. Their ambush had been sloppy but Taker-like in its implementation. Had he been anything less, he would have been dead. He would not underestimate these "dead" things again.

Vescus could see a break in the trees, and he increased his speed. Using his paw-like hands and feet to propel him, he jumped across the chasm and landed with one cheeky hind paw dangling over the reach. He turned and waited.

One soldier cleared the trees and dove toward Vescus. His arms and legs flailed wildly, and he dropped his sword midair to reach the ledge. He struck the side of the chasm wall with a thud, hanging over the ledge with only his fingers to hold him. The other guards stopped on the opposing cliff and shrieked.

Vescus pulled his ears back and growled, "Well, that's a long jump. I'm surprised you made it this far."

The dangling soldier grunted and flailed his legs wildly, trying to get traction against the smooth granite. His fingers slipped, and Vescus grabbed his arm.

"Not so fast."

The soldier's flesh squished through his fingers like boiled meat. Vescus was disgusted. "Do you speak?" Vescus asked.

The creature looked down into the darkness then up at Vescus. With his free hand, he lifted the mask.

The guard's jawbone was rotted away, leaving a mass of droopy flesh that opened up to his throat. What remained of his nose was gangrenous and plastered to the left of his cheek, where it rested on a bed of confluent pustules. Only his eyes remained, and Vescus recognized them well: yellow, like Taker's eyes.

"Those who did this to you will die," Vescus said, releasing his grip.

The creature fell but did not shriek. Vescus heard a thud, then nothing.

"Anyone else?" he regarded the guards on the other side of the chasm. The soldiers stared at Vescus defiantly, and then one by one, they disappeared back into the darkness of the forest.

Vescus rested on his haunches and wiped his hand on a pile of damp leaves. This was why the Gilian were clearing the Old Kingdom of bodies. In living subjects, Galen's potion turned men into Takers, but giving it to the dead created something less, neither monster nor man, neither alive nor dead, an endnote in creation, spoiled and incomplete.

A forest rat scuttled over Vescus's toes, and he grabbed it by the neck. The rat squealed, and Vescus looked into its eyes, mesmerizing it. He cracked its neck between his fingers and dug his claws beneath its fur, tearing skin from muscle. The flesh was warm and steamed in the cold night. Vescus ate as two dark figures approached him.

"Where have you been?" asked Pelagus, sniffing Vescus's hand.

"Right here, waiting for you," he said, twisting off the rat's head and tossing it aside. "We got separated."

"How is that possible? You were right behind me," Pelagus snapped.

Vescus bit off the rat's forefeet and spat them at Pelagus. He swallowed the rest of the rat whole. "Does it matter?"

"No. It doesn't," answered Arkax. He loomed over Vescus like a great shadow. "We heard shrieks."

"Some of Galen's experiments. One thought it could follow me." Vescus gestured with his snout toward the chasm.

Arkax looked over the edge then across the reach. He sniffed the air. "You ran from them?"

"I was outnumbered."

"Weakling." Pelagus lifted his nose.

Arkax leaned closer until Vescus could not escape his rank breath. "And why did they follow you?"

"I got too close, that's all."

"They guard the sea witch. Are you sure you weren't getting too close to her?"

Vescus shrugged dismissively, avoiding Arkax's eyes. "What would I do with her, eat her?"

Pelagus peeked over the lip of the chasm. "We should destroy all these rotting freaks."

"They are a small threat." Arkax moved off. "The rot will eventually reach their brains, and not even Furius will be able to control them then."

"I'm hungry." Pelagus shifted with an expression of discomfort.

"Yes, me too." Arkax wetted his nose with his tongue. "Let's see what prize Furius brought us for leading him out of the Apennine Kingdom. Come."

Arkax bounded over the chasm, and Pelagus shook the dew from his fur. "I hate jumping. You go first."

Vescus did, and Pelagus got a bounding start before clearing the reach. His hind paw slipped off the edge, and he scurried ahead.

Arkax chuckled and ambled into the forest on all fours.

Vescus slowed. "Arkax. The wind is carrying our scent down the ridge. If we pass this close to Atius's house, the dead soldiers may detect us."

"It doesn't matter. We're expected," Arkax said without looking back.

"Move," growled Pelagus, shoving Vescus from behind.

Vescus snapped at the air in front of Pelagus's face. "Don't tell me what to do."

Pelagus crossed in front of Vescus and farted in his direction.

"Sorry. I couldn't help it. It must have been something I ate."

Vescus snarled and sniffed the ground to clear his senses. The scent of the forest was clarifying and overwhelming.

First, there was the forest floor. Vescus could distinguish at least four seasons of rotting detritus, but everything beyond that seemed to blend together. Then there were the scents of the small animals of the forest, each with its characteristic markings and territories, which Vescus found endlessly amusing, both in the painstaking effort they put into creating them and at the complete disregard humans had for them. The scent of the lake was also on the air—a fishy, pleasant scent that made Vescus's stomach growl. And then there was Aggersel itself. He had never considered humans to be unclean, but now that he was a Taker, he found humans to have the most obtrusive scent of all. Despite their predilection for bathing, a human's scent was detectable for kilometers. Not to mention that they clustered together. The overall effect was nauseating in its intensity. Vescus was not surprised most wild things avoided people.

Arkax and Pelagus paused at the tree line. Their forms appeared as shadows in the darkness.

Vescus held his ears back. The shouts of Furius's soldiers echoed up and down the ridge. Even the way they swung their torches was loud. Just the annoyance of it made Vescus want to bite them.

"Hoy! Stop here," Atellus called out, pulling on the yokes of the bull-driven wagon.

Behind him, two lines of soldiers with long spears flanked the cart. Furius's retinue trailed behind. To Vescus, it seemed like an excessive show of force, but then again, Corvus had nearly just burned them all to a crisp.

Arkax motioned silently with his snout, and Vescus approached on all fours. A long, metal cage lay flat on the wagon's bed. It reminded Vescus of something he had seen on the weapons ship. Vescus could hear someone sobbing from within.

"These soldiers are uneasy. I can smell their fear. Something is wrong. We should go," Vescus whispered.

"Don't be foolish," Arkax spoke dismissively.

"Let us hunt; it is safer."

Arkax shook his shaggy head. "I want my meal, and I want you to fetch it. Go." Arkax nipped at Vescus's leg.

Vescus evaded the bite and slowly entered the torchlight. The soldiers' eyes widened, and he could see the whites around their irises. They shifted uneasily, and Vescus scrutinized each one in succession. Their fingers were white from their grip on their spears.

The bull pulled against its reins, and Atellus got down from the driver's box and patted the beast on the neck, quieting it. He looked from Furius to the soldiers to Vescus.

"He's yours, take him," Furius said to Vescus.

Gurges came around from the rear of the wagon and undid a series of latches on the cage. He swung it open like a trap door and backed away.

Vescus stopped.

"What are you waiting for?" Gurges asked. "Take him."

The soldiers around the wagon edged back. Vescus could hear their hearts beating against their chest walls. He did not move. "No, tall man. Bring them to me."

Gurges looked from Atellus to Furius. Furius cleared his throat. "You have no reason to act so suspiciously among friends. Your master and I have an arrangement."

Vescus looked to the forest where Arkax's yellow eyes glowed. The beast nodded.

Vescus growled and tiptoed forward, not taking his eyes and ears from Furius's forces. He rose up on the tips of his toes and looked into the cage. "Enius?"

Enius threw a handful of powder at Vescus's face. Vescus choked and scrambled away, sneezing. He reached the forest edge and fell face down in the leaves.

"Keep his head up, or he'll suffocate," ordered Furius. "The powder only paralyzes his muscles. He can still hear, see, and feel everything—can't you, Vescus?"

Vescus tried to growl, and Furius laughed. He held Vescus's snout and peeled back his eyelids. "You are weak, Vescus, but from your blood, we will create a few loyal servants. That was the arrangement I made with your master, Arkax."

ICABUS

"The bats have returned." Zrilla pointed her spear heavenward.

The Fire Spirit waved its iron fists as the swarm of bats emptied their fish baskets onto its fiery core. The water evaporated in billowing bursts and condensed, forming puddles that slid over the dry earth like mercury. Icabus stepped back in amazement.

The Taker cackled. "Do they think some buckets of water would put out this fire? These bats are so stupid I'm doing them a favor by eating them."

Shrail swooped down to join Icabus, while the remainder of the bats settled on the colonnaded rim of the amphitheater. They looked to the horizon intently.

"You didn't." Icabus eyed Shrail with surprise.

"Shrail almost dies twice, but Shrail does. Looks!"

At the far end of the amphitheater where Icabus had entered came a great tumult. Torrents of waters erupted from the doors and drains, swirling together in a living wave.

"Who dares steal my body and carries it to this cursed place? I will drown you!"

The Fire Spirit uncoiled its fiery tendrils from the stones. Drawing itself to its core, it resembled an expressionless giant covered in flame. Patches of its body were charred over with wheals of ash.

The puddles of water joined the wave, which formed the pseudo body of a giant man. As it spoke, the sound came not from its mouth but from a ripple that passed over its entire body. "Fire! You are alive."

"I survive," hissed the Fire Spirit, speaking from its fiery core. “It is good the Water Spirits still endure.”

“Endure? After Earth and Fire destroyed themselves, the mana springs dried up like leaves on a cut tree. Only now that mana returns have I gained the strength to collect my essence into forms. How did you survive?”

“I survive by Prax’s mouth; as he devours life, I live and grow stronger.”

“You have joined yourself to the same monster who deceived you. It is his kind who are responsible for all this destruction.”

“The past is inconsequential. Once this beast has devoured these lesser beings, I will have the strength again to draw mana on my own.”

The Water Spirit split into two serpents and encircled the Fire Spirit in a ring of water. “Have you learned nothing? We were once the protectors of this land.”

“If you will not help us, then stay out of our way, brother. I do not wish to harm you.”

“It’s too late for that. I’m sorry.”

The ring of water constricted around the Fire Spirit’s body. The Fire Spirit shrieked, sending forth fiery tendrils into the crowd. The Taker flailed backward with a roar and dropped Nubis onto the ground. Steam billowed into the air as fire and water destroyed one another.

Icabus and Zrilla knelt beside Nubis. The dragon knight looked around, confused.

“Icabus... is that you? I must be dead,” he mumbled.

“Not quite yet.” Icabus smiled. “Zrilla, take Nubis and lead the Vlorka to the other side of the theater. Shrail, have the bats fly them to safety.”

“What are you going to do?” Zrilla asked.

“Yes, Shrail does not likes.”

Icabus tightened the grip on his sword. “I’m going to end this.”

Zrilla barked a few orders at the Vlorka. Those without spears followed her, but a handful of Vlorka did not move.

“These lizards will not abandon you,” said Zrilla.

Icabus recognized Herh, Freh, and Erilla of House Srehk. Accompanying them were Zrilla's brothers, Hress and Sercxal.

"Alright." He nodded to the assembled Vlorka. "Let's go!"

The Vlorkas' footfalls were inaudible over the shriek of the Spirits, and they followed Icabus into the mist surrounding the pit. Erilla touched Icabus's shoulder and pointed toward the edge of the hole, where Prax crouched amid the rubble.

Gashes crisscrossed Prax's body where the Water Spirit had injured the Fire Spirit. Icabus rested his sword on the monster's shoulder so that its tip touched Prax's jugular vein. The other Vlorka moved in, surrounding the beast.

"You will become just like me, boy." Prax spat up a mouthful of blood.

"I used to fear that but not anymore. I am a man, and that's what I choose to be."

A rash of boils broke out over the Taker's body and spilled their contents on the dusty floor. "No! What's happening?"

A deafening blast shook the amphitheater. Bits of fiery essence rained down, and the flesh covering Prax's muzzle and shoulder tore away. Prax howled and lunged for Icabus's throat. It happened so fast, Icabus didn't feel his sword pierce the monster's chest. Even with his sword buried up to the hilt and Vlorkan spears piercing the monster's sides, the Taker's jaws snapped shut just centimeters from Icabus's face.

The Taker gasped as if trying to escape an imaginary lake. Icabus watched with pity as the creature took its final breaths; to suffer was horrible, even for a monster.

Erilla helped Icabus up, and he pulled his sword from Prax's heart. The mists parted as the ash of the Fire Spirit's remains settled onto the floor. Icabus steadied himself and lopped off the beast's head.

Cheers erupted from the far end of the theater where the bats and Vlorka celebrated. Standing with them, supported by Zrilla and Shrail, was Nubis. The dragon knight looked at Icabus thoughtfully, with what Icabus thought was an air of surprise.

Icabus waved and immediately felt silly.

Nubis smiled awkwardly and looked past Icabus to where the remains of the Fire Spirit smoldered.

Icabus sheathed his sword and walked over to the rubble. There was no trace of the Fire Spirit's essence. At the center of the devastation was a small puddle.

Icabus knelt over the water. The liquid shifted but did not rise.

"Little Taker. Have you come to end me?"

"No," Icabus shook his head. "I want to help if I can."

"Essence for essence. That is the only way to kill a Spirit. I could not stop the devastation that took this city, but the same evil will not return."

"Can mana restore you?"

"Mana returns to the land, but no spring is strong enough yet to restore me. I suffered so long to hold the memories of my line, and now they will fade with me."

"There must be something I can do."

"I wish there was. There is much water in you. Don't lose it."

Icabus looked to Prax's remains and back to the puddle. "If Prax could join with the Fire Spirit, could you do the same with me? Like you said, I'm mostly water. I will protect your memories until you are stronger."

"I will not become an abomination." The liquid rippled.

"I don't want to be one either, but what choice do you have? If these memories are worth more to you than your life, then join with me. We owe you our lives."

Icabus extended his hand to the Water Spirit. The water recoiled, and Icabus relaxed. He began to pull away, and a translucent hand rose up from the liquid. Icabus hesitated and took it with his own.

The touch was cold, but Icabus did not pull away. He could feel the Water Spirit's essence enter through his hand and into his arm. He began to receive impressions and feelings that were not his own.

Much of what he felt and saw he could not interpret; the Water Spirit's senses and consciousness were so different from his own. It frightened him.

"We can't do this," said the Spirit's voice in Icabus's mind.

A sense of relief passed over Icabus as he felt the Spirit retreating from his body. He didn't want to join with this being.

As their connection faded, Icabus felt the Spirit's fear. The Spirit was going to his death, and Icabus could sense it.

Icabus's relief broke. "Wait," he said to the Spirit in his mind. Ignoring the strange thoughts and sensations he could not understand, Icabus let down his mental guards.

"What are you doing?" asked the Spirit.

"I want you to know me for who I am. I give you permission."

"You would open up your mind to me? I could wipe it away and take your water for my own."

Icabus could feel his fear projected outward into the Spirit's conscious. "Yes, I'm willing to risk that for this to work."

Icabus could feel the Spirit hesitate and then slowly return its essence to his body. The feeling was intimate and terrifying, but Icabus held his mind open and did not retreat.

"Don't be afraid, Icabus. I will not harm you. See me. We are now brothers."

Icabus saw the Spirit, and the Spirit saw him, and they were reflections of each other one and the same.

LUCIA

"You're awake." Lucia stepped into the kitchen.

"Aye." Atius faced her. "Furius's men are gathering. We should probably wake the others."

"They're getting dressed." She kissed his forehead. "Do you want to talk about what happened?"

Atius rested in her image. "No, not now, maybe never."

She rubbed his shoulder and embraced him. "Is what Cana said about Vescus true?"

"Aye. It's true. Vescus saved Corvus and me from the fire. We were dead men, and he came back for us."

"How could you send them into the woods, Atius? They are children."

"How could you send Icabus?"

Lucia pulled back. "Shame on you. I had no choice. You know that."

Atius lowered his face. "I'm sorry. I know. I thought the monster in the woods had Icabus, but that might have been a lie all along."

"What are you saying?"

"Vescus told me he followed Icabus's trail to a fortress in the mountains. He said Arkax wouldn't enter the ruins."

Lucia covered her mouth. "The gate?"

"It's just a legend."

Corvus and Cana appeared in the doorway; in their shadow stood the Lady Tulia. Tulia was already fully dressed and wearing a light powdering of clay dust.

"There are men going door to door," said Tulia. "You all need to hide."

A loud rap came at the door, followed by Atellus's voice. "Open this door now, or we'll kick it in."

"Hold your chaps," hollered Tulia. "I'm coming." She pointed to the kitchen table, which Corvus and Atius moved. "Now, the mat," she said.

Lucia and Cana slid the mat aside, revealing a large trap door. Tulia crossed her arms. "Can't say I've been down there since I was a child. Try not to sneeze."

Atius pulled open the door, revealing a dark stairwell. He grabbed Lucia by the back of the neck and kissed her cheek. "Will you be alright?"

She nodded, and he slowly descended into the darkness. Corvus followed with Cana in hand.

"No, the girl has to stay," said Lady Tulia. "We can't move the table back otherwise."

Corvus squeezed Cana's fingers and kissed her on the head. "Be careful," he said.

Corvus disappeared into the darkness. Lucia and Cana lowered the door and placed the mat back into position. The table was heavy, almost too heavy for the three women to move, but slowly they edged it into place. Cana and Lucia sat down, and Lucia placed Amara on her lap.

"Coming, coming," called Lady Tulia. "Men are so impatient."

She unlatched the door and opened it.

Atellus was leaning forward with his head down and one hand resting on the doorframe. "What took you so long?"

"Young man, do you think this powder attaches itself to my face naturally? Trust me; you'd be in for quite a shock if I answered the door without it."

"I see." Atellus looked past her. "I have been sent by our master, Furius, to search houses for traitors and deserters. Is there anyone in this house that fits that description?"

Lady Tulia shook her head. "No, unless you consider us ladies a threat."

"Then you shouldn't mind if we take a quick peek, will you?"

"Not at all. Come in."

Lady Tulia opened the door, and Atellus stood in the entryway. He instructed one soldier to search upstairs and another the ground floor. He turned to Lady Tulia and smiled. “Now where is Atius’s wife? We are old friends, she and I.”

“Here,” said Lucia. She held Amara in her arms. “What do you want?”

“Your daughter may not wish to hear what I have to say.”

“Come, come, Amara,” Lady Tulia said, holding out her hand. Let us try to get the fire going.

Lucia waited till they were in the den and cleared her throat. “I know what it is you’re going to say. My husband came to me in a dream to say goodbye. His spirit is no longer with us.”

“Aye. The fire claimed many. I am happy to see your grief has not consumed you.”

Lucia lowered her head, and Atellus closed the distance between them. He took one of Lucia’s hands in his own and kissed her fingertips. “I know I have been a source of grief for you. I would have you know Atius and I became friends near the end. He was a good man.”

“And you would give me no time to grieve him.” Lucia pulled away.

“There is no time to give, Lady Lucia. Galen is also dead, and Furius is giving out prizes to those loyal to him. You are a beautiful woman.”

“And a prize for you?”

“I hope it will not come to that. If Furius gives you to another, there is nothing I can do. Before all of this, I was a married man. I know that in time we could be happy together and I a good father to that child.”

One of the soldiers descended the stair and shook his head. The other soldier appeared behind Lucia and said, “No males, Master Atellus, just this young girl.”

“Let go.” Cana jerked her arm away.

Atellus shook his head and gestured to the two soldiers. “Go on to the next house; I will meet you there.”

The soldiers left, and Atellus laughed. “Well, well. I’m not sure what Furius would do if he found out you were still alive, little Cana. We thought Vescus ate you. I suppose there is still time for that, given that he is now Furius's prisoner."

"You're a liar. Vescus is too strong for you to capture."

"That's what I thought, too, but Galen's numbing powder did quite a number on him. He must not have made a good monster if all the other monsters were willing to sell him out."

Cana balled her fists, and her face grew pink with anger. Atellus watched with amusement.

"Atellus." Lucia stepped in front of Cana and placed her hand on his chest. "This girl is an innocent. She is no harm to anyone. Please."

"Lady Lucia, if this girl is an innocent, then I'm a saint. But let her be my gift to you. Consider all I've said. You have less time than you think."

Atellus kissed her on the cheek and backed away. Lucia watched him through the window until he was out of view.

"He's gross." Cana wrinkled her nose.

"Come on, dear," said Lucia.

Together they dragged the table back and swung open the trap door. Corvus came up the stairs and wrapped his arms around Cana.

"No, you're all dusty," she giggled, trying to wriggle away. Corvus kissed her on the forehead and released her.

"Lucia, hand me a lamp," Atius said from below.

"What do you see?" she asked.

"I'm not sure."

"Did he turn his ankle?" asked Lady Tulia.

"No, I don't think so. What's down in the tunnel?"

"I don't know. My father forbade me from ever going down there, and until this moment, I quite forgot it even existed."

"Ooo, scary cave," said Amara. "Are there spiders inside?"

Lucia handed Atius the lamp and lifted Amara. "Only if they can eat dust."

"Corvus, Lucia, come down here and see this," said Atius.

"Stay here with Lady Tulia, Amara," said Lucia, placing her

on the ground.

"I'm going, too," said Cana.

"Come on then," said Corvus.

They descended the stair and entered a room that looked like the upturned belly of a ship.

"It's like being inside a ribcage," Cana remarked.

Atius sneezed. "Lucia, do you remember what our grandparents used to say—that our ancestors made their first homes from their ships?"

"Yes." She coughed. "Gods, Atius. What is that?"

"That's what I want to find out." Atius winked, handing her the lamp.

Against the far wall was a large mound covered with heavy woven fabric. Atius, Cana, and Corvus began removing the cloth, which fragmented in their hands. They stopped, and Cana smiled at Lucia.

"What is it?" Lucia asked.

"Weapons," said Cana.

ICABUS

"Firewood Princess lives."

"Stop it, Shrail. I'm tired." Morning sunshine passed through the oculus and rested on Icabus's forehead. He lifted himself upright, sending shockwaves of pain radiating out from his left shoulder. "Ouch!"

"Be careful," came a familiar voice.

Icabus rubbed his eyes. "You're alright?"

Nubis smiled. "Yes, I'm fine."

The dragon knight admired the view of the sea. He appeared completely healed. "I'm impressed, Icabus. I've been trying to get the bats and Vlorka to work together for decades."

"Stinky lizards," Shrail spat.

Icabus laughed, and he immediately regretted it. "Ow, stop. Please don't make me laugh, it hurts."

"You are very bads. That's what you gets." The bat waddled around the fire, doing his best impression of a human gait.

Nubis shook his head. "You have visitors."

Icabus looked over to the stairwell where a dozen Vlorka crowded in the entrance of the dragon keep. Icabus waved, and they beat their spears and erupted in a joyous chorus of hisses and reptilian chatter. A few eyed Nubis cautiously from across the room. Icabus could sense they feared but also respected the dragon knight.

"The Vlorka put up quite a protest when I had the bats bring you here to the Giants City instead of the village." Nubis appeared amused. "For some reason, they think you're their leader. An injured king is not permitted to lead the clans. You must choose a successor."

"Is this a temporary replacement?"

"No. The custom of succession began at a time when injuries often resulted in death. Don't take it personally."

"I'll try not to. Do you want to lead the Vlorka?"

"No." Nubis crossed his arms. "Even so, I do not believe they would approve. You must pick from among the major houses. I should warn you. This choice is not an empty gesture. It is the equivalent of marriage into the family."

"What? Does that mean that I could be called upon to fight again?"

Nubis nodded.

"Well, I suppose it won't be so bad as long as I'm not forced to marry a Vlorka."

Nubis blinked thoughtfully.

"Wait. That can't happen, right?"

"I don't think the females would find you tall enough."

Shrail chirped something in Vlorkish, and the Vlorka entered the keep. Fourteen males, each representing the various houses, lined up before Icabus. They stood high on their toes and exposed their necks. Kneeling beside them were Vlorkan females, who were less adorned.

Icabus turned to Shrail. "Where is Azfrell? Is he not yet recovered?"

"Balance is bads," said the bat, acknowledging Azfrell's son, Sercxal. Kneeling beside Sercxal was his sister, Zrilla.

"So how does this work?" Icabus asked Nubis.

"You call forward a Vlorka and give them your crown."

"That's it?"

"That's it," said Nubis.

"I can choose anyone."

"Anyone."

Icabus let his eyes wander over the Vlorka. "Are only males permitted to lead?"

Nubis relaxed his arms. "There was a time before the fall of the Spirit City when Vlorkana led the clans."

Icabus motioned to Shrail, who helped him to his feet. "Then

I have made my choice. Zrilla, please accept this crown. May your rule be long and prosperous."

Zrilla raised her eyes, and Shrail translated. Disquiet fell over the group, and Zrilla spoke a few words to the other Vlorkana, who slowly rose to their clawed toes. As Zrilla stood, Sercxal and the other males knelt.

Zrilla touched her brother's shoulder and tiptoed forward. She glanced to Nubis, who raised the corner of his mouth, and knelt before Icabus. Fear and anticipation blazed in her diamond eyes, and she lowered her face.

"With your help, Zrilla, the Taker is dead. You saved my life, Nubis's life, and many others. My family and my village still have hope because of you. I will be honored to call you my queen."

Icabus placed the crown on Zrilla's head and sat back down. She revealed an even line of white serrated teeth and exposed her neck to Icabus.

"Thank you," she said. "Storytellers will speak of our victory and the brother I gained from a king's lost toe."

Icabus smiled, exposing the tips of his not so sharp teeth. Zrilla barked a few orders to the assembled Vlorka, who bounded down the stair, leaving Icabus, Shrail, Nubis, and her alone. She approached Nubis and touched the black scales on his neck.

Covering her hand with his own, Nubis leaned forward and spoke into her ear. Icabus could not hear their secret exchange, but they both smiled as Zrilla turned away. She shook her spear in Icabus's direction before hopping down the stair.

"What was that about?" Icabus asked Shrail.

The bat cringed slightly. "Scales, yucks."

"Nubis, is Zrilla your girlfriend?"

"Just conferring my blessing. It may keep you from having to fight any more Vlorka for a while."

"Give me a break. I saw sparks."

"We will not discuss this any further." Nubis crossed his arms.

"Tell me then, why do the Vlorka act so weird around you? We are not that much different."

"Different smells," injected the bat.

"Aye. It is clear to them we are not related." Nubis turned back to the sea.

"Maybe so, but it's almost like they're interacting with a deity or something."

Nubis faced him and laughed. "I'm no deity. I've been around a long time, Icabus. Anyone who doesn't die in this land is considered special. May I ask you something?"

"Sure."

"Why did you come for me? You could have returned to Aggersel."

"I thought about it, but I decided you're the only one who can help me save my village."

Nubis studied him. "And if I agree to train you and help you find the dragons, you will follow my instructions?"

"Of course."

"Then you must trust me when I say your primary concern should be the trials ahead. You have already proven to be brave beyond your years. There is a fine line between bravery and recklessness. If you follow my instruction, I promise there will be no veil between us when your training is complete."

"Even about Kail?"

The dragon knight regarded him with a sad expression. He looked away toward the beach. "Yes. Before we leave, I will tell you about Kail."

Icabus could feel the dragon knight's pain as it were his own. "I'm sorry. Shrail told me how much he meant to you. If you never wish to speak of him, I'm alright with that."

"You remind me of him," Nubis spoke softly. "He was spirited, courageous, and at times foolhardy. His presence brought me comfort and made me complete. Every day that has passed without him I have despaired. I never thought I would find these qualities in another. That is, before today, Icabus." Nubis offered him a gentle smile.

The warmth of Nubis's words made Icabus feel special. Something about the dragon knight had changed, and it changed him, too. "I don't want to disappoint you."

"I trust you won't. Does your wound hurt?"

Icabus rotated his shoulder slightly in the sling. "Only when I make sudden movements. It itches like terrible, though."

"Goods," said the bat, who was now wrapped in his wings and dozing by the fire.

"That means it is healing," said Nubis. "We recover quickly in this land. The process will occur faster now that mana returns. It should only be a matter of days before you can wield a sword again. For now, rest. There's been enough talk for one day."

LUCIA

They sat around the table in silence, waiting. Lucia took a sip of her tea and shifted in her seat. A piercing cry like death or birth echoed from outside. Cana squeezed her father's arm reflexively.

"That's the fourth one," said Corvus. He turned to Cana and brushed away the loose strands of hair from her face. "Are you certain that's was it is?"

Cana nodded. "Yes, that's the same cry Vescus made when he changed."

"Could it be him again?" asked Atius. "Or perhaps Pelagus?"

Cana thought about it and shook her head. "These cries sound different."

"Yes, I agree with Cana," said Lucia.

Corvus frowned. "That last scream almost sounded like Furius's squire, Enius."

"That might be so," said Atius. "The poor boy trusted Furius like a father."

Corvus tapped the edge of his teacup. "Aggersel is no longer safe. The women and younger children must leave."

"And where should they go?" Atius grumbled. "There is no safe path, no refuge anywhere on Apenninus for them."

Corvus smiled slyly. "There is, Atius. Only you have forgotten it exists. I still remember how scared you were when we found it; you threatened to turn us in if we got any closer, remember?"

Atius's eyes brightened. "The old watchtower? Gods, how could I have forgotten? The walls around it were massive, at least a meter thick or more."

"Where?" asked Lucia.

“In the northern fields, half buried in the forest, or so it was when I was young,” Atius answered.

Lady Tulia cleared her throat. “The old hunters used to camp there.”

“Old hunters and adventurous boys,” added Atius, with a half-hearted smirk.

Corvus wrapped his knuckles on the table. “It is half a day’s travel on foot. The old may not make it.”

“Don’t be foolish, gentlemen.” Lady Tulia furrowed her already creased brow. “There is not an elder in this town who would not trade their lives for the future of their kin, even myself. If you plan to go, know that it is with our blessings.”

Lucia shook her head. “Atius, we aren’t warriors. Even if everything goes right, how will we survive? How will we protect ourselves?”

“There is a spring and an orchard within the guarding wall. There are pheasants and other game that have taken the tower as their home. I know it’s not ideal, but I promise you it is safer than waiting here. These monsters Furius is creating eat people.”

Lucia looked into her teacup and sighed. “I counted six iron wood bows below. We should restring them and re-fletch the arrows. Others may have bows, too. The women of Aggersel may finally use them for more than shooting targets.”

Corvus took a sip of tea and rested his forearms on the table. “My wife was skilled with the bow, and Cana tells me you have taught her to shoot, Lady Lucia.”

“Yes, she is a good little huntress.” She winked at Cana. “If we had a bow for each, the women of Aggersel could make quite a stand.”

“Five will have to do,” said Atius, squeezing Lucia’s hand. “It’s for you to decide who shall protect the others. Choose wisely.”

LUCIA

"The dress looks good, dear. But you don't look too happy." Lucia covered her mouth to hide her smile.

Cana fidgeted. "It's fine. I just am not used to it, that's all."

"It does make you look different."

"Yeah, it's girly." Cana wrinkled her nose. "And if the wind blows too hard, someone might see my underwear."

Lucia giggled. "Furius may no longer be looking for you now that Galen is gone, but it's better to be safe than sorry."

"So, this is my disguise?"

"Yes, I suppose." Lucia adjusted Cana's dress at the shoulders.

"Fine, I like it better then. Just as long as I don't have to wear it inside."

Lucia made a crossing motion over her heart and led Cana into the town square.

"Do you think Atius's plan will work?"

"Well, I suppose that will depend on how many of the women we convince to join us. It's a dangerous business all around."

"I hope Father and Atius don't get betrayed."

"I think that's what they're counting on," Lucia sighed.

Bartering tables lined three sides of the square and surrounded a collection of wood stump tables, where a few villagers gathered to play Castle and drink lake leaf tea. Lucia traded some dried herbs for a few biscuits and sat with Cana at one of the tables.

"Just as I said." Marina leaned her broad arms against the table adjacent to Lucia.

"You don't say," said Junia, turning to her sister, Jovita. Both women were tall and skinny like their late father, Maro the Elder.

Jovita's eyes widened. "It's just too terrible to imagine."

"Believe it," said Marina. "I had that skinny soldier so drunk and stuffed with food he would have told me the color of Furius's underwear if he knew."

Jovita covered her mouth. "Marina!"

"Aye, I stand by it. This man, Gurges is his name, thief and murderer, second under that fiend Atellus, said they were turning our kin into monsters."

"How?" asked Junia, skeptically.

Marina straightened her back. "Using Galen's blood and the blood of one of our own, Vescus, son of Cilo."

"That doesn't make any sense. Vescus is not a monster," said Junia.

"Was not." Marina leaned in and motioned out to the docks with her pudgy nose. "Gurges said the boy was transformed after he burned Furius's ship; my brother's boy, Pelagus, was turned, too. Selfish as his father that one was."

"I can't believe that." Junia shivered.

"It's true," Cana said. "I was with Vescus. He saved my life, but your nephew, Pelagus, escaped the fire. He made Vescus drink a potion in exchange for letting me go. Vescus became a monster just like Pelagus."

"You saw this with your own eyes?" asked Jovita.

Cana nodded.

Marina turned to Lucia and eyed her from head to toe. "I heard about your boy, Lucia. Icabus was a fine lad. I'm happy he did not see his father's sins."

Cana opened her mouth, but Lucia squeezed her thigh tightly, silencing her.

Lucia looked down. "It sounds like both of us cannot escape the shadow of our families' deeds."

Marina regarded her with a look of intrigue and suspicion. She turned to Cana and said, "Do you trust her?"

Cana smiled at Lucia. "With my life."

Marina raised her eyebrows and took a sip of tea. "I'll speak my mind then. Lady Lucia, before your husband met his makers, did he tell you what Furius was planning?"

Lucia leaned forward. "Nay, but he said enough for me to know that each day we remain in Aggersel, our families are at risk."

"What would you have us do? Run away?" Junia scoffed.

"I would have us protect each other. We cannot stay."

Jovita held her trembling hands together. "And where would we go? The Old Kingdom? The forest? Some other cursed place that is no refuge at all?"

"Nay, I say steal one of the ships and leave Aggersel for good," said Lucia.

"You're mad," said Marina.

Junia rolled her eyes. "And how might we do that Lucia? With kitchen knives and good looks?"

"Cana and I have found a cache of weapons below Lady Tulia's house. There are bows, daggers, and blades of all makes," Lucia whispered.

"What, you want us to abandon our homes and risk it all on the forest lake? You may as well walk us into the forest and feed us to Pelagus and Vescus." Junia flicked the side of her teacup.

"Furius made it here. We can make it out." Lucia eyed each woman in turn. "Aggersel is no longer safe. You've seen how Furius's men look at us. They will come for us, and we will mourn this day we failed to act."

The women shared silent gazes. "What do you think, Jovita?" Junia patted her sister's hand.

"I don't know, but I think Lucia has a point. None of us are safe. Marina, what do you think?"

"You do not ask us an easy thing, Lucia, daughter of Marcellus. It will surely be too much for some; others with families might join you. What of your sister, Junia? Julia has a son. What do you think she would want?"

Junia offered Lucia a hard, unblinking eye. "I cannot speak for my sister. She might be willing."

Marina knocked the table with her fist. "If others are willing to risk it, I think we should help them."

"I can't believe I'm hearing this," said Junia. "The lake is certain death."

Lucia rested her palms together as if in prayer. "I don't deny the danger. Our ancestors made the crossing to this island long ago when their need was greatest. Such a time has returned."

Jovita placed her thin fingers over Junia's hand. "I shall speak to Julia and those I know with children."

"I want to see these weapons," said Marina.

Lucia smiled. "As the lady wishes."

ICABUS

"You appear troubled," said Nubis, looking into Icabus's eyes.

"Thinking of home, that's all," said Icabus, resting in the dragon knight's image.

Icabus could see the glimmer of morning sunlight rise behind Nubis's silhouette. This was how the dragon knight liked to start each day of training.

Nubis blinked thoughtfully. "If you want to progress in your training, you must put your fears aside."

"How? People I love could be dying."

"They might, but to help them, you must train. Remember, time moves more slowly here."

"All we do is meditate and stretch. We hardly spar at all."

Nubis's expression did not change. "Kail did not like to sit either. He preferred action over reflection. It made him reckless."

Icabus cracked his neck. "I just want to learn how to fight better."

"Great warriors are balanced and focused. Balance comes from physical training, and focus comes from meditation. To fight well is simply an extension of the two."

Icabus straightened his back and slowly released his breath. "I was thinking about asking Zrilla and Shrail if they would fight with us. This threat also affects them. Together, I think we can defeat Furius and Galen."

"The bats and the Vlorka will fight, but they can't pass through the gate. Those bones you saw in the dragons' cave were from creatures that wandered into our world. Time moves slower for us here, but the reverse is true for Shrail, Zrilla, and others born to this land. If they pass through the gate, they will grow old and die before our eyes."

"That's horrible."

"It is what it is. I sense there is something else bothering you."

Icabus placed his hands together on his lap and studied the lines on his palms. "I always wanted to grow up, to be different, but now I'm afraid of change. I'm afraid if I change, everyone else will, too, and they'll be gone."

"Change is inevitable, Icabus. Even when change is good it represents a loss. If you resist it, you will always be disappointed when it comes. Accept it, and it might be used to your advantage. The boy you were is not the man who can save Aggersel."

Icabus met Nubis's gaze. "I wish Kail were still here. Having a dragon around would be very useful."

"It would..."

FURIUS

Furius reached into the coffin-sized cage and stroked the fur on the back of Vescus's head. "Not much longer."

Vescus exposed his teeth and drifted off into a weary delirium. Leather straps bound him in place, restricting his movements.

Four chains attached the corners of the cage to the ceiling. Goblets, chalices, and other vessels were arranged beneath to catch the blood dripping from Vescus's canalized veins. At first, Vescus's struggles helped draw the blood from his body, but as he weakened, the flow became no more than a gradual drip.

Furius raised a bloody glass and took a sip.

"Mind and body are brothers. If you break one, the other will follow," said Galen.

Furius looked behind him, but no one was there.

"Leave me alone. You're not real," Furius cursed.

"I'm very real." Arkax ambled down the stairwell and sniffed around with interest. "Is Vescus dead yet?"

"No." Furius frowned. "His blood is valuable. Shouldn't we keep him alive to harvest more?"

Arkax waved his hand dismissively and flopped down in an old cart filled with empty cloth sacks. "The Icabus lived in this house. He sat in this cart often."

"You mean Atius's son? I assume he was a nice snack for you."

"He escaped me to the gate."

"I thought you said—"

"Shut up," Arkax snapped. "The Nubis is mad. He will kill any human who enters the Golden Land."

"Is this Nubis a dragon, a man, or something else?"

Arkax tittered. “A dead man.”

“He’s lying,” said Galen.

Furius looked behind him, and Arkax squinted. “What’s wrong with you?”

“Nothing. I just thought I heard something,” said Furius.

Arkax yawned and closed his eyes. “Ghosts. Kill enough people, and you’ll collect a few.”

ICABUS

"Anything to report, Shrail?" Nubis asked.

"Not," said the bat, dropping his basket in front of Icabus.

Icabus went to work filleting Shrail's catch. "It's nice that the bats and Vlorka are guarding the gate."

"Bats do work. Vlorka lazies and sits on mountain."

Icabus smiled. "Well, it's good that you are working together."

The bat cursed something in his tongue and looked out to the sea. The fur on Shrail's head rose, and Icabus stood up with his sword. Two fair-skinned figures stood in the shallows facing them. "Nubis, we aren't alone."

"Put away your blade. They're Gilian. They will not attack us."

"Gilian?" Icabus sheathed his sword. "I never thought they'd show up."

"Stinky sea peoples," Shrail spat, stuffing his mouth with raw fish.

Nubis rose. "Wait here, Icabus."

"Why? I deserve to know why they let Furius cross the lake."

"Your anger clouds your judgment. Wait here."

Icabus sat on his haunches. "Fine."

The seawater lapped against the Gilians' feet. Nubis approached them slowly, and they bowed.

"The Gilian look different from each other," Icabus noted.

"Warriors and shamans." Shrail pointed with the tip of his wing.

Icabus thought the Gilian Shrail identified as the warrior could not be much older than himself. He wore only a pair of shark-leather shorts and carried a silver trident. Where the light reflected off his shoulders, Icabus discerned the faint pattern of scales.

The shaman appeared older than the warrior, with white hair and intricate scar-like tattoos. He wore an assortment of jewelry made from gems, shells, and rose-colored metals. Even as he bowed to Nubis, he never took his eyes off Icabus.

Icabus thought both Gilian looked remarkably human.

"Can you hear what they're saying, Shrail?"

The bat turned his ears in their direction and wiggled his nose. "Sea language. Shrail does not understands."

The warrior Gilian spoke without raising his eyes, and the shaman reached out and touched the black scales on Nubis's neck. Nubis gestured for Icabus to approach.

Icabus stood and wiped his hands off on his trousers. "I guess now I'm invited. What should I call them first, Shrail, murderers or cowards?"

"Stinky fish heads."

"Thanks for the fish, Shrail."

The bat swallowed another fillet and took flight in the direction of the gate valley. Icabus stepped into the sun and kept his gaze locked on the newcomers; Nubis was right—he was angry.

The shaman bowed to Icabus, and Icabus rested his hand on the pommel of his sword. The warrior Gilian frowned and tightened the grip on his trident.

"Icabus," said the shaman. "I am Herms, and this is Urms. Master Nubis tells us you are from Aggersel. You have truly come far to be here."

"Yes, so have you. Why are you here?"

"Icabus!" Nubis frowned.

Herms raised his hand while keeping his eyes on Icabus. "We are here for the same reason, to stop Furius and Galen."

Icabus's throat felt dry, making it difficult to swallow. "If that's true, then why have you done nothing? Your people haven't let a ship cross the forest lake for a hundred years, but you let Furius and his men through—why?"

Urms glowered at Icabus. "You should keep an eye on this

human, Master Nubis. He may yet become a Taker."

Icabus started forward, and Nubis raised his arm to Icabus's chest, stopping him.

"Urms." Herms frowned. The shaman said something to Urms in his language, and the young warrior stepped back a few paces.

"I'm sorry for that, Icabus." Herms bowed again to him. "I feel your pain, and I empathize with the suffering of your people. We did not wish for Furius to cross."

"Then what happened?" Icabus asked. He found it difficult to speak.

Herms turned back to Urms. "Tell Icabus of our failure."

"Master Herms?"

"Speak to Icabus as if to me," said Herms.

Urms shifted in place and exhaled forcefully. "We found Furius's ships adrift. We boarded the vessels to look for survivors. We were ambushed and taken prisoner.

"Furius knew of our queen, Arwa. She agreed to meet with him to negotiate for our safe return. Furius abducted her. Herms saved my life, but others perished. It is my fault. All of it."

Icabus glared at Urms.

"It's not your fault," said Nubis. "If Furius knew of Arwa, then Galen already had some control over him. If anyone is to blame, it's me. I was responsible for Galen. I should have made sure he was dead."

"We should not blame ourselves for the evil deeds of others," said Herms.

Icabus crossed his arms. "So Furius takes Arwa, and you open the path to Aggersel. Why haven't you tried to rescue her?"

"Furius threatened to kill her if we intervened. She is being held in the farthest house from the sea, guarded by the dead given life. There is no way for us to get close enough." Urms looked to Nubis.

"You want our help?" Icabus scoffed.

Urms gave Icabus a dismissive glance. "We want Master Nubis's help."

Nubis rested his hand on Icabus's shoulder. "How do the people of Aggersel fare?" he asked Herms.

"Things have worsened since Icabus fled. We believe Furius and Galen now have an alliance with the monster, Arkax, and have discovered a way to make more Takers without crossing into the Golden Land. It is only a matter of time before they move on the gate."

"What of the people... the families?" Icabus asked.

"Many have joined with Furius. A great many men perished in a fire in the Apennine Kingdom. We believe the target was Furius and Galen, but Furius has been seen alive."

"Nubis, we have to go back," said Icabus.

Nubis shook his head. "You are not ready."

"You heard what Herms said. Things are getting worse. We can't stay here any longer. I'm ready."

"You don't even know how to properly defend yourself."

"Then teach me."

Nubis scratched his chin and eyed Herms, who glanced toward Urms and nodded. "If I train you to fight, Icabus, you will stay?" Nubis asked.

"Yes," said Icabus.

"Urms, do you remember your lessons in swordplay?"

"Yes, Master Nubis, I have not forgotten."

"Good. Then if you wish for my help, you will help me train Icabus."

"Him?" Icabus's jaw dropped.

"Him?" Urms frowned at Herms, who nodded with approval. Urms fidgeted and bowed his head quickly, avoiding eye contact with Icabus.

"Fine then," said Nubis. "I was never much of a swordsman anyway. Icabus and I meditate until noon. You may come join us after that, Urms. Be happy; both of you are getting what you want."

LUCIA

Lucia went to the window and stood in the sunshine. White blossoms covered the apple trees, and the air smelled of pollen.

I'm dreaming, she thought.

A melody in the distance drew her attention. At first, she thought it was the wind whispering through the apple branches, but as the wind died down, she realized it was a voice—a child's voice.

Lucia took her shawl and descended the stair. The front door was open, and warm wind made her dress tickle her legs.

A young girl, dressed in white lace, skipped past the house up the ridge. She was singing a skipping tune that Lucia knew.

Sun is bright
Clouds away
Wind is warm
Time to play
Day is long
Blossoms bright
Time to play
Till sunset's light

"Lepida, wait!" Lucia ran to the door. "Don't go pick flowers near the forest. Come back!"

The girl in white did not turn around, and Lucia attempted to catch her. She was not moving fast, but every time Lucia blinked, the distance between them increased until Lepida was far up the ridge and gone.

Lucia fell to her knees and sobbed. "Don't go near the woods, Lepida, or you'll die."

"She's safe here," said a voice from behind.

Lucia shielded the sun from her eyes. "Who are you?"

"My name is Arwa." She smiled, offering Lucia her hand. "I am sorry for bringing you here without your permission, but I had no choice. We have little time. Will you walk with me?"

"Yes," Lucia whispered, taking the woman's hand. Arwa led her hand-in-hand through the apple trees. Lucia thought Arwa bore an uncanny resemblance to herself.

"Furius must not be allowed to reach the Golden Land, Lucia. His strength is growing, and soon even my people will not be able to stop him."

"The Gilian?"

Arwa stopped and nodded. They had come to a promontory overlooking the forest lake. Along the shore and coming out of the water were rows of men with tridents. Some wore shiny mail, appearing almost human, while others wore only loincloths and looked more like amphibians than men.

"My kin have protected these waters for a thousand cycles, but they will not act while I am a prisoner. I am too weak to reach them with my mind."

"How can I help?"

Arwa looked back over her shoulder, and Lucia held her breath. Below the white-blossomed canopy of the nearest apple tree was Lepida. She sat amid a blanket of violets and spring grass, weaving a braid of flower stems. Under her breath, she hummed an old tune Lucia had forgotten.

"Go to her," said Arwa. "She will not run. I told her you were coming."

Lucia held her breath and knelt beside the girl in white. "Hi..."

Lepida stopped her humming and glanced over her shoulder. "Hi." She smiled and turned back to her work.

"What are you making?"

"A braid for my friend, Lucia. She's coming."

Lucia held back a wave of emotion. "It's very nice. Do you come here often?"

Lepida looked around and thought about it. "No. I was lost in the forest. That lady showed me the way out." Lepida pointed to Arwa.

"Were you scared?"

Lepida nodded. "The lady says I don't have to go back. She says the Old Kingdom has kids who like to play. She'll show me how to get there if I help my friend."

"How does she want you to help her?"

"To save her from the monster that got me." Lepida pointed toward the mountain.

Lucia brushed a single tear from her eye.

"Done," said Lepida, holding up her braid.

"It's nice," said Lucia.

Lepida handed her the braid.

"I thought you said this was for your friend."

"It's alright. I can make another."

Lucia took the braid and traced it with her finger.

"What's your name?" asked Lepida

Lucia hesitated and smiled. "Lucia."

Lepida paused. Her expression was a mixture of sadness, recognition, and confusion. "You're old."

"I know," said Lucia.

"I've been lost a long time, haven't I?"

Lucia nodded. She did not bother hiding her tears. "I've missed you."

"Me too," said Lepida. "Don't cry."

Lucia nodded and wiped her eyes.

"Will you make me a flower braid for my hair like you used to?"

"Yes. How does lavender sound?" Lucia smiled.

"Yeah, that's good. Make sure it won't come out when I'm running."

"I will."

Lepida removed her white bonnet, and her golden hair fell

onto her back. "If I go to the city, will you come and visit me?"

"Whenever you like," Lucia said.

Lepida smiled and started humming another song. Lucia ran her fingers through Lepida's golden hair and hummed along, weaving in her own melody as she braided the strands of Lepida's golden hair with the soft lavender stalks.

Lucia opened her eyes, and Atius smiled. "It looked like you were having a good dream," he said.

"It was a good dream" She kissed his forehead. "You were right. Furius has Arwa. We need to free her before Furius hurts her."

"She came to you in your dream?"

A tear escaped Lucia's eye. "Yes. Someone else, too."

Atius rubbed away the tear with his thumb. "Icabus?"

"No. Lepida."

"Your old friend who was taken?"

Lucia nodded. "Her spirit has been wandering the woods. Arwa reunited us. She wants to help." She sat up in bed and put on her slippers.

"Hey, hey, hey, where are you going?" Atius pulled Lucia close to him with both arms.

She kissed him on the nose. "Marina and a few others want to see the weapons this morning. I'm hoping they will help me restring some of the ironwood bows. Besides, no one wishes to risk their lives on an empty stomach."

"Aye, including me."

"Then let go," she said, swatting his arm.

Atius sighed and released her.

Lucia wrapped her shoulders in a shawl. "Did Cana come back with you last night?"

"No. She wanted to see her brothers. I'm glad I took her along. Caelius almost put a blade in my back. Tonight, there's going to be a meeting at Corvus's. Caelius and Caius are summoning any man they think might join us. It's a dangerous business."

"Be safe." Lucia squeezed his toes and left the room.

ICABUS

Icabus sat in the sand and yawned. "Shrail, tell me again why the bats have moved into the Giants City?"

"Caves are for scaredies. Bats are strong nows, like Giants."

"Do Giants have to wake up before the sun is even out?"

"No," said Nubis, sitting cross-legged beside him. "But those in training do."

Icabus rubbed his eyes. "Look, Urms is already here."

"Shrail goes. Brings lunches."

Icabus waved, and the bat flew off toward the Giants City.

Urms slowly walked out of the shallows onto the shore. It had been almost two weeks since they began training together, and in that time Urms looked more and more human.

"Your skin looks darker than before," Icabus acknowledged.

"You don't look any different." Urms eyed him with indifference. "Master Nubis, I am ready to train. May we begin?"

Nubis gestured with his chin to Icabus, who stood with a groan. Urms was instructing Icabus on the various stances necessary for swordplay. Icabus thought he was a good student, but Urms scrutinized everything he did. At first, Icabus looked to Nubis for support, but the dragon knight said nothing, which irritated him further.

"Shall we spar today?" asked Icabus.

A thin smile appeared on Urms's lips, but Nubis shook his head. "Not yet. I don't want you to hurt Urms."

Urms's eye's widened, and Icabus shrugged. "Fine."

"Master Nubis, I believe I—" Urms began.

Nubis raised his hand and stood. A retinue of Vlorka waited at the edge of the forest. Icabus recognized Zrilla and her two brothers, Hress and Sercxal, behind her.

Since becoming queen, Zrilla had stirred up Vlorkan society. She invited the bats to her coronation, which Icabus was told had not happened since before the fall of the Spirit City, and sat their leaders, including Shrail, at her table, making them equals to her family in all manners of respect. In her brief address as the new leader, she shocked the clans, and her own family, by restoring the honor of those indentured through past challenges, who had fought alongside her in the battle against the Taker, Prax. This act endeared some families to her but created enemies in others. No choice, however noble, is without consequences, Icabus concluded.

Zrilla's visits to the Giants City usually amounted to quick meetings with the bats and council with Nubis. Icabus tried to join them, but Nubis's body language made him quickly excuse himself. He didn't know the scope of Zrilla and Nubis's relationship, but he suspected they talked about more than politics. The only time he ever saw either of them smile was after a long walk on the beach.

Icabus waved to Zrilla, and the Vlorkana raised her spear in salute.

"Give me a moment," Nubis said.

Icabus turned to Urms. "This might take a while. You want to sit?"

Urms stood at attention and ignored Icabus. Icabus rolled his eyes and sat in the sand. After a few minutes, Zrilla and Nubis approached them.

Zrilla regarded Urms. "Nubis says you are of the Gilian race. I am Zrilla."

Urms made the gesture of respect, touching his left thumb to his ring finger and raising the others, and bowed slightly. "Yes, my people and I know of you, Queen Zrilla."

"Nubis says your people have a warrior class. Need I be concerned by your race, Urms?"

"No, Your Highness," he replied.

"I am told you are training Icabus to be a swordsman."

"He is a poor pupil, but he is learning," said Urms.

"Perhaps you are a poor teacher," said Zrilla.

Icabus looked down to hide his smile. Urms was silent but bowed his head slightly.

Zrilla continued to regard Urms sternly and said, "Nubis says Furius abducted your queen. Why have you not tried to free her?"

"Furius has threatened to kill her if we intervene, and our shamans cannot reach her mind. My people have decided on restraint."

"It sounds like your people wish for Nubis and Icabus to do the work for you."

Urms raised his eyes. "I think our inaction is shameful, Queen Zrilla. Time has made us wise but also slow to act. I would have our queen rescued and Furius defeated, but I am one Gilian, and I must follow my orders."

"Yes, you must," Zrilla held her position. "My people's children are safe today because of Icabus. Remember that next time you would speak poorly of him in my presence."

Urms repeated the gesture of respect with his hands. "I understand. Thank you, Queen Zrilla.

Nubis addressed Urms and Icabus. "Take rest for the remainder of the day. Icabus, practice your guards. I don't like how you are exposing your left flank during Urms's attacks."

"Sure, Nubis." Icabus got up and brushed the sand off him.

"I should return by midday tomorrow," said Nubis. "We can resume your training then."

"Where are you going?" asked Icabus.

"I am accompanying Zrilla to the valley of the Glitkha. Their king is receptive to a new alliance, but he has requested that I consecrate any agreement."

Icabus crossed his arms. "Are these Glitkha dangerous?"

"They are not warriors, but they are not defenseless."

"What do they look like?"

"You've seen a turtle on the forest lake, haven't you?" Urms replied.

Icabus's eyes widened. "Turtle people?"

Nubis nodded.

"Whoa. Are the Vlorka going to train them to fight, Zrilla?"

"Possibly. This land needs more warriors to protect it."

"Fighting turtles. Who would have thought?" Icabus scratched the back of his head.

Icabus watched as Nubis and the Vlorka disappeared into the forest. Behind him, he heard the crunch of sand beneath Urms's feet.

"Where are you going?"

Urms looked back over his shoulder. "Where do you think? Back to the sea."

"Don't you want to spar?" Icabus placed his hands on his sides.

Urms twirled the sword in his hand and looked at the shoreline. "Are you sure you're up for it?"

"I can't think of a better time."

"Alright, neither can I." Urms smiled slyly. "But not here. I'd rather Herms not appear and report this to Master Nubis."

"Great. I know a place. Follow me."

LUCIA

"This is quite a cache, Lucia," said Marina. She pulled a short sword from its scabbard and examined the blade's edge. "Dull but not a speck of rust. A few of us could have these sharpened in less than a day."

"That's what I hope. What about these bows? Can they be restrung?"

Lucia handed Marina a bow, which she grabbed at the ends and bent with great force. "The wood still has its oil. It should hold a new string. Where are the shafts?"

"Here." Lucia handed Marina a quiver. She pulled an arrow from the lot and examined it, then another.

"These arrows have seen better days. Some are true; others have been ruined by moisture. We'll have to sort the good from the bad and re-fletch them. Any metal arrows?"

"Aye," said Lucia, holding up a single quiver gilded in bronze with a matching bronze bow. She pulled an arrow from the quiver and handed it to Marina.

"Tarnished but strong. Yours, I presume?" Marina winked.

"You may have it if it gives you the will to fight."

"Keep it. My will kindles itself. I remember the show you used to put on at the summer solstice. You could strike an apple from a dock pole three hundred steps away. If anyone should carry that bow, it's you."

"My aim is not what it used to be."

"Let us pray you find it again," said Junia. "I was never good with a bow. Father didn't like us using weapons. On the other hand, my sister here is a great shot."

"Me?" Jovita shook her head. "Where did you get that silly idea?"

"I watched you practice in hiding, little sister. There was never a target you set up that you couldn't hit. Why did you stop?"

"Father found my bow and made me burn it. He made me swear never to use one again."

"He was a good man, but he could not have anticipated this day. If we fight, will you shoot for me?" Junia offered Jovita a bow.

"I don't remember how?" Jovita's voice trembled.

"Then we'll practice. Down here if we have to." Marina shook Jovita by the shoulder.

Jovita took the bow. "I can't promise I'm good, or that I'll even hit anything."

"I'm just asking that you try." Junia rubbed Jovita's back.

Marina took her place beside Julia, who was still staring at the weapons. In her arms, she carried her infant son, Marcus, who was fast asleep.

"What do yah think?" asked Marina.

Julia sighed. "It's an impressive cache. If only we had warriors enough to wield them."

"They would be for protection mostly," said Lucia.

Julia looked at Lucia and then to her sisters. "You know, 'twas her husband Atius who led my husband Mattia into that accursed city and first joined Galen and Furius and convinced others to join him, too. Now you would have us follow her as blindly as they followed him?"

"Sister," said Junia. "I would not ask you and the other mothers of Aggersel to consider this if I thought there was any other choice. Aggersel is no longer safe for us."

Julia eyed Lucia. "And you believe we can cross the forest lake?"

"I do."

"Why?" Julia spoke sternly.

Lucia held her gaze. "My husband said that Furius had many maps."

"And who among us has the skill to read them?" Julia eyed each woman.

"I can," said Marina. "My father passed the knowledge to me, good-for-nothing as he was, although I never thought it would be of any use," she chuckled.

Marcus shifted in Julia's arms. She rocked him slightly. "I will speak to the other mothers. What of those women whose husbands have joined Furius?"

"For now, tell them nothing," said Lucia. "We will give them the opportunity to join us when the time is right."

"Yes, for now, they must know nothing," said Junia. "It's too dangerous."

Marina nodded. "I know of some trustworthy widows who could help us restore these weapons today. Shall I fetch them?"

"Yes." Lucia started up the basement stair. "I'll bake some biscuits."

Marina laughed. "You do that. I'm starving."

ICABUS AND URMS

"Are you ready?" asked Icabus.

Urms twirled his blade. "Ready for what?"

"Stairs."

"Stairs?"

"Giants stairs."

Urms sheathed his sword and bounded past Icabus. Urms looked like a man, but the spring in his legs was more frog-like.

"Hey, wait up," Icabus called ahead.

"This passage smells like dragons. It's uncanny," Urms called down.

"It's the mosses. They hold the scent of whatever they come in contact with."

"I hope they don't end up smelling like you."

Icabus stopped. "Hey, I heard that."

"Oh, I guess there must be an echo in here."

"You really should be nicer to humans."

"Humans kidnap my queen and kill my friends. Your race is volatile and unpredictable."

"We're not all bad," Icabus panted, reaching the landing.

"So, what will you become, Icabus?"

"What do you mean?"

"This land will change you. It is inevitable," said Urms.

"I just want to be myself."

"And who is that?"

"I don't know... me."

Urms groaned and looked around the dragon's roost. "Is this where we're going to spar?"

"No. This is where Nubis and I sleep. I've got a better place. Come on."

Noonday sunlight cast a dazzling display of shadow and light on the colonnaded walkways. The frosty breath of the dark, abandoned passages, mixed with the warm sea air, condensing it into dew to nourish the lichen-covered everything.

Behind Icabus, the dull patter of Urms's feet sounded on the stone. "I hope you know where you're going."

"Don't worry." Icabus picked up his pace. "I've only gotten lost three times."

"What?"

"I'm kidding. You're not afraid of the dark, are you?"

"No, I'm afraid of the land. I've never been this far from the water."

"Really?" Icabus turned down a winding stair. His eyes strained to adjust to the surrounding blackness. Slowly, the pale green lichen light brought everything into focus.

"So, what do you think?"

"It's dusty—" Urms sneezed. "Should I be impressed?"

Icabus pulled himself on top of a shelf of wood whose edge reached his chest. "This, my good Urms, is the dining hall of the Giants. And this..." He stamped his foot. "This is the table of the Giants. You can't tell me you've never wished to stand on a set table or, better yet, fight on one?"

"We don't eat at tables."

"Then where do you eat?"

"On land, we eat on grass mats."

"On grass..." Icabus shook his head. "That won't do. You need to know about table eating if you're going to have more dealings with us land folk."

"I thought we were going to spar?"

"Yes; but first, I need to teach you how to set a proper table."

Icabus kicked a silver cup toward Urms, which whizzed past his head and rattled off the wall. "That is a chalice. You serve water in it. It goes at twelve o'clock to the plate."

Urms smirked. "Oh, I see how this is going to be."

"Pay attention. This is a goblet." Icabus pointed his sword at the vessel. "Goblets hold cider and drink. They should be held by the stem, like so." Icabus raised the glass with his sword through a metal loop on its stem. "Cider should be served before the course that accompanies it. Goblets go to the right of chalices. Got it, fish head!" Icabus flung the chalice toward Urms's head.

Urms ducked and raised a brow. "A little slow. I hope your sword is as quick as your tongue. Prepare yourself."

"Then quit your talking and hippity-hop up here, frog-boy. You can't see anything from down there."

"Gladly," said Urms, leaping onto the tabletop. "Master Nubis may favor your fighting skills in his mind, but I have experience on my side."

"Ah, but no table manners. You just kicked your bread plate. Tsk, tsk."

"Where did it belong?"

"Top left-hand corner above the forks."

"What, these metal spike sticks?"

"Yes. Here, have some bread with it."

Icabus stepped onto the lip of an empty bread bowl and flipped it up into his free hand. Inverting it, he flung it like a disc toward Urms's feet.

The Gilian lifted his foot and shook his head. "Bad aim."

"Who said I was aiming at you?"

Urms examined the table setting beneath him. "My knife and spoon are gone."

"Which is closer to the plate, the spoon or the knife?"

"The spoon?"

"Wrong!" Icabus jumped up and cut the rope holding a massive, bronze chandelier. It crashed down between them onto the table, sending spoons, chalices, and plates clambering off in every direction. "Knives go before spoons, sharp edge in."

Urms hopped over the wreckage. "And you say I have no table manners." He thrust his sword at Icabus.

Icabus locked their blades and pushed Urms back. "I'm disappointed, Urms. You just broke the golden rule. There is one last thing you should know about table etiquette. Whatever you do, never, I say never, strike before your host."

"I think I'm done eating." Urms tapped his sword against his hip. Icabus thought he was reconsidering his decision to fight when Urms took in a deep breath and cried, "On guard!"

Urms led with a series of jabs driving Icabus back to the edge of the table.

"Ha! You retreat."

"That's what you think, fish brains." Icabus stepped into Urms's attack, allowing the Gilian's momentum to drive him headlong off the table.

Icabus twirled his sword and shook his head. "It's not a trident, Urms."

"Again." Urms lifted himself off the floor.

Icabus scratched his head. "Are you sure? You look a little frayed around the edges. I wonder if you've been out of the water too long."

Urms emitted a spitting snarl and leapt up onto the table. Plates, bowls, goblets, and tarnished silverware crashed over the table edge as Urms advanced on Icabus.

With his back foot planted, Icabus parried Urms's attack and kicked him in the stomach. The Gilian lurched over and gasped for breath.

"What was that?"

"A dirty human trick, I suppose." Icabus bowed.

"Despicable human!"

"Frog."

"Peasant!"

"Fish-head!"

"Rhar!" Urms charged, attacking Icabus with a series of overhead strikes.

Icabus lost ground and leapt backward off the table.

"Where are you going?"

"I'm tired of the scenery up there. You're a sloppy eater, Urms. Catch me if you can."

Urms jumped down from the table, and Icabus ran past him down a long, winding corridor. Icabus slid to a stop and felt the tip of Urms's blade poke his back.

"Ouch. Wait, Urms."

"Do you yield?" Urms panted.

"Yes, I yield."

Urms appeared satisfied by this response and twirled his sword expectantly in his hand. "What is this place?"

"I don't know. I have the strangest sense I've been here before." Icabus put away his sword.

Alcoves crisscrossed with iron bars formed makeshift cages along the hall's length. Dim light penetrated those cages whose doors hung open. Toward the end of the hall, the light dimmed, and the cage doors were rusted shut. Icabus was glad he could not see into the cells. It seemed even the lichen knew not to grow in a tomb.

"Icabus, draw your sword," Urms insisted in a hushed tone. "I smell Taker."

"Your nose is right, Urms. But the Takers are dead. Only the lichen remembers their scent."

"How can you be sure?" Urms lowered his sword slightly.

"When the Water Spirit tried to join with me, I experienced his memory of the attack that destroyed the Spirit City. During the battle, the Takers let loose monsters against the Vlorka. These monsters were Vlorka and other creatures covered with the essence of fire and earth."

Icabus rested his hand on one of the iron doors. "The Water Spirit killed one of them but not before extracting its memories of this place. This dungeon is where the Water Spirit was going before the Spirit City was destroyed. He wanted to stop what Galen and the Takers were doing here, but he never made it."

Urms spat onto the floor. "Do you have a flint?"

"Yeah. Why?"

"Let's destroy this place."

Icabus looked up surprised. "What?"

"You heard me."

"How are we going to do that?"

"Like this." Urms pushed over the shelf behind Icabus. Jars

and potion bottles crashed to the floor. "Smells flammable to me."

"It does." Icabus crouched over the rubble. "Thank you, Urms. In my village, we commit our dead to fire. I always thought it was a way to remember them, but I think it's also a way to let them go..."

"To ashes," Urms said.

"To ashes," Icabus repeated.

Icabus struck the flint, and the solvent sprang to life with a *swoosh*. Green, red, and blue flames slipped across the floor and consumed the tables in a spectral lake of fire. Brief memories of unspeakable horror flashed before Icabus's eyes but disappeared as the fire spread into the closed cages and ignited their contents in a bright yellow fire.

Urms placed his hand on Icabus's shoulder. "We should go."

"We can't let Galen do this again, Urms."

"I know."

FURIUS

"Master Furius."

Furius looked over his shoulder and then back to the mountain. "Yes, Atellus."

"One of our spies reports that the sons of Corvus, Caelius, and Caius are planning a revolt. They are meeting tonight at the fig tree above the gristmill. May I take care of it?"

"Yes, but first, did you bring me what I asked for?"

"Yes." Atellus motioned over his head, and Gurges pushed a skinny man forward. The man was gagged and blindfolded, and his hands were tied in front of him. His clothes had been stripped off to his undershorts. Fresh whip marks covered his back.

"After the fires, this man hid in a house to escape his duty. We found—"

"I don't care what he did, Atellus. Remove the gag and blindfold."

Atellus did, and the man fell before Furius's feet. "Sir, I hurt my leg in the fire. I have served you loyally. Please, give me another chance."

"I am," Furius spoke calmly. "All you must do is cross this meadow, touch the rock wall bordering the forest, and return here."

"Yes, Master Furius, anything."

Furius extended a hand. "You may go."

The man bowed and stumbled forward with an evident limp. After a few steps, he focused on the wall ahead and picked up his pace. He reached out and touched the stone and looked back to Furius, who nodded agreeably.

Atellus took a step back and tapped Gurges on the chest, who also stepped back.

The man picked up his pace again, half dragging his gimpy leg behind him. Somewhere in the forest, a crow called out. If it was a warning, it was too late. Four Takers leaped from the forest, falling on the man and driving him to the ground. There was no scream, no chance to flee or fight, not even time to wipe the stupid grin off his face.

Perched atop the rock wall were two other Takers, Arkax and Pelagus. Arkax watched emotionlessly as the young Takers fed voraciously, while Pelagus fidgeted and drooled.

They slunk down the wall and approached Furius. Pelagus took a moment to tear a piece of flesh from the man's calf, which elicited half-hearted growls from the younger Takers. Pelagus was dominant, and they knew it.

"When you asked for children, I thought you were going to eat them, not turn them into monsters." Furius looked away from the carnage. "How are they developing?"

Arkax cleared his nostrils. "Stupid and hungry. Have you made more potion?"

"Yes, but if I keep drawing from Vescus at this rate, he will die soon."

"It doesn't matter." Arkax used his claw to pick a piece of skin out of his twisted, yellow teeth. "Once we take the Golden Land, we won't need a potion to make Takers. Your men will become the animals they already are in their hearts. So will you."

"We will see," said Furius.

"Yes, we will," Galen laughed in Furius's head.

One of the Takers gagged up a piece of bone, and the rest stalked forward like mountain cats. Licking the blood from their muzzles, they settled behind Arkax and Pelagus, admiring Furius with curiosity and, Furius thought, hunger.

"Once all the children turn, I will lead your men to the gateway," said Arkax. "Nubis will fall before us."

Atellus cleared his throat. "What of the town?"

"What of it?" asked Furius disdainfully.

"Some of your men would like to stay behind and govern in your absence. Not all of us wish to live forever."

"And you think that man should be you, Atellus?"

Atellus raised his chin. "Yes, Majesty. My family has served your house for generations. Let me safeguard this town in your name."

"Very well, Atellus. End this little insurrection the townspeople are planning, and you may have this place if you desire it. I'm sure our new friends here will require human sacrifices from time to time."

The Takers grinned widely, and Atellus bowed. "Thank you, Master Furius."

CANA AND URMS

From behind a row of empty apple crates, Cana listened to the villagers argue.

"I am certain Dulius is a still loyal to Furius. We should not invite him to the meeting," Caelius said.

"What of Tullius?" Caius paced. "You trust him, but I have my reservations."

Caelius threw up his arms. "Very well, we won't invite either of them."

"No," said Corvus. "If we go on this way we won't have anyone to fight with us. It will not do."

"He's right," said Atius. "We need these men, but we must take precautions. I've told anyone whose loyalty is in question to meet me at the lookout instead of here. If they betray me, then our purpose will not be lost."

Corvus nodded.

"What if Furius captures you?" asked Caius.

"Then it was good we didn't meet as one. Whatever happens, tonight we plan our move. May the Gods favor us."

"Aye," said Corvus.

"Has your wife taken any precautions in case we are betrayed?" Caelius asked Atius.

"Yes, but I know only that in case I am captured."

Caelius nodded. "Tis best, I suppose. Let me check in on Cana before we go."

Cana lay down on a bed of hay.

Caelius pushed aside the curtain and Cana sat up. "You're awake... or pretending to have been asleep?" He smiled.

Cana grinned and picked at the dried wheat between her

feet. “I need your help, Caelius.”

Caelius sat beside her. “What is it, little sister?”

“Vescus needs our help.”

“I was afraid you might say something like that. If what you tell me is true, little sister, no one can help Vescus.”

“He’s different, Caelius. I know it.”

Caelius rubbed Cana’s back gently. “If that’s true, then what makes you think he’s still alive?”

“Marina says Gurges says so.”

“I know you care about Vescus, but he is beyond our reach. I want you to promise me you will go with Lady Lucia and the others when the time comes. Promise me.” He raised her chin.

“I promise.” Cana embraced him. “I need to go.”

“Where?”

She stood. “To help Lucia.”

“The sun hasn’t fallen. It isn’t safe.”

“You think it’s safer at night? Are you crazy?”

“I guess you’re right.” He got up and placed his hand on her shoulder. “Stay off the road, aye?”

“Alright.” She kissed him on the cheek.

Cana left the barn and ran across the field between her house and the lake road. She kept to the reed bank, skirting the marsh to avoid Furius’s guard. Somewhere beyond her vision, a goose honked and fell silent. She shaded her eyes and looked out to the water.

“Hey, girl.”

Cana turned back to the road where Gurges sat on the edge of the bridge. He smiled and winked. “Come here.” Gurges motioned with his finger.

Cana stopped. “I can’t. My friend Lucia is waiting for me in town.”

Gurges jumped down. “I only want to talk for a minute. Where are you coming from? There’s only one house out this way and the dead city.”

“The fire took some of my friends; I just wanted to—”

“What? See if they were still alive?”

Cana nodded, and Gurges caressed her cheek. He loomed over her like a leafless tree.

"Can I go, mister?"

"Yes, but first I need your help with something. It's right over here under the bridge. Come now," he said, grabbing Cana by the wrist.

"No!" Cana screamed and kicked him in the shin.

Gurges let go and growled. "You little tramp! I'll show you rough."

Gurges reached out, and Cana tripped. Her back hit the reeds, and she looked around frantically.

"Nowhere to go is there? Come here, and I'll forget everything, I promise."

"No!" Cana dashed past him toward the road.

He dove and seized her ankle. "Gotcha!" he laughed, pinning her to the ground. "The Gods must favor me today. I was about to take a nap, and look what I find: a pretty little girl."

"Leave me alone." Cana rolled onto her back.

"You know the rules. Nobody is supposed to be wandering about, especially this close to the ships."

"I'm sorry. I'll go home. I won't do it again."

"Oh, I know you won't do it again," said Gurges, licking his long incisors. "You're a good girl, and good girls should get a second chance. That's why, if you do what I say, nobody is going to know you were snooping around down here. Got it?"

Gurges stroked Cana's cheek. His fingers smelled like rotten cabbage, and Cana struggled, pushing against his chest.

"Feisty. That's alright. You can fight me all you like, pretty girl, but if you make a peep, I'll put your face in the water and no more Mama and Papa for you."

Cana shuddered. Even if she screamed, no one would hear her, not here. She looked at the narrow path behind Gurges, and the soldier shook his head.

"Don't get any funny thoughts now, pretty girl. Gurges caught you fair-and-square, and now it's time to play."

Gurges straddled her abdomen and fiddled with the buttons

on his tunic. Cana saw her chance. She threw herself forward and pushed him as hard as she could. Gurges fell backward, and Cana scrambled away from him on all fours.

"Come back here, you little tramp!"

Gurges grabbed at her pant leg, and Cana screamed and kicked him in the face. Something inside his nose made a crunching sound, and he recoiled, bringing his hands to his face.

"Ah! My nose! I'll kill you!"

Blood poured from Gurges's nostrils. He gingerly touched his deformed nose. He looked at Cana, and his eyes were murderous.

"You little..." He lunged forward again, but this time Cana evaded him altogether and pushed herself to her feet. Gurges threw himself at her and grabbed her shirt. She tried to pull away, but Gurges wrapped his arms around her.

"Let go of me!"

She hit the ground, and Gurges covered her, half resting, half holding her against the reed bed with his oppressive weight. Blood gushed from his nose into her hair; he panted; droplets of his hot breath, foul like rotten cider, fell upon Cana in nauseating waves. He kissed her forehead and covered her mouth while she screamed.

"Good girl," he said, loosening his belt.

A floating island drifted to the shore.

"You thought you'd get away, didn't you?" He pushed himself up and pinned her arms with his knees.

"Stop," she whimpered.

"Hush. No more talking." He covered her mouth with his bloody fingers. "Not a peep now, not ever again."

Gurges winked, but his gaze faltered, and his lips trembled as if he'd forgotten how to speak. He looked down at his chest and touched his tunic, where a sword penetrated his chest. Gurges slumped forward, and Cana scrambled back.

"Are you hurt?"

"Urms?"

"Yes, it's me." He took her by the hand and lifted her.

Cana embraced him and began to sob.

"It's alright." He embraced her back.

Cana wept, and Urms led her to a stone and sat beside her. "Thank you," she sniffled. "You look different."

Urms touched his forearm. "I'm training more on land."

Cana tasted blood in her mouth and spat between her feet. "I thought I was going to die like Icabus."

"Icabus? Icabus is not dead. He's in the Golden Land. I saw him only a day ago."

Cana's jaw slackened, and tears escaped her eyes again. "That's impossible, Icabus is... He's gone. Arkax got him."

"No, Icabus evaded the monster. He is well, I assure you." He touched her back.

Cana wrapped her arms around him. "He's alive. Gods, he's alive. Wait till I tell Lucia and Atius—they'll be so relieved."

Urms placed his hands upon Cana's shoulders. "Lady Cana, do you agree that I saved your life?"

"Yes."

"Then I must ask you for one thing in exchange for my deed."

"Of course, whatever you want."

Urms's expression was hard. "Say nothing of Icabus or me. When the time is right, he will return."

"And when will that be?"

"Soon." Urms grabbed Gurges leg and lifted him over his shoulder. "And hopefully not alone. What say you, Cana, do you promise?"

"Yes."

"Do you swear it to the Gods?"

"Aye, I swear."

"Thank you." Urms turned away.

Cana stood and blocked his path. "Wait. Vescus is being held captive. I need your help, Urms."

"You mean that disagreeable human who was with you before?"

Cana nodded. "He's not so bad. After his father died, he hasn't been the same. Cilo was Vescus's only family."

"I'm sorry, Cana. I can't risk Arwa's life by being seen."

"Vescus is being held in the same house as her. We can rescue them both."

Urms shook his head and waded out into the water. "If you cherish your life, Cana, you will stay away from that house. If Vescus is truly there, then you should pray for him and not trust a hope."

Cana watched as Urms disappeared into the lake. She knew what she had to do but just didn't know how to do it.

ICABUS

Morning light woke Icabus from a dreamless sleep. He sat up and yawned.

"Good morning," said Nubis.

"Hi." Icabus rubbed his eyes. "I didn't hear you return last might. How did things go with the Glitkha?"

The dragon knight sat cross-legged, overlooking the sea. Against the morning light, he appeared like negative space in the outline of a man. "Well enough. The Glitkha have accepted an alliance with the Vlorka. Herh and Freh of house Srehk will stay on to train them. Zrilla has asked that you go to the village at midday. The Air Spirits have requested you."

"Really? Do you know what they want?"

"No. Zrilla did not know. They left their sanctuary to see the Spirit City. I am told they took the loss of the Water Spirit with great sadness. He was the last of that line of Spirit."

Icabus tossed a handful of dried thimbleberries in his mouth and stirred the embers in the firepit with a stick. Even though he failed to join with the Water Spirit, Icabus could still feel the Spirit's presence like an old memory.

"There is something I've meant to ask you, Icabus."

Icabus wiped his mouth. "What?"

"Can you tell me what you experienced when the Water Spirit shared his mind with you?"

"Well... The first time I felt his consciousness it was scary. His mind was so big, it felt it would be swallow mine up. The second time was different. This may sound strange, but it felt like waking up, as if a part of me had been asleep my whole life and, all of a sudden, I was aware of it. It was the weirdest thing;

I've never felt more alive."

Nubis did not move and continued to look out to the sea. "When a dragon chooses a human companion, he also shares his mind. What you describe is similar to this experience. When an older and stronger mind is shared, there is at first a sense of being lost in it, but then there is an awakening into that consciousness. The reflection of the other mind becomes a part of you. It is a precious gift."

"Whatever it was, it didn't last. I'm just me again."

Nubis looked over his shoulder. "You remember none of the Spirit's memories?"

Icabus picked at his bootlace. "Yesterday, I found a room in the city where Vlorka and others were tortured. I shouldn't have known it, but I did. That's it."

Nubis raised an eyebrow. "What was the Spirit's intention in sharing its mind with you?"

Icabus exhaled slowly. "I should have told you this before, but it didn't seem to matter anymore because it didn't work. He wasn't just trying to share his mind with me; he was trying to join with my water. I got the idea from Prax and the Fire Spirit. I knew the Spirit was dying, and I wanted to help keep him alive."

"That was a dangerous choice, Icabus. You don't know what could have happened with such a joining. The Spirit could have overtaken your mind, or you could have died."

"I just wanted to help. I'm sorry."

Nubis's frown softened. "Don't be sorry. It was foolish of you to try to save me, too, but you did it anyway. I have found that foolishness and goodness often occur together." He regarded the sea and let out a soft sigh.

"When I first touched Kail's mind, I was afraid. We found out things about each other that embarrassed us, but as you experienced yourself, the companionship and experience of another's mind is a profound and intimate thing.

"Being without Kail has been like missing a piece of myself. I have tried desperately to hold on to his memories, so much so that I have lost a part of myself in the process. I used to think protecting this land from Arkax, and others like him, could fill that void. I realize now that this was my mistake."

"What made you realize it?"

Nubis paused and offered Icabus a warm expression. "You did, Icabus."

CANA

Cana pushed open the door, and the women gasped.

"Gods, child, you frightened me!" said Marina, righting herself on her stool. "Lucia, you didn't latch the door?"

Around the kitchen table, Lucia, Junia, Jovita, and Marina exchanged relieved glances. Before them was a collection of bows, strings, shafts, and arrowheads.

Lucia dropped the latch. "Gods, you gave me a shock. Are you hurt, dear?"

Cana smiled meekly, but tears filled her eyes.

Lucia kissed Cana's forehead and brushed the hair from her face. "Cana, you smell like you fell in a swamp. And look at these bruises on your wrists. Who?"

"Someone didn't..." Junia began, but Cana shook her head fiercely.

"He tried, but I fought him off, and I ran. I thought I was fine but seeing all you..." Cana shook her head. "I don't know why I'm crying."

"Well, isn't it obvious?" Marina asked. "You've got guts like nails, dear, but none of us fights for our life without getting a little put-down. Now, come here." Marina stood up, grabbed Cana by the arms, and crushed her between her massive breasts. She smelled like cinnamon and clean fabric. "Come and sit by me, dear, and I'll make you an arrow to fire into his heart. Aye?"

"You won't have to; he's dead," Cana said without thinking.

Lucia looked at her. "Did you?"

Cana shook her head, searching for something to say. "No, I mean, I don't think so. We were struggling, and he slipped. He stopped moving, and I ran. I didn't look back."

"Gods, that's horrible," said Jovita.

"Not as horrible as him finishing his deed," Marina spoke with an air of distaste.

"Better he's gone," said Junia. "Did anyone else see you come here?"

"No. I'm sure."

Junia sighed in relief and handed Cana a bow and cloth covered with apple oil. "Here, join us. A little work will get your mind off it."

Cana took the bow, and Marina made a place for her at the end of the bench. Lucia watched her intently like a worried mother, and Cana found it hard to look her in the eyes.

"Is there anything else, dear?" Lucia asked.

"Icabus is alive!" She looked at Lucia and wished she had spoken the words she had said in her mind.

Lucia squinted with concern.

"No, I'm fine."

Cana stroked the bow with the cloth, and the work did seem to calm her. In total, they were able to salvage four bows and twice the number of arrows.

Junia crossed her arms. "What are we going to do, throw the arrowheads at them when we run out of arrows?"

"Is that supposed to be funny?" Jovita's hand shook.

Marina crossed her arms. "Are there any other arrows in town?"

Lucia shook her head. "Furius's soldiers took anything that might be used as a weapon when they searched the houses."

"Take their arrows," said Jovita.

"What?" asked Junia.

Jovita cleared her throat. "Take their arrows," she repeated.

"If only it were that easy," said Junia.

"She's right." Marina struck her fist against the table causing Jovita to jump. "We're going to take Furius's ships anyway. We'll have all the arrows we need right there."

Junia straightened her posture. "And, how do you suppose we take the ship if we only have eight arrows?"

"Carefully," said Marina.

"Carefully is right," Cana added.

"You're looking a little white around the gills, Lucia," noted Marina.

Lucia forced a smile. "It's just dangerous, that's all."

The women eyed each other uneasily, and Marina nodded to each of them in turn. "Well, it's settled then. We use what we have and take the ship."

"Alright, we take the ship, but just the four of us," Lucia insisted. "Once we have it, we can send word to Julia and the other mothers that it's safe."

"What about me?" asked Cana.

"I want you to look after Amara and Lady Tulia, dear." Lucia patted Cana's hand. "When we send word, I want you to help them and the others move as quickly as possible."

Cana tried not to look disappointed. For Lucia's real plan to work, she knew the ships would have to burn.

FURIUS

"Tie down his arm!" shouted Furius.

Enius grabbed Vescus's arm and held it in place. Furius palpated the flesh above Vescus's blown vein.

"Knife!"

Enius handed him a small paring knife. Furius pushed it through the skin without hesitation. A pool of blood formed, and he forced the cannula into place.

Vescus yelped.

"Make sure the arm is secure this time," said Furius. "He still has fight in him."

Enius went to work, and Furius left the basement. Last week Furius hadn't known anything about veins or surgery, but somehow, now he did. It was a strange sensation to know something you never learned and to be confident in the knowing.

There were other things he knew, too, things about Arkax, the Gilian, and the gatekeeper, Nubis. How such a transmission was possible, he didn't know, but he had a good idea where it was coming from. He also had a good idea of who might know more.

Furius stepped into the parlor where Salvius, Seius, and Minius rested on the soiled furniture. He smiled as they stood to attention. The one thing these men feared more than anything else was he.

"Any requests from our guest?" asked Furius.

Minius cleared his throat. "Water and fruit, sir, nothing else."

"I trust that wasn't too difficult."

"No, not at all, sir. I had the men fetch it for me. She, well, liked it very much."

"Good, I want my guest handled well. You three may leave. I've no need of you 'til morning."

The men shuffled out the front door like three obedient dogs. Two of Galen's rotten soldiers stood idly by in the shadows at the top of the stair. Their stench made the whole house stink.

"Soch jah," commanded Furius, and the dead left the house. He closed the door and smiled. When he killed Galen, Furius thought he would need Arkax and Pelagus to dismember the dead soldiers because only Galen knew the words to control them; however, like many things Furius used not to know, he found the words.

Furius ascended the stairs to the upper bedrooms. The ceiling upstairs was vaulted. A single hallway separated a large master bedroom on the mountainside and two smaller bedrooms to the right. His guest was in the master bedroom.

Furius rapped on the door. There was a stirring within, and he entered. Arwa sat at the edge of Lucia's bed, staring at him with piercing, grey eyes. She ran her fingers over the bed quilt and frowned.

"You have caused this family and the people of this village great pain. By harming them, you have cursed yourself."

"I was cursed long before now," he said, sitting beside her. "I once lived in a castle with a son I loved more than the world. Are the men who took that away from me cursed as well? I have yet to see their bodies upon a pyre or their families torn away from them."

"And you bring upon these people the same violence that hurt you. You are a fragment of a man, Furius. Your appearance hides the emptiness inside you."

Furius's smile settled like stagnant water. "Those who survive will be stronger for it, as I have become. The rest are in the hands of the Gods. I will return to the Golden Land."

Arwa looked into Furius's eyes. "Galen...? How can this be?"

"Galen is dead. I killed him. His knowledge lives within me. That is all."

Arwa touched Furius's cheek. "Your eyes say different. Let me help you. My people—"

"Get away from me." Furius pushed her away. He looked at his own hands in shock. "I didn't do that."

"He's growing stronger, Furius. He will grow in you like a cancer until there's nothing left but him. I can help you. Take me back to the lake."

"No." Furius pressed his fist to his forehead. "You're trying to trick me! Galen tried to trick me, and now you're trying to do the same."

"Furius. End this, and I promise to lead you from this darkness."

"I..." Furius got up and fell to his knees. Burning pain enveloped him, and he could neither move nor call out. If hell was a feeling, he felt it.

"Forever, if you oppose me," said Galen in his head.

The pain stopped, and Furius looked up, confused. He was on his back and Arwa standing over him. An uncomfortable wetness told him he'd soiled himself.

"Get back." Furius rolled away from her.

"Furius, you must listen."

"No! You can't help me." He crawled through the door and slammed it shut.

CANA

"Cana, it's dark. After what happened today, I think you should stay here tonight," Lucia addressed Cana in her motherly tone.

"I'm sorry, Lucia, but I have to do something."

Cana grabbed a biscuit and stole out the kitchen door before Lucia could block the exit. Soldiers came and went between the town and hill, where a great many men had congregated around Icabus's house, fortifying it with a perimeter of torches. Cana watched them from the shadows of the apple grove.

"Have any of you seen Gurges?" Atellus stopped three soldiers, whom Cana recognized as members of the group who'd killed the Elders.

"No, I have not seen him," said Minius, coughing. Soot still covered his face.

"What about you two?"

Salvius shook his beard.

"Nay," Seius said.

Atellus placed his hands on his hips and looked around with an irritated expression.

"Shall I pass on a word if I see him?" asked Minius.

"Tell him Atius survived the fire. He's trying to rally the townspeople, but they sold him out. What errand does Furius have you on?"

"None," said Minius. "We've been dismissed for the night. Furius has had us guarding the sea witch and that beast, Vescus, while he's bled. I don't know how anything can still be alive after losing that much blood, but I suppose it won't be much longer."

Seius shook his head. "Monsters, rotting soldiers kept alive by potions, people crawling out of the lake, what's next?"

"Dragons, I suppose," offered Salvius.

Seius shook his head. "Gods save us."

Atellus rolled his eyes and patted Minius on the shoulder. "Have a drink for me."

"Two," said Minius, following Seius and Salvius down the hill.

Cana watched Atellus until he disappeared over the ridge. She leaned against a tree and stared at the ground. She didn't know what to do. Atius was in danger, but if what Minius said was true, Vescus had little time.

"I gotta help Vescus," she whispered to herself.

A hundred meters up the ridge, Cana could see the silhouettes of Furius's men through the trees. Cana thought that if she had any chance of getting into the house, it would have to be from the forest side.

She stayed out of the firelight and crossed under the dark canopy. Four of the corpse guards stood motionless behind Icabus's house.

"Maybe I can scare them off?" Cana considered.

A twig snapped behind her, and before she could stand, a dead arm had her by the throat. She clawed at the forearm. Layers of flesh squished between her fingers like spoiled butter, and she gasped, feeling her strength slip away. A flash of silver cut across her vision, and the corpse's head landed in her lap. The soldier's arms slackened, and its headless body fell toward her. She scrambled away to face her new enemy.

"Urms?"

The lake boy put his finger to his mouth and knelt beside her. Behind them, three of the other dead guards lay decapitated. Urms examined Cana's neck and arms. He took her hand and attempted to lead her away from the house.

Cana held her ground and shook her head.

Urms leaned close and whispered in her ear. "If you could hear what I hear in that house, dear Cana, you would not linger."

"My friend is inside; I have to help him."

Urms regarded her gravely. "He may have already succumbed to Galen's magic and been turned into a monster himself."

"I don't care; I'm going. Don't you want to save Arwa?"

"I can mask my scent only from a distance. Any closer and I risk detection."

"Then help me get inside," Cana said. "Give me a distraction to lead those guards away. I'll try to help Arwa after I rescue Vescus."

"Lady Cana, if I let you go in there, I cannot rescue you."

The concern Cana saw in Urms's eyes momentarily shook her resolve. She looked at the house, and the fear of death crept into her heart. "I love him, Urms."

Urms lowered his head. "Very well. May the Gods protect you, Lady Cana, and your friend."

Urms picked up the head of one of the dead soldiers and hurled it in the air. It crossed Icabus's backyard and fell in the forest beyond, making a loud *clack*, where it struck the branches. Cana watched as two of the guards shrieked and sprinted into the wood.

"There are still more," Cana said, but Urms was already gone. A moment later, a loud crash, like a limb breaking, sounded in the forest. The remaining soldiers sprang into action without hesitation.

Cana moved into the clearing, hyperaware of her surroundings. It was scary and intoxicating. She guessed this was how people felt when they were about to go into battle.

She approached Icabus's back porch and took the stairs quietly. The door to the kitchen was ajar.

A foul smell, like rotting garbage, wafted from the kitchen. Cana peeked in. Seeing nothing dead or alive waiting inside, she slipped in, locking the door behind her.

The kitchen was not as she remembered it. A layer of mud covered the floor. Its moisture climbed the walls in grotesque stains. Amara's toys and a collection of broken dishes were piled up in one corner.

A long knife stuck in the table. Cana pulled it free and

examined her reflection in the metal. She didn't know if she had the guts to use it, but having it made her feel safer.

Moonlight and memory were her only guides as she made her way out of the kitchen to the front door. Two narrow stained-glass windows, as tall as the door itself, stood on either side. Through these, Cana could see the outlines of two figures guarding the entrance. She tiptoed closer and examined the door's sliding latch. As long as she could remember, the front door of Icabus's house had never been locked. For this reason, the latch looked strange to her.

Cana held her breath and took the latch in her hand. She lifted it and slid the bolt into the locked position.

One of the figures beyond the glass lifted his head. Cana held her breath and waited. Seconds passed like minutes, but after a few moments, the dead soldier lowered his head. Cana backed away into the shadows.

Up the stairwell where the stairway bent, Cana could see a flicker of firelight against the stained wood. The slow creak of the floorboards overhead indicated that someone was upstairs. Cana listened intently, and she thought she could make out two voices: one male and another female. The male voice sounded like Furius, while the other was unknown to Cana. She guessed it was Arwa.

Another sound drew Cana to the basement door, where a trail of blood led down into the hold. "Vescus?" she whispered, tiptoeing down the stair.

The blood led to a long, rectangular cage, elevated by chains connected to the rafters. Bloody footprints coursed the perimeter of the enclosure, where vessels collected the blood dripping from above.

Cana rushed forward. She removed the locking pins from the top of the cage and swung open the lid. "Vescus," she shook him.

Vescus's ears twitched, but he did not open his eyes.

Ropes bound his neck, arms, and legs. His veins had been cut down where they had collapsed or coagulated, creating long, vertical wounds. Where the veins were still open, cannulas were placed to encourage the flow of blood.

Cana removed the cannulas. She pressed her hands against the wounds, stopping the trickle of blood.

"The ropes," Vescus whispered.

Cana smiled and cut the bonds with her knife. Vescus opened a golden eye.

"Vescus, come on."

Vescus closed his eye.

"Hey, wake up." Cana shook him.

"He's not going anywhere," came a voice from the darkness beneath the stair.

"Who's there?"

"Who or what? Do you think Furius would leave the house unguarded or let his prize pin cushion escape?"

Cana held up her knife. "Show yourself."

The Taker stepped into the light, and Cana knew it to be Enius by the tattered vest he wore. The rest of his clothes had been stripped away, replaced with a thick, reddish-brown fur.

He held back his ears and wiggled his wet nose in Cana's direction. His thin lips parted, revealing a deadly collection of pointy, white teeth. Cana wasn't sure if he was smiling or trying to appear menacing. She guessed both.

"Stay away, Enius, or else."

"Or else... what?" Enius approached.

"I'll hurt you."

Enius laughed. "You should thank me, Cana. I could have eaten you the minute you came down those stairs, but I was curious about what you would do. I admire your devotion to Vescus. You can be just like him, too."

Cana edged around the cage, and Enius picked up a blood-filled challis.

"Still fresh," he said, lapping up the contents. "A new world awaits you, Cana. You just have to drink." Enius reached for her.

"No." Cana stabbed in his direction. Enius evaded the strike, and seized her by the wrist. She dropped the blade, and he pressed her against the cage.

"Sorry about this, but you'll forgive me." Enius pried open her mouth. "Say cheers."

"Cheers," said Vescus, rising up and taking Enius's neck in his jaws.

Enius's eyes widened, and Cana could tell he was afraid. He flailed ferociously, tossing the cup aside and clawing at any part of Vescus he could reach.

Vescus held on, but Cana could see his strength failing. She grabbed her knife and threw herself in Enius's direction. Enius backhanded her to the ground. She looked for the knife, but it was gone—buried to the hilt in Enius's back.

Cana looked on in shock. Enius snarled and reached for the knife in vain. Already his breath was quickening as blood filled his lungs and escaped his mouth.

"I'll... kill you," he managed, choking on the words. He slumped backward, limp.

Vescus released his bite. "Cana, turn away and cover your ears."

Cana did, and Vescus tore Enius open and ate his muscle. Even with her fingers in her ears, she could hear Vescus's teeth scrape against Enius's bones.

"Cana." Vescus touched her shoulder.

Cana started, and Vescus stepped back. "Vescus," she embraced him.

Vescus hesitated and wrapped his arms around her. "You should not have come."

"You were awake the whole time, weren't you?"

"It was the only way I could get him close enough. I'm sorry you got hurt."

"It's alright, I forgive you." Cana tried to smile. She expected to see Enius's blood on him but she didn't see a drop. "Were you scared you were going to die?"

Vescus blinked thoughtfully and nodded once.

She reached out and touched the fur on his cheek. "What's it like... being like this?"

Vescus studied her silently for a moment. "It's not so bad. I can see and hear things I never could before. What Enius told you is true. You would not regret the change, but I do not wish this for you. There are things I miss..."

Vescus looked into Cana's eyes, and Cana blushed. She wrinkled her nose. "Well, you might think you see and hear better than me now, but I think your nose is broken, Vescus. You smell really bad."

"I've been tied in a cage," Vescus said in a hurt voice.

Cana pushed him. "Gosh, Vescus, don't be so sensitive. You're almost as bad as Icabus. I'm just fussing with you."

Vescus regarded her with affection. "Thank you."

"Furius? Are you alright?" came a voice from outside.

"It's Pelagus." Cana jumped. "He's trying to get in the house."

"You locked the door?"

"Yeah. It seemed like a good idea at the time."

A steady rap of feet sounded on the stairwell above. Vescus growled.

"It's Furius. He's upstairs," Cana whispered.

Vescus made a move toward the stair, and Cana grabbed his arm. She shook her head and pointed to a narrow passage lined with shelves and jars. "Atius's cider cellar goes right under his workshop. Icabus and I used to spy on him through the cracks in the floor. It's just wood. We might be able to get through, but it's dark."

"Maybe for you." Vescus winked. "Follow me."

Vescus took Cana by the hand and led her through the darkness. At the end of the passage was a small square room with a round table on which stood a candelabra and an empty goblet. The ceiling was a series of wide floorboards set upon a foundation of intersecting beams. Vescus got up on the table and pressed on a few of the boards. The floorboard closest to the right wall creaked, and, with a single thrust, Vescus pushed it up.

Standing on his clawed toes, Vescus stuck his head through the opening and took Cana's hand. "Let me help you up," he said.

Cana let him lift her through the opening. He followed her and put the board back.

The sound of feet on the basement stairway echoed like broken piano keys. "Enius is dead! Vescus is gone!" Pelagus shouted.

The guards surrounding the house broke formation and moved away. The dead guards were nowhere in sight.

Cana pointed to the doorknob, and Vescus shook his snout once and pointed to the window. Out of the woods stepped a handful of Takers Cana had never seen before. The pack moved back and forth in an unsynchronized swarm. Their yellow eye-shine told Cana that they had already tasted human flesh and now had an insatiable craving for it.

The Takers crossed the open space between the orchard and the house toward the backyard. They were nearly out of sight when a straggler stopped and turned to the workshop.

Vescus tensed and tightened his grip on Cana's shoulder.

The Taker sniffed the ground and disappeared around the edge of the house.

"That hurt, Vescus."

"I know. He would have heard you if you'd moved."

Cana rubbed her shoulder. "How do you know?"

"Because I would have, too. We need to hurry."

Vescus led them out of the workshop and into the shadow of the apple grove. They hadn't gone far when Vescus stopped.

"Do you hear something?" asked Cana.

"I hear shouts from the direction of the lookout."

"It's Atius. Atellus knows he's alive."

"Why can't that man just stay hidden?" Vescus cursed.

"Like you?"

Vescus squinted disagreeably but said nothing.

"We've got to help him, Vescus. Come on."

Vescus followed Cana down to the stream above the grist-mill. He lapped up the water greedily and waded across a deep pool.

"Watch out," he said, shaking the water from his body like

a giant wolf. Leaves and other detritus covered the bank, and Vescus exposed the deeper layers with his paws and rolled his entire body in the earth.

"Great, now you smell like dirt."

"You should do the same. They will follow our scent."

"I'll roll in the leaves, but if you think I'm going in that freezing water, you're crazy."

Vescus pawed away a fresh pile of leaves and rolled Cana back and forth over it.

"Alright?" she asked.

Vescus smelled her and rolled her back and forth a few more times. "There," he said, dropping a handful of leaves on Cana's head.

She grinned. "Let's go."

Cana ran along the side of the stream, while Vescus hopped from boulder to boulder. They had not gone far when Vescus jumped in front of Cana's path.

"Hey, what gives?"

"Someone is hiding ahead. He smells like the lake."

"I bet it's Urms. He helped me get into the house. Where is he?"

Vescus gestured ahead with his muzzle, and Cana squinted but saw nothing. She motioned for Vescus to 'stay' and stepped forward.

"It's too dangerous, Cana," Vescus objected.

"Stay," she said emphatically.

The skin on Vescus's muzzle creased, but he did as Cana said.

"Urms is that you out there? This is my friend Vescus I told you about. Hello?"

A hand reached out from behind a tree and grabbed Cana by the collar. "You won't have her, beast."

"Hurt her, and I'll pull your heart through your gills," Vescus snarled.

"Let go, Urms." She shook him off. "This is my friend, Vescus."

"Your friend is a Taker?"

Cana hesitated. "Yeah, but he's only been like this for a few days."

"Cana, you can't trust him. He's not a person anymore. He will hurt you."

"No Urms. Look at his eyes. They aren't yellow."

Urms looked. "Why does that matter?"

"If a Taker eats people their eyes turn yellow."

"It's true," said Vescus. "If a Taker tastes human flesh, it changes them and they serve only their hunger."

"You must come with me, Cana. The monster has you jinxed."

"No, Urms. If Vescus were going to hurt me, he would already have done it."

"You don't know that."

"No, but I do," said Vescus.

"Cana?" Urms held out his hand.

Cana took up position beside Vescus and placed her hand on his shaggy shoulder. "My choice."

Urms backed away. "And what of Arwa? Is she dead?"

"No, she's alive, Urms. I overheard her talking to Furius, but we couldn't get to her. I'm sorry."

"No, you had another errand. Goodbye, Cana."

"Wait, Urms. Atius, Icabus's father, is in trouble. We could use your help."

Urms shook his head. "I've already done too much to endanger Arwa."

"Go hide in your lake then. That's what your kind has done so far." Vescus glared at Urms.

Urms raised his sword, and Vescus exposed his teeth. Cana stepped between them.

"No, I won't let you both fight." She turned to Vescus. "Please."

Vescus closed his mouth, and his gaze softened.

Cana raised her hands to Urms. "Stop it, Urms."

Urms returned his sword to its sheath. "Goodbye, Cana. I do not think we will see each other again."

Vescus leaned over and whispered in Cana's ear. "Can I eat him now?"

FURIUS

"Furius? Are you hurt?" Pelagus called out.

Furius stumbled down the stairs. He fell against the door and unbolted the latch. The door swung open.

Pelagus caught him. "Furius!"

Furius steadied himself on the doorframe. "Search the house. Someone locked the door from within."

Behind Pelagus, a handful of soldiers drew their swords and entered the house. "Sir, the rear door is locked as well," one soldier shouted from the kitchen.

"Check the basement!" Furius ordered.

More soldiers were coming toward the house, and Arkax crept out from the woods, yellow eyes blazing. Behind him, the young Takers fanned out in the shadows.

"Sir," screamed a soldier. "Enius is dead! Vescus is gone!"

"The doors to the house are locked! Find them!" Furius shouted.

The soldiers cleared a path for Arkax. Walking beside the beast, his men looked puny and insignificant. Arkax sniffed Furius and fixated on his trousers. "Had a scare, I see."

"Vescus has escaped. Put your nose to good use and find him."

Arkax nodded to Pelagus, who barked and sprinted around the back of the house. The young Takers followed in tow.

"If you ever give me an order like that again, Furius, I'll make sure you lose more than your dignity." Arkax pushed past the Authian king and lumbered down the stairs, sniffing the air. A moment later, he reappeared with a piece of Enius's severed leg in his mouth. "There's a secret passage beneath leading to the shed."

"Aren't you going after him?" Furius asked.

"Why? If Pelagus finds him, the young ones can practice dismembering him and the girl."

"Girl?"

Arkax leaned past Furius and sniffed the door latch. "Her stench is everywhere. She's of childbearing age now. A shame. It spoils the meat."

"You got all that from a door latch?"

"As I said, her scent is everywhere." He sniffed Furius. "Except on you. You have another's scent on you. How did Arwa hurt you?"

Furius wiped his cheek with his hand and looked at it. "I don't know. All of a sudden, I just felt very sick."

Arkax licked his chops. "You should let me talk to her. I'm tired of this foreplay."

"That's not our arrangement. Once you lead me to the Golden Land, she's yours. Unless you can't deliver."

"We're almost ready," said Arkax. "Vescus's blood is still down there. Use it."

"I plan to. Atellus is about to crush Atius's little insurrection. I'll prepare more potion and turn the rest of the village brats. Once you have your Takers, I want to move on the gate. I despise this village."

"Fine." Arkax sauntered back toward the woods.

Furius leaned against the doorframe. Three soldiers scurried to his side.

"Draw me a bath," Furius directed. "The rest of you clean this house. I'm not Galen; I won't live in a troll pit."

"Yes, sir," said the men, out of unison. They scurried off, and Furius shut the door. His body felt tired and overworked.

"Not much longer," Galen's voice whispered. *"Not much longer at all."*

ICABUS

Icabus wiped the sweat from his brow. Around him, the ferns drooped, and the ground crunched under his feet like crackers. Ahead of him, the tracks of the Vlorka were no more than indistinct dust puddles. Luckily, he knew where he was going.

"Two on the left, one on the right."

Icabus spun around. No one was there.

"Gosh, I'm starting to hear things. That sounded like the Water Spirit."

"Behind you—two left, one right. Pull your sword! Turn!"

Icabus pulled his sword and swung around just as two spear-bearing Vlorka jumped from the foliage. They landed within striking distance and simultaneously thrust their spears at his chest.

Fast as water, Icabus pulled left, and the spears crossed. He drew his sword across his body and decapitated the sharp ends of the spears, causing the Vlorka to hiss and bound backward.

"Behind you! Duck!"

Icabus did, and a spear whizzed past his right ear and stuck squarely in the bark of a redwood. The other two Vlorka were gone.

"What the heck? What kind of welcome was that?" Icabus panted. "That definitely wasn't an official challenge. It was more like an assassination."

Icabus poked around in the ferns with his sword. "Water Spirit? Gods, the heat must be making me hallucinate."

Icabus released the spear from the tree and examined its shaft. The dart was dark and indistinct save for a row of small glyphs carved from its base to mid-shaft. He lopped off the pointed end and rapped its blunt end against the earth. “At least now I have a walking stick. We’ll see what Zrilla has to say about it.”

Warning barks announced Icabus’s arrival at the village. Three Vlorkan warriors appeared from the shrubbery, including a particular guard from House Ker Icabus cared not to remember and Zrilla’s brother Sercxal, who showed his teeth in a thorny grin. Icabus wished he had such an impressive smile.

“Hi,” Icabus said.

Sercxal eyed Icabus’s walking stick, and his grin vanished. He grabbed the stick, fingered the runes on its shaft, and barked a few orders to the other Vlorka, who disappeared into the underbrush. Icabus heard a succession of barks and hisses as the perimeter guards were alerted to danger. Sercxal handed back the broken spear and looked Icabus over.

Icabus lifted his hands and turned around in place. “Don’t worry, I’m all in one piece.”

Sercxal nodded, and his sharp grin returned. He patted Icabus on the shoulder and hissed something that sounded congratulatory, but Icabus wasn’t sure.

“Where’s Zrilla?” Icabus asked.

“Zrilla,” Sercxal repeated with a backward nod of his scaly head.

Icabus understood the gesture and followed Sercxal into the heart of the village.

GIZA

Ripples of heat blurred the First Tree like a mirage. Zrilla and the old shaman lizard, Giza, sat on their haunches in the shade. The old lizard rattled a handful of bones between her long fingers and dropped them between her clawed feet.

"Icabus is here."

Zrilla looked surprised. "You see that in the bones?"

"No, he's walking up behind you."

Zrilla hissed and turned her head.

Icabus tried not to smile too broadly. "Queen Zrilla." He exposed his neck.

"You're becoming as quiet as Nubis. What's that you're carrying?"

"I was hoping you could tell me. Sercxal seemed to recognize it, didn't you, Sercxal?"

Icabus handed the spear to Zrilla, and Giza quickly grabbed it from her hands. The old lizard said something to Sercxal in Vlorkish. His reply made Zrilla's eyes widen.

Zrilla rose to her toes. "Are you uninjured?" She turned him around and moved his head from side to side with her hand.

"Yes, I'm fine. Sercxal already examined me. I hope that's the last group of Vlorka I'll be fighting today."

Giza grunted. She traced the runes with her claws and handed the spear shaft to Zrilla. "Lost tribe."

"Lost tribe?" Icabus raised an eyebrow.

"A story to scare children, or so I thought." Zrilla stared off into the woods.

"They are quite real," said Giza. "They are the remnants of the Vlorkan families whose bloodlines ended when the Takers came. They have sworn an oath to destroy any creature that threatens the Spirits."

The old lizard looked again at the bones between her toes. "You didn't kill any of them."

Icabus wasn't sure if it was a question or a statement of fact. "No, they fled after their ambush failed."

Sercxal spoke up, and Zrilla translated. "Warriors led by the tracker Erilla have been sent to intercept."

"That will accomplish nothing." Giza waved her hand. "The scent of these Vlorka is the forest itself. You may as well go searching for a tree."

"Should we warn Nubis?" Icabus asked.

Giza scooped up the bones and tossed them again. She grumbled and repeated the act. "These Vlorka are no threat to him."

"Why did you toss the bones twice? Is something wrong?" Icabus asked.

The old lizard picked up the bones one by one and placed them in her bag. "There is only one threat to your master's life, and it is you."

"Me?"

"Him?" Zrilla eyed Icabus.

Giza grunted. "I said nothing because the threat is unclear. The bones show drastic change. That usually means death."

Icabus lowered his head. "Are the bones ever wrong?"

"The bones show possibilities—that is all."

"Then this fate can be avoided?"

Giza placed the last bone in her satchel and scratched a rune into the dust. "You choose your path every day."

"Zrilla..." Icabus looked to her.

"What?" she answered curtly.

"You know I wouldn't knowingly threaten Nubis's life."

Zrilla cursed something in Vlorkish and flicked her tail. "He is a free being, just as you and I. We cannot make decisions for him."

Giza nodded. "Yes, don't be naïve. In the end, all paths lead to death. It is far more important to choose how best to live than how best to die. The wise prefer to live well rather than long."

Icabus looked at his feet. "So, why am I here?"

"You have been requested by the Spirits. Since their return from the Spirit City, they have allowed no one to enter the First Tree. They have barred their minds to me and sealed the passage until now."

"They must have taken the death of the Water Spirit badly," said Icabus.

Giza regarded him gravely. "To harm a Spirit is forbidden, and you have killed two. Our queen will not hear my words, but she cannot deny the will of the Spirits."

"Am I here to be punished?" Icabus asked Zrilla.

"I do not know the will of the Spirits. Nor does Giza know it." She regarded the old shaman lizard sternly.

Giza growled under her breath. "I do know it. As I know the creature Shrail will also have to answer for his part in this crime."

"No, he won't." Icabus came toe to claw with her. "If anything happens to Shrail, I'll make sure justice comes to you, law or no law."

The old lizard twitched her tail. "That is what I thought you'd say."

"Good. Then we understand each other. I think I will see the Spirits now."

Icabus crossed her path, and Giza pinned him against the bark. She closed her fingers around his neck, and Icabus could feel the throb of her heartbeat through her scales.

"If you harm the Spirits, I will spill your guts," she hissed.

"Giza!" Zrilla gasped, raising her spear to the shaman's neck.

"Be still, My Queen. I have sworn to protect you, but my fealty also extends to the Spirits."

"And to the lost tribe?" Icabus choked.

Giza flared her nostrils, exposing the rosy flesh within. "I am not yet too old to forget the suffering your kind brought to this land. I survived the fall of the Spirit City within an inch of my life. I was only a child, but I remember."

An impossible memory arose in Icabus's mind. "Wait... You're the child the Water Spirit rescued the day the Spirit City fell? The earth had opened up in the rotten hallows, and he carried you to safety. You were so afraid that you drank of his essence. A part of him is still inside you."

The old lizard slackened her hold. Moisture glistened around her eyes and dampened her moss colored scales. "Impossible. You can't know that."

"He's a part of me now, too, Giza. If you kill me, you kill him, too."

Giza pushed Icabus aside and let out a piercing cry.

Icabus touched the end of Zrilla's spear, and she lowered it. He lifted his hand to Giza's shoulder, but she evaded his touch and raised her neck.

"My sacred oath is broken. I have shamed the Vlorka and the Spirits. I accept your judgment, My Queen."

"You dishonor me, but it is to Icabus that your disgrace is greatest. Your punishment is his to decide."

Icabus picked up Giza's spear and undid the leather wrapping along the shaft. Glyphs similar to those of the lost tribesman's spear lay hidden beneath. Icabus examined the glyphs and ran his fingers down the worn shaft. "I accept your spear, Giza, and I return it to you," he said, extending the spear to her with both hands.

Giza lowered her snout. Her diamond pupils widened, and she searched Icabus's countenance with disbelief. She took the spear with a trembling hand.

"You forgive her?" Zrilla gasped. "She tried to have you killed! At the least, you should banish her."

"I know what it feels like to lose everything, Zrilla. I can't do that."

Zrilla struck her spear against the earth. "Something must be done. I cannot lead when my shaman subverts my orders and commands a lost tribe against us."

"How about you let them come home? Let the lost tribe form a new house and swear fealty to you," Icabus suggested.

"Why would they want to do that?" Zrilla scoffed.

"Because they are lost," whispered Giza.

Zrilla cursed in Vlorkish and scratched the earth with her toe claws.

"Zrilla, I know I am no longer king, and I am young, but as a friend, please consider my request. I would be in your debt."

"You are beginning to act like Nubis," Zrilla hissed. "Whenever I'm sure I've figured him out, he surprises me. I'm not yet as skilled a leader as I hoped to be.

"Stand, Giza. If I accept the lost ones, you will pass your authority over them to me?"

Giza raised her head. "I will."

"Then I will not banish you, despite my wish to. I want this new house presented to me before the next twin moon."

Giza bowed, and Icabus smiled weakly. Zrilla shook her head at him and said, "I would not keep the Spirits waiting."

ATELLUS

Atellus knew Gurges was dead.

Some people had an intuition when it would rain. Others could sense droughts or earthquakes. Atellus could sense death. Even as a boy, Gurges had been a fiend. Atellus knew such vice would eventually lead to ruin. For better or worse, Gurges was always there when Atellus needed him, and now he was gone.

"Hail, Atellus," said a soldier, raising his spear in salute.

Atellus entered the firelight and sat beside the man. He was fat and bearded, with a missing right eye covered by a poorly fitting patch.

"Fish," said the soldier, lifting an already cooked fillet at his side.

Atellus took it and swallowed it in two bites. "Thanks, Morelius. How are things here in town?"

Morelius looked over his shoulders and laughed. "Quiet. So far. You seem troubled."

"Gurges is dead. There is no body, but I know it."

Morelius pulled a fish from his spear, bit off its head, and spit it into the fire. "I see. I remember when we were all boys. He was a bastard even then. If not for you, he'd have been hung by the neck long ago."

"Aye, a bastard he was," Atellus remarked, with a weak smile. "Did you know Furius back then, before the war?"

"No. Suppose not many did. His father was grooming him to lead as yours was grooming you to be his stable master."

Atellus looked at the dirt. "Those times are only a dream to me now. Marius and Arx Caeli made sure of that."

"They did, but we'll have our vengeance. Galen said the power to destroy Arx Caeli was in the Golden Land. Do you doubt it?"

Atellus regarded him. "I think there is power there," he said, noting the concern in the man's remaining eye, "but not the kind we think."

Atellus tossed a stick into the fire and watched it sizzle. He understood now why Galen wanted them to destroy Aggersel. In the dungeons of Arx Caeli, they were only martyrs imprisoned for defending their homeland. Galen made them murderers. Why? Because Galen needed an army, and not just any army—an army of Takers like Arkax. That was Galen's dirty little secret: immortality with a hairy price. Atellus wouldn't have it.

"I gather you're not here for conversation, Atellus." Morelius offered him another fish.

Atellus waved his hand. "Conversation was never one of my strong points. I need a hand with a loose end before we push ahead for good."

"Does your problem bear a sword?"

"Well, if he did, it probably wouldn't help him, but he is more cunning than most."

Morelius's left eye flickered in the firelight. "I'm intrigued. Anyone, I know?"

"Atius."

Morelius choked. "He's still alive?"

Atellus patted Morelius on the back. "Aye."

"Cursed be the Gods. We lost many comrades in the fire. What I would give to put my ax between that man's eyes. Sword wielder or not, Atius is not one to be underestimated."

"Agreed." Atellus stood.

Morelius cleared his throat. "Authians! Commander Atellus needs our spears. Let us not forget our oaths."

The men around the fire rose up and struck their spears against the earth. At one time, Atellus would have taken pride in such customary signs of respect, but no longer. Such pageantry only reinforced his hopelessness. For who would follow a man like him unless they were either a fool or damned?

"Where to?" Morelius stood at attention.

Atellus pointed to the darkened orchards. "On that hill is a lookout that faces the Old Kingdom and the lake. Atius and the other traitors are up there right now planning our destruction. Furius commands that we end this little insurrection. What say you?"

"Death to the traitors!" Morelius cried.

"Death to the traitors!" the men repeated.

ICABUS

"*Bring her,*" the Water Spirit spoke in Icabus's mind.

"I want you to come with me, Giza," said Icabus.

The old lizard looked surprised. "I've not been summoned."

"You have. You just don't know it." Icabus extended his hand.

Giza hesitated and took Icabus's hand. The passage into the center of the tree smelled sweet like orange oil. Icabus felt a strange sense of elation he could not explain. He smiled at Giza and said, "It feels like waves of energy are moving through my body."

Giza hummed contentedly. "This is how I remember the mana flow as a child. It is returning."

"Is it dangerous?"

"No, being in tune with the source can extend life and prevent illness."

"Giza, why are those of us who pass through the gate so sensitive to mana's effects?"

"I believe your land is old, and the mana source there is deep or no longer exists. For you, being in this land is like giving a malnourished lizard a king's feast and expecting him not to grow."

Icabus nodded. "Giza, what happened to the Spirits when the source was damaged?"

"When the source receded and the mana springs dried up, many Spirits could no longer hold their mind essences together and became elemental earth, fire, water, and air. I wish you could have known our world before the Takers came. You would have marveled at it."

Icabus smiled. "I'm marveling right now."

In the hollow center of the tree, a gossamer web of leaves, supported by some unknown energy, filtered the sunlight in a natural kaleidoscope. The Air Spirits, who appeared in the form of the Elders, stood with their backs to Icabus around a pedestaled stone basin.

"Icabus," said Maro, smiling wearily. He appeared just as Icabus remembered him, with long grey hair and airy white robes bordered with green embroidery.

The other Elders turned to Icabus and smiled, save for Vetus, who only furrowed his brow. Their faces looked gaunt and pale, as if under a terrible strain.

"We did not call you, shaman." Vetus glared at Giza.

"The Water Spirit asked her to come," said Icabus.

The Elders exchanged curious glances, and Silana waved them forward. "Come close; there is little time," she said.

Icabus and Giza stepped between Maro and Ralla and closed the circle. The large woman embraced Icabus, and he momentarily got lost in the warmth of her rose-scented bosom.

Cilo pointed to the bottom of the basin, where a glistening pool of water undulated. "This is all of the Water Spirit's essence we could recover from the Spirit City. We've used our energy to maintain it, but it continues to evaporate. Soon it will be gone."

"For a Spirit, body and mind are inseparable," said Maro. "When our brother used his essence to extinguish the Fire Spirit, he willingly sacrificed his memory of beginning, which is what binds any Spirit together."

"We have tried to give him our memories, but those of an Air Spirit are different than a Water Spirit's," Ralla sighed.

"And he is the last of his kind?" Giza touched the edge of the basin.

"Yes," said Vetus. "He is the last. With him ends the line of Water."

Maro regarded Icabus. "We asked you to come, Icabus, because we found a strange memory in this water, a human memory of us."

Icabus stared at the Spirit's essence. "After the battle, I tried to join with the Water Spirit as Prax did with the Fire Spirit, but something went wrong, and when I woke up I couldn't sense him anymore."

"Maybe it did work. Give me your hand," said Vetus.

Icabus extended his hand, and Vetus pulled an obsidian blade from his cloak and cut into Icabus's palm. Icabus tried to pull away, but Vetus held his wrist. Blood mixed with the clear essence in the basin, staining it red.

"I'm sorry. I was wrong," said Vetus, releasing his wrist.

"Gods, why did you do that?" Icabus closed his fingers over the wound.

"Oh dear." Ralla cupped Icabus's injured palm in her own. Blood trickled from between his fingers, but washing it away was clear water.

"Gods, he's bleeding water!" Cilo gasped.

Ralla held his hand over the basin as a rush of alien memories moved through him. The world as he knew it fell away, and he found himself aware of himself not as a product of elements but as only water and space.

Icabus could feel the mana channels running through the earth. Everything–land, plant, animal, light, and space–he perceived through its sum of mana, which reverberated through the different elements in waves of energy.

"Icabus, open your eyes," said the Water Spirit.

Icabus blinked and laughed at the sensation. "I feel like I haven't used my eyelids in ages."

"I must agree with you. It is a strange sensation," said the Water Spirit, blinking.

Icabus rubbed his eyes. "You are me, or is this a mirror?"

"We are now a part of each other," said the Spirit. "Goodbye."

Icabus's vision blurred, and he heard Maro's voice calling to him. The Elder's face came into focus, and he felt Ralla's breast brush against his cheek. "He's waking up," she said.

Maro stood and placed his hand over the Water Spirit's essence, and it shuddered. "Too little essence remains. Even with our collective strength, we cannot restore the Spirit."

"Great Air Spirit," Giza addressed Maro. "When I was young, this Spirit saved my life. In my fear, I swallowed part of him that day, and it has given me the gift of many life cycles. I would let you draw this water from me if it might save the old one."

Maro searched her eyes. "If you do this, you may die or age naturally. Are you willing to make this sacrifice?"

Giza nodded and looked to Icabus. "My life's work is almost complete, thanks to the wisdom and forgiveness of others."

"Give me your hand," said Vetus.

Giza did, and Vetus cut into it with the obsidian blade. The old shaman didn't flinch, and the water poured from the wound with only a few drops of blood.

Beneath them, the earth began to shake, and Icabus fell forward onto a patch of grass. Above him, the leaves dropped from their spectral web as the Air Spirits broke their circle.

"Get away, Icabus," said Silana.

"Hold the circle," cried Vetus.

Giza lifted Icabus and pulled him back just as the earth beneath him fissured and fell away. The rock pedestal holding the Water Spirit's basin cracked, dumping the essence into the soil.

"No!" Ralla reached out.

Around the pit, the plants browned as moisture left the earth. Icabus choked, feeling his own water drawn away.

"Look!" Silana screamed.

A pillar of water grew out from the pit. Vetus, Cilo, and Ralla surrounded the water, and Icabus felt his strength return. "See my mind, brother," said Cilo. "We mean you no harm."

A jet of water struck Cilo against the chest, dashing him against the bark of the First Tree. Vetus and Ralla moved in, and the Water Spirit cut them down with a watery scythe.

"Icabus, Giza, run!" Silana stood between them and the Spirit. A band of water seized Silana by the neck and struck her against the bark of the First Tree, causing her human form to fade into air.

"Stop!" Icabus cried.

"Little Taker!" The Water Spirit pressed him against the ground.

"What are you doing?" Icabus's words were hoarse and barely audible.

"You steal my water and use these Spirits to attack me. The Takers must die."

"I am not a Taker. I... am... your... friend."

"Lies!"

"No, not lies, great Spirit." Giza raised her hands. "Do you remember me? I was the Vlorkan child you saved from the fall of the Spirit City. The boiling water was touching my scales, and you rose up and carried me to safety. Do you not remember?"

"I remember such a one, but she took essence from me, and I sense naught in you. Do not deceive me!"

"The essence I took is returned. Look within yourself, and you will know it to be true. This human, whom you call a Taker, saved you from death. He risked his life to restore you. Do not kill him. He is your ally."

Silence fell between Giza, Icabus, and the Water Spirit. The weight of the Spirit was still upon Icabus, but the hold lessened, and he no longer felt as weak as he had a moment before.

The water over the Spirit's body rippled. "Impossible... these memories."

"Wait!" Icabus reached up, but the Spirit passed over him like a wave drawing itself up the bark and out of the hollow center of the tree.

"Let him go," hissed Giza. "He is confused and not himself."

Icabus stood using the bark of the First Tree, and Giza rose on her toes. Silana materialized next to Icabus and looked him over. Behind Icabus, a familiar spear poked its head through the dark entrance.

"Hi, Zrilla." Icabus brushed himself off.

"Icabus, what happened? The sounds were terrible, and then I saw..." Zrilla lowered her spear and brushed the dirt and grass off Icabus. "Icabus, who are these humans?"

"The Air Spirits. How do they normally appear to you?"

"As my ancestors," said Zrilla. "Are these humans your ancestors?"

"No, they are the leaders of my village whom Furius killed. That's Maro, Silana, Cilo, Ralla, and not to mention Vetus."

"Don't mention it," Vetus said gruffly.

Ralla passed her fingers through her curly hair. "Are you hurt, Icabus?"

"I'm not hurt. Are you all alright?"

The Spirits nodded.

"What happened?" Icabus asked.

Maro scratched his head. "It worked, I think."

ATIUS

"Gotcha," Atius whispered. He aimed the arrow at Atellus's head and released his bowstring.

Morelius stepped in front of Atellus and the dart bisected the bearded man's neck, painting Atellus in blood.

"It's a trap!" Atellus cried, diving into the leaves.

Atius cursed and drew another arrow. The three soldiers in Atellus's guard fanned out. Caius shot one through the eye, whilst another soldier retreated toward the canyon where Caelius sprung from the shadows and stabbed him in the heart.

"Where's Atellus?" Atius fired an arrow into the leg of a last soldier. The man cried out in agony, and Caelius ended him with a cut across the neck.

"I see him; he's climbing through the fig tree." Caius aimed his bow at the thicket.

"Save your arrows?" Atius touched Caius's hand. "There's only one way out of that thicket, and that's over the cliff facing the Old Kingdom. Unless Atellus has a death wish, he won't be doing that."

"Where'd he go?" Caelius ran forward, panting.

A single yelp sounded over the cliff edge.

"Gods, did he fall?" Caius released the tension on his bow string.

"I think I heard a branch break," said Caelius.

"Aye. Come on," said Atius. "We need to make sure he's dead."

"Oh, Gods." Caelius turned around and froze.

Five pairs of yellow eyes glowed in the darkness of the canyon. Crossing in front of them was a badly burned creature with only one eye.

"Pelagus?" Atius held his ground.

"In the flesh, or what's left of it, Atius. Did you kill Furius's favorite servant? Don't tell me he got away."

"Atellus fell. What do you want?"

"Not you, surprisingly. Have you seen Vescus?"

"No." Atius pulled out his sword. "Be gone with you."

"Or what?" growled Pelagus, shifting his gaze to Caius and Caelius. "Hello, old friends. Don't you have anything to say to your old pal, Pelagus? You know, I was going to feed your sister to my hungry pups, but you two will do just fine."

"Try it." Caelius raised his sword.

Pelagus rolled his eye and barked at the Takers behind him, who spread out. "You may wound one of us if you're lucky, but you'll never get off another shot. I look forward to finding out what your bones taste like."

VESCUS

From where he hid, Vescus could see everything; he saw Caelius and Caius bring down Atellus's men and Pelagus and the other Takers approach. He knew Cana could not see any of it. Part of him wanted just to watch and wait. Caelius and Caius might get off one shot, but in the end, they'd die. Atius might survive the night long enough to be tortured and turned into a Taker. The truth was Vescus didn't care much about humans anymore. In fact, the only thing holding him to this human world was Cana, and how she felt mattered to him.

"Do you trust me?" he asked Cana.

"Yeah, why?"

"Atius and your brothers are up there. Pelagus has them surrounded. I need you to count to one hundred and go to them, but not before then."

Cana grabbed his hairy arm. "No. Where are you going?"

"I'll lead them to the lake. Maybe your fish-head friend, Urms, will pick one or two off on the way."

She grabbed Vescus around the neck and held him. "Come back."

"I will if I can," he said, resting his long snout against her back. "Now start counting."

Holding the Takers in his peripheral vision, Vescus bounded down the hill toward the mill. Pelagus swung his head around and growled.

"It's Vescus. Get him!"

Moonlight washed over Vescus as he broke from the orchard onto the lake road. The pack of Takers emerged from the tree line, and Vescus cut into the reeds.

The floating trees drifted near, and Vescus allowed his lips to curl back in a monstrous smile. These Takers were young and energetic but not yet wise.

Cold lake water touched Vescus's toes, and he froze, allowing the nearest Taker to leap toward him. Vescus could see the hunger in the monster's eyes, the all-consuming moment of satisfaction that comes right before you get what you want. Then it was over.

Vescus fell to his side, and the Taker's head landed in his lap, jaws still biting. Its body lay limp in a bed of mowed reeds. The weapon that had severed the Taker's head spun overhead and arced back to the lake. Several others whirred above him, clearing paths of reeds and dismembering any Taker within reach.

"You," said a voice behind Vescus.

He turned and saw his reflection in the moonlit blade.

Urms looked at him with distaste. "Where's the girl?"

Vescus considered having one last go at the lake boy's neck but resisted. "On the hill with her brothers."

"Is she safe?" Urms pressed the blade to Vescus's neck.

"Now that I'm gone, she is."

Urms's expression briefly softened, then he pushed the cutting edge of the blade to Vescus's skin, drawing blood. "Where are you leading these Takers?"

"To you, to die. I'm too weak to fight."

"I don't believe you. You are a Taker the same as them. There is nothing you can say I can trust."

"Behind you!"

The Taker in the reeds pounced, driving Urms to the ground. Urms's blade fell from his hand into the mud.

"Vescus," said the Taker. "Do you recognize me?"

Vescus sniffed the air. The stench of lake mud and old fire made his nose almost useless, but the Taker's scent was stronger still.

"Artus?"

"In the flesh." Artus bowed. "Pelagus wants you dead, but I'm having too much fun. I'll give you a head start while I have this little snack. Go!"

Vescus snarled and slunk into the reeds.

Artus turned back Urms. "You should have killed him faster."

"Yes, he should have," said Vescus, wielding Urms's blade with two hands and decapitating Artus where he stood. The headless body convulsed and fell into the mud. Vescus lingered just long enough to savor the surprise on Urms's face before dropping the lake boy's blade and slinking into the darkness.

The lake road was dark, and Pelagus was out of sight. The floating trees drifted back from the shore, indicating the Gilians' retreat.

Vescus sat in the shadows and swallowed forest mice as they attempted to cross the lake road. A heavy mist already covered the lake and would soon come ashore and give him the cover he needed to enter the Old Kingdom. For now, he was happy just to rest and feast on the mice.

ATELLUS

Atellus watched as Vescus tossed mice into the air and silenced them with his jaws. To Atellus's surprise, and subconscious dismay, the fall had not killed him. In fact, he had barely suffered a scratch. A bramble of thornless prairie vine cushioned his fall like a feather pillow.

When he first saw the commotion by the lake, Atellus thought he should run, but the survivalist in him told him otherwise, and now he stared his enemy in the back while Vescus gorged himself on field mice. Atellus thought he was going to be sick.

After what felt like an eternity, Vescus sauntered off toward the Old Kingdom on all fours. Atellus brushed himself off and reached for his sword, which was missing. He looked around briefly, cursing himself for losing his blade, and crossed the road. He hadn't gone far before he found the severed hand of a Taker amid the reeds. Whatever happened down here was a massacre.

"Atellus," came a growl from across the road.

Atellus jumped and reached instinctually for his sword.

Pelagus's wolf-like head appeared in the underbrush. "Come here."

Atellus hesitated and crossed the road. Behind Pelagus, one Taker held the stump of a missing hand, while another licked a laceration on his shoulder.

"What happened to his hand?" Atellus asked.

Pelagus stalked back and forth. "He lost it."

"Yes, I see that. How many were you?"

"Five. The rest are dead. Did you see Vescus?"

"Aye. He went off toward the Old Kingdom.

"We should return to town. Your companion is going to bleed out unless you cauterize that wound."

Pelagus gave Atellus a hateful, hungry look. Atellus didn't care whether Pelagus or any of these monsters were alive or dead. He reasoned any place was safer than in the dark with a bunch of homicidal Takers.

"Arkax will be expecting us. We need to return to Atius's house. Do what you will. Come on, you stupid beasts," Pelagus growled.

Atellus watched them go, and he set off to town. He stopped before the well and splashed water on his face. His clothes stunk of stress and detritus. The odors oppressed him, but a part of him didn't care.

Atius had escaped his grasp; Atius's wife, Lucia, would not. He would have her whether she wished it or not. Atellus only hoped Atius lived long enough to know the anguish of his loss—a loss Atellus lived with every day.

"Sir, is that you?"

Atellus lifted his face from his hands.

Minius looked at him with wide eyes. Behind him were Salvius and Seius. "I heard you went off with Morelius. Where is he?"

"Dead," Atellus laughed, rubbing his eyes.

Salvius's jaw dropped. "Dead? How?"

"Atius and the Corvan boys ambushed us. Even Furius's furry freaks got sliced and diced. It was a bloodbath."

"The Gods have spared you," Seius said.

"The Gods." Atellus shook his head with a chuckle. "The Gods mock me!"

The men fell silent.

Atellus glowered. "All of us should have died in the dungeons of Arx Caeli. At least then we were men. At least then the name Authian stood for something."

"But what of our revenge?" asked Salvius.

"Revenge." Atellus's voice fell. "None of us are ever going to leave this island. Don't you see that? This is hell."

Minius shook his head and began to protest, but Seius placed his hand on his shoulder, silencing him.

Salvius kicked the dirt. "I'm used to hearing this garbage from Seius but not you, Atellus."

Seius took up position beside Atellus. "The Gods have a plan for us all. You will see."

Minius threw up his hands. "I'm tired of hearing about the damned Gods! I'm getting a drink. Salvius?"

Salvius stroked his beard and eyed Atellus. "Aye. I'm coming."

Atellus laughed half-heartedly as the two men moved off into the shadows. "You should join them, Seius."

"Nay. Come with me to the gate."

Atellus glared at him through the strands of his dirty brown hair. He saw in Seius's eyes the reflection of his own emptiness, but there was a glimmer there that Atellus did not share, something he had lost along the way. "Why do you want to do that?"

"Atonement."

Atellus regarded the mountain in silence. He could not believe he was considering it.

"The beast lies," said Seius. "He is not the gatekeeper. He is a castoff like Galen. I wish to profess my sins to the true gatekeeper. What he does with me is beyond my will."

"And, what if there's nothing up there? No gate. No gatekeeper. Just the beast."

"Then he may have me. I deserve no better."

"Are you willing to fight your way there?" asked Atellus.

"Aye."

"What of Furius?"

"The Gods have a path for him, too," Seius replied.

"As long as his path and our path don't cross in the next hour, then I'm satisfied," Atellus remarked.

Seius nodded.

Atellus shook his head with fatalistic abandon and raised his face to the heavens. "Find me a sword and meet me where the orchards, wheat fields, and forest come together in an hour. I need to collect something for our journey."

"As you wish. There are more swords about than men to carry them."

"Then bring me two lest I lose another." Atellus smirked with a touch of madness in his eyes.

ATIUS

"Atellus's gone. You can see where he fell. Lucky devil, and look, here's his sword." Caius pulled the blade from the branches and handed it to Atius.

Atius swung the sword at a clump of vines. "He couldn't have gone far. If only my aim were better."

"The rest are dead," said Caelius. "That has to count for something."

Atius looked past them, searching the foggy darkness. "The more of Atellus's men we kill, the more dangerous Furius will become."

"And the more arrows I have, the more dangerous I will become," Caius said with a smile. "Admit it, Atius. It was a good victory. And it didn't cost you your life or freedom. Let us see if our father has done his part and convinced others to fight with us."

Atius smiled weakly and placed his hand on Cana's shoulder. "Vescus is craftier than either of us. He'll be fine. Come."

A single lantern burned outside Corvus's barn. The fields around it were quiet and covered in a layer of mist. To the south, the Old Kingdom's guarding wall rose like a nameless tombstone. A goat bell sounded somewhere between and then fell silent.

"Are you sure no one followed us?" asked Atius.

"Only the crows." Caius pointed.

A murder of crows roosted in a dead walnut tree behind Corvus's house. At the center of the group was a huge crow.

Caelius rapped his fist against the barn door recreating a rhythm Atius knew from childhood. After a moment, the door creaked open, and Corvus's pale face appeared.

"Cana? What are you doing here? Is Lucia alright, Atius?" Corvus asked.

"Aye, Cana and Vescus found us. A good thing, too, because he saved your sons and me."

Corvus frowned and embraced his daughter. "Tell me about it later. All of you inside."

The barn was dark, and Corvus led them through the apple crates to a hidden door among the boxes. He pressed against the wood and light surrounded them.

"Atius!" several men shouted, taking up their weapons. Caelius and Caius guarded Atius.

"What? Is he your prisoner, or are we his?" asked Livius, holding up his fish spear.

Livius was the late husband of Ralla the Elder. Other relatives of the slain Elders were in attendance. In all, Atius counted twenty heads, and not one of them looked like they'd miss the chance to skin the hide from his back.

"I understand why you wouldn't trust me..." Atius began.

"Trust you!" snapped Cyprian.

Cyprian was brother to Silana the Elder. Atius was sure the man's hair had greyed since the Authians had come.

"Shame on you." Cyprian spat on the ground. Behind him, other men threw insults until the room became so loud that Atius could not even hear his thoughts.

"That's enough!" Corvus shouted. "If anyone has an ax to grind with Atius, it's me. Let the man speak and then render your judgments."

Cyprian, Livius, and the others grumbled contemptuously and, one by one, took their seat on a circle of apple crates. Corvus turned to Atius and nodded.

Atius cleared his throat. "I do ask for your forgiveness, as I do not forgive myself. When Icabus went missing, I could not accept he was gone. Galen knew it and used it against me.

"I tried to end it all with the fire: Galen, Furius, the Authians, the Takers, all of them, but when Furius killed Galen, everything changed. Furius ordered many of his men to leave the Old Kingdom. I would have been content to die there, but thanks to Corvus and another, I escaped. I only ask you to help me end this. What comes of me afterward I leave to the next Elders to decide."

"And if they choose banishment or death, then what?" asked Cyprian.

"So be it," Atius replied.

The crowd spoke among themselves, and Livius motioned them to silence. "Corvus, you ask us to trust this man. After everything that has happened, I would ask why."

Corvus fell silent, and Cana took his hand. Behind him, Caius and Caelius rested their hands on his shoulders. Corvus faced those assembled.

"When I watched what Atius did to Celsus, I swore to myself I would never forgive him. In the name of all the Gods, I cursed him. If fate had put me in his path then, I would have sacrificed my own life to take his. To obsess for a man's death is like being addicted to the foulest cider, no matter how much you hate it, you are compelled to drink again and again."

Corvus shook his head. "To save Celsus and protect my family, I took Furius's oath. Like Atius, I would sacrifice anything for my children... but to watch them make the same sacrifice broke my spirit. I know some of you experienced the same."

Corvus paused and scanned the crowd. "The truth is it's not Atius's fault. He was compelled to act for the sake of his family, as we did for ours. Would any of you have chosen differently? All along, Furius wanted to turn us against one another. Let us not allow him to succeed in death where he didn't in life."

Corvus faced Atius. "Atius will have to atone, as all of us who took Furius's oath must. But today is not the time for atonement. We need to act and act as one. We are one tribe, and this island is our home. For the sake of our families and future, we must come together again. Otherwise, we should give up now...

"I've got nothing else to say."

Livius stroked his beard. "Even if we succeed, nothing will

ever be the same."

"I'm sure that's what our ancestors said when the Old Kingdom fell," said Corvus. "Somehow they worked through it. I suppose we will, too."

The men in the room huddled together and spoke. Atius rubbed Cana on the head, messing up her already unruly hair. She looked concerned but smiled anyway.

"How's Lucia? Has she been busy?" Atius whispered.

Cana's eyes widened, and she nodded. Atius winked, and Cyprian cleared his throat.

"We will fight with you," Cyprian spoke with reservation, "but only if we know the plan to protect our wives and children. Those are our terms."

ARKAX

Arkax let drool drip from his mouth. He wanted to tear out the Furius's throat and drink the draught of his still beating heart. Men, particularly older ones, were not a meal he typically craved; it was a tough and sour meat. But something about the Furius's scent was different. It stunk like a finely-aged cheese. The Galen had smelled this way when he was masquerading as a human.

Arkax left the light of the torches and nestled in the shadows. He exhaled slowly, focusing on the sounds around him. On one layer was the hum of the insects: predictable, monotone. On another were the larger creatures: men and beasts toiling about as loud as drums in a catacomb. And then there were the hidden things, animals that were old but not necessarily wise: birds and reptiles, waiting in the shadows like him, hunting or just waiting for their prey to come to them.

There was a particular creature Arkax was listening for: a large crow perhaps as old as the island itself. At some point, it had passed through the gate and out again, becoming immortal and as large as a fat child. Arkax didn't care for the taste of crow either, but this crow had helped the Icabus, and once Arkax had it in his mind to kill something, he could hardly think of anything else.

The wind blew up from the forest lake, carrying its perfume. He inhaled deeply, dissecting the scents and uncovering the fainter odors of decay that were his focus. Since Galen had returned, the smell of death around the village had increased enough to hide Arkax's scent.

The hair on Arkax's neck rose and fell. He licked his nose

and inhaled again. There was blood in the air. Fresh blood. Not beast blood—human and Taker blood, and more than a little.

A series of tracks led away from the Atius's house, and Arkax examined each set with interest. The Vescus had gone this way, and if his nose was right (it always was), so had the Cana.

Arkax hated that the Vescus hadn't eaten her yet. She had been a perfect age and large enough to keep for several meals.

The Vescus, however, was a defect. He had the body of a Taker but not the mind. That's why Arkax had given him to the Furius to make more Takers.

The trail went cold at the edge of the stream, and Arkax bared his teeth disagreeably and looked around.

Caw!

Every hair on Arkax's back stood on end. He lifted his muzzle straight up and met the fat crow's black eyes. He had never been surprised by his prey. This infuriated him.

Caw! Caw! Caw!

Arkax dug his claws into the mud and lapped up water from the stream. The fat crow was just beyond his reach (he knew it well).

"Where is the Vescus?" Arkax spoke without raising his face.

Pelagus crept out of the darkness, followed by the two injured Takers. "He led us into a trap."

Caw!

Pelagus looked up and snarled, and the bird took flight toward the Old Kingdom.

Arkax sauntered through the stream. He paused before the Taker with the missing hand and ran his nose over the monster's body. When he reached the Taker's right heel, he bit down, tearing out a chunk of the Taker's Achilles tendon.

"No!" The monster shrieked, flopping in the stream like a fish out of water.

"The Golden Land can't heal missing limbs, but Furius can still use your blood. Bring him to the house. If he struggles, bite off his other hand."

Pelagus nodded and struck the Taker on the head with a

rock. The monster convulsed and fell limp, and Pelagus dragged him away.

Arkax shuffled silently up the hill to the cliff's edge. A small orchard of black walnut and apple trees surrounded Corvus's house and barn. Arkax could hear the humans moving around inside the barn like plump plums ready for plucking.

Scaling the rocks with arachnoid ease, Arkax settled in the shadow of the apple branches and waited. A familiar sound drew his attention to the sky, where the fat crow landed in a nearby walnut tree surrounded by a platoon of his smaller kin.

Arkax's paws moved before his mind could think to act. He leaped, landing on a lower branch and immediately springing upward. The smaller crows took off first, forcing the fat crow to stall momentarily. It was only a small lapse, less than a second, but for Arkax it was enough (it was always enough).

Arkax snapped his jaws shut and crushed the fat crow's leg between his teeth. The crow shrieked. The sound was not that of a crow but a man, terrified and seeing his end.

The crow pecked at Arkax's back, drawing blood, but Arkax did not flinch and tightened his bite. He landed on his paws and shook his head ferociously. Something in the crow's neck snapped, and Arkax tore open its belly without hesitation. High above them, the lesser crows circled and dispersed with a few despondent cries. Arkax ignored them and focused his yellow eyes on Corvus's barn.

CANA

"Caius, did you hear that?" Cana tugged on his arm.

Caius turned away from the circle. "What, little sister?"

"I thought I heard a cry from outside."

"All I hear are the crows."

"What do you think startled them?"

"I don't know. They're crows. Would you be satisfied if we took a peek?" he asked.

Cana nodded, and Caius rose, letting her take the lead. They weaved their way through the maze of apple crates and out into the main hold of the barn. Caius made for the barn door, but Cana grabbed his hand and shook her head.

"Let's go up." She pointed to the ladder. Caius raised his hand, gesturing for her to lead, and followed her up the ladder.

Two opposing lofts ran parallel to the open center of the barn. An old pulley system hung from the rafters to lift apple crates, hay, and other goods into the attic.

Caius placed his hand on Cana's shoulder. "Wait. It looks like someone has been living up here."

"Vescus stayed up here for a while."

Caius frowned but relaxed his posture. "Where are we going?"

"To the windows," Cana whispered.

They walked along the edge of the loft to the front of the barn. Cana lifted the rusty latch and pushed the shutter out just far enough to peer out.

Caius peeked out over her shoulder and made a satisfied grunt. "You see? Nothing."

Cana grabbed his arm. "Look on the ground. It's the fat crow. He's dead."

"Let me see." Caius scanned the ground. "I don't see—"

"Caius!" Cana screamed, pulling him away from the window. They fell back as Arkax's arm swung down at them from the roof like a hairy scythe.

"Get up! Run, Cana!" Caius pulled Cana to her feet and pushed her backward, toppling apple boxes and upending whatever else he could turn over to block their path.

Arkax growled and slipped down through the window. His yellow eyes scanned the overturned debris and he laughed.

Caius stopped and pulled out his knife. "Cana, get down the ladder and warn Father."

"No, Caius, you can't fight him."

"Cana, don't argue! Go!"

Cana grabbed the ladder, and Arkax leaped. He parted his jaws and let his yellow eyes roll back into his head. Caius tried to right his blade, but Arkax's paws reached him first, driving him backward against a row of apple crates.

"Caius!" Cana cried.

Caius didn't move and Arkax offered Cana a malign grin.

"Go away!" She screamed and hurriedly descended the ladder. Arkax scrambled away from the boxes and swatted at her from over the ledge. She jumped away, landing on a small tuft of hay.

Curling his toes over the loft ledge, Arkax sprang toward Cana like an inescapable ending; she froze, watching in disbelief as something struck the monster from the air in a tumbling mass of fur and fang. Corvus, Atius, and Caelius appeared from the darkness, brandishing bows. Caelius drew back his arrow.

"No, it's Vescus!" Cana screamed.

The two Takers rolled away and separated momentarily with a squeal. Vescus stood in front of Cana, panting. Claw marks cut across his face and chest, and part of his ear was bitten off.

Arkax looked at Atius and chuckled. "Just the man I was looking for."

"Vescus," Atius said. "Get Cana out of here. Now!"
"Yes, Vescus, run. I'll finish you soon," Arkax snarled.
Vescus panted with exhaustion. He looked to Cana.
"No," she said, backing away.
Vescus seized her. "I'm sorry." He broke through the barn door and stole into the night.

ARKAX

Arkax crouched. "Take your best shot, Atius."

Livius and Cyprian joined Atius, brandishing spears. Behind them, Corvus and Caelius steadied their bows. Atius grabbed Cyprian's tunic. "Get everyone else to the Old Kingdom."

"Go!" Livius nodded to Cyprian.

Cyprian hesitated and ran back into the darkness, knocking over boxes and crates as he went to block his path.

Atius turned back to Arkax. "Fire!"

The bolts whirred past Atius toward Arkax. The firers' aim was true, but Arkax was faster and jumped up into the rafters.

"To him," shouted Corvus. "Don't let the beast escape."

The rafters creaked above, and Corvus and Caelius drew their bows again. "I can't see him!" Caelius spun around.

"There!" hollered Livius, pointing up.

Corvus fired, and his arrow rattled off the beams. Arkax laughed and fell behind them. He backhanded Caelius unconscious, causing the boy's bow to fire into Corvus's leg. Corvus screamed and fell to the ground. Livius roared and struck out with his spear. Arkax bent his body backward like a contortionist, dodging Livius's strike and snatching the man's neck with his forepaws. There was a crack, and Livius fell limply to the ground.

"No!" Atius drew his sword and charged.

Arkax rolled right, but Atius got a piece of his left hip. The pain only accentuated Arkax's bloodlust and he wiped the bloody wound with his forepaw and licked it. "Do you think I'm afraid of your pathetic sword, Atius? Before I turn you, I'm going to chew off your ears and nose."

Atius swung the sword across his body, catching only the fur on Arkax's chest. Arkax cackled and pounced, pushing Atius against a beam and stunning him.

"Die, beast," Corvus cried, planting Livius's spear in Arkax's thigh.

Arkax yowled and spun away. Corvus fell onto his side, and Arkax pulled the spear from his leg and drove it into Corvus's stomach. Corvus shuddered in agony.

"Corvus..." Atius reached out his hand and Arkax pummeled him with both fists.

Atius stopped moving, and Arkax flung him and Caelius over his shoulders. "You and this boy will make good Takers, Atius," he grunted, leaving Corvus writhing on the floor.

Pelagus was waiting for Arkax in the clearing behind Atius's house. Arkax tossed Atius and Caelius before his feet. "Gifts for Furius. Did you do as I said?"

Pelagus shifted uneasily. "Yes, Furius is drawing the blood now."

Arkax sauntered away on all fours.

"Arkax," Pelagus said. "There is something different about Furius. Even his scent has changed."

Arkax stopped without turning around. "Anything else?"

Pelagus paused. "He refuses to make more Takers until you swear allegiance to him."

Arkax growled low and disappeared in the shadows of the apple grove. He scaled the cliff and emerged from the forest near Atius's house, where the dead guards stirred and fell back to rest against their spears. He inhaled, seeking out Furius's scent—which, as Pelagus rightly noted, was different—and followed it into the basement.

The handless Taker whimpered as Furius probed his arms for veins. Metal thread bound the beast's arms, legs, and snout. Arkax guessed the Taker must have snapped at Furius.

"Arkax," Furius said without looking up from his work.

Arkax walked around the table. He picked up a silver chalice collecting blood and drank it. The wounds on his body closed without a scar. "I have brought you the Atius and one of the sons of the Corvus."

Furius lowered his knife and opened the Taker's forearm. The beast struggled against his bonds. A steady stream of blood pooled on the skin, and Furius fitted the metal cannula into the vein and placed a chalice beneath it. He sighed and regarded Arkax. "What of the other rebels?"

"They ran away to the Old Kingdom. They are no longer a threat."

Furius picked up a cloth from a table and wiped the blood from his hands. Sitting on the floor with their backs against the wall were the corpses of Morelius and his men. Furius walked over to them with a funnel and bowl of blood in hand. He forced the tube into Morelius's mouth, past the hole in his throat, and poured in a cupful of the Taker's blood. He repeated this same process with the three other corpses, one of whom still had an arrow protruding from his eye.

Furius stepped back and waited. The corpses began to shake and gasp. "Authians," said Furius. "Remember your oath. In life and death, I command you."

The corpses struggled to their feet and fixated their stare on Furius. They regarded him with unconscious obsession and dropped their gaze.

"Guard this house," said Furius, handing each corpse a spear. "Kill anyone who would harm my bannermen."

The corpses took the spears and filed up the stairs.

Furius smiled at Arkax. "You were saying?"

Arkax sprung at Furius.

Furius stepped aside, and Arkax struck the wall. Furius grabbed the beast's neck and lifted him.

"Move, and I will snap your spine."

Arkax gasped. "How did you...?"

"Move so fast? Galen taught me secrets even you don't know. I am not your servant. You are mine. If you betray me like you betrayed Galen, I will find a pit so deep and dark even time will forget you. Now, swear to serve me or die."

Arkax squinted, and Furius tightened his grip. "I swear to serve you."

Furius dropped him. "Now, that wasn't so hard, was it?"

CANA AND VESCUS

"Put me down, Vescus!" Cana protested, striking his back with her hands.

Vescus passed through the gate and ascended the stair to the wall walk. He eyed the burned-out structures and leaned forward, allowing her to slide off his shoulder onto her feet.

"Vescus, why did you do that?" She pushed him.

He looked at her for a moment and said, "I don't care about them, only you."

"Well, I care about them. What do you think about that?"

Vescus grimaced and looked past her toward Aggersel. A low mist cradled the edges of the mountains and stretched all the way to the docks. From the side of Corvus's barn, a small group of men ran across the field toward them.

"Some men have escaped. They are running to us now," Vescus said.

"Father?" Cana ran down the stairs and waited near the portcullis. Vescus settled above her on the parapet like a gargoyle. To his disappointment, neither Atius, Corvus, nor Cana's brothers were among the party.

"Hey," Cana called out.

The men slowed and tightened the hold on their weapons. "Who goes there?" Cyprian asked.

"It's me, Cana. Where're Father and the others?"

Cyprian knelt beside her. "They fought so that we might escape. Give them time, and they might yet come."

"No." Cana attempted to run, but Cyprian grabbed her arm, and she fell, striking her side.

Vescus bounded off the wall. "Hurt her again, and I'll tear your arm off!"

"Gods!" Cyprian gasped.

"No ripping off arms, Vescus." She stood in front of him.

"Vescus, son of Cilo?" Cyprian shook his head. "It can't be."

Vescus rested on his haunches. Some of these men had been friends of his father, Cilo. Their horrified stares gave him sadness. He knew that whatever limited role he had in the world of men was quickly fading.

An older man with deep wrinkles and long gray hair pushed through the group. Vescus knew him as Iulius the trapper and pelt maker.

Iulius rested his hand gently on Cana's shoulder and stepped around her. "Vescus?"

Vescus regarded him blankly. He could see Iulius's eyes scanning him. It wouldn't have bothered him so much if fur didn't cover his body. "See something you like, Iulius?"

Iulius took a deep breath. "If you are who you say, then let me see your arm."

Vescus blinked thoughtfully and extended his left arm. "You'll have to get closer if you want to see."

Iulius hesitated and stepped into Vescus's reach. He gently held Vescus's wrist with one hand and parted the fine fur on his forearm with the other, running the tips of his fingers against the borders of an old scar. Iulius released his hold and moved away. "It's him. He bears the scar he suffered as a boy from one of my traps."

The men whispered among themselves, and Vescus interrupted. "It's dangerous to stay here in the open. We should go inside the gate."

A red-haired man, whom Vescus knew as Rufus, addressed the crowd. "Vescus or not, we can't trust him. The Old Kingdom is cursed. If we go inside, we may become like him.

"No, Vescus is right," said Iulius. "There's no refuge for us out here in the open. We should fortify the gates."

Cyprian put his hands on his sides and looked around displeasingly. "Gods curse me; I'm following a Taker into the Old Kingdom."

Rufus stood stoically until all the men had joined Cana and Vescus beneath the barbican.

Vescus walked back to Rufus and said, “Do you remember when I used to climb that oak tree behind your house? I was never afraid of going up, only coming down. How many times did you have to rescue me?”

Rufus eyed Vescus suspiciously. “Three, maybe four times.”

Vescus nodded, and Cana led the men through the gate.

Rufus looked back to Aggersel and scratched the back of his head. “This is madness. If you plan to kill me, Vescus, do you promise to make it painless?”

“Sure,” said Vescus, turning back.

Rufus sighed. “Alright then, lead the way.”

Vescus sauntered through the group of men and sat in the warm ash of a burned out villa. “The stairs there lead to the wall walk. There’s only one way up and down. If anything comes from Aggersel, you’ll see it. Don’t bother fortifying these buildings. The paths here are narrow and maze-like. A trapper might find an opportunity to set a few traps.” He smiled at Iulius, exposing the tips of his teeth.

“Aye,” said Iulius, leading a few men off into the shadows. Mattia and those men with bows climbed onto the wall walk, while Rufus, Cyprian, and the others examined the half-shut portcullis.

Vescus’s jaw dropped. “Where’s Cana?”

The men shrugged, and Cyprian turned to Vescus. “We will search for her.”

“No,” Vescus barked. “She’s gone back to her father’s. I should have never taken my senses off her.”

“Let me go with you,” said Cyprian.

“I can go faster without you.” Vescus bounded up the steps and scanned the moonlit field. Far ahead, the mist swirled around a solitary figure. “Cana...”

Vescus leapt off the wall, landing silently on his paws. The mist swirled around him and he took off on all fours. Ahead of him, Cana turned around the corner of the barn and vanished.

Ten seconds later, he did the same and froze.

The barn door was ajar, and radiant lamplight emanated outward in pulses. Arkax's paw prints were visible going toward the mountain. Vescus pointed his ears in that direction and examined the hillside for any signs of him. The beast was gone.

Vescus poked his head through the barn doorway and slipped in like a furry shadow. The scent of blood was heavy on the air, and Vescus cursed himself for the drool that pooled in his mouth. Atius and Caelius were gone, most likely taken as prizes for Furius. In the center of the barn lay two dead men: Livius, whose neck had been rent, and Corvus, who had a spear buried in his stomach. Cana held her father's head in her lap and sobbed.

Vescus's claws clicked against the clay floor.

Cana looked up. "Get away, Vescus!"

"It's not safe here." Vescus examined the rafters tensely. "We have to go."

"No! They needed you, and you ran. I don't want to see you anymore."

Vescus suppressed his anger, sat on his haunches, and stared at her.

Cana grabbed an apple and threw it against his chest. Vescus didn't flinch.

"Go away!"

Vescus shook his head. "I promised myself I would protect you. I don't care about anyone else."

Something shifted in the loft and Vescus rose to all fours. Cana gently placed her father's head on the floor. "It's Caius."

"Cana, wait—" Vescus rose up on his toes.

Cana ignored him and ascended the ladder. "Caius, can you hear me?"

Something below a pile of broken boxes moaned, and Cana tossed aside the debris. Vescus joined her and used both forepaws to hurl the junk between his legs.

"Little sister?" said Caius, not opening his eyes.

"Yes." She wiped the tears from her cheek.

Caius tried to move. "I can't feel my legs." He winced.

Cana grabbed his ankle. "Feel that?"

Caius shook his head. He blinked and rested his weary gaze on her. "Little sister, you have to go. I'm very tired. All I want is to sleep. Let me rest."

He shut his eyes, and Vescus lifted Caius's tunic, exposing his belly, which was distended and bruised. "He's bleeding inside," he said.

Cana sat on her heels and stared at Caius's stomach.

Vescus lowered his ears. "The Gilian may be able to heal him."

Cana looked at Vescus, barely perceiving his words.

"They still carry the knowledge of the Old Kingdom."

"Why would they help us? Urms already abandoned us."

"That fish-head owes me a favor. If I do this, you must promise to go back to the gate and stay with Cyprian."

"Vescus, I want to come with you."

Vescus shook his head. "No, and you must swear on your brother's life not to follow."

Cana placed her hand on Caius's. He turned his head from side to side, somewhere between sleep and delirium. "I swear," she said.

Vescus lifted Caius over his shoulder, and Cana descended the ladder. Vescus used his claws to descend from a support post and grabbed a lamp and container of oil. Cana went to her father's side and kissed his forehead.

"We need to burn the bodies," said Vescus, handing Cana the lamp and oil.

Vescus pulled the bodies out of the barn, and Cana doused Corvus and Livius from head to toe with oil. She tore away a piece of her shirt and lit the frayed end using the lantern. When she began to feel the touch of the flame on her fingers, she tossed it onto Corvus's chest. "Bye, Father. I love you..."

Vescus took her hand and led her back into the mist. Near the entrance to the Old Kingdom, they stopped. Vescus sniffed the air. "Cyprian?"

Cyprian stepped out from behind the shadow of the portcullis. Above him on the wall walk, Mattia and the other archers relaxed their bowstrings. "Who is that on your back?"

"Caius." Vescus nudged Cana toward the gate with his snout.

She leaned over and kissed Caius on the cheek and hesitantly walked to Cyprian and the others.

"Don't let her out of your sight. Not even for a moment." Vescus eyed Cyprian.

Cyprian nodded. "Where are you going?"

Vescus ignored him and disappeared into the mist. He slowed his pace near the lake road and took a few shallow breaths.

"I want to speak with Urms." Vescus entered the reeds. The mist hid the Gilian from his eyes, but his nose told him they were close. "Urms?"

"It would do you right not to move." Urms parted the reeds.

"I don't have time for this." Vescus started forward but found himself surrounded by a circle of trident tips.

"As I said, I wouldn't move. Who is that on your back, a victim?"

"It is Caius, son of Corvus, Cana's brother. Arkax broke his back. In exchange for saving your life, I want you to help him."

Urms raised two fingers, and the tridents disappeared back into the mist. "Place him on the ground."

Vescus laid Caius at Urms's feet and backed away. Urms knelt beside the man and placed his hands on his forehead and belly. "It is forbidden to do what you ask. You should have let him die in peace."

Vescus dug his claws into the mud and snarled. "You're a fish-bellied coward, Urms. How can you just let him die?"

"How dare you judge us? Don't think yourself so unique. There were others like you in the Old Kingdom when Galen turned the city. One by one, they gave into their desires until every human in the city was turned or dead. You should kill yourself now before you hurt someone you love."

Urms pulled a dagger from his belt and held it out to Vescus. "Kill the boy. It is mercy. Do it for Cana. Don't you see how he suffers? Soon he will drown in his own blood."

Vescus lowered his head. "I won't hurt him."

"Then take the knife and end yourself. Here." Urms held out the blade. "You think you can protect Cana from what's coming? You can't. Only my people can protect her. End your life, and I will protect her and bring her brother to our healers."

Vescus hesitated and took the knife. He held the sharp edge to his neck. "You swear it?"

Urms nodded. "On Queen Arwa's life."

Vescus shut his eyes and tightened his grip on the coral handle.

"Stop!"

Vescus opened his eyes, and standing over him, was a lake man he didn't recognize. Unlike the other Gilian, his scent was indistinguishable from the lake itself.

"I am sorry to do that to you, Vescus, son of Cilo, but I had to see for myself what Urms told me about you. My name is Herms."

Herms cupped Vescus's hand in his own and removed the blade. He passed the knife to Urms and knelt beside Caius, resting his hand on Caius's forehead. "Urms, bring this boy to our healers. He doesn't have much time."

Urms raised three fingers, and two Gilian adorned with jewelry similar to Herms stepped forward and lifted Caius.

"What do you want from me?" Vescus asked.

"To listen," said Herms.

Vescus shifted uneasily.

"What keeps you here is impossible to possess, son of Cilo. I fear that if you continue in this fight, you will lose not only yourself but also the one person you love."

"How do I protect her?"

"Let her go." Herms touched Vescus's shoulder.

"I'm afraid if I leave her, I'll lose myself."

"Love is eternal," said Herms.

Vescus saw no lie in the shaman's eyes. "I understand."

Herms offered him a gentle smile and followed the Gilian

carrying Caius into the lake. Urms waited behind long enough to nod in Vescus's direction.

Vescus stared at the earth between his clawed toes. He had never felt so alone.

FURIUS

Furius looked at his hands. Somehow, they seemed different to him. Throughout his life, he had never doubted that these were his hands, but now he was no longer sure. When Galen came forward to attack Arkax, Furius's will was brushed aside like a piece of rubbish. He felt Arkax's fur against his hand and the beast's pulse as he tightened his grip, but a part of it wasn't him, it was Galen.

Furius wiped the sweat from his brow and ascended the basement stairs. His guards, Valens and Tatius, met him at the landing.

Valens stood at attention. "Sir, we have bound Atius and Caelius outside."

"Are they conscious?" Furius asked, pulling open the door and stepping into the night.

"Atius is," said Valens. "The boy is out cold."

"Make me some tea and bring me a chair," Furius ordered Valens. He motioned for Tatius to approach and took that man by the shoulder. "Send for Atellus and order all my men not guarding the ships here, now."

Tatius's eyes widened. "All the men, sir?"

"All the men."

Tatius ran off, his armor clinking in the darkness, and Valens returned with a chair. "The water has been set to boil, sir. Is there anything else I can do for you?"

Furius sat in the chair facing Caelius and Atius. "When Tatius returns, have those townspeople who've sworn oaths to me stripped of their arms and brought to the basement. I have thought of a new way for them to serve us."

“Yes, Master Furius,” said Valens.

“And don’t forget my tea.”

“Sir.” Valens bowed, running back to the house.

Furius smiled at Atius. “Disappointed I’m not going to make you a beast?”

Atius spat a piece of grass out of his mouth. “What are you going to do with us?”

“You, I haven’t decided. The boy, on the other hand, is going to be lunch for my hungry little Takers.”

“Let him go, Furius. It’s me you want.”

“Not really. But every time I turn around, you’re getting in my way. You seem to suffer most when others suffer in your place, so, for now, just sit back and enjoy the show, Atius.”

Valens returned with Furius’s tea. Furius took a sip and looked at the forest.

“What are you going to do?” asked Atius.

“You’ll see.” Furius smirked. “I just thought of it. At least, I think I did.”

ATELLUS

In the end, Lucia came with him without a fight. Amara had answered the door, foolish child as she was, and seeing her in his arms was all the convincing Lucia needed to go with him. He let Lucia pack what she needed and put the child to bed. That old hag, Tulia, cursed him in the old tongue. He would have cut out her tongue had she not agreed to tend the child.

"I packed enough food and supplies for a night's march. Where are we going?" Lucia frowned.

"I hate surprises, too, but that answer will have to wait," said Atellus.

Lucia hugged Lady Tulia and covered her mouth.

"Come," said Atellus, holding open the door. She did, and when she was close enough, he grabbed her bag and reached in, pulling out a long knife.

"For cooking, I presume."

"For protection," said Lucia.

Atellus threw the knife at the floor, where it stuck handle up. "Don't worry; I will protect you. Bye-bye, witch." He waved at Tulia, who cursed him again.

Atellus kept Lucia in front of him and guided her with the gentle tap of his walking stick. They came to the edge of the town, where the fields of wild wheat stretched for kilometers up the northern shoreline.

Lucia regarded him blankly.

"Into the grass and up the hill." He motioned with his stick.

Lucia parted the grass and stopped.

"Who goes there?" said a voice within the wheat. Three men appeared in the tall grass, each with a bow in hand. Atellus knew them as Giles, Leros, and Cos. Cos was the eldest brother of Leros. Giles was a bastard son, who lived in Leros's shadow. Before the war with Arx Caeli, the three brothers served in Atellus's fields for poaching the king's flock. The sentence should have been death, but Atellus argued for their life.

"I, Atellus."

"Well, if it isn't our old lord master Atellus," said Cos. "Come to put us to hard labor in your field, have you?"

"Don't be foolish. Put down your bows."

Cos hesitated then relaxed his string. Leros and Giles followed in turn. Cos stepped out of the grass. "And to what do we owe the pleasure?"

"Passing through. Who stationed you here?"

Cos chuckled and glanced over his shoulder where a woman sobbed in the tall grass out of view. "Who stationed us here? Well, we did. You see, we found this woman wandering around after dark and, good soldiers that we are, we're looking after her. I see you have someone to look after, too."

"Please, let me go," the woman cried.

"Julia?" Lucia stepped forward.

Giles raised his hand. "Where do you think you're going?"

"Don't mind her," said Atellus. "She's spirited, that's all."

"Really," said Cos, grabbing Lucia's ponytail and pulling her close. Lucia struggled briefly but then relaxed and averted her gaze.

"You don't want to do that," said Atellus.

"Why? You want her all to yourself, do you? Do you think you can defend her with that little dagger of yours?" asked Cos.

"No, but she might with hers."

Cos looked down, but before he could move back, Lucia buried her dagger under his rib cage. He gasped and pushed her away. "Kill her."

Giles raised his bow, and Atellus threw his walking stick aside and drew a knife from his belt. Before Giles could shift his aim, Atius threw his dagger into the soldier's neck. Blood erupted from the wound, and he fell backward.

Leros looked on, stunned.

Cos touched the bloody wound with his hand. "Witch! Leros, shoot them."

Atellus pulled Lucia behind him. Leros raised his bow, and Atellus grabbed Cos by the tunic and used him as a shield. Leros's arrow stuck in Cos's back, and he dropped to his knees, dead.

Leros attempted to draw another arrow, but he was too slow. Atellus released the dagger from Cos's chest and threw it in Leros's eye. The man opened his mouth as if to speak then slumped forward in the grass.

Atellus released the dagger from Leros's eye. "For protection?" he asked Lucia, placing her knife on his belt. "Are there any other knives I have to worry about hidden beneath your skirt?"

"I guess we'll have to find out," she said.

Julia lifted herself out of the grass, and Lucia went to her. The woman had a large bruise on her face, and grass stains covered her dress. She embraced Lucia and wept.

Lucia touched Julia's bruised face. "Did they hurt you?

"It didn't get very far," she said.

"Where's Marcus?" asked Lucia.

"With my sister, Jovita. Where are you going?" Julia rubbed away her tears.

"With him." She gestured to Atellus. "Go back to the village. Take care of your son and be ready. Understand?"

Julia nodded and looked upon Atellus with hatred before retreating toward town.

"She should thank me—I saved her life," Atellus said, retrieving his blade from Giles's neck. "After you." He pointed up the hill.

They came to the place where the fields, orchards, and forest met. The light from Lucia's house rose above the grove as a warm glow in the distance. Atellus could hear the telltale sounds of gathering soldiers. It was a sound that made him nervous and told him he was running out of time.

"Seius?"

Seius stepped from the tall grass with a bundle under his arm. He regarded Lucia coolly.

"We have an additional traveling companion." Atellus smiled at Lucia licentiously.

Seius handed Atellus the bundle, which contained two swords, one broad and one short. Atellus fixed the swords to his belt.

"There is a gathering where this woman once lived," said Seius. "Furius summons all men to bear. Something is amiss."

"Furius has gone mad. That's what's amiss," said Atellus.

Lucia started, and Atellus and Seius drew their swords to the woods.

"What did you see—one of those beasts?" Atellus asked, looking back at her.

"No. I thought I saw... a ghost."

"A ghost?" Seius stepped back.

"A ghost," growled Atellus, sheathing his sword.

"Whose spirit?" asked Seius.

"A childhood friend, Lepida. The Taker took her when we were only children. She was never seen again."

"Until now," said Atellus dismissively. "Which way did she go?"

Lucia pointed up the hill into the forest.

"Good. That's where we are going, too. After you."

Lucia brushed past him, and Seius whispered. "Sir, this is a bad omen, a warning."

"Don't be a fool, Seius. It's that beast, Arkax, we have to be concerned about. Last I checked, ghosts don't have razor sharp teeth."

"Should I light the lamp?" Seius squinted.

"No, I don't want to draw attention to ourselves." Atellus pushed away a branch. They came to a fork of three paths, and Lucia chose the one on the right. Atellus stopped at the fork. "Lucia, the center path is brighter. Are you going that way to gut us in the dark?"

Lucia looked back wide-eyed. "This is the direction that the child's footprints lead."

Atellus and Seius looked down, and Seius covered his mouth. "Gods, she is right. There are footprints."

"So there are. That doesn't mean a ghost made them. The center path has better light, and that is the path we will take."

Seius touched Atellus's shoulder. "Sir, I think the footprints are a sign. It may be dangerous to ignore them."

"Then follow them alone, Seius. Lucia." He pointed in the direction he wished her to go.

Lucia gave him a disagreeable look and took up the center path. Seius followed closely behind.

Lucia stopped.

"What is it now?" Atellus hissed. He stepped in front of her and examined the path ahead. A wide chasm split the forest in two. A fallen oak tree, whose bark had been stripped away by rain and age, spanned the reach and acted as a bridge. Animal tracks crisscrossed the surface; one pair was undeniably Taker, another human.

Lucia reached down and touched the footprints. "Icabus?"

"Light your lamp, Seius." Atellus led Lucia across the reach.

Above them, the columns of trees merged in broad canopies, blotting out the light. The forest floor itself was dry and barren.

"Extend the wick." Atellus glared back at Seius.

"It is." Seius shivered. "The darkness is devouring the light. Gods protect us."

"That's absurd." Atellus took the lamp.

Lucia shivered and kept her eyes forward. The path twisted up the forest slope, but the scenery itself was stagnant and unchanging, a horrific reminder of what eternity looks like for the damned.

They passed between a collection of large boulders, and Atellus grabbed Lucia's shoulder and stepped ahead.

"What do you see?" Seius asked.

"Nothing. It's what I smell."

Seius stepped forward and covered his nose. "Gods, that's awful."

Atellus pulled out his sword and raised an eyebrow at Lucia. "If you have another knife down your dress, now might be the time to find it."

"What is this place?" Seius turned around.

"Arkax's home," said Atellus, handing him back the lamp.

Lucia knelt before a pile of children's shoes strewn against the side of a boulder. "Gods..." she covered her mouth.

"Come." Atellus touched Lucia's shoulder. "Let us be through this place."

"Why are you in such a hurry?" Arkax stared down at them from atop a boulder. His yellow eyes blazed in the lamplight.

Atellus pulled Lucia behind him and raised his sword.

"Really?" Arkax chuckled. He licked his nose and sniffed in Lucia's direction. "You smell familiar. That was your brat boy who came here, wasn't it? I tore out his heart before he stopped breathing."

"You're lying. Icabus's not here." Lucia spoke flatly.

"You're right. Pieces of your son are scattered all over the mountain."

Lucia bit her lip and cast her gaze away.

"Well, a woman who does not cry. Isn't that something?" Arkax grinned.

"We don't wish to disturb you any further," said Atellus. "May we pass?"

"Furius would be mad if his henchmen made it to the Golden Land before him. I can only imagine what he might do if that happened."

Seius stepped forward to speak, and Atellus put out his hand and shook his head. Atellus sheathed his sword and gestured for Seius to do the same. "May we pass?"

Arkax blinked, allowing the silence to become uncomfortable. "Very well, but the woman stays."

Atellus looked back at Lucia and laughed uncomfortably. "Arkax. There are so many women in Aggersel for you to choose.

Why must you take this one from me?"

"She wants to know what happened to the Icabus. I will show her."

"There are many other women in Aggersel... younger women to match your taste."

"The only pleasures I want are the ones that try to escape me." Arkax winked at Lucia.

Seius rested his hand on his sword and looked to Atellus, who shrugged him off. The concern Atellus felt for Lucia was the first genuinely good emotion he had felt since arriving in Aggersel.

"Go," said Lucia. "I'm not afraid."

Atellus's face reddened. "We are supposed to be together."

"I could never love you. Not in this life." Lucia spoke sternly.

The hair on Arkax's neck rose. "Don't make me wait, knight of Authia. This is not a negotiation."

Atellus held Lucia's gaze. His love for her was only a dream and a wish. In her eyes, he saw his reflection, and it disgusted him. "Let's go, Seius."

ICABUS

Nubis sat cross-legged, watching Icabus. "You are acting rashly."

Icabus mulled over the armor pile searching for a pair of bracers that were his size. "My mother is in danger. I have to go."

"Your dream might only be a manifestation of your fear."

Icabus stopped and faced Nubis. "You know that's not true."

Nubis did not avert his gaze. "What do you plan to do?"

"Rescue her," Icabus said, pulling a shield from the pile and tossing it aside.

"That's not a plan."

"Do you have a better idea?"

"Join the bats and the Vlorka in safeguarding the gate. The enemy will come to us."

"And what about everyone else? In my dream, I saw Arkax kill my mother and Aggersel burning. I can't stand by and do nothing."

"Don't throw your life away, Icabus. Some fights cannot be won alone, no matter how much we wish it."

Icabus kicked a breastplate and put his hands on his sides. "When I first saw you, I thought you were going to kill me. A part of me didn't care, because I was ashamed of having run. I vowed to myself that, if I lived, I would never run again."

"Is that why you saved me from Prax? You could have returned home then."

Icabus shook his head. "I believed you could help me, and you have. I'm stronger now than I was. I'm ready."

Nubis looked past him to the pile of armor. "I'm not ready,

Icabus. I can't protect you. I was foolish to send the other dragons and knights away. What I haven't given away, grief has stolen from me. I'm sorry."

Icabus looked at the ground between his feet. "You don't have to apologize to me, Nubis. I forgive you... for everything."

He met Nubis's emerald eyes; he wondered how he could have ever been afraid of these eyes, which looked upon him with such love and concern. Their connection grew stronger every day, and Icabus now began to understand what it meant to care for someone unconditionally and be willing to sacrifice everything for their safety.

"Wait. For one day," said Nubis. "It is not smart to travel under the sun. I will journey with you at dawn. It is time for me to stop running, too."

Icabus slowly let out his breath. "Alright."

FURIUS

In less than one hour, Tatius had assembled the bulk of Furius's force. The villages, who'd swore allegiance to Furius, were stripped of their weapons and brought to the basement where Pelagus transformed them into Takers. The remaining men gathered around Furius in a disjointed throng, brandishing weapons and long torches. Furius walked up the rise to the edge of the forest and addressed them.

"Authians, hear me! In the dungeons of Arx Caeli, I promised you vengeance. Tonight, I fulfill my promise to you!

"Arx Caeli took everything from us: our families, our homes. They kept us alive only to let us suffer in our loss. In my grief, I cursed them and called upon the ancient Gods to send us a redeemer. That night, Galen came to me in a dream. He gave me the knowledge to escape our prison and cross the forest lake. Many of you did not believe we would survive the crossing, but here we stand, and now our journey is nearly complete."

Furius placed his arms at his side and crossed in front of Atius and Caelius, who lay bound on the ground before him. "In exchange for the sea witch, Arwa, Galen promised us the power to enact our vengeance against Arx Caeli. He spoke of a Golden Land where we might find the strength and wisdom of the Gods. Galen promised to share this power with us, but in secret, he plotted to turn us all into mindless monsters for his ends.

"I cut out his heart before he could act against us." Furius raised his fist in the air and shook it at the crowd. "Galen's power rests in the heart of this mountain. It is now ours for the taking! Let us burn this forest and have it!"

Furius's men cheered and shook their torches.

"Fools!" Pelagus left the house. Behind him, a pack of Takers followed with blazing eyes, their mouths red from their first human blood meal.

The Takers circled Furius, and Pelagus leaned close. "Arkax will have your heart for this," he said.

"Not if I have yours first." Furius grabbed Pelagus's muzzle and drew the beast forward.

Surprise filled Pelagus's only eye, and he thrust his jaw downward, only to meet Furius's knife. He slumped forward, legs and arms twitching with the last throws of life.

Furius pulled the knife from Pelagus's neck and pushed the monster aside. "None will stand in our way! Burn the forest!"

The young Takers lowered their heads and averted their gaze in a show of subservience, while Furius's men shook their torches with desirous shouts and moved off toward the wood. Furius winked at Atius.

"You're not yourself," said Atius.

"You're right; I'm not. What do you think of this face? Does it suit me?"

Atius's eyes widened. "Galen? How?"

"The blood is the life, Atius. Care for a drink?"

"I think I'll pass."

"No matter. Your story is almost at an end. Tatius! Valens!"

The two men came down from the forest edge, which now blazed bright with orange light. "Sir," they said in broken unison.

"Tatius, bring me a chalice of Taker's blood from the basement. Valens, bring Arwa down here. I don't want her to miss this."

The two men scurried off, and it was Tatius who returned first. He handed the chalice to Furius. "The Taker below is dead. Bled dry."

Furius shrugged and took the chalice. He lifted the chin of each dead guard and poured the blood into their mouths. "Hear me," he said. "Gather all your brethren. Live men are hiding in the Old Kingdom. Kill them and feast on their flesh."

The dead guards moaned and slipped into the darkness

behind the house. A minute later, Valens forced Arwa from the house and pushed her to her knees. The Takers yipped and bobbed their heads with hungry excitement.

"They like you." Furius smiled at her.

Arwa glanced at the fire and down at her bound wrists. "Do you mean to kill me now?"

"Kill you! Nay. You're my ticket through the gate, my lady. Even Nubis would not dare oppose my army with a blade at your throat."

Furius signaled to Valens and Tatius, who stood at attention. "Atius and his pathetic band of rebels hoped to distract us while their women and children attempted a crossing. Rally a company of men and join the guards on the ships. Allow the women and children to board then kill them all."

"No! They are innocents!" Atius struggled against his bonds.

Valens struck Atius in the face, silencing him. "Sir, I understand killing the rebels, but these are women and children."

"If you do not wish to accept my orders, Valens, I can find other uses for you." He glanced back at the Takers.

Valens shook his head. "No, sir, your will is my own."

"Good, Valens. Proceed."

Tatius and Valens bowed again and went to collect soldiers from the fire line. Minius and Salvius broke away and greeted Furius on one knee.

"Sir, I am told you are looking for Atellus," said Minius.

"Where is he?"

Minius and Salvius rose. "I don't know. I spoke with him earlier, and he wasn't himself. No one else has seen him or Seius since."

Furius faced the forest. "No matter. If he's where I think he is, he's in for a surprise. Are you capable of fulfilling my orders?"

"Aye, sir," said Minius. "It's an honor to serve you."

"Before we move on the gate, have our men take whatever they want from Aggersel and burn the village to ashes."

"Minius, don't do what he says!" Atius cried. "He's lost his mind! Minius!"

Minius walked away, and Furius kicked Atius in the nose. "Be quiet, Atius, or I'll break something of more importance next time." Furius sipped his tea and sat back in his chair..

Furius gazed at the mountain, and the fire reflected yellow in his eyes. "Soon it shall all be mine again."

CANA AND VESCUS

Cana rested her arms on the top of the parapet and stared in the direction of the forest lake. Below her, the men of Aggersel cursed as they tried to loosen the ancient portcullis. The torchlight reflected off the mist, blinding her to almost anything beyond it. The portcullis groaned and shifted down a few centimeters.

"Stop, I say stop," snapped Cyprian.

Rufus gave the grating a final desperate pull and wiped his brow. "It's stuck."

Cyprian frowned. "It's worse than that. It's rusted in place. It would take a dragon to move it."

"Speak not of dragons," said Iulius with a shiver. "We have enough problems."

"We'll have more if we can't get this gate down," Cyprian cursed.

Rufus pulled out his sword and struck the side of the portcullis, freeing a chunk of rust. "It's soft enough. We should try to clean it along the sides where it's stuck."

"And dull our blades to uselessness?" Cyprian spat at the metal.

"As you said, we'll have it worse if we can't shut it," said Rufus.

"He's right," came a voice from the mist. Vescus's golden eyes announced his position.

Iulius pulled out his sword and nodded to Rufus. "You work on this side, and I will work on the other."

"Vescus!" Cana called down.

Vescus looked up, and she disappeared from view.

"I wasn't sure if we would see you again." Cyprian smiled thinly.

"Me either," said Vescus.

"Are we safe for now?" Cyprian looked to the mist.

"For now." Vescus turned his head back toward Aggersel.

Cana came around the edge of the wall, panting. "What happened?"

"The Gilian agreed to help him."

Cana smiled and threw her arms around Vescus's neck. The men looked at each with repulsion and astonishment. Vescus could sense their collective unease and pulled away.

"Are you hurt, Vescus?" Cana asked.

"I'm fine, but I need to go. We can't afford anything sneaking up on us."

"Look to Aggersel!" called someone from the wall walk.

Rufus and Iulius stopped their chipping, and all the men behind the wall gathered beneath the portcullis. A radiant orange glow rose from the mountain.

"Is that fire in town?" asked Rufus.

"No," said Vescus. "It's the forest. Furius is burning it. Cana, go back to the top of the wall and stay there. The rest of you, get that gate down."

Iulius and Rufus began chiseling again. Vescus trotted off into the mist. Cana watched him go.

"You heard him," Cyprian said to Cana, looking to the wall walk.

"Yeah, yeah, I'm going. Get that gate down."

Cyprian shook his head. "Kids today."

Up on the walk, Mattia paced back and forth, twirling an arrow in his hand. Cana climbed up and leaned over the parapet.

"Take care, Cana, or you'll fall off the side." Mattia eyed her with a mixture of concern and annoyance.

Cana pointed into the mist. "I saw something down there."

Mattia looked. "What? I don't see anything. The only thing that troubles me is that awful rotten smell. It smells like something died."

Cana's eyes widened. "Cyprian, I think Galen's dead guards are here!"

"Where?" He held his sword with two hands and faced the gate. The other soldiers on the ground did the same.

"I don't see anything," said Mattia.

"Open your noses," said Cana.

"'Tis foul," said Rufus. "What is that in the dark? It's not moving, but I swear it wasn't there before."

All eyes turned to the mist. Iulius stepped forward. "I think your eyes are playing tricks on you. It looks like a post or something."

Rufus extended a hand. "Then go have a look."

"I might," Iulius said.

Cyprian blocked his path with his arm. "No. It's a trap. Mattia, light up an arrow and burn that thing."

"With pleasure," said Mattia, dipping the end of his arrow in oil and lighting it with a torch.

"Mattia, look out!" shouted Cana.

Mattia relaxed his bowstring and ducked as a spear grazed his cheek. Above him, a dead soldier leaped over the parapet and rolled onto the wall walk. He reached for Mattia's neck, but Mattia kicked the dead thing in the chest, driving him back. Cana grabbed a well of oil and doused the guard's decaying face. The dead soldier reached out for her, but Mattia stabbed him in the side and lit his face with a torch. The guard shrieked and spun around in a dizzy display. He tripped over the parapet and fell to the ground below.

"Burn them," Mattia called out. "They fear fire!"

Cana leaned over the wall where Cyprian and the others grappled with three spear-bearing soldiers. "Mattia, shoot these things."

"I'm a little busy, Cana," said Mattia.

Cana swallowed her words as two dead soldiers climbed over the wall and rushed toward their position. Mattia released a burning arrow, which stuck in the first soldier's head. The thing didn't even flinch, and Mattia dropped his bow and pulled out his sword.

"Cana, get behind me!"

Cana moved in Mattia's direction as the first of the two dead guards reached them. Mattia parried the soldier's spear and drove his blade into the guard's neck. A drought of black blood issued forth, and the soldier dropped his spear and stepped into the sword and wrapped his hands around Mattia's neck. Mattia gasped.

"Let him go," Cana shouted, kicking the dead thing in the leg. The second guard shrieked and struck out at Cana with his spear. Cana fell back against the parapet wall and doused the dead soldier with the bucket of oil .

"Cana," Mattia choked, kicking the torch toward her.

Cana raised the torch to the soldier's chest, and flames erupted over his body, illuminating the entire wall walk like a hellscape. He spun wildly in place, screeching, and waving his arms hopelessly. The flesh over his face was melting away, and he froze, fixating his melting yellow eye on Cana before throwing himself in her direction.

A thundering growl came from over the side of the wall and struck Cana breathless. She imagined only Arkax could make such a sound, but it didn't come from Arkax–it came from Vescus.

Vescus hit the dead soldier so hard that both of them tumbled over the parapet and into the Old Kingdom. The soldier strangling Mattia released his hold and Mattia freed his blade and decapitated the guard where he stood. Cana gawped at him speechlessly.

"Are you alright?" he asked.

Cana nodded with her mouth still agape. She scrambled to her feet and looked over the edge of the wall from where Vescus looked back. He had torn out the dead soldier's neck with his teeth. She didn't know whether to cheer or to shriek. She found she couldn't do either.

Within the gate, at least two of Cyprian's men were dead or wounded. Cyprian and the others were surrounded. "Help them," Cana called down to Vescus.

Vescus squinted his golden eyes and pounced like a hell-hound. The dead soldiers dispersed, and Vescus went after them, tearing each one to pieces.

Black, stagnant blood dripped from Vescus's fur. He breathed heavily with a half-crazed glimmer in his eye. Vescus focused on Cana and then sprinted off into the Old Kingdom.

"Hey, where is he going?" Mattia asked Cana.

"Killing isn't good for him. He needs a break." Cana watched him go.

"Well, he sure is good at it," said Mattia, retrieving his archer's cap.

ATELLUS

"It's wrong to leave the woman," said Seius.

"She doesn't want to be with me anyway." Atellus kept his eyes on the forest ahead.

"I remember your wife and daughter. They would leave offerings at the temple. You were always in their prayers."

Atellus stopped and pulled out his sword. "Don't speak of my family!"

Seius held his ground, expressionless.

Atellus gritted his teeth. "You think you are still a holy man. You have the blood of their Elders on your hands. We all have their blood on our hands."

"As I told you, we are here to redeem ourselves. The Gods have given us a second chance."

"The Gods..." Atellus's voice cracked. "I hate the Gods."

"Then do it for your wife and child who would see you again."

Atellus collected himself and scanned the woods with his eyes. "My wife believed in the Gods. She told me she could feel their presence all around her. I watched her die, Seius."

"She was a good woman."

"From the moment I stepped foot on this island, I have felt the presence of the Gods. It made me so angry to finally feel them and to know that they allowed my family to die. Everything I have become has been to spite them, everything."

"And now?"

"Now? Now all I want is blood." Atellus balled his fist.

Seius crossed his arms. "Even Furius could not equal your skill with a blade. If anyone can kill that monster, it is you."

Atellus raised his face to the canopy. "Do you smell that?"

Seius turned and sniffed the air. "Smells like smoke."

Atellus sheathed his sword. "Furius is burning the forest."

"I think it's a sign."

"Of what?"

"The end." Seius smiled.

"Not yet." Atellus touched Seius's shoulder and stepped past him. "First, we have to hunt."

"Aye," said Seius. He followed after Atellus, and under his breath, he whispered, "Praise the Gods."

LUCIA

Lucia sat and stared at the ground. She could hear Arkax breathing and feel his eyes on her: searching, watching, yearning. It made the hair on her neck stand up and the skin on her arms tingle uncomfortably.

"Furius is burning the forest," said Arkax. "Soon you'll be nothing more than ashes."

"What about you? Can't you die?" She raised her face to him.

Arkax made a throaty chuckle. "The forest has many secret places. Fires pass, as do overconfident men. Are you prepared to see your son?"

"My son isn't here. Somehow, he escaped you. How is it that, with all your strength, you can't even catch a boy?"

Arkax scaled the boulder, and Lucia let her hand slip between the folds of her skirt where a small dagger lay hidden.

"Let's see if you call out for your mama the way your Icabus did for you." Arkax slunk forward. A sound like a branch snapping sounded in the forest behind them, and Arkax raised his ears and swung his massive head in that direction. "Those fools," he said, scaling one of the boulders and bounding up the ridge.

Lucia scrambled to her feet. She saw the shadow of a man running through the forest away from her at the top of the hillside. "Run! Arkax knows you're here!"

A hand seized her shoulder and she gasped, drawing the dagger from her skirt. Atellus grabbed her wrist and looked at the blade. "Ouch... For me?" He winked.

"Atellus? Who was that?" Lucia looked up the hill.

"Seius, giving the beast a needed distraction. Come." Atellus tugged her arm in the direction of the fire.

Lucia resisted. "We can't go that way."

"You must trust me." He released her.

Lucia stepped back. "Why?"

"Because I came back. Because you have no choice." Atellus extended his hand to her.

She took it without releasing his gaze, and together they skirted off into the darkness. Somewhere a man shrieked, and Lucia stopped.

"No, don't stop," Atellus demanded, pulling Lucia forward.

She stumbled and picked up the pace again. Already, the roar of the fire made it hard to hear her footfalls. The air itself was hot, and its acrid vapor burned her eyes and nose.

Atellus stopped ahead of her. "Get behind me, but be mindful of the chasm," he said.

Lucia did and tore off a piece of her dress to cover her mouth. On the other side of the reach, a wall of flame reached for the heavens. Lucia knew it was only a matter of time before the fire jumped the chasm. She had never felt so utterly trapped in all her life.

"Stay down," Atellus said, pulling out his long sword.

Up the hill, Arkax's glowing eyes appeared. He swaggered forward on all fours, licking his teeth. "Tsk, tsk. I see you reached a dead end. I guess for you there will be no crossroads."

Atellus circled Arkax. "This is my crossroads."

Arkax lowered his head and growled. "I will tear out your throat and throw you into that fire."

Atellus said nothing. He matched Arkax's movements foot for paw keeping a sword's length of distance between them.

"Enough!" Arkax leaped.

Atellus rolled left, unable to right his sword quickly enough to strike. Arkax swung around and clawed Atellus's left shoulder. Atellus screamed and stumbled backward. Blood poured down his arm.

Lucia moved toward him, and he raised his hand to her. "Stay back, Lucia."

"I'm going to make you watch me kill her. Then I'll break

your legs and eat your liver."

Atellus began to circle Arkax again. His held his left arm to his side and dropped the point of his sword and sighed.

"Giving up so easily? Very well... Die!" Arkax sprang.

Atellus held his ground as the full force of Arkax's forepaws struck his chest. He fell backward, not trying to roll or save himself in any way. Arkax buried his claws in Atellus's chest, and he cried out, righting his sword and plunging it upward through Arkax's abdomen and into his chest.

Arkax made a hideous, inhuman cry and tore out part of Atellus's neck with his teeth. He fell to Atellus's side, motionless. The light of the flames reflected in his dead yellow eyes.

Lucia rushed to Atellus's side, elevating his head onto her lap and covering his neck with the piece of cloth torn from her skirt. He coughed up a mouthful of blood and regarded her with a dreamy stare.

"Good. Tearless. As it should be." He touched Lucia's cheek. "You remind me of my wife. Gods keep her."

"Thank you for coming back," she said, releasing a single tear.

"Come, come now. What did I say? No tears."

Lucia fell silent. Surrounding them were children, too many for Lucia to count.

"Atellus, do you see them?" she whispered.

"Aye." He coughed. "What are they doing?"

"Bearing witness. They're the ghosts of Arkax's victims. The violence of their deaths bound them to the forest. Now they are free."

One by one, the children came near to look at Arkax's remains and vanished. Atellus looked up at Lucia and shuddered. "I don't want to be trapped here. Please, Lucia, say a prayer for me."

Lucia raised her eyes and there, just beyond the last of the children, was a woman and a girl not more than five years in age. Unlike the others, their eyes were on Atellus and not Arkax. Lucia placed her hand on Atellus's cheek and pointed.

Atellus looked, and his whole body shook once as tears filled his eyes. The two ghosts smiled, and Lucia felt Atellus's body go limp in her arms. In the light of the burning forest, Atellus's spirit embraced his family, and together they vanished from the world forever.

LUCIA

"Milady."

Lucia yelped.

Seius raised his palms to her. "I mean you no harm. We must go." He offered her a hand.

Hot ash burned the back of Lucia's neck, and she brushed it away and rested Atellus's head on a flat stone. Lucia took Seius's hand and he lifted her to her feet. He knelt and closed Atellus's eyes.

"You're alive?" she asked with surprise.

"Aye." Seius spat on Arkax's body and stood. "The beast almost had me, but he must have heard Atellus and turned back. I suspect he thought I wouldn't get far."

"Where should we go?" Lucia faced the wall of flames. Where the canopies touched, fire already crossed the chasm.

"Away from the fire." Seius pointed uphill.

They ran up the ridge as fast as they could. "Stop," said Lucia.

"Milady, there's no time."

"Look." Lucia pointed to the edge of Arkax's lair, where the pile of children's shoes lay.

"Gods, it's an apparition."

Lucia stepped forward. "Lepida, is that you?"

The ghost nodded and began to run away from them along the edge of the hill.

"We must follow her!"

Seius looked up the hill and back at the fire. "She'll lead us right into the fire."

Lucia ignored him and took off after Lepida. She heard Seius's footfalls close behind.

The wall of fire climbed closer, and Lucia could feel her skin burning. Smoke filled her lungs, and it became difficult for her to see. Behind her, Seius coughed and prayed aloud. Ahead of them, Lepida rounded a boulder and vanished.

"No!" Lucia called out. She spun around and fell to her knees. "Lepida."

Seius came to her. "Milady." He pointed. At the base of the boulder was a cave covered in brush. Lucia and Seius pulled the branches away and crawled inside.

Lucia slathered the cold mud onto her singed skin and handed Seius some to do the same. Tree roots penetrated the roof of the cave and dangled into the passage.

"We should go deeper," he said, applying the mud to his arms and neck.

She nodded. "Alright but stay close. Wait... Help me; I'm sliding!"

Seius grabbed her hand. "Hold on," he said, reaching out for a root.

Lucia screamed, and they fell into the darkness.

ICABUS AND NUBIS

Icabus rose before dawn and set out from the Giants City. Strange constellations still spun above as he left the seashore and climbed into the mountains where he had first met Shrail and the Water Spirit. At daybreak, he watched the sunrise in the east and then descended into the gate valley. Hot noon sun glimmered off the waterfall, and Icabus stopped, seeing a familiar sight.

There, sitting at the edge of the pool and staring into the falls, was Nubis. Beside him, his armor was folded in a small pile. Shrail and Zrilla stood not far away under the shade of an apple tree.

Icabus descended into the clearing and sat beside Nubis. The dragon knight continued to watch the falling water.

"If you plan to evade your friends, you should at least include those who can fly in your plans," said Nubis.

"Shrail brought you here?" Icabus asked.

"Yes, me first, then Zrilla. He may have strained a wing."

Icabus addressed Nubis's reflection in the falls. "I'm sorry. I didn't want you to get hurt."

"I understand. I have brought you a gift." Nubis placed his hand on his armor.

"Your armor? It's too big for me."

"I had the Glitkha modify it from the measurements Zrilla knew from your coronation. It should fit you well."

"Thank you," said Icabus, turning to Nubis. "I know, Nubis."

"What do you know?" he asked calmly.

"That this is not your armor."

Nubis turned his face and met Icabus's gaze, and Icabus saw

the sorrow in Nubis's eyes.

"He has become a reflection of his grief. That is what the Air Spirits told me about you. It took me a while to figure out what they meant, but when I did, it all made sense.

"You warned me about the power of the Golden Land to transform me. I thought you were only talking about the Takers, but you were also speaking about yourself. Kail was the knight, and you were the dragon."

Nubis shed a tear and smiled at Icabus with a mixture of sadness and relief. "When I found Kail, he was barely alive. I carried him to the Water Spirit's pool, hoping for a miracle, but Kail's wounds were too severe. I blamed myself and sent the rest of the dragons and knights away.

"I could not accept Kail's passing and became a reflection of him. I forgot what it was to be a dragon. I had accepted this until you came through the gate. After you rescued me from Prax, I sought to restore myself, but neither the Air Spirits nor any of the other old races of the Golden Land could help me."

Nubis placed his hand on Icabus's knee. "I am sorry for not telling you myself. You have grown in so many ways. From a scared boy, you have become a man capable of greater deeds. I never thought I would share the kinship I had with Kail again, but in you, I have found a companion and a friend.

"If you accept this armor, no longer will there be the path of Icabus and the path of Nubis; there will only be one path, together."

Icabus rested his hand on the armor. "Together." He smiled.

Nubis patted Icabus's knee. "Good," he said, turning to Shrail and Zrilla, who walked over.

"I see you have accepted," said Zrilla. "A smart choice."

"You both kept his secret well," said Icabus.

The bat furrowed his brow. "Shrail hates secrets. Makes Shrail's head hurts."

"There are no more secrets between us," said Nubis.

"You plan to go?" Zrilla asked.

"We must," said Nubis. "Are the bats and the Vlorka ready

for what's coming?"

"Bats ready. I don't knows about stinky lizards." Shrail regarded Zrilla with a toothy grin.

"We're ready," said Zrilla.

Icabus stood and hugged Shrail. Shrail whimpered.

"I'll miss you, too," said Icabus.

Zrilla stood straight and exposed her neck to Icabus, and he did the same. She took Icabus by the shoulder and pulled him close, embracing him. "I like this human custom, too. There is one other who would like to thank you," said Zrilla.

"Who?" asked Icabus.

Zrilla turned to the reflecting pool, where a column of water rose to Icabus's height. The water moved to the edge of the pool, where it assumed Icabus's form. It appeared as an exact copy of Icabus in every way.

"Little Taker," said the Water Spirit with a bow.

"Wow, you look and sound just like me." Icabus grinned.

The Water Spirit looked at his hands. "The solidness is unsettling, but I'm becoming accustomed to it. Your red water has given me the potential to assume this form when I wish. Why are you turning red?"

Icabus scratched his head and looked to Zrilla and Shrail who were staring wide-eyed at the Spirit. "Well, because you're not wearing any clothes and, well, some parts like those are private."

The Water Spirit looked between his legs. "Oh, I see. You mean these parts?"

"Yes," Icabus looked down. He reached into his pack and offered the Spirit a pair of silver shorts that Urms had given him as a gift after their adventure into the halls of the Giants City.

The Water Spirit put on the shorts and smiled. "A strange custom. Have you experienced any changes yourself?"

Icabus shook his head. "No. I'm not sure I want to, either."

"It may be for the best," said the Spirit. "When you revived me, I was very confused. I'm sorry if I hurt you. I am grateful to be alive."

"You're welcome. Promise me that if Furius comes through that gate, you will stop him in my form. I want the last face he sees to be mine."

"I promise," said the Spirit.

Icabus lifted Kail's armor and regarded Nubis. "Give me a head start so I can change.

Nubis nodded, and Icabus walked to the gate. He touched the fluid darkness and turned back just long enough to wave goodbye before the blackness swallowed him.

NUBIS

Nubis approached Zrilla and took her hands in his own. "May your reign be long and prosperous."

"Fight hard," Zrilla said.

Shrail embraced Nubis in his wings. "Shrail misses Black Scales."

Nubis smiled. "I know Shrail. I will miss you, too."

The bat joined Zrilla at her side. "Protect them," Nubis said to the Water Spirit.

The Water Spirit nodded and touched Nubis's cheek. "This man whose form you've taken—you brought him to me long ago. I was too weak to heal him, but before he died, he asked me to keep memories for you. Do you wish to have them?"

Nubis raised his eyebrows. "You have Kail's memories?"

"Only a few. Drink if you wish."

The Spirit extended his right palm to reveal a small handful of glistening water. Nubis looked at the water with disbelief. He cupped the Spirit's hand with his own and drank.

"Nubis, wake up, you beast," said Kail.

"Dragons are not beasts," said Nubis, opening one eye.

Kail looked down at him and smiled. "Come on, let's go flying. The Takers are dead, and there is mist in the air. It'll be good for those itchy scales on your backside."

Nubis yawned and closed his eye. "How about I use you as a pillow, and we both take a nap?"

Kail shook his head. "You know, for being the fiercest thing in the skies, you dragons sure do sleep a lot."

"It's a form of meditation that dragons happen to be very good at. Come back after noon."

"Alright. I'll go on a hike instead. The view will have to do."

"No! Don't go!" Nubis shouted.

The scene froze, and Nubis found himself in human form again standing beside the Water Spirit. He stepped into the scene and knelt in front of Kail. Tears filled his eyes, and he covered his face with his hands.

"Why make me relive this? This was the day when Galen and Arkax killed Kail."

"He wanted you to remember that it was his choice," said the Water Spirit.

The scene around them dissolved, and they appeared in front of the forest pool of the Spirit. Before them Kail lay, his armor rent, deep lacerations covering his face and neck. Overhead, a black dragon roared in anguish. Kail touched the waters rippling around him.

"Spirit, I know you can't save me. I worry that Nubis will blame himself for what's happened. I fear that he will forget himself."

"What do you wish me to do?" asked the Spirit.

"Take all my memories of him and show him through my eyes how I see him. If he knows this, he will never grieve for me."

The water over Kail rippled. "If I do this, it will kill you."

Kail coughed. "I'm already dying. Spirit, please."

The scene froze again, and Nubis knelt beside the image of Kail.

The Water Spirit knelt beside him. "By the time you returned from hunting Galen and Arkax, the mana spring had dried up, and I passed into a dreamless sleep. It wasn't until Icabus restored me that I remembered Kail."

"I loved him so much," said Nubis.

"And he you," said the Spirit, extending his hand. "Let me show you."

Nubis took the Spirit's hand, and Kail's memories poured into Nubis like stars filling the night sky. There was no resisting the flow of feeling and memory. Every happy experience, every positive thought, surrounded and entered Nubis in a kaleidoscope of inescapable love.

"The dragon you were is gone," said the Spirit. "You have forgotten him. Let me show you the dragon Kail remembers. Open your eyes."

"Black Scales!" Shrail shrieked.

"No," screamed Zrilla, going to the place where Nubis had stood. "What happened? Where did he go?"

The Water Spirit looked at his hand. "I don't know."

"Black Scales is dead," cried Shrail.

"Stop it, Shrail," Zrilla hissed. "Spirit, what did Kail show him."

"Himself as Kail saw him."

A great roar shook the birds from the treetops. Zrilla stepped back. She looked at Shrail and then to the sky.

Shrail hid his face and shook uncontrollably. "Is it black magics?"

"No, it's Nubis," Zrilla called out, raising her spear.

The black dragon circled the canyon, releasing a stream of molten fire above the falls. Sunlight shimmered off his scales, and he dove backward into the canyon. His massive body twisted like an arrow, and he threw out his wings, capturing the air with a resounding "Clap!" and landed squarely on his clawed toes.

"Impressive," said Zrilla.

"Scary," said Shrail, peering over Zrilla's shoulder.

Nubis retracted his wings fully and licked his lips. "It's been so long since I tasted fire," he said. His voice was deeper and richer but still his own.

Zrilla moved closer and ran her finger along one of the spikes protruding from the back of Nubis head. "Sharp," she said approvingly. "How is this possible?"

"Kail gave all his memories of me to the Spirit so I would not mourn him. I forgot the dragon I was, but Kail's memories helped me become the dragon he remembered."

"Bigger, scarier dragon," said Shrail, shivering.

"I suppose," said Nubis, showing off a mouthful of pointed teeth.

Shrail squawked and shut his eyes.

"What do you think?" said Nubis, turning his emerald eye to Zrilla.

She rested her hand against his jaw and ran her fingers across his scales. "It is right."

Nubis placed his snout on her shoulder, and she leaned in and embraced his long neck.

"I do think Icabus might smell of urine again when he sees you," she hissed amusedly.

"Look," said the Water Spirit.

Along the stream, beneath the trees and along the cliff faces, the Vlorka and the bats had silently assembled. Zrilla tapped the base of her spear against the earth, and soon every Vlorka in the valley did the same.

"We will protect this valley as you once did. All who pass will be judged," she said.

"Bats helps," said Shrail. He released a shriek that echoed through the valley. The bats repeated his cry with deafening intensity.

Nubis balanced on his toes and lifted his head high. He extended his wings fully and roared, shaking the earth. The Vlorka and Bats erupted in a cacophony of calls.

Nubis settled on all fours and moved toward the gate. For the first time in an age, he felt fully content. Everything he needed was ahead of him, and he had no urge to look back ever again.

CANA AND VESCUS

Cana saw two golden eyes flash in the dark streets and jumped to her feet.

"Where are you going?" asked Mattia.

"I see Vescus. Don't shoot us."

Cana ran down the wall walk stair and entered the shadows of the ancient buildings. "Vescus?"

Something behind her shifted, and two golden eyes appeared in one of the broken windows. "It's dangerous here, Cana."

"Why are you still hiding?"

"The scent of the blood affects me. I didn't want to hurt you."

"I know you wouldn't hurt me, Vescus."

"You don't understand, Cana. I could barely think."

"I'm sorry." Cana fidgeted, suddenly unsure of what to say. "Are you alright now?"

"Yes, I've been eating rats."

"Ugh, gross Vescus. Now I know why your breath stinks," she giggled.

Vescus snorted in amusement. "You should go. I'm fine."

Cana shook her head. "We need to go help Lucia and the other women."

"You want to board the ships?" Vescus said, almost despondently.

"No, Vescus," she whispered. "That's only what Lucia told the women in case someone betrayed them. The plan was to come here. They're probably on their way now."

"Here?" Vescus's eyes widened. "This place is barely secure."

"Better than the lake."

Vescus leaped out of the window. "Climb onto my back and

hold on to my fur. I'd leave you here, but I doubt Lucia would listen to me."

"I think you're right."

Vescus knelt, and Cana climbed onto his shoulders. "Hold on."

Cana tightened her grip and pressed her knees tightly against Vescus's sides. They came upon the gate, and Vescus slowed.

"Your wives and kin are seeking refuge here. Prepare to defend it to the death."

"Here?" Cyprian gasped.

"Here." Vescus sprinted through the gate.

MARINA

"Look," said Marina. The last of Furius's soldiers are leaving their posts and making their way to the fire front. Is everybody ready to go?"

Jovita rubbed her forehead. "Junia and I counted over thirty families. Lucia's sleeping potion has done well to keep the younger ones quiet. They are waiting in the fields, ready to make for the ships."

"We should get Lucia and go. We will not find a better time," said Junia.

Marina grunted in agreement, and they set off through the streets. Against the backdrop of the fire, Lady Tulia's house looked forsaken.

"Wait," said Marina, touching Jovita's hand. "The door, it's ajar."

Jovita raised her hand to her mouth. "Oh no. You don't think we're discovered, do you?"

"There's only one way to find out," said Marina, pulling a dagger from her dress. "Come on."

The door creaked on its hinges. "Lucia?" whispered Marina.

"She's gone," said a voice from the dark.

Marina dropped the knife to her side. "Tulia, where is Lucia?"

The old woman emerged from the shadows. "That evil-eyed man, Atellus, took her. To what end I don't know. Her child was inconsolable, and I had to give her a potion to sleep."

"Did he take the weapons?" asked Junia.

"No," said Tulia. "He came for her alone, the snake."

"Lucia..." Jovita shook her head.

Tulia brushed the front of her dress. "I placed the weapons

in a large kindling basket."

"Thank you, Tulia." Marina exhaled. "We don't have time to delay.

"Jovita, get the child. Junia, help me with the weapons."

Jovita disappeared up the stairs, and Junia and Marina went into the kitchen where a wicker basket, fashioned with a shoulder strap, sat against the hearth.

Marina tested the weight. "Heavy, but I can manage it." She smiled.

"I won't argue with that," said Junia.

"Here," said Lady Tulia, handing Marina an old, folded parchment. "Tis a map of the Old Kingdom. I pray it may help you."

Marina took the map in her hand. "The Old Kingdom?"

"Yes, that's right," Vescus's voice rumbled from behind.

Marina extended her dagger and stepped in front of Junia and Lady Tulia. "Stay back, beast."

"Stop it." Cana appeared in the doorway. Vescus rested on his haunches, and she placed her elbow on his shoulder. "This is Vescus, Marina. He's here to help us."

"Vescus?" gasped Junia. "No!"

Jovita descended the stairs, holding a sleeping Amara in her arms. She reached the bottom of the steps, looked up, and let out a strangled cry.

"Hush!" said Marina.

Jovita fell back onto her backside and covered her mouth. "What... is... that?"

"Vescus, if Cana speaks true," said Marina.

Cana waved her free hand at Jovita, who raised a trembling hand in return.

"Lucia didn't want to attempt the crossing. She wanted to move everyone behind the walls of the Old Kingdom. Lucia thought we had a better chance to defend ourselves there," said Cana.

"We can make the crossing, I know it," Marina said sharply.

"It's folly," said Vescus. "Nothing escapes this island while the Gilian queen is in Furius's hands. It's suicide."

Marina frowned. "What you ask of us is suicide. If Lucia had told me, I would never have agreed."

"Behind the walls of the Old Kingdom, you have a chance," said Vescus. "Your husbands are already there. They have already repelled one attack. They need more weapons and more archers."

"I think Lucia was right and wise not to tell us." Jovita's voice shook. "Furius would have never given us peace. At least now we are in control of what happens to us. I want to fight."

Junia pulled the bronze bow and quiver from the basket. "I thought Lucia should have these, but I think you'll do fine, little sister."

"Will you fight with us, Marina?" asked Jovita.

"Fools... all of you... even beast boy here. Gods, curse me, but I won't let you face this alone. I suppose life isn't much fun if I'm the last one living."

"Thank you." Junia hugged Marina. "I will carry Amara, Jovita."

Jovita handed over the sleeping child and took the bow and quiver. "Are you ready, my lady?"

"I do not need adventure," said Lady Tulia. "If Aggersel's time has come, I will go with it."

"Come now," said Marina. "We aren't going to leave you here."

Lady Tulia raised her hand in a gesture of silence. "I never intended to follow you. My place is here in my home. If the Gods are just, we will see each other again in this world or the next."

Cana ran over and embraced Lady Tulia. "We're going to win."

"I hope so," said Tulia, turning to Vescus. "Keep that child safe and do not forget the face of your father, Vescus, son of Cilo."

Vescus dipped his snout and the women gathered around Lady Tulia to say their goodbyes. Marina hoisted the weapon basket onto her back.

Cana returned to Vescus's side. "We have to do something. Don't stop for anything," she said.

Marina frowned. "Let's do this before I change my mind."

VESCUS AND CANA

"Can you hear them?" asked Cana, looking up the hill.

"I hear them," said Vescus, glancing over his shoulder. "Takers. They're coming."

"We have to hurry, or they'll get Marina and the others."

Vescus kept to the shadows and made for the town square. The storefronts were empty and looted. Vescus trotted along the debris and entered one of the buildings.

"What are you looking for?" asked Cana.

"Iulius distills pure alcohol to remove the smell from his animal hides. I remember he blew up the entire back of his shop once making it. Ah ha!" Vescus raised two corked ceramic jugs.

A piercing cry, followed by a cacophony of guttural barks, stole Cana's breath. "Gods, Vescus, we're too late."

"Not yet. I need cloth."

"Got it." Cana grabbed an old rag stained with tanning solvent from Iulius's workbench.

"Follow me," he said, taking the jugs and leading Cana out from the back of the shop to the docks.

Vescus placed the vessels on the ground and removed the corks. Cana leaned forward and coughed.

"Be careful. It will choke you." Vescus closed his nostrils.

Cana handed the cloth to Vescus, who tore it in two and stuffed a piece into each jug like a wick. Using his claws, he climbed onto the deck of Furius's lead ship, and Cana handed him the containers.

"If something happens to me, run to the reeds. Urms will protect you. Now, hide," said Vescus.

Cana nodded, and Vescus crossed the deck making no

attempt to hide himself from inquisitive eyes. Across the harbor, Vescus could hear the whispers of Furius's men on the other ship, which was drifting closer under the power of oars. Vescus settled beneath a smoldering torch cup and lit one of the jugs.

"You're too slow," Vescus whispered, raising the jug over his head and aiming it toward the adjacent deck.

"It is you who are too slow, beast!" screamed Valens.

Vescus spun around as Valens and Tatius rose from behind a row of garum barrels and released a volley of arrows. Valens's bolt whirred past Vescus's ear, but Tatius's hit its mark, piercing Vescus's shoulder.

The burning vessel fell from Vescus's hands and rolled toward Tatius. "He means to burn the ships! Put out that flame, Tatius!" Valens pointed.

Tatius pushed over the barrel in front of him, spilling garum over the deck. The jug began to slide back toward Vescus, and Tatius scrambled forward, falling face forward in the fishy muck. He grabbed the vessel in both hands and raised it to Valens. "I've got it!"

"Actually, I do." Vescus seized the container and threw it with all his remaining strength toward the other ship.

"No!" Valens screamed, drawing another arrow.

The burning container hit the flanking deck and exploded, sending wooden shrapnel in every direction and illuminating the surrounding waters with Stygian brilliance. Valens released his bolt into the air and shielded his face from the explosion.

On the neighboring ship, the men screamed as fire consumed the deck and sail rigging. Tatius regained his feet and Valens drew his sword. "You will make a fine rug," said Valens.

"Don't touch him," screamed Cana, reaching over Valens's head with a rope and using her weight to pull him over the edge of the ship. Tatius reached for Valens, and Vescus pounced, striking the man in the chest and sending him flailing over the side of the vessel.

Vescus peered over the railing and saw Cana sitting on the dock staring back at him. She waved, and Vescus saw Valens's body hanging limply in the rigging. Tatius floated face down in the lake.

"I told you to hide," he said.

"I'm tired of hiding," said Cana.

Vescus gritted his teeth and pulled the arrow from his flesh. He threw it into the water and raised his pointy ears. "Hurry, move!"

The burning ship collided into the starboard flank of Furius's flagship, sending its burning mast crashing down over Vescus. The force of the strike pushed the lead ship against the pier, splintering it and forcing the dock boards upward.

Vescus fell into the flames, and Cana scrambled back on all fours. "Vescus!" she screamed, watching the ships begin to sink.

In the town square, the Takers howled, and Cana watched them join together like a mad pack and race toward her. She brushed the hair away from her eyes and picked up Valens's fallen sword with both hands.

"Come and get me!"

The Takers hit the shore running, and Cana saw something shift in the corner of her eye. One of the floating islands had separated from the others and struck the dock. Cana took two quick strides and leapt for the clump of floating trees. She grabbed one of the hollow boughs, and her momentum drove the little island out into the harbor. The trees bobbed, and Cana scrambled to right herself, careful not to drop her sword.

The Takers reached the end of the pier, and some nearly tumbled into the lake as their numbers crowded every available surface. They moved among each other incoherently, wary of the black waters separating them from Cana.

Cana drifted slowly in the direction of the reed marshes. Furius's fires had evaporated the lake mists, exposing the entire field between the gristmill and the Old Kingdom. Cana climbed one of the trees and looked out over the reeds. She saw groups of people moving out of the orchards and onto the lake road toward the Old Kingdom. One of the figures leading the charge was a large person that Cana assumed was Marina.

"They made it across town. Now they just have to be quiet and not be seen," Cana whispered.

Hope filled her heart and quickly died as a child's cry cut through the night air. The Takers howled in answer.

MARINA

From the shadow of the meeting hall, Marina and Jovita watched the Takers enter Aggersel, tearing down locked doors and killing those within.

They entered Lady Tulia's house, and Marina said a prayer under her breath. "It's only a matter of time before they find the rest of us. Get ready to use that bow, Jovita."

Jovita pulled out an arrow and an explosion shook the ground beneath them.

"Hold it," whispered Marina. "Look."

The aura of the burning ships rose above the buildings, casting an orange glow against the sky. The Takers began to move away toward the light, and Marina sighed deeply.

"They've done it," said Jovita.

"Appears so," said Marina. "We aren't out of this yet. Come on; I don't think we'll get another chance."

Junia and Julia waited for them at the edge of the wheat field. "Is it time? Everyone is ready."

"Aye, the monsters are moving toward the burning ships. Let's hope Vescus and Cana are safe," said Marina.

Junia waved her hand, and one by one, a steady line of women, children, and Elders, sixty in total, moved out of the wheat. Infants and toddlers stirred silently in their mothers' arms. Marina had fretted about whether to drug the older children, too, but fear held them more silent than all.

They came to a group of fenced houses, and Marina raised her hand. She gestured to everyone to sit down and motioned to Jovita, pointing to the closest house on her left.

The house was dark, but firelight revealed a horrific scene.

The front door was shattered, and lying in the debris was Laelius, father of Blandus. His stomach was torn open, and pieces of his bowel littered the yard. Crouching over him with its muzzle buried in his belly was a Taker. The creature's back was facing them, and it growled as it feasted.

Marina leaned close and whispered into Jovita's ear. "If it calls out, we're dead."

Jovita placed an arrow to her bow. Her hand trembled, and she drew back the string to her ear, having no clear shot at the monster's heart.

A loud crash sounded from the lake, and the Taker raised its head. Its eyes widened with surprise at the sight of Jovita, and she fired. The arrow pierced the beast's right eye and penetrated the skull at the rear. The monster fell limply to the ground, arms and legs twitching like a dog running in its sleep. Jovita dropped the bow to her side and sighed.

Marina tapped Jovita on the shoulder and pointed to the house. There, in the silhouette of the doorway, stood Laelius's wife Aeliana and Blandus. Aeliana hid the boy's face in the folds of her dress.

A white picket fence surrounded the yard, and Jovita opened the gate and stepped inside, waving Aeliana toward her. Aeliana guided Blandus around the bodies and ran into Jovita's open arms. Jovita led them from the yard and into the arms of the other women.

Marina took Jovita and Junia aside. "I need your bows at the end of the line. Let's keep everyone moving down to the mill. Once we reach the lake road, we must move fast. We are going to be exposed."

Jovita and Junia held their position, encouraging those with a free hand to help the younger and older alike, while Marina led them down to the mill. They moved cautiously along the river, holding to the muddy banks and avoiding the light of the burning ships.

Marina stopped at the bridge. "Children and mothers to the front."

Once she was satisfied with their arrangement, Marina climbed up the bank and eyed the docks. Nothing recognizable remained of the ships; fire had spread to the masts, which burned brightly like crooked candles.

On the docks, the Takers growled, yipped, and bit each other for position. Marina followed their attention to a small island floating in the harbor. She looked carefully and saw Cana among the trees. "Good girl," she said.

Marina climbed down the bank. "Hurry now. It's time. Go to the road above and make for the Old Kingdom. Don't look back. Go quickly."

Marina, Jovita, and Junia helped everyone ascend the bank. Aeliana carried Blandus against her chest and stuck close to Jovita at the rear of the line.

Tears stained Aeliana's cheeks red. "Those monsters killed my husband."

Jovita took Aeliana's hand. "Come."

Blandus stirred in Aeliana's arms, and she put him down. "You keep your eyes forward and don't look back," she said.

The boy ran forward and turned back to his mother. The light of the fires illuminated his face, and he looked past her to the ships and screamed.

The Takers' ears rose, and they howled in a melancholy chorus. Marina and Junia stopped, and the rest of the group turned back in horror.

"They're coming!" screamed Mariana. "Run!"

FURIUS

Through the same eyes, Galen and Furius watched the fire burn high up the mountainside. The walls of Furius's mind grew thinner by the hour, and there was no longer a veil between Galen's thoughts and his own. Furius knew that if he offered any resistance, the sorcerer's mind would come forward and take control for good.

"Kill them," said Galen's voice in his head. Furius glanced at Atius and Caelius. *"Kill them both."*

Minius and Salvius trotted forward from the burned waste and bowed. "The bridge is complete, sir," said Minius. "The ground beyond still burns. I don't see how anything could have survived."

"Do not underestimate Arkax. The land is full of caves."

"What are your orders?"

"Move our men across the bridge and then throw Atius and the boy into the chasm. Arwa will come with us to the Golden Land."

"Sir," said Minius. He turned to Salvius, who nodded and ran back to conduct the men over the reach. They moved slowly at first but quickly picked up their pace as their footing became sure.

Minius cut the rope binding Atius to Caelius and pulled Atius to his feet.

Atius struck Minius in the face with his elbow and charged Furius. Furius tripped him, driving him face forward into the ground.

Furius shook his head. "Really, Atius?"

Minius kicked Atius in the face and drew his dagger. "Get up, or I'll cut your neck."

"Furius, stop this," Arwa pleaded.

"Shut up." Furius shoved her forward.

Salvius returned and Atius struggled to his feet. In the harbor, the burning ships had imploded and sunk to their masts. Somewhere in Aggersel, a child's scream cut through the air.

Furius chuckled. "Could that be the last child in Aggersel, Atius? Perhaps your daughter?"

Atius grimaced and lowered his face. "Let Caelius go. He's no threat to you now."

"You're right. He is not a threat anymore, but like you, he betrayed his oath. Disloyalty begets vengeance, Atius."

"You speak like a man with honor, but you are neither," said Atius.

A dark form passed over the moon, covering Furius with its shadow. The Authians shuddered in horror.

"No," Furius gasped. "It can't be."

LUCIA

Seius covered Lucia, and they crashed into a pile of bleached bones. "Are you hurt?" Seius asked, helping Lucia to her feet.

"I don't think so." Lucia brushed the cobwebs away from her face.

"What is this place?"

Lucia looked up. Far above her, a natural oculus allowed moonlight into the cavern. "It's a dragon keep."

"Look, milady." Seius pointed.

Beyond the light of the oculus was an arched passage. The blackness within appeared absolute, absorbing the light around it.

"It's the gate." Lucia covered her mouth.

Seius stepped forward and extended his hand. The surface was like air, neither deforming nor resisting his touch.

"Oh no," said Lucia. "Something is happening."

The blackness of the gate began to bend in their direction, and a shadowy figure joined their reflection.

"Get behind me. I think something is coming through." Seius drew his sword. The shadow pierced the edge of the gate and became a man.

Lucia felt her whole body weaken.

"You," said Icabus, dropping his armor and drawing his sword. "You killed Maro..."

"Icabus?" Lucia stepped in front of Seius.

"Mother..." Icabus lowered his sword.

Lucia ran forward and embraced him.

"How did you get here? Were you kidnapped?" asked Icabus.

Lucia began to cry and kissed Icabus's cheek. "Aye, but Seius rescued me. We followed Lepida here. You look... taller."

"It's mana, I guess." He smiled.

Lucia touched the stubble on his face. "You've come back to fight?"

"Yes, and I'm not alone." Icabus faced the gate. A shadowy form appeared in the distance, and the gate's surface began to deform. Icabus took a step back.

"What is it?" asked Seius.

"I don't know. Something big," said Icabus.

Ebony talons like hand scythes pierced the gate.

Behind Icabus, Lucia gasped. "Icabus, what is that?"

"Dragon. Get back!" Seius held up his sword with both hands.

The dragon stood on its hind paws and beat its wings, sending a rush of wind in Icabus and Seius's direction. Dust struck Seius in the face, and the dragon swatted away his blade. Seius backed up, guarding Lucia.

"Icabus," said the dragon, falling to all fours.

"Nubis?" Icabus hesitated and lowered his guard. "How?"

Nubis closed his wings. "Before Kail passed, he shared his memories of me with the Water Spirit hoping, if I received them, I would not mourn him. The mana springs dried up before the Spirit could pass on this gift. Thanks to you, the Spirit is restored, and I was able to remember the dragon I was through Kail's eyes."

"Kail must have remembered you to be quite formidable." Icabus smiled anxiously.

Nubis shook his tail and raised his wings slightly at the shoulders. "Shrail agrees."

Icabus held out his hand. "May I?"

"Of course," said Nubis, lowering his spiked head.

Icabus touched the scales on Nubis's neck and giggled.

"What's so funny?"

"It's amazing. You're amazing."

Nubis blinked thoughtfully and sniffed the air in Seius and Lucia's direction. His pupils remained round, but his irises were more colorful, like emerald starbursts. "Your mother. And a friend?"

Icabus faced Seius. "Not a friend. This is the man who killed Maro the Elder. I would have already made him answer for his crime, but my mother says he saved her life." Icabus offered his hand to Lucia, who slowly moved in his direction.

"My lady," said Nubis the dragon.

Lucia embraced Icabus, and Nubis regarded her with an emerald eye.

"May I?" she asked, placing her hand a few inches above Nubis's scales.

"Of course," said Nubis.

Lucia rested her fingers on the dragon's neck. The scales were warm and smoother than polished metal, and she ran her fingertips over them to the dragon's jaw, feeling the almost imperceptible flutter of muscle beneath. "Thank you for saving my son." She kissed his snout.

"You're welcome, my lady, but it was your son who saved me."

"We saved each other." Icabus winked, leaning against Nubis's shoulder.

The dragon snorted cordially and regarded Seius sternly. "What do you seek?"

"I seek what I deserve and nothing else."

"And if that is death?" asked the dragon.

"Gods willing, I will accept whatever judgment you give." Seius lowered his face.

"Only the Spirits can know whether you are a beast or something else. Go. Your judgment awaits there beyond the gate."

Seius removed his quiver and bow and handed it to Lucia. "May your aim be true, milady."

Lucia touched his heart, and Seius removed the dagger from his belt and dropped it on the ground. He turned to Icabus. "I'm sorry."

Icabus said nothing, and Seius lifted his hand to touch the gate. His hand moved effortlessly through the surface, and he walked forward and disappeared.

"What will happen to him?" asked Lucia.

Nubis regarded her sympathetically. "If he is not a Taker, he will find a new life."

"What if he is?" she asked.

"Then the end will come swiftly," Icabus replied.

Nubis lifted his head and flared his nostrils. "They are burning the forest. Coming here?" he asked Lucia.

"Yes, they're coming."

Icabus sheathed his sword. "Should we warn Shrail and Zrilla?"

"No need," said Nubis. "The Water Spirit will know Galen's intention from Seius's mind. They will be ready."

"Galen is dead," Lucia said to Nubis. "Furius killed him."

"Do you know this to be certain?" asked the dragon.

"My husband saw the corpse himself. He said Furius tore Galen to pieces."

"What of Arkax?" asked Icabus.

"Dead, by Atellus's hand. He saved my life."

Icabus shook his head disbelievingly. "Atellus saved your life?"

"Yes. He meant to kidnap me, but at the end, he sacrificed his own life for mine."

She grabbed Icabus's hand and squeezed it tightly.

"What's wrong?" he asked.

"I was to lead the women and children out of Aggersel. I told them we would attempt a lake crossing, but it was a ploy in case someone betrayed us. Only Cana and Lady Tulia knew otherwise. If Marina and the others attempt to board the ships, Furius will capture them or worse. Your father was to lead our men to the Old Kingdom to fortify it for our arrival. We must help them."

Icabus exhaled slowly. "It's not too late then. What do you say, Nubis? Are we ready?" he asked with confidence.

"I am. Are you?" Nubis eyed Icabus's armor.

Icabus picked up the armor and raised his eyebrows to his mother. "He's always like this."

"I'm not sure what you mean, dear."

Nubis rumbled jovially. “I think I like your mother.”

Icabus waved his hand dismissively and disappeared behind a pile of giant bones. A few minutes later he emerged into the light of the oculus.

“What do you think?” He adjusted his bracers.

“Like a dragon knight of old,” said Nubis.

Lucia covered her mouth and wiped a tear from her eye. “You look so grown up.”

Icabus’s jaw dropped. “Oh, come on.”

Nubis unfolded his wings slightly. “There’s only one way out of this cave, and it’s not with those.” The dragon glanced at Icabus’s feet. He turned his long neck back toward Lucia and crouched on his forepaws. “You first, my lady.”

“Alright.” Lucia slowly mounted Nubis’s back.

“Did I ever tell you I was afraid of heights?” Icabus climbed up in front of Lucia. He held on to the dragon’s chest with both knees, while Lucia wrapped her arms around him.

“We’re ready,” Icabus said half-heartedly.

“Hold on to my neck, Icabus.” Nubis extended his leathery wings.

Icabus did, and the dragon crouched down and leapt into the air, scattering the bones with the thrust of his wings. Dust and wind swirled around them, and Lucia squeezed Icabus’s torso tightly, feeling a rush of fear and elation as they climbed out of the cave to the moon.

Nubis passed through the oculus and dove downward. A vast gulf opened between them and the land, and Lucia saw the forest lake from above: enormous and green with moonlight shimmering off the waterways.

“It’s beautiful,” said Lucia, relaxing her hold.

“Aye,” Icabus said, opening one eye, then the other. “It’s like a dream I used to have long ago.”

“And I,” said Nubis.

The wind reverberated under Nubis’s wings, and the dragon adjusted his pitch to silence them. He turned an eye toward them and grinned in what Lucia thought was embarrassment.

"These wings are bigger than I remember them."

Nubis turned left, lifting his right wing and banking at a shallow angle. The steep rock faces of the mountainside zipped past so close that Lucia thought she could touch them.

"Gods, Icabus, look," said Lucia, pointing below. The forest above Aggersel was a blackened wasteland. A host of Furius's men gathered in the desolation.

"Nubis, they're marching toward the gate," Icabus spoke fretfully.

"I see them. Look to the shores."

"No!" Lucia gasped. "It can't be."

In the harbor, the tangled masts of Furius's ships burned like floating candles. Lucia covered her mouth with her hand and watched the Takers climb over themselves as they tried to snatch bits of burning carcasses hanging from the ships.

"I don't think those are your people. There are women and children emerging from the orchard near the mill," said Nubis.

"Thank the Gods! Amara may be with them." Lucia leaned forward to get a better view.

"I think they're in trouble," said Icabus. "The Takers are on to them. They won't outrun those beasts to the Old Kingdom."

"They have a little time," said Nubis. "Right now, we have another problem. Furius's soldiers have spotted us. We need to keep them on the other side of the reach, or we'll be fighting them, too."

"Take out the bridge," said Icabus.

"My thought exactly," Nubis rumbled, covering Furius's men with his shadow. "There's a group who haven't yet crossed the chasm. Arwa is among them. Do you recognize the others?"

"Your eyes are better than mine." Icabus leaned forward. "That's Furius with the red cape, I think."

"One of them is Caelius... The other is your father," said Lucia, dropping her voice.

Icabus looked back over Nubis's wing. "Father?"

"They're dragging them to the edge of the chasm," said Lucia.

"Hold on!" Nubis brought in his wings in and dove to the earth.

The air whirred around Lucia and Icabus, and they leaned forward, deflecting it over them. Salvius and Minius released Caelius and Atius and ran across the bridge. The host of soldiers moved up the hill in retreat.

The dragon pulled back and caught the wind beneath his wings like two large sails. Lucia felt herself lift off Nubis's back, and she squeaked, tightening her hold on Icabus's waist. Nubis extended his talons and dug them into the bridge. With a roar, he pulled the timbers up with a mighty wing stroke and released them into the chasm. He landed on the cliff's edge facing Furius.

"Release them," Nubis growled.

Furius pulled Arwa to her feet and put his sword to her neck. "Another step, and she's dead."

"Lucia! Icabus!" Atius struggled against his bonds.

Icabus jumped down from Nubis's back. "Nubis. You have to stop the Takers. Take my mother and go. I'll take care of this."

"No, Icabus." Lucia shook her head. After everything she had gone through, she could not bear the thought of losing Icabus again.

"Yes, fly away, Nubis. I'll put some more holes in that armor," Furius sneered.

"Galen..." I should have filled that well with dragon fire after I threw you in it," Nubis snarled.

Icabus reached up and touched Nubis's neck. "Go. You must. There's no time. Please trust me. I can do this."

Lucia reached out her hand to Icabus and he squeezed it tightly. She saw no fear in his eyes and this gave her strength.

"I love you," Icabus said to them, pulling away.

Nubis roared and leapt into the air. Lucia held onto the dragon's neck and looked back catching the warm brown glimmer of her husband's tearful eyes. "My love," she called out to him. She didn't know if he heard her.

ICABUS

Furius laughed and threw Arwa to the ground. "Well, well, Atius. Your son has returned. The Golden Land has made him less a boy. Care to watch as I cut him down to his old size?"

Icabus drew his sword and tossed a dagger in his father's direction. His hands shook with anger at the sight of the Authian king, but he willed himself to focus.

Atius grabbed the knife and began cutting his bonds. "Be careful, Icabus. Galen has taken over his mind."

"Shut up, Atius." Furius took a few cautious steps forward and pointed his sword at Icabus. "I've cut into that armor before. Don't make me do it again."

"Drop your sword," said Icabus.

"Really, Icabus?" Furius chuckled in a voice not his own. "How about you drop yours? I never wanted to hurt you. It was your dreaming that awoke me. I am connected to all the descendants of Apenninus and they to me."

Icabus stood his ground. "You're a nightmare."

"No, I am your destiny, Icabus." Furius extended his hand. "Join me, and I will call off my Takers and spare the people of Aggersel. There are forces at work here beyond your conception. Don't be a fool."

Atius steadied Icabus's knife between his feet and worked his wrist bonds against the sharp edge. "Don't listen to him, Icabus."

"Nubis is an endnote in this story, Icabus; it's not too late for you. You wear Kail's armor, but you will never equal Kail in Nubis's eyes. To him, you will always be a shadow of what he lost. Our fate lies far beyond this island, Icabus. Let me show you."

Icabus stared into Furius's eyes, which were now also Galen's. He knew on a deeper level that the sorcerer spoke truth—that their path was connected. "If you are so wise, how did you lose the Golden Land and end up at the bottom of that well, Galen. You're no more omniscient than I. I'd rather die than join you."

"Imp!" Furius seethed. "What hope do you think you have against me? I have the strength of five men and Furius's skill with a blade. I will cut you down and feast on your flesh."

Icabus steadied his sword and willed the tension in his muscles to fade. His heart had found its place and he would stand firm regardless of the consequence. "Then what are you waiting for?"

Furius's face contorted, and he moved forward with inhuman speed; he led with a barrage of overhead strikes, testing Icabus's guard. Icabus blocked instinctively, quickly losing ground and stumbling perilously close to the chasm's edge.

"Icabus!" Atius shouted.

Icabus checked the king's thrust and pivoted away from the cliff. Off-balance and flat-footed, he stabbed at Furius's chest, hoping to force separation between them. Furius did not yield and instead stepped into the attack, locking swords and punching Icabus in the face.

Icabus staggered back and fell to one knee. Blood ran over his lips and down his chin. A wave of nausea passed over him, and he wobbled back into a fighting stance, feeling unsteady and in a daze.

Furius shook his head disapprovingly. "Is that all you have, Atius's son? Did Nubis teach you nothing?"

Icabus wiped his nose with the back of his bracer and held his sword in front of him with both hands. The grip on the leather hilt gave him focus, and he took slow, deliberate breaths to clear his head.

"Give me your best shot, dragon knight?" Furius said mockingly; he brought his sword down to his right side.

Icabus attacked Furius's exposed flank, thrusting out at the Authian king's stomach, then heart. Furius voided the strikes and twirled away like a lithe spirit.

"You have the higher ground, boy." Furius raised his hands.

Icabus dropped the end of his sword and panted. The blade felt heavy in his hands, and his shoulders ached. He felt overmatched and unsure of himself.

Furius winked. "Come on. Are you a warrior or a weakling?"

Icabus summoned his strength and swung his sword overhead. Gravity added power to his strike, and he brought it down with a fierce, "Hrah!"

Furius planted his foot and leaned into the attack. The Authian king's over-the-shoulder block looked unsteady, but Icabus's blade slid over Furius's like rain down a slick roof.

Icabus could feel his momentum carrying him forward and there was nothing he could do to stop it. He fell forward, yielding the high ground to Furius, who kicked him in the calf, causing his knees to buckle and the sword to fall from his hands.

"No!" Atius cut more fiercely at his bonds.

"Pathetic," said Furius, twirling his blade and raising the hilt above his head. He stabbed downward, and Icabus rolled away. Furius laughed, and Icabus retrieved his sword and scrambled to his feet.

"Mana has made you strong and fast, but that will not save you." Furius thrust his sword toward Icabus's heart, and Icabus barely turned to avoid the attack. "You expose your left flank, Atius's son."

"So, I'm told," said Icabus, not dropping his guard. In the distance, he could hear the yips and yowls of the Takers followed by the cries of the townspeople and a dragon's roar. It made his whole body feel weak.

"You see, it is hopeless. Twenty Takers against one dragon. Shall we wait to hear your mother scream before I cut you down?"

"Monster!" Icabus charged Furius, driving him back with a flurry of angry thrusts. Furius's smile became thin as he lost ground. Icabus aimed for Furius's leg, and the king slipped on the gravel, dropping his sword.

"No." Furius raised his left hand.

Rage filled Icabus, and he directed all of it through the point of his blade. The king rolled right and Icabus planted his sword in the ground. Icabus struck again, and Furius pulled a dagger from his belt and lunged forward, burying it into Icabus's side. Icabus twisted away in agony and fell to his knees, facing his father.

"Icabus!" Atius freed himself and rushed to Icabus's side.

"Stupid boy," said Furius. "You see only what I wish you to see. It will be fun to watch you bleed out."

The fear Icabus saw in his father's eyes stole his hope. This was the same horror he saw in the Elders' faces the day Furius executed them. Everything he fought for and everything he'd hoped to defend felt as it were suddenly slipping out of his reach.

Atius's hand shook with anger and he looked at the Authian king with bloodlust. "Monster!" Atius rushed him, swinging his dagger wildly across his body. Furius seized Atius's wrist and struck him in the head with the hilt of his sword. The dagger fell from Atius's hand, and he collapsed onto his hands and knees.

Furius shook his head and laughed. He raised his hands high. "Behold, the saviors of Aggersel!"

Arwa crawled to Icabus. She pulled the dagger from his side and applied pressure over the wound. Icabus whimpered and coughed. "Hold it," she said.

"Murderer!" Atius picked up Icabus's sword and attempted to stab Furius in the gut.

Furius shirked the strike and backhanded Atius back to the ground; he pulled on Atius's hair, exposing the man's neck. "Good, now stay that way while I cut your throat."

"No, Furius!" Arwa took up the fallen dagger and stabbed Furius in the heel.

Furius shrieked like a Taker and kicked her in the face. Arwa fell backward, and Atius forced himself up. He held Icabus's sword high in both hands and thrust it down between Furius's shoulders. The strike was true, but Furius's attack was quicker, stunning Atius with an underarm thrust that punctured his liver. Atius froze, dropped Icabus's blade, and fell over onto his side.

"Father..." Icabus crouched over Atius. Hot tears of anger streaked his cheeks.

Atius's breath quickened. Blood pooled around his wound and expanded with each heartbeat. Icabus placed his hands over the injury, and Atius shook his head. "There's nothing to be done about it."

Atius touched Icabus's nose and rubbed his fingers before his eyes. "No blood... just water." He stared at Icabus's wound. "Healed? How?"

"A gift," said Icabus, wiping his eyes.

Atius touched Icabus's face and wept. "I've done terrible things, Icabus. I'm so sorry."

"Stop it. I don't care."

Atius coughed, and blood escaped his mouth.

"No." Icabus's voice sank, and he lifted his father's head.

"Do you forgive me, Icabus?"

"Of course, I do."

Atius squeezed Icabus's shoulder. "Protect your mother and sister. End this." He released his grip and fell back limply.

Icabus shook him. "Father!"

Furius's shadow fell over Icabus. "This is your last chance, Icabus. Join me, and I promise that no more harm will come to the people of Aggersel."

Icabus grabbed his sword and shot up, swinging at Furius with fluid fierceness. He moved like a river, unimpeded by any block Furius gave him. The Authian king stumbled and Icabus backhanded him onto one knee.

"Fool," Furius growled. Icabus made to strike again, and Furius grabbed a rock and threw it at Icabus's face. The rock hit Icabus in the temple, and Furius stabbed him in the shoulder.

"Ah!" Icabus covered the wound with his hand.

"Any final words?" asked Furius.

Icabus lifted his hand from his wound. Water dripped from his armor and quickly reentered the injury, closing the flesh around it.

Furius stepped back. “Impossible. I killed all the Water Spirits.”

“You missed one,” said Icabus.

Furius gritted his teeth, and Icabus could see the yellow spill into Furius’s irises like a sickness. Claws began to sprout from the king’s fingertips, and hair grew over his face where a small snout began to protrude.

Icabus raised his sword. “Galen! You have betrayed your sacred oath as a protector. You brought death to this island and the Golden Land. You murdered Kail, my father, and the people of the Apennine Kingdom. I am a dragon knight, and I am here to stop you.”

“Arrogant wretch!” Furius snapped. He lunged forward, cutting into Icabus’s thigh and arm. No blood flowed from the injuries, and Icabus stabbed Furius in his shoulder. The king recoiled and held his wound. Icabus lowered his sword, and Furius charged, claws-out, driving Icabus toward the edge of the cliff and knocking him onto his back.

“You can’t kill me,” Furius laughed. “Nubis shook me lifeless, and I survived. My corpse rotted in a well for a century, and I survived. Furius stabbed me in the heart, and I survived. Let’s see how bleeding water helps you when I cut off your head.”

Furius lifted his sword, and his arm froze in place. He grabbed his frozen wrist and let out a guttural wail. “Furius, no!” He dropped the sword.

Icabus grabbed Furius’s collar in both hands and rolled the Authian king onto his back. Mana as ancient as the Golden Land surged through his body, and he took up Kail’s sword feeling that man’s strength and that of the Water Spirit guide his hands.

Furius blinked, and the yellow left his eyes. “For Authia… for my son… kill me,” he begged.

Icabus yelled and drew his sword over his head. Furius blinked again, and the yellow returned to his eyes; he reached for his sword, but Icabus had already made his cut, decapitating him. The Authian king’s sword hit the ground, and his body fell back lifelessly; his head rolled off the edge of the cliff into the chasm.

LUCIA

Lucia watched Icabus and Atius from Nubis's back. In her heart, there was an emptiness that troubled her. It was the same feeling she had the night the Elders died and Icabus left.

Nubis beat his wings ferociously, gaining speed and altitude. He leveled out and glanced back at Lucia. "I feel it, too," he said. "Do not despair, mother of Icabus. Such feelings are inexact and cannot show us the future."

Lucia sighed. "Aye, we have our own task."

"Yes." Nubis leveled out his wings.

Lucia leaned forward over the dragon's shoulder and saw the throng of women and children moving along the lake road toward the Old Kingdom. They were halfway across the field, and the pack of Takers was closing in quickly.

Nubis flew over the Takers, allowing his shadow to pass over them. Some of the beasts looked up, causing the entire group to halt and move about in disarray. Farther ahead, the woman and children cried, having seen the Takers behind them and a dragon above them. Shouts arose from the gate where the men lined up with their bows along the wall, and others ran forward through the gate, swords in hand, toward the approaching group.

The Takers yipped and yowled, and Nubis let out a roar. The beasts scattered like a colony of disrupted roaches. A few stayed their course, and the rest returned to them, bounding forward in a full speed attack.

The fastest of the women and children had already reached the armed men, while a majority trailed behind. A few of the men lifted children and elderly onto their backs and made for the gate. Others ran to the end of the group to face the oncoming Takers.

Lucia saw Junia, Jovita, and Marina forming a line of bows at the tail of the group. Jovita bore the bronze bow, and she fired a bolt into the Takers. The arrow passed through one of the monsters entirely and stuck into the heart of another, felling them both.

The Takers did not stay their charge, and Marina and Junia fired into the group with uncertain effect. Jovita raised her bow to Nubis and held her position.

"Be careful. Those are bronze bolts," said Lucia. "Can you fly around them, so they can see me?"

"I can," said Nubis. He circled from above, exposing his back and Lucia to them. Jovita relaxed her aim and said something to the others. She adjusted her target to the Takers and fired off another shot. The Takers were less than twenty meters ahead, and Marina, Jovita, and Junia took off for the gate.

"They won't make it," said Lucia.

Lucia felt a warmth grow in Nubis's neck. He turned and dove steeply, firing a torrent of liquid flame between the Takers and the women.

The Takers closest to the fire halted, but the momentum of the others was too strong to stay. They collided into one another and fell into the flames with horrible cries.

"Oh my," said Lucia.

The majority of the women and children had crossed the threshold of the gate and Marina, Junia, and Jovita were close behind. Some of the Takers ran around the fire, while others jumped over the flames. Shouts rose up from the walls of the Old Kingdom, where the men of Aggersel pulled desperately against the iron grating of the portcullis, moving it only a few inches.

"They can't close the gate," said Lucia. "They'll be overrun."

Nubis growled and descended to the earth. "When I touch the ground, jump off and run under the gate."

"What about you?"

Nubis struck the dirt hind paws first, shaking the earth. He bared his teeth to the men at the gate, who jumped back instinctively, and Lucia slid off his back. She ran under the gate, and Nubis grabbed the portcullis with his forepaws and pulled down. The grating lurched, giving way and sinking to the ground. The Takers came and enveloped him.

Nubis whipped his tail and dashed one of the Takers against the wall. Another buried its jaws in Nubis's wing, and he arched his long neck backward and seized the beast with his jaws, flinging it lifelessly against the grate. Other Takers piled onto him, and he spun around, making one desperate attempt to fly before being driven into the ground.

Looks of shock and abject horror surrounded Lucia. Only Marina greeted her with a semi-crazed smile. "Marina, Jovita, anyone with a bow, to me!" shouted Lucia.

She led them up to the wall walk, where she met Cyprian, Iulius, and Mattia. Mattia had his bow drawn and was arguing with Cyprian and Iulius.

"If you're not going to shoot the dragon, then give me your bow," said Iulius. "You won't get another chance."

"No," said Cyprian, grabbing Iulius by the arm and pulling him back. "The dragon saved them. I saw it myself."

Mattia released an arrow, and Lucia cried out. She looked over the parapet and saw a Taker fall lifelessly off Nubis's back—an arrow buried in its heart.

"My lady," said Mattia. "That was quite an entrance."

Lucia pulled an arrow from her quiver and joined Mattia at his side. "Aim for the beasts. Save the dragon. Fire!"

The bolts flew from the wall walk, and the Takers fell from Nubis's back with yowling cries. Nubis crushed one beast against the road with his forepaw and snatched another off his back by the foot with his teeth. He flung it into the air before closing his jaws on its neck. The dragon roared, sending the remaining Takers scrambling back toward Aggersel.

CANA AND CAIUS

Blandus cried, and the Takers' ears rose to the new sound. "No, you stay away from them!" Cana shouted.

The Takers took off, kicking up dust and sand as they left the docks. Marina and the others picked up their pace, but Cana knew they couldn't outrun the beasts.

Cana fell to her knees and covered her face. She could hear some of the women beseech the Gods aloud, while others wept; Cana wished she could fill her ears with wax to not hear the horror to come.

A shadow swept over Cana's position, and she pulled herself up, disbelieving beyond hope the thing she saw. She rubbed her eyes and grabbed one of the small trees to steady herself. The dragon above her roared, and goosebumps spread over her skin. Its wingspan was as wide as one of Galen's ships.

The dragon swooped low, apparently taking notice of the Takers and the others. Cana recognized the figure on the dragon's back.

"Get 'em, Lucia!" Cana raised her hands.

The dragon and the Takers passed out of view behind the floating trees, and Cana rested against one of the trunks. Something stirred in the greater floating forest behind her.

"Who's there?"

"Just me," said a familiar voice.

"Caius?"

"Aye," he said, stepping out of the shadows. "How are you, little sister?"

Cana ran to embrace him. "I thought you were dead."

"I was very close to it." Caius smiled. "You would not believe what I've seen, little sister. The Gilian are remarkable."

"Were you the one who rescued me?"

"Yes, but I had a little help." Caius passed a fleeting glance over his shoulder. Cana caught the faint sign of movement in her peripheral vision. If the Gilian were there, they blended perfectly into the setting.

"Most are not warriors," said Caius. "For decades, control of the floating islands was enough to protect Apenninus, but when Arwa was kidnapped, they were divided. Try not to judge them too harshly."

"I won't. Just Urms. That guy has issues." Cana managed a fleeting smile. She turned back to the ships and frowned. "Have you seen Vescus?"

Caius held her hand. "I've not."

"He saved you, you know. And me, too, several times."

Caius held her gaze. "He cared for you very much. I will miss him, too."

Cana hugged him tightly. "What now?"

"Now, my little sister, we wait."

ICABUS AND ARWA

"Caelius!" Icabus shook him.

Caelius opened his eyes and recoiled from Icabus's touch. "Icabus? You're alive! Or am I dead?"

"You're not dead," said Icabus, cutting his bonds.

"You look... taller."

"I've heard. Time moves differently where I've been."

"The Golden Land?"

Icabus nodded.

Caelius rubbed his wrists and stood up. He wobbled and nearly fell.

"Careful. You took a hit on the head."

Caelius nodded and rose more slowly. He shaded his eyes and looked at Furius's headless corpse. "You did this?"

"We did this." Icabus stepped aside where Arwa said prayers over his father's body.

"No... Atius." Caelius's voice was no more than a whisper.

"It still does not feel real to me. None of this." Icabus gestured toward Aggersel.

"Much has happened." Caelius grasped Icabus's shoulder. "My father and brothers will make sure Atius is well received."

Icabus's eyes softened with understanding. "I'm sorry."

Caelius nodded and looked to the mountain, where Furius's men climbed. "What will happen if they find it, this place you came from?"

"They will regret the day," answered Icabus.

"Good." Caelius heaved a sigh.

From the direction of the Old Kingdom, a shrill cry and a roar made Icabus cringe. "Nubis. He's hurt. We need to go."

"What form of creature makes a cry like that?" asked Caelius.

"A dragon."

"Dragon?" Caelius stopped and stared at him with wide eyes.

Arwa closed Atius's eyes. Icabus knelt and touched his father's shoulder.

"May you find rebirth in the Golden Sea," said Arwa.

"I must get you to the water. Climb onto my back, and I'll carry you." Icabus knelt down.

"There's no time for that. Cover your ears."

Caelius and Icabus did, and Arwa unleashed a high-pitched cry that gave Icabus goosebumps.

"My warriors will end it," she said.

VESCUS AND URMS

Vescus could taste blood and lake water in his mouth. Every part of him hurt from snout to tail tip. Mud blinded him, and he blinked rapidly to clear his vision. Urms stood with his back to him, looking at the lake.

"You're alive. Happy?" asked Urms.

"I remember the explosion and being stuck underwater. Where's Cana?" Vescus rose to all fours, wobbled, and slumped back onto his side. He hung his head over the ground and left his mouth agape, while a wave of nausea passed over him.

Urms turned to him. "She's safe."

Vescus focused on him and looked back at the ground. "I feel terrible."

"I can still end your suffering if you like. It would appeal to my better judgment."

Vescus tried his best to laugh, but it made him dry heave.

"After the explosion, you hit your head. You were more fortunate than most."

"Why did you help me?" asked Vescus.

Urms looked back out to the lake. "At the time, I thought it a crime to let you die. I wish I weren't the one who found you."

"Lucky me." Vescus cleared his nostrils, expelling a cupful of lake water from his sinuses.

"I do have a request."

Vescus looked up thoughtfully.

"Let Cana go. She loves you. Do not let her follow you to where you are going."

"And where is that?"

"Away."

In Aggersel, smoke still rose from the buildings, and the last remains of Galen's ships barely appeared above the surface of the forest lake. Vescus raised his pointy ears as a single note echoed forth from the mountainside. Its frequency cut across the human range of hearing, but Vescus imagined that it would draw man and beast alike like a siren's song. Vescus followed Urms's gaze to the docks where Gilian were now rising from the waters. Row after row, they ascended onto the shore with tridents in hand and armor glistening like silver scales.

"Icabus has defeated Galen and his puppet, Furius. Our queen calls us to her side," said Urms.

"Cana's Icabus?"

"He is not as you remember him. The Golden Land has changed him."

A great roar sounded out from the Old Kingdom. Vescus's hair rose on his back then fell.

"That's not Icabus, is it?"

"No, that's Nubis, the dragon," said Urms, smiling. "You would do well to avoid him."

Vescus gave Urms a horrified look. "Dragons... Cana will be happy Icabus is alive. He will protect her."

Urms nodded. "Yes. He's a fine swordsman, but I'm better."

Farther along the shore, Vescus saw the Takers come up the lake road from the Old Kingdom. Fear moved them blindly toward Urms's brethren, who were gathering at the bridge. They spun about incoherently, and in their moment of indecision, a hundred silver boomerangs cut through the reeds and ended them in pieces.

Vescus sighed. "I would have enjoyed hunting them."

Urms faced Vescus. "Where will you go?"

"I don't know..."

"The gate is guarded. The Water Spirit there will kill you in this form."

Vescus fell into silence. He scanned the mountains disdainfully.

"I am told that the dragons once enjoyed the hot springs on

the other side of the mountain. Our elders say the springs connect to the Golden Land. I have never been and cannot say for certain." Urms lifted the corner of his mouth in a thin smile and turned back to the lake. "Be well, Vescus, son of Cilo. You are a beast but have the heart of a dragon." He walked into the reeds and disappeared into the waters of the lake.

Vescus sat up and moved into the wheat on all fours. The wind blew through the grasses, whispering in the voices of his father, his mother, and others long passed but not unremembered. He followed them far into the wilds, and there he forgot what it was to be a boy and to dream a boy's dreams; he forgot the warmth of fires and the sound of rain against rooftops; he almost forgot himself but for an image burned into his mind like star fire against the night sky.

And when he called upon this image of the girl he loved, he remembered his name and the warmth of fires and the sound of rain on rooftops, and in his own way he lamented these things without missing them, longing only for the girl's touch, whose embrace now felt as distant as the light of the flickering stars.

SALVIUS AND MINIUS

The dragon's shadow covered Minius, sending shivers down his spine. "Away from the bridge!" he shouted.

Salvius, wild-eyed and pale as a ghost, waved his hand, coaxing the others to move faster up the hill. "Is it coming around?"

"Aye, it is," said Minius.

"What of Furius?"

The dragon landed squarely on the bridge and raised it into the chasm.

"We can't help Furius," said Minius, leading the men up the hill. He saw the dragon take off again and head toward the Old Kingdom.

Salvius came up beside him, panting. "The dragon moves away. Should we return for Furius?"

"And what if the beast returns? Do you want to be dessert?"

"Minius?"

Minius stopped and grabbed Salvius by the collar. "Furius is good as dead. Do you wish to join him?" He pushed Salvius away. "Authians! I seek the Golden Land! Anyone who cares to be a dragon's meal may stay here. All others to me."

The men looked to each other, and after Minius moved again, none tarried behind. Minius stopped and crushed a skull beneath his foot.

Salvius looked around. "'Tis the beast's lair?"

"What's left of it," said Minius. "Spread out! Report back quickly if you find something."

"Sir, I've found some corpses," called out one of the soldiers.

Minius went back down the hill to where the two bodies lay. One was a man, severely burned beyond recognition, while the other was that of a beast—the man's sword still buried in its chest.

"Atellus and Arkax," said Minius.

"How do you know, sir?"

Minius crouched beside the bodies. "The beast speaks for itself, but that armor belonged to Atellus."

"Minius," shouted Salvius, running forward. He stopped and looked at the corpses then handed a shawl to Minius.

"What's this?"

"The men found this garment in the mouth of a cave over that rise. It belongs to Atius's wife. I remember the pattern distinctly."

"And no sign of the woman or Seius?"

Salvius shook his head. "The dragon may have devoured them."

"Gather the men and show me," said Minius.

Salvius led Minius to the cave and gave him a torch. A short distance within, Minius raised his hand and knelt. "Look," he said, holding out the torch in front of him.

Two sets of footprints were visible in the mud. The tracks moved in parallel for a short distance and then became exaggerated and indistinguishable.

"Did they fight?" asked Salvius.

"No." Minius extended his torch. "It looks like they slipped and fell."

Salvius reached up and grabbed a root. "Where do you think it leads? I can't see the bottom."

The passage sloped downward into the darkness like a muddy slide. An alternate passage crested away from the former and descended in a spiraling stone staircase.

"Make some torches," Minius ordered. "Touch nothing. Abandoned places are the refuge of things older than ghosts."

The men did as commanded, and Minius and Salvius led them down the ancient stair into the maze of bones. He stopped briefly to stare up through the oculus at the stars.

"Gods, what is this place?" asked Salvius.

"A dragon's keep," said Minius.

"These are strange creatures indeed," said Salvius, examining the bones.

"Aye," Minius said, looking around. He knelt, picked up a skull, and hurled it through the air.

"Gods, where did it go?" Salvius started. "It disappeared."

Minius approached the wall of liquid darkness torch first. The men gasped as the torch head vanished. Minius stepped back, and the light returned.

"It's sorcery," said Salvius.

Minius shook his head. "No, it's the gate. I'm sure of it."

"How can you be certain?" asked Salvius.

Minius reached out and let his hand pass into the darkness. He felt nothing, saw nothing. "What else could it be?" He smiled madly.

"Authians!" Minius faced them. "Join me now! We stand before the gate to the Golden Land. Arx Caeli took everything from us: our homes, our families, our very lives. We gave up everything to be here. Vengeance cannot replace our loss, but I will have vengeance nonetheless. Come to me now! Power equal to our sacrifice awaits us. To me!"

Minius threw down his torch and passed into the gate. Salvius and the other Authians followed after him.

A bright light blinded Minius, and he stumbled forward. The air was sweet like slightly rotten apples, and a waterfall sounded nearby. Minius shaded his eyes and let the world slowly come into focus. Salvius and the others gathered around and spoke words of astonishment.

"Silence," said Minius, raising his hand. Across the meadow, sitting cross-legged before the waterfall's reflecting pool, was a man. He wore only a loincloth, and a long staff of polished redwood lay at his side. His hair was long and white and tied back with a leather string. Minius recognized him immediately.

"Seius," said Minius, stepping into the center of the meadow. He stopped suddenly, realizing the changes in the man. Scales of faint green had grown in place of skin on his shoulders, neck, and back; his hands and feet were elongated and distorted with short claws displacing nails; and, beneath his scales, new muscle filled in Seius's form, giving him a youthful, strong appearance.

"You may go no farther," said Seius.

"What sorcery has done this to you?" asked Minius.

"No sorcery," said Seius, standing to face them.

Minius stepped forward. "My friend, you are not yourself."

"You are right, Minius; I am not. I was not myself when I abandoned the teachings of the Gods and participated in Furius's madness. I was not myself when I stood by as Furius kidnapped the Gilian queen and brought death and suffering to the people of Aggersel. No, my friend, I have not been myself for a long time. But I have been given a second chance, and I would offer you the same."

Minius gestured with his hand to the soldiers behind him. "These men abandoned every oath to reach this place so that they might find the power to destroy Arx Caeli, and now you would ask them to forget their purpose. Who are you to judge us?"

"It is not I who will judge you. It is they."

Seius raised his staff, and the harsh screech of hundreds of bats rang out from the cliff sides. They took to the air and swarmed overhead, blocking out the sun and casting deep shadows in the valley. Seius beat the base of his staff against the ground, and the earth shook as countless Vlorka joined him, appearing from behind tree and shadow and striking their spears against the ground in a powerful union.

Minius stepped back, and the soldiers clustered together and raised their weapons. The wind whipped through their numbers, displacing sword, knife, and shield. Minius's own blade was torn from his hand and tossed meters away.

"Retreat to the gate," hollered Minius.

The soldiers abandoned ranks and made for the gate, but before they could reach it, a gust of wind knocked several rows of men to the ground.

"No, it can't be," said Salvius. "Ghosts! Ghosts!"

In front of the gate, the Air Spirits materialized in the form of the Elders. The men retreated, falling upon one another and scrambling to the center of the meadow.

A watery figure rose from the pool and towered behind Seius. Minius and the others gasped.

"Damn you, Seius," growled Minius. "This is a trap."

Seius halted the rapping of his staff, and all the other Vlorka stopped in turn. The bats settled along the cliffsides and looked down at Minius and the others.

"Authians!" Seius silenced them. "The power of the Golden Land is change. Galen and Furius made you commit unspeakable acts, knowing that none of you would willingly become Takers. He plotted to take away your humanity and have this land transform you into his slaves.

"We followed him blindly to our ruin and the ruin of countless others. Our actions bind us, but our regret has the power to set us free."

Minius knelt to pick up his fallen sword. He spat in Seius's direction. "Have your regret, Seius. I will have my vengeance. Authians! To the gate! Fight! Fight for vengeance! Fight for life!"

Minius ran through the center of them. A handful of soldiers joined him, Salvius not among them. They ran toward the Elders, swords held high, screaming as only madmen could. The Elders raised their hands, and the running men fell dead, their necks broken by an unseen wind.

Salvius took a knee facing Seius and the others joined him. The Water Spirit took Icabus's form and moved toward the group. Seius spoke a prayer for the Takers hiding among the flock.

ICABUS AND URMS

The Gilian piled what was left of the Takers on the shore and lit them ablaze. Arwa and Icabus walked hand in hand. The Gilian knelt and bowed in her presence.

"These creatures were once villagers, weren't they?" Icabus asked.

"Yes," said Arwa.

Icabus shook his head. "If only I had come back sooner."

"If you had, even more might have died, including you and Nubis."

Icabus lowered his head. "That doesn't make me feel any better."

She rested her hand over Icabus's heart and whispered in his ear. "Your greatest power is your hope, Icabus. Do not give in to despair. Nubis needs you; your people need you. There is no greater charge or burden than to lead, and the greatest leaders are those who never wished for it."

"I'm afraid."

Arwa took his cheek in her hand and kissed his forehead. "Then you are more prepared than you think." She smiled.

Icabus led her to the water's edge, and the Gilian followed behind. Urms cut through the crowd and knelt before Arwa. "My queen."

"Please stand," said Arwa.

Urms did and bowed to Icabus. Icabus laughed and embraced Urms firmly. "Don't bow to me. I won't have it."

Urms hesitated and embraced him back.

Behind Urms stood Herms. He made the Gilian hand gesture of respect, touching his left thumb to his ring finger and raising the others. “Thank you for saving our queen,” he said.

“Icabus! Is that you?”

“Cana?”

The crowd parted, and Cana ran to him. She stopped and inspected Icabus from head to toe and laughed. “You look old.”

“I’m finally taller than you.” He smiled.

Cana jumped into his arms, almost knocking him over. “I’m so happy to see you.”

“Me too.”

She laughed, and Icabus set her down. Caelius embraced her in turn, and she kissed him on the cheek. “Guess who I found?”

Caelius looked up and began to cry. “Caius, you’re alive. Praise the Gods.”

“Praise the Gilian,” Caius said, moving through the crowd to hug Caelius.

Caius bowed to Icabus.

Icabus laughed. “Stop with the bowing.”

Caius looked up the hill. “Where is Atius, Icabus?”

Icabus followed his gaze. “He helped end this.”

Caius squeezed Icabus’s shoulder. “May my father and brother receive him.”

“Atius...” Cana’s eyes watered, and she stared off into the distance. “It’s not going to be same without them.”

Icabus nodded. “No, it’s not.”

The Gilian whispered to each other, and Icabus followed their attention to the lake road, where Nubis and Lucia led the villagers toward them. The dragon had some bites along his neck and forelegs that had already stopped bleeding. His left wing was bound with garments in a makeshift sling that was secured around his neck. Amara sat on his back, beaming.

“Icabus!” said Amara. “Look at Mama’s dragon.”

“I don’t think he’s anybody’s dragon,” Icabus replied. He lifted Amara off Nubis’s back and placed her on his shoulders. “His name is Nubis.”

“I know. You got bigger and stinky.”

“Stinky?”

Amara nodded. She reached out, took a wreath of flowers from Nubis's head, and placed it around Icabus's neck. "Your dragon smells like Mama's cakes. These flowers will make you smell good."

Cana laughed.

He grabbed Amara's nose. "Alright, I'll wear them."

Several Gilian bearing satchels approached Nubis and spoke to him in Gilian. Nubis grunted in assent, and they began removing his bandages and tending his wounds. His eyes widened when they applied a white salve to his bites.

"Stings a bit," said Nubis. He spoke to the healers again in their tongue and a few dispersed into the crowd to help the sick and wounded. Nubis looked over Icabus. "You are uninjured?"

"Apparently, I bleed water now."

All the Gilian within earshot backed up and whispered to one another.

Amara laughed. "Like pee pee?"

"No, not like pee pee." Icabus tickled her. She squirmed, and Icabus set her down. She ran over to the Gilian, took some of the white salve from their hands, and applied it to Nubis's wounds. Nubis winced.

"Kids." Icabus winked.

The people of Aggersel gathered around the shore and shared curious stares with the Gilian. Icabus heard them whispering his name, but it was Marina who broke the silence and seized him with her thick arms. "Wow, didn't you get big?" she said, sizing him up.

"And stinky," Amara laughed.

Lucia came forward and hugged Icabus tightly. "Where's your father?"

Icabus shook his head, and his mother covered her mouth. Icabus held her tightly and looked to Arwa, who nodded. Icabus cleared his throat.

"Hi, everybody. I'm not good at this sort of thing, so I'm just going to say what I feel has to be said. Forgive me if I lack Maro's eloquence or Cilo's wit. Any of our Elders would have spoken better than I.

"I'm here to tell you it's over. Furius is dead. His head lies at the bottom of the chasm; what's left of Furius lies beside my father, who died to end this." He paused, feeling the weight of the words draw away his breath.

"Furius's men may find the gate, but they will find more than dragons protect the Golden Land. Judgement will come to anyone who makes that crossing. That land will not suffer Takers again." He regarded the burning pile of corpses.

"I see who we are without and..." Icabus bit his lip and slowly surveyed the faces in the crowd. "I know it's never going to be the same."

Icabus cast a tearful eye on Nubis. "In the Golden Land, I met someone overcome by sadness. Galen had also taken someone from him, and his loss transformed him into an image of his grief. He might have stayed that way if not for the love of another. So, grieve but do not hold to your loss." Icabus surveyed the villagers. "It will bind you in despair.

"Our tribe once crossed the forest lake with only the clothes on their backs and the apple seeds from their homeland. Without anything, they built the Apennine Kingdom and all that we are today. Let us rebuild this place, so our children might know the peace we once shared. I hope we are strong enough to give them that. That's what I hope." He forced a smile.

"I ran into the woods a boy. Now, I feel very different. Your eyes see true. Time moves slower in the Golden Land, but the land has also changed me. Nubis and I faced many trials there before we could return. I want you to know that I spent every moment thinking of you and wishing to return here. The faces I do not see here today will haunt me forever. Forgive me. I would have given myself without question to save them." Icabus took his mother's hand, and she kissed him on the cheek.

Arwa whispered in Herms's ear. The Gilian shaman bowed his head and addressed the villagers. "There is a ceremony of lights to honor our sacred dead. My queen offers it to any family who wishes to commit their loved ones to the lake tomorrow at sunset."

"Thank you." Icabus bowed his head to her.

Arwa took Lucia's hands in her own. "It's nice to meet you again."

Lucia smiled, and Arwa touched Amara's head. The young girl giggled, and Arwa held Icabus's hands. "You spoke well," she said.

Arwa crossed in front of Nubis, and the dragon lowered his head.

"Perhaps the time of the dragons is not over after all." Arwa kissed his snout.

Herms linked his arm with Arwa's and led her into the water. The Gilian slowly broke ranks and followed them. Torchlight glimmered off the lake like a golden tapestry showering them with radiance.

Urms took up the rear and bowed slightly to Icabus, Nubis, and Cana in turn. "My lady," he said to Cana before turning to the lake.

Cana chuckled, and Icabus raised an eyebrow. "You know him?" Icabus asked playfully.

"Yeah, he's the grumpy Gilian."

"I heard that," said Urms, entering the lake.

Quiet surrounded Icabus and the villagers, and even the insects in the forest lake held their wings. A breeze came down from the mountain, shaking the apple branches and going north to the wheat fields, where it carried the voices of the departed through the wind-bent grasses to the Golden Sea.

NUBIS AND ICABUS

"Don't go in the cellar," said Icabus, closing the door behind him. "Should I have Nubis burn the place to the ground?"

"No," said Lucia, running her hand down the doorframe. "Your father planed each board in this house by hand.

"I remember when you were just a baby." She smiled. "Your father and I spent all day molding roof tiles out of clay. We had set them along the hillside to dry in the sun, and you decided to run right over them. You laughed every time one cracked. He ran after you and probably ended up breaking more tiles than you.

"There are good memories here, Icabus. I know you have them, too."

"Yeah, I do. Promise me then you'll let me deal with the cellar. I don't think you want to go down there."

"Alright, dear."

Icabus looked around. "Where's Amara?"

"Outside with Nubis. I think he's teaching her numbers."

"Really?" he laughed.

Icabus stepped outside and saw Nubis lying on a patch of grass in the shade of the house. Amara reclined against his neck and counted the scales on his forepaw. Nubis watched intently.

"...ten, eleven, twelve..."

"Thirteen," said Nubis.

"Fourteen, fifteen... twenty-ten hundred."

Nubis's eyes widened, and Amara laughed.

"Twenty-ten hundred?" Icabus said with surprise.

"Mr. Nubis has one, two, three, four, five claws and twenty-ten hundred scales."

"That might be an exaggeration," said Nubis.

"Yeah, I think you have ten-twenty hundred scales," Icabus said.

"Ten-twenty hundred thousand two," said Amara, arching backward in laughter.

Icabus shook his head. He picked her up and gave her a gentle pat on the bottom. "Go bug Mother. I think she's playing your favorite game, clean the house."

Amara put her arms at her sides and frowned. "That's not my favorite game. If you're not nice, Mr. Nubis will bite you." She looked back and pointed to his mouth. "He has a thousand million teeth."

"She's right." Nubis grinned.

"See?" Amara raised her eyebrows.

"Alright, I'm sorry."

Amara patted Nubis on the shoulder and whispered in his ear. "Tell Icabus we played castle house."

"We played castle house."

"See, you said dragons don't play castle house." Amara raised her chin.

"I guess I was wrong. Who played the dragon?"

Amara's eyes widened. "Nubis."

"Then who were you?"

"She was the princess, of course," said Nubis. "Run along, little one; we'll play again soon."

Amara smiled and swatted Icabus's leg and ran around the house. Icabus sat down and leaned against Nubis's belly. Nubis rested his chin on his foreleg.

"You should see the cellar," said Icabus.

Nubis flared his nostrils. "I can smell it."

Icabus looked out over the forest lake. The sun was just beginning to touch the horizon. "It's almost time. I hope I don't have to make any more speeches."

"Your people will look to you until things are rebuilt. It is inevitable."

"I don't want to stay, Nubis. Mother can sense it. I'm not the same."

Nubis regarded him silently for a moment and let his gaze wander out toward the horizon. "My wing will be mended soon. There are many places from my youth I would like to show you. Places that I was never able to show Kail."

"Ask me then," Icabus said, not looking away from the horizon. He clasped his hands behind his head and leaned back.

Nubis farted.

"Gods." Icabus waved his hand in front of his face. "That doesn't smell like vanilla. What did Mother feed you?"

"Chicken." Nubis burped. "Not to mention all the other things the villagers have been bringing me today."

"I guess the nuts and berries diet is over?"

"Yes, but I may try to become a carrion eater."

"Dead things? Please don't. I can't even imagine what your farts would smell like then."

Nubis and Icabus laughed. They settled back into silence, and Icabus gazed into the distance. "Mother said Arx Caeli burned the Authians' lands before they made the crossing. I think it's time they knew there's a dragon around."

"And a dragon knight who bleeds water," Nubis added. He cocked his head slightly and turned his long neck. "Cana and Caelius are coming." He sniffed the air. "And they're bringing chicken."

"Great." Icabus stood up and brushed the grass from his leather pants.

Cana and Caelius walked around the side of the house. They wore loose fitting linens that reminded Icabus that summer was near. In Caelius's hands he held a clay pot with a matching cover.

"Nice dagger," Nubis said to Cana, noting the coral hilted blade attached to her leather belt.

"Thanks. It was a gift from Urms," she said.

Icabus smirked. "I may be older now, Cana, but something tells me you might still be more mature."

"That wouldn't be hard," said Nubis.

Cana giggled. Icabus put his hands at his sides and looked back at Nubis. "Easy for you to say, dragon farts-a-lot."

"See, he still tells tall tales like a child." Nubis gave a throaty chuckle.

Icabus's jaw dropped. "Don't listen to a word he says."

"Good try, Icabus," Caelius laughed.

"I think we should head down to the lake now," said Cana.

"Oh, I almost forgot. I roasted this chicken for you both." Caelius extended the pot to Nubis.

The dragon took it delicately in one paw and lifted the lid with his talon. He offered the chicken to Icabus, who tore off a leg and raised it to Caelius.

"Cheers," said Nubis, turning the vessel upside down and swallowing the chicken with a single bite.

"He doesn't even taste it." Icabus shook his head.

"Dragons can't be bothered with chewing," said Nubis, licking his upper lip. He lifted himself up and stretched. "After you."

"Mother, we're heading to the lake!" called Icabus.

"Don't yell, dear." Lucia left the house with Amara in hand.

"Don't yell, Icabus," said Amara.

"Fine, fine, let's go," said Icabus, waving his hand.

They had barely started downhill when Nubis farted. "Icabus," he said.

Everyone laughed.

The Gilian began to surface as soon as the shadows of the forest lake touched the shore. At the edge of the harbor, the floating islands parted, and six long rafts, each guided by two oarsmen, glided into the harbor. At the center of the rafts were large copper vessels glowing with radiant flames of purple and gold. Surrounding these vessels were collected several rows of unlit paper lanterns, each with its own small raft at its base.

The oarsmen docked their rafts, and a white boat entered the harbor, moving silently without the power of oars. Standing near its pointed bow were Urms and Herms, clad in delicate silver mail. At its stern, before a copper vessel of glowing white flame, was Arwa. She wore a white dress, the material of which was so fine that it seemed to float over her thin body. Against the white flame, the dress sparkled like blue stars suspended in an opal sky.

"Beautiful," Icabus heard Cana say under her breath.

The ship docked, and Arwa came to shore with Herms and Urms following a few steps behind. A sense of calm fell over Icabus. Even the children quieted in the presence of Arwa. He looked back to Nubis, who winked. There was magic in those burning vessels.

"Thank you." Arwa lowered her head to those present. "I am alive because of your sacrifices. This ceremony is a way to remember, a way to forgive, and a way to move forward. Impermanence follows us everywhere. Each day we have together is a blessing. Let us join together and honor those who are no longer with us. May their memory empower us now and forever."

Herms handed Arwa a paper lantern, and Urms lit it using the white fire from the cauldron. The oarsmen on the rafts lit their lanterns and passed them out among the townspeople. Icabus took his lantern and felt his body lighten as he breathed in the scent of the flame within. Memories of his father passed over him like a warm breeze, and for a moment, they did not feel like memories at all but time relived. He giggled and looked around him. Not a frown could be seen. Even Nubis looked like he was smiling.

"Some memories are eternal in love. They are the breath of the Gods and the force that holds us all together. Here, our loved ones rest with us where the good find eternity."

Arwa walked to the water's edge and placed her lantern on the surface. She touched the lake, and a small ripple began from her finger and pushed the lantern out into the bay. The villagers and the Gilian joined together behind her and released their lanterns onto the water, speaking the names of their departed loved ones. The lanterns followed Arwa's into the bay, where the floating islands drifted apart to form one long waterway stretching out to the starry horizon.

"Until we meet again," said Arwa. "I love you."

CANA AND ICABUS

"So, you're really going?" Cana spoke softly. She sat down next to Icabus under the apple tree. They watched Nubis glide by, floating from one thermal to the next.

"Nubis's wing is strong enough to carry me. Now that Aggersel is rebuilt and safe, there is no reason for us to stay."

Cana shoved him. "What about me?"

Icabus steadied himself and smiled. "I will miss you, Cana. You'll help Mother, won't you?"

Cana nodded and picked at the fallen apple leaves between her knees. "Where will you go?"

Icabus pointed to a crop of hazy hills beyond the forest lake. "Nubis says there used to be dragons there. I guess we'll find out."

Cana's gaze hung there in the distance. Nubis banked back to the shore and glided toward them. "He's beautiful, you know?" said Cana.

Icabus smiled at her. "Yeah."

Nubis landed before them hind paws first without a hop and pulled in his wings like an obsidian accordion. "Hi," he said casually.

"Hi, Nubis, how's your wing?" Cana asked.

Nubis turned his long neck and flexed his left wing slightly to expose the joint for all to see. Small, dull scales covered the area. "Feels good. The scales will mature with time thanks to the Gilian's medicine. At first, I was afraid it would scar."

Icabus laughed. "That might be the first vain thing I've ever heard you say."

Cana shoved Icabus again. "You're so insensitive, Icabus.

You wouldn't want Nubis to have an ugly scar, would you?"

"No, of course not. It's just a little funny because Nubis is not vain."

"I suppose it is a little vain. A dragon's body is his only possession."

Icabus got up and ran his hand over the new scales. "It may be vain, but if anyone ever messes with your scales again, they'll have to answer to me."

Cana stood and brushed off her pants. "Stay safe, Icabus," she said, hugging him. "You too, Nubis." She embraced his long neck and whispered something in his ear.

Nubis laughed and winked. "I'll try."

"Take care of Mother, will you?" said Icabus. "She doesn't want me to go."

Cana nodded. "It's alright, Icabus. Caelius and I will help her; she won't be alone. Where is she anyway, with the other new Elders?"

"Right here," said Lucia. She led Amara by the hand.

Amara ran to Icabus, and he embraced her and spun her around. She giggled, and Icabus set her down. "Are you going to be bigger when I come back?" Icabus asked.

"Bigger than Mama's dragon," Amara laughed.

Icabus smiled. "We'll see about that."

Lucia handed Icabus a knapsack and embraced him. "Dried meats and fruits. Try to save the meat for Nubis."

"Thanks," he said.

Lucia kissed him again and held out her hand to Nubis, who lowered his head. She rubbed his cheek and kissed his snout. "Keep him safe," she said.

Amara raised her arms to the sky, and Lucia lifted her. She touched Nubis's snout and covered one of his nostrils with her hand. He wiggled his nose and exhaled, displacing Amara's fingers. She laughed.

"You will make a fine Elder for your people," Nubis said to Lucia.

Lucia touched the green stole that distinguished her as an

Elder. "I will be in good company," she said.

She embraced Icabus again, kissing him three times on the forehead and hugging him tightly. She wiped her eyes and took Cana and Amara by the hand. Cana waved and, together, the three continued down the hillside toward the village. Icabus crossed his arms and exhaled deeply, leaning against Nubis's firm shoulder.

"I'm going to miss them."

"Me, too," said Nubis.

"What was that Cana whispered in your ear, Nubis?"

Nubis nudged Icabus's back with his snout, causing him to start forward and release his crossed arms. "She wants me to find you a girlfriend."

"A girlfriend? No thanks. You see how they are."

Nubis considered this. "I once knew a dragoness with the prettiest blue scales who wanted me to fertilize her eggs. She was very persistent—"

"Gross. Stop, Nubis. I don't want to imagine you fertilizing anything."

"That's not the point. The point is that sometimes things just happen, but you have to be open to them."

"Did you give Kail love advice?"

Nubis glanced up in thought. "Well, yes. Kail had the hardest time talking—"

Icabus covered his ears. "La, la, la, la, not open, not open."

"Well, now I see where you lack in your training. We're going to have to work on this."

"Gods, I hoped you weren't going to say that."

Icabus climbed on top of Nubis's back and settled into position. Iulius had fashioned a leather saddle to Nubis's specifications, with saddlebags on either side. It was fastened over the dragon's shoulders and across his chest. The studs and buckles were all made from polished silver donated by the villagers. A stiff horn wrapped in woven leather extended from the head of the saddle to form a handle.

"Here we go," said Nubis.

Icabus held onto the horn and leaned forward. "Ready."

Nubis grunted agreeably and began to trot to the edge of the sloping hillside. He picked up speed swiftly, and Icabus could not help but close his eyes as the dragon bounded forward and left the ground. The butterflies in Icabus's stomach rose and fell, and he opened his eyes to the vastness of earth below him.

Nubis tilted his head to Icabus. "You alright?"

"More than alright," Icabus said, taking in the air.

Nubis cut right, circling back over Aggersel. The Gilian had expanded Aggersel's bay by rearranging the floating islands and erected docks there as a gift from the queen. Around the town square, new houses rose from the rubble, and already the young grasses and field flowers softened the blackened landscape above the village.

Along the docks and the shore, the Gilian and villagers gathered. Arwa was there along with the new Elders of Aggersel: Lucia, Marina, Junia, Cyprian, and Caelius. Icabus waved, and the gathered crowd waved back, calling out their goodbyes.

"Wow, isn't that something?" Icabus said, wiping his eyes. "Goodbye, everyone! 'Til we meet again!"

The crowd answered with a cheer, and Nubis leveled out with the horizon, catching a thermal that pushed them higher. Icabus looked back down the length of Nubis's impressive tail. He took in the entirety of the island for all its beauty one last time and committed it to his memory.

A shifting shadow drew his vision to the wall walk of the Old Kingdom. Icabus held his breath.

"What do you see?" asked Nubis.

"Just a shadow," said Icabus. "Nothing to worry about." He looked back one last time and never again.

The End.

ABOUT THE AUTHOR

Jame grew up on their family vineyard in Calistoga, where they explored the Napa Valley hillsides, reading, writing poetry, and stunting their growth with too much espresso. Despite Jame's desire to be a dragon when they grew up, they resigned themself to a career in medicine and writing. Inspired by the fantasy books of their childhood and their adventures in the military and abroad, they began their Dragons of Apenninus book series.

Come visit Jame at
www.dragonpublications.com

or

Find Jame on Facebook, Twitter, Instagram
@dragonnovelist

www.ingramcontent.com/pod-product-compliance
Lightning Source LLC
Chambersburg PA
CBHW030828310726
48980CB00006B/678/J

* 9 7 8 0 5 7 8 2 6 0 2 3 5 *